THE PENNY WEDDING

Alex stroked his wiry hair thoughtfully with the palm of his hand. 'Could she be – a doctor, for instance?'

'I don't see why not.'

'Never been a doctor in our family,' Alex said and then to Jim Abbott's astonishment suddenly doubled over and began to weep. 'Her mother always said – Och, this's terrible, bubblin' like a bairn. I'm sorry, sir.'

'I understand.' Jim Abbott put his hand on Alex's shoulder.

'Mavis always had such high hopes for the lass. Hopes she'll never see fulfilled.' Alex rubbed his nose and looked up, wet-eyed. 'Ally got her brains from her mother, not from me.' He forced a moist self-deprecating laugh. 'You just have to look at me to know that. Takes no brains to be a bloody riveter.'

'It takes other qualities, Mr Burnside. Toughness, determination, strength of character . . .'

Also by Jessica Stirling

About the author

Jessica Stirling, one of Scotland's foremost writers, was born in Glasgow. Her most recent novels have had settings as diverse as Edwardian Glasgow and eighteenth-century Ayrshire.

The Penny Wedding

Jessica Stirling

CORONET BOOKS
Hodder and Stoughton

Copyright © 1994 Jessica Stirling

The right of Jessica Stirling to be identified as the Author of
the Work has been asserted by her in accordance with the
Copyright, Designs and Patents Act 1988.

First published in 1994
by Hodder and Stoughton

First published in paperback in 1995
by Hodder and Stoughton
A division of Hodder Headline PLC

A Coronet Paperback

10 9 8 7 6 5 4 3 2 1

A CIP catalogue record for this title is available
from the British Library

Typeset by Keyboard Services, Luton, Beds

Printed and bound in Great Britain by
Cox & Wyman Ltd, Reading, Berks

Hodder and Stoughton Ltd
A division of Hodder Headline PLC
338 Euston Road
London NW1 3BH

Contents

ONE

A Sunday in September

Fans of 'Our Gang' would have identified the Burnsides' dog immediately. Pete may have lacked a circle of black greasepaint around his left eye but he had enough of the ham in him to justify his nickname and certainly had star quality when it came to begging for titbits. None of Alison's brothers – with the possible exception of Henry – would ever be mistaken for a matinee idol, however, nor were they sufficiently engaging to uphold Alex Burnside's claim that his offspring had once been just as frolicsome as the highly paid little clowns of the silver screen.

Alison nurtured no illusions about her own appearance. At sixteen she was sallow and solemn, oval-faced, with dark brown eyes and dark brown hair cut plain and short and she could no longer kid herself that she might suddenly develop into a voluptuous beauty.

Brenda envied Alison her slender figure. Brenda was for ever moaning about her own unfashionable chubbiness and the fact that she was only five feet dot and, as Brenda put it, still shrinking. Brenda was Alison's best chum and near neighbour. They had known each other for years. On that particular Sunday afternoon, however, Brenda had chosen to go her own way and Alison was out alone with Davy, the youngest of her brothers, and, of course, the dog.

They had meandered up to the towpath of the Forth and

1

Clyde Canal, a favourite haunt, and had stopped at Mrs Kissack's little shop to buy sweets.

The plank wall of the hut-like building was warm under Alison's fingers. She balanced herself against it, bicycle raked at an angle, floral print dress tucked modestly between her thighs, one long brown leg extended to touch the toe of her sandal to the ground.

The bicycle was an old Raleigh Sports, complete with crossbar and narrow saddle. It had belonged to each of Alison's brothers in turn and had accumulated over the years a large number of accessories including two bells, a celluloid pump, plump red rubber handlegrips, a wicker basket, and a greasy canvas pannier clipped above the back wheel.

Alison had inherited the machine from Davy before she had been quite tall enough to reach the pedals. She had been given her first lessons in cycling deportment in the quiet back streets of Partick as a passenger on the crossbar, Davy's strong arm about her waist, her teeth chattering, her bottom bruised by the streets' uneven cobbles. But that adventure, like so many others, seemed like ancient history for in April the Burnsides had flitted from tenement town and out of Partick for good.

The family had been part and parcel of Glasgow Corporation's new suburban housing policy and Alex, a respectable working chap, had applied for and had been duly allocated a brand-new, four-in-a-block, cottage-style house in Flannery Park, near the city's boundary with the Burgh of Clydebank.

To Alison's surprise she missed the bustle of Dumbarton Road and Sutton Street's crowded tenement hardly at all. The luxury of a five-apartment house with an indoor toilet and bathroom, a separate kitchen and a garden front and back more than compensated for the upheaval and disorientation that the move had caused. Besides, she had not left everything behind. Quite a number of her Partick schoolmates, including Brenda, had been part of the exodus to the suburbs and many familiar faces from the old days were to be seen in Flannery Park's spacious avenues. Alison's contentment with her lot had increased after Easter when her mother had promised her a further full year of education and she had gone on to Flannery Park's neat new school instead of being packed off to work.

The only fly in the Flannery Park ointment was that the influence of fresh air and unimpeded sunlight had caused her to sprout an extra couple of inches during the summer. When Alison's brothers teased her about her height, though, Henry, the eldest, who was altogether too dogmatic for his own good, told them they were imagining things and that it was an established medical fact that growth in the female stopped long before the age of sixteen.

Alison didn't much care how her brothers tried to put her down. She was happier now than she had ever been, particularly on that warm, late-September afternoon when she had Davy, her favourite, all to herself.

Davy, followed by Pete, appeared from inside the shop.

Pausing in the doorway he ostentatiously opened the brown paper bag of wine gums which he'd bought at the cluttered counter. Scent of the gums drove the black and white mongrel frantic. Crouched on his hindquarters, forepaws draped across his hairy chest, Pete emitted a series of practised little whines, so desperate and pleading that no one in the Burnside family – Bertie excepted – could ignore them for long.

'What's his favourite flavour?' Davy asked.

'Port,' Alison answered.

'Are they the black ones?'

3

'No, the red.'

'I thought the red ones were burgundy?'

'They all taste the same to Pete anyhow.'

'No, they don't. Got a nose like a bloodhound, Pete has. He can tell port from burgundy any day of the week.' Davy scuffed the dog's ears lovingly. 'Can't you, champ?'

'Bet he can't.'

'Bet he can.'

'What's at stake?' Alison said.

Davy gave the matter careful thought.

Although he was barely nineteen, work as a bricklayer and an obsession with sports had given Davy broad shoulders, a deep, muscular chest and a clear complexion. He was fair like his mother and his hair tended to fall into crinkly curls in spite of all he did to discourage it. He disdained the sober suits in which most young men sauntered forth on Sunday afternoons.

He preferred casual flannels, a collarless white shirt with rolled-up sleeves and, in lieu of shoes, a pair of black rubber gym pumps. He peered into the candy bag, poked among the gums with his forefinger, then glanced at his sister and winked.

'If you're wrong,' he said, 'you get the green ones.'

'I hate the green ones,' Alison said.

'That's the bet. Take it or leave it.'

'How many green ones are there?'

'Three.'

'Oh, all right,' Alison agreed reluctantly. 'But how are you goin' to prove it?'

'Ah-hah!' said Davy. 'Just you watch.'

Tail sweeping the dust and tongue lolling, Pete whined pitifully when Davy tucked the sweetie bag out of sight in his shirt pocket.

Alison rested her shoulder against the sun-warmed

4

wood, watching, curious and amused, to see what her daft brother had dreamed up now.

Distracted by chatter behind her she glanced over her shoulder and saw three small boys in cub scout uniform trek over the canal bridge and gather in a huddle that spoke of important business. She realised at once what they were up to, pooling their Saturday pennies for a transaction with grim-faced Mrs Kissack from whom no charity and no quarter could be expected.

The boys seemed distinctly different from the urchins who roamed Partick's backcourts and canyon-like alleys. They were neat, clean and well nourished, not thin, whey-faced and rickety. What was more, they had money to spend. In the past few months Alison had become conscious of social gradations and tended to exaggerate them. In fact, as Henry was never done telling her, the shiny new citizens of Glasgow's garden suburbs were just yesterday's tenement dwellers lightly toasted by a summer in the sun. Fathers and brothers still worked in Beardmore's or Barclay Curle's, in Brown's, Fairfield's or Ransome's and trudged off each working day to earn a living by the sweat of their brows. Alison, of course, would have none of it. She had long ago acquired the family habit of taking everything Henry said with a pinch of salt which, as it happened, was not always a wise thing to do.

From the railed bridge that topped the lock-gate came a little shriek and, looking up, Alison saw a girl, hardly older than she was, clinging in mock terror to her boyfriend while, with hands about her waist, he steered her over the planks and at the same time tickled her. In the soft vaporous warmth of the autumn afternoon Alison felt suddenly enveloped in the odour of weeds and sluggish brown water and very conscious of the fabric of her dress brushing her bare skin.

'Hoi, dreamy,' Davy said. 'Are you payin' attention?'

'Of course I am,' said Alison.

Bending, Davy offered his closed fists to the dog. Although used to performing for the Burnsides' amusement, Pete was puzzled by the idiotic delay in doling out the Sunday treat and prowled, sniffing suspiciously, round Davy's legs.

'See,' Alison said. 'The poor mutt doesn't have a clue.'

'C'mon, champ.' Davy weaved his fists cajolingly. 'Find the red one.'

Intrigued by Pete's antics, the cub scouts in their tight green jerseys and skipped caps drew closer.

'Ah've got a dog,' on. of them informed Alison.

'Have you? What's his name?'

'Spot. But ah call him Killer.'

'Quiet, pul-ease,' said Davy.

Now that he had gathered a crowd of sorts, Pete was finally willing to perform. He stiffened, craned out his neck, opened his jaws and lightly fixed his fangs on Davy's left hand.

'Told you – the dog's a genius.' Davy opened his palm and showed his sister the red-coloured gum. 'Got it straight off, like I said he would.'

He tossed the sweet to Pete who, to the delight of the small boys, plucked it neatly out of the air, carried it to earth and, slobbering, devoured it.

'That's all very well,' said Alison, 'but what about your other hand?'

'What other hand?' Davy said, innocently.

'*That* other hand.'

Davy grinned, popped the errant wine-gum into his mouth, sucked it for a moment then stuck out his tongue.

'Red!' Alison cried. 'Oh, you big cheat! You horrible, rotten cheat. I want my share of those sweeties.'

'You shall have it, honeybun,' Davy said, 'but first you'll have to catch me,' and with that he sprinted away towards Rowan Road with Pete and Alison in hot pursuit and the cheers of the three little cub scouts ringing behind him in the soft beige air of the September afternoon.

If Sunday was a day of relaxation for her family, for Mavis Burnside it was only marginally less active than any other day of the week. She did, however, make time to attend morning service in Flannery Park's Congregational church. She left the boys to struggle with the mysteries of frying pan and gas grill while she put on her best coat and hat and joined the folk heading up Wingfield Drive towards the Congregational or, like the Rooneys from next door, setting off on the trail to the Roman Catholic chapel at Scotstoun.

Mavis no longer expected to be accompanied by her husband or sons. She was used to presenting herself at the kirk door like a war widow. When the boys had been young she'd insisted that they rolled out for Sunday School and Bible Class. In those days they had not been unwilling to take religious observance at face value. She held no sway over them now though. They were grown men with minds of their own and had a right to decide what they did with their spare time and what they did, or did not, believe in terms of a God and an afterlife.

Alison still fell in with her mother's wishes in church matters as in everything else. Alison had always been a kind and thoughtful child. Since the move to Flannery Park, though, Mavis had intentionally slackened the reins on her daughter, had encouraged her to attend evening service and stay on for the Fellowship meeting that followed where, Mavis hoped, she might meet a nice, respectable young man.

Mavis was sensitive to the fact that her daughter's youth was passing like a flash and that in two or three years Alison would be married and gone. No absolute rule decreed that Ally had to marry young, of course, and as Alex never tired of pointing out they hadn't managed to get shot of any of the boys yet and Henry was already kicking twenty-five.

Girls were different, though, very different.

Mavis glanced up from the sink as Alex, whistling cheerfully, rattled the back door and came into the kitchen from the garden.

He wore a Fair Isle cardigan, old flannels and an open-necked shirt. He was small in stature, only an inch or so taller than Mavis, but thickly muscled. He had big square hands, all scarred, and a head which seemed a shade too large for his body. His face bore reminders of many accidental injuries, including the youthful calamity of a broken nose. Summer weather and an outdoor life had weathered his skin to the colour of mahogany and the tan, combined with all that scar-tissue, gave the impression of stalwart character and toughness, of a man well able to take care of himself.

'Wipe your feet,' Mavis told him.

'Aye, right.' He manufactured a vague scraping motion on the mat behind the door then sauntered past his wife into the living-room.

It was mid-afternoon, a little after three o'clock.

Mavis had eaten a bacon roll and drunk three cups of tea on her return from church before changing out of her best frock. There was an evening meal to prepare, clothes to wash and, Sunday or not, she could not afford to be idle. She did not dare hang clothes on the ropes between the poles in the garden in case she gave offence to God-fearing neighbours but she had no conscience about washing stockings and shirts, light things which could be hung to dry on the pulley indoors.

Up to the wrists in foamy warm water, Mavis kneaded away at Bertie's vest. She took pleasure in simple domestic chores like ironing, sewing and polishing furniture, particularly in the new house where there was space to move about.

Smiling to herself, she glanced out of the back door at Henry and Jack who were crouched on the grass by a lawnmower which their father, for some reason known only to himself, had stripped to its oily parts. Dismantling machinery was much more fun than using it, Henry had told her, but Mavis had long since given up listening to anything Henry said.

Alex, in the living-room, was raking through the sideboard drawers.

The sideboard occupied the wall between the room's two doors and the drawers were crammed with string and wire, pliers, knives, screwdrivers and other small tools. Alex had stopped whistling. Mavis listened to him muttering impatiently until he found what he was looking for and resumed the tuneless aria once more.

He came back into the kitchen with a spanner in his hand, paused and asked, 'Where's Alison?'

'Out on her bike.'

'She's not on her own, is she?'

'Davy's with her.'

'Should she not be home by now?'

'Time enough,' said Mavis.

Alex asked casually, 'How's your head then?'

'Oh, it's fine,' Mavis answered.

Middle age, or at least its first dark sign, was the cause of her occasional migraines. Alex and she had celebrated their silver wedding last March; she was, after all, nearly forty-four years old. Dr Lawrence had told her that a woman at her time of life must expect certain functional disturbances, had given her a prescription for pills and had arranged an eye test which had led to the purchase of a pair of spectacles which she seldom bothered to wear.

Alex leaned his chin on her shoulder and slipped an arm about her waist. 'An' how's the rest of you then?'

'Perfect,' Mavis said. 'As always.'

She had always been inclined to be stout but this past six months she had put on an extra half stone and felt cumbersome because of it. Easy living in Wingfield Drive probably had something to do with it. No flights of stairs to clatter up, no baskets of clothes to lug to the washhouse, no steps to scrub every Friday night. She didn't have to search for reasons why her beam had grown broad and her bosom, never exactly petite, had begun to expand in all directions, mainly downward.

She glanced towards the open door.

'Alex,' she whispered coyly, 'stop that.'

'Stop what?' said Alex. 'What's wrong with givin' you a cuddle?'

She struggled to maintain the air of modest gentility behind which women of her generation hid their true feelings. 'Not in broad daylight.'

Playful amorousness had always been part of Alex's charm. There had been more evidence of it of late too. It was as if Alex had left some of his masculine conceits behind in Sutton Street and twenty-five years of marriage had not quite killed his desire for her.

Up to the elbows in suds, Mavis wriggled again. Alex drew back, gave her bottom an appreciative pinch, resumed his whistling then swaggered off into the garden to argue the theory of nuts and bolts with his sons.

Mavis leaned her plump elbows against the edge of the

sink and sighed. She had told Alex a little white lie. Her headache had not quite gone. In spite of Dr Lawrence's medication she regularly suffered a creeping ache which, if she did not lie down at once, swiftly developed into a blinding pain which made her squint and squinch for ten or fifteen minutes and then, thank God, passed away almost as swiftly as it had arrived.

She'd had a blinder in church that morning. She'd been relieved when service was over and she was free to totter out into the fresh air. She'd scoffed two of Dr Lawrence's pills there in the street and before she'd reached home the worst of the pain had eased. Tea and a bacon roll had put paid to the rest of it, except for a faint trickling sensation, irritating rather than painful, behind her left eye.

As she rested against the edge of the sink, however, she felt a sudden wave of giddiness.

To steady herself she stared from the open doorway and tried to focus on the houses across the backs, on paths and lawns, net-curtained windows, all hazy and tinted by autumn sunlight.

Alex, Jack and Henry were kneeling on the grass, muttering and tinkering, so that it looked as if they were praying over the components of the lawnmower.

Mavis smiled at the men's simplicity then, without even being aware of it, slid downwards and flopped with a soft thud on to the kitchen floor.

Davy was walking by Alison's side, one hand upon the back of the bicycle saddle. He had, of course, shared the wine gums with her and had even taken all the green ones for himself. No longer quite so young as he used to be, Pete panted along at Davy's heels, a half yard from the edge of the pavement.

The motorcar was big, upright and expensive. It roared around the corner from Wingfield Drive, past the new row of shops and pulled away up Shackleton Avenue in a terrific cloud of dust.

Private automobiles were rare in Flannery Park and Alison wobbled, braked and swivelled to stare after the vehicle as it vanished into the distance.

'Jeeze!' Davy exclaimed in admiration.

'What on earth was that?' said Alison.

'It's a bloody great Lanchester,' said Davy. 'Not much change out of a thousand quid after you buy one of those. You could build two houses for what that car cost him.'

Alison pedalled slowly forward, Davy holding the back of the saddle and Pete padding behind. 'Cost who?'

'Dr Lawrence.'

'Mam's doctor?'

'Aye,' Davy said, 'but he's not makin' his dough from treatin' the likes of us at thirty bob a whip. He's got a posh practice in Bearsden too. I expect that's where the real money comes from, from the toffs.'

'I wonder where he's been,' said Alison.

At that moment she caught sight of Jack loitering at the garden gate and knew intuitively that something awful had happened.

Jack's complexion was even more flushed than usual, the cornet-player's embouchure white as chalk against it. His candid features were crumpled and secretive and all the tunefulness had gone out of him.

Pete bounded forward and pawed against Jack's legs. Jack shouted '*Down*,' so sternly that Pete obeyed without a whimper.

It was uncannily quiet in Wingfield Drive, the atmosphere musty with the odours of mown grass and clipped privet. Somebody had drawn the window blinds at 162. Neighbours were gathered at front doors, not gossiping but, like Jack, silent, watchful, and somehow embarrassed.

'What's all the excitement?' Davy enquired.

Alison dismounted, bumped the bicycle's tyres over the kerb, brought the machine as close as she dared to her brothers and listened, almost like an eavesdropper.

'It's – it's Mam,' Jack said.

'Mam? What about her?' Davy said.

Jack's eyes swam with tears.

'She's – she's – dead.'

'You're kiddin'?' Davy said.

'I wish to God I was,' Jack said.

Everything seemed to crowd in on Alison, reduced in scale, distorted and hostile. She was already weeping inside herself. She suffered an almost overwhelming urge to scream at her brothers, to accuse them of tormenting her with a hideous untruth.

Instead she bit her lip hard and in a sharp and nagging voice that made her sound horribly callous, asked, 'How did it happen? Was it an accident? Was she run over?'

'No,' Jack said. 'She fell down on the kitchen floor. Somethin' burst in her head, a blood vessel. We were out in the garden when it happened. She just keeled over at the sink, an' that was it.' Jack wiped his nose with his wrist. 'Dr Lawrence says she never knew what hit her.'

'Where's Dad?' said Alison.

'In the back bedroom,' Jack answered.

Tears seemed frozen in the space behind Alison's eyes. An icy lump hung deadweight in her chest. Even when Davy broke down she remained unnaturally calm, on the outside at least. She had never seen her brothers weep before, not even Bertie. She appeared to observe the phenomenon dispassionately. Jack put an arm about

Davy's shoulder and helped his brother up the path towards the front door. Alison, pushing the Raleigh, followed on behind. She was aware of Mrs Rooney and her husband at the door of 164. Mr Rooney was holding back two of the smaller children with his forearm. The children's eyes were curious but uncomprehending.

Alison walked faster, head up. She ignored Mrs Rooney's attempts to communicate. She wheeled the bicycle along the path before the front window and through the covered close that separated the Burnsides' house from the Donaldsons' next door. She stored the bicycle in the brick shed by the kitchen step then paused to tug up her socks, smooth her rumpled dress and comb her hair with her fingers.

She felt that she would be required to make herself presentable, though she could not think why. She did not know how to behave in this situation and had it in mind to ask her mother what she should do next. When she opened the kitchen door and stepped inside, however, the emptiness was palpable, a great vacuum that extended into nothingness. The closed door of the living-room seemed miles away.

Pete rubbed himself against her heels, whining softly. His tongue lolled out and his black rubbery nose was dry. She fished the dog's water dish from beneath the sink, filled it from the tap, put it outside on the doorstep and gave the dog a gentle nudge with her foot to coax him back outside.

She paused in the doorway, looking out, trying vainly to rationalise everything and bring it into perspective. But the weight of the afternoon continued to impress itself upon her like a fist thrust into clay.

From the kitchen window of the Wilsons' house she caught the strains of a wireless orchestra playing. She listened without guilt to the music until Mrs Wilson yelled, 'Billy, turn that dashed thing off. Show some respect. Don't y'know Mrs Burnside's just passed away?'

'Alison?' Henry emerged from the living-room behind her. His oblong features were gaunt and far back in his dry, dark eyes was something that Alison had never seen there before. 'Did Jack tell you?'

Alison nodded.

She expected some sarcastic remark, some patronising comment but all Henry said was, 'You'd better come with me.'

In the living-room she could see a whisky bottle and glasses upon the dining table, brown paper blinds, mottled like parchment in the slanting rays of the evening sun, Davy and Jack, slumped and silent, no sign of Bertie or her father.

Henry touched her shoulder. 'Are you okay?'

'Yes.'

'Go on then.' Henry gave her a little push to project her into the living-room. 'Remember, I'm right behind you, if and when you need me.'

'Well, I'm glad it's not me,' Brenda said. 'I wouldn't know what to do if you were took sudden.'

'You'd cope,' Ruby McColl told her daughter. 'You'd have to.'

'Suppose so,' Brenda conceded.

Stationed three or four feet back from the upper-floor window and seated on the room's only chair, she could observe through a gap in the net curtains the Burnsides' house across the edge of the tiny triangular park which divided Wingfield Drive from Foxhill Crescent.

It was Brenda's favourite post on those evenings when her mother was at work. She liked to watch the children at play and the menfolk trudging home from the bus stop or railway station.

From here too she could also spy on Alison's brothers and mark their comings and goings. Silly, really. All she had to do to encounter Jack or Henry was cross the road and ring the bell. She had always been made welcome in the Burnsides' house but somehow it was more exciting to watch them without their being aware of it.

Once, not so long ago, she'd quite fancied Jack Burnside. When she'd been ten or eleven he'd playfully tugged her plaits and asked her when she was going to grow up so he could marry her. She was grown up now, though she was hardly much taller than she'd been at eleven, and Jack paid her even less attention than he'd done when she was at primary school.

Jack was a real busy-bee, of course. In addition to working at Ransome's shipyard, he'd be out four or five nights a week tootling his cornet in one band or another. He never seemed to be home for more than ten minutes at a time before flying out again in his spotless white shirt and black bow-tie with his precious cornet case clutched under his arm.

Lately, she'd found herself more attracted to Alison's oldest brother, Henry, who was undoubtedly the best-looking of the Burnsides and had about him an air of knowingness that Brenda, without being able to define it, found increasingly magnetic.

Brenda, however, did not confine her daydreams to the Burnside boys. Since moving to Flannery Park she'd begun to pay attention to more attainable males, like the builders' mates who gave her the eye as she sauntered home from school or the brash shipyard apprentices who lounged about Ferraro's Café on Sunday afternoons.

'What's happening now?' Ruby asked.

She was seated behind her daughter, on the edge of the bed, a cigarette in her mouth and an ashtray in her lap.

'Nothin'.'

The Burnsides' front door was closed, blinds drawn. Nosy neighbours had crept back indoors. In fact, nothing of consequence had occurred since Bertie had arrived home from his afternoon shift at the GPO sorting office.

Brenda didn't like Bertie. Nobody did. He'd always been a mama's boy, the softie in the family. But it couldn't have been much fun for him to come home to find out that his mam was dead.

He'd been greeted at the gate by Henry and had been given the bad news there and then. He'd shrieked and squealed like a lassie and had dropped to his knees on the pavement. When Davy and Henry had tried to lift him he'd flattened himself full-length on the ground. Not right for a grown man to behave that way in public, no matter how bad he felt. Eventually Davy and Henry had had to lift him by the arms and legs and lug him into the house feet first. Brenda had thought it comical and might have laughed out loud if her mother hadn't been in the bedroom.

Ruby lit a fresh cigarette. Brenda smelt the waxy smell of the match and smoke from the Woodbine and saw the beady bright eye of the cigarette's coal reflected in the window.

'You're not working tonight, are you?' she asked.

'No, thank God,' Ruby answered. 'I'm on two to ten tomorrow, unless I can wriggle out of it.'

Ruby was employed by the management of the Argyll Hotel in Glasgow's Queen Street. She had gone there soon after her husband had been killed at Cambrai in 1917 and had graduated from kitchen skivvy to chambermaid to dining-room waitress. She was currently a barmaid in the residents' salon and, since she was a handsome outgoing woman, earned more in tips than she did in wages.

'So you can go to the funeral?' Brenda said.

'The funeral won't be until Tuesday,' said Ruby. 'It might even be later if there are doubts about how she died.'

Brenda glanced round. 'Doubts?'

'Sudden deaths sometimes have to be reported.'

'Hey, you don't think Mrs Burnside was murdered?'

'Who on earth would want to murder Mavis?'

'Well, I just thought – you know – for the insurance.'

'Don't be a bloody idiot.'

Ruby's tart manner and salty tongue stemmed from too long an association with commercial travellers and out-of-town businessmen and meant nothing. Brenda was undaunted by the reprimand.

She shrugged. 'What'll they do with the, you know, the body?'

'Keep it in the house, I expect,' Ruby answered.

Brenda made a grueing sound to indicate distaste. 'I don't fancy sleepin' next door to a dead person.' As a new thought occurred to her she glanced round again. 'Will Alison have to see the body?'

'She might want to,' Ruby said, 'to say goodbye.'

Brenda had never seen a corpse, not even in the depths of the influenza epidemic when they'd been carrying them out of Horsefield Road Primary School by the barrowload. She'd been just too young to distinguish dead from dying, unfortunately.

As if she'd picked up her daughter's thought waves Ruby said, '*You* certainly won't get to see Mrs Burnside lyin' out, that's for sure.'

'Why not?'

'Women don't,' was the cryptic reply.

18

Brenda pretended not to care, an act which practice had brought to near perfection. She stared out of the window into the gloaming which had settled stealthily over the park. 'When will the undertaker arrive?'

'As soon as it's dark,' said Ruby.

'Why?'

'To measure Mrs Burnside for her coffin and settle funeral arrangements with the family.'

'I mean,' said Brenda patiently, 'why won't he come until it's dark?'

Ruby answered, 'Because he won't.'

Twilight tinted Brenda's whisky-coloured hair and imparted a temporary ruddiness to her cheeks that made her look, Ruby thought, like one of those sturdy lassies that stook corn at harvest time.

Ruby drew smoke on to the back of her throat and let it linger there. She'd been smoking since she was twelve years old and, at thirty-four, still took pleasure in the habit. Pouting, she ejected a ball of smoke and watched it float towards the ceiling.

Why, she wondered, was Brenda so keen to see the undertaker's men arrive? There would be nothing much to see except a mannie in a long black coat and a lum hat walking up the path and, a half hour later, walking back down again. Ruby hadn't been all that close to Mavis, not one to pop in for tea and a blether. Even so, she found it disturbing to realise that Mavis Burnside was gone for ever, her time on earth over, her race run, while she, Ruby McColl, was still here, waiting for her life to begin.

Brenda stirred and stretched her arms above her head.

She's bulging out of that dress too, Ruby thought, and it certainly won't see out another summer.

'Are we goin' over there to, you know, pay our respects?'

'You're not,' Ruby answered.

Brenda swung in the chair, carefully extracted the Woodbine from between her mother's fingers and took a long expert drag on the cigarette before handing it back. 'Just as well, really. I haven't a clue what to say to Ally.'

'Perhaps I'll look in later.' Ruby cleared her throat. 'No, come to think of it I'll wait until tomorrow.'

Ruby had exercised patience for years; a few more weeks would make no difference. In a month or so she would begin a serious pursuit of cocky Harry Burnside who had always seemed to her like an ideal mate and who, amazingly, had suddenly become available.

'Why not go tonight?' said Brenda.

'Because I won't,' said Ruby and to her relief saw Brenda turn towards the window again to watch for the arrival of the undertaker's men.

'Swallow these,' said Henry. 'And drink this.'

Bertie wiped his eyes with the back of his hand and glowered at the pills his brother held out to him. 'What are they?'

'Poison,' said Henry. 'For God's sake, Bertie, just take them. They'll calm you down.'

Bertie glanced uncertainly at Jack, who shrugged. Bertie extended his palm. Henry tipped the four pills into it and everyone in the living-room watched Bertie slip them one by one into his mouth and swallow. His prominent little Adam's apple bobbed and bristles scratched against his celluloid collar. Nobody knew why Bertie persisted in wearing such old-fashioned shirts or why, when he was so pernickety in other respects, he somehow never managed to shave properly.

It was Mam who'd kept him neat, of course. Mam who'd brushed his shoes, ironed his handkerchiefs, put his trousers into the trouser press every night. Mam who'd trimmed his fingernails with her own special scissors. Mam, no doubt, would have shaved the little blighter too – and Bertie would have let her – if his brothers had not been there to shout him down. According to Henry's theory, Mam had thought Bertie might be her last child and, because he was so puny, had fallen into the habit of treating him like a precious piece of porcelain.

Bertie choked down the last pill and reached for the glass that Henry held out to him. 'What's this?'

'Brandy.'

Unlike many Glaswegians, the Burnsides were not heavy drinkers. But not even Bertie was daft enough to turn down brandy. He accepted the glass, sipped its contents and managed, with an effort, not to pull a face.

'Better?' Davy asked.

'A bit,' Bertie answered.

They had gathered around the dining table which filled the long window bay. Now and then Jack would touch the blind and squint out at the gate.

'No sign?' Henry would say. Jack would shake his head.

'I wish they'd come,' Davy would say, 'and get it over with.'

The boys were tense, Alison no less so. She'd been in the house for almost two hours and so far had seen nothing of her father who remained resolutely locked in the back bedroom.

Twice Henry had crossed the living-room and had knocked on the bedroom door, 'Are you okay, Dad?'

'Aye, lad. Fine. Fine.'

They were willing to let Dad have his way. As soon as the Co-operative Society's undertaker arrived Mam would no longer belong to any of them.

Alison had fed Pete and had coaxed the dog upstairs. She had watched him settle to sleep on Davy's bed. She was full of tears, deep, hurting sobs. She tried desperately to control her emotions and to feign a purposeful efficiency just as her mother would have done. If she fell apart completely she would become useless to her father, her brothers and herself.

So far Henry had done all the work. He had made the trip to the public telephone box to call the Co-op funeral service. He had also called a neighbour of Aunt Flora's who had a telephone in the house. He had told Aunt Flora the stark truth and had left it to the oldest of the Gilfillan sisters to break the news to Granny Gilfillan who lived near Flora in Clydebank. Soon after Henry had returned to the house Mrs Rooney had appeared at the back door to see if there was anything she could do and, to Henry's consternation, had promised to light a candle for Mam's departed soul. Then Bertie had arrived home and had had to be carried inside and brought out of his swoon and revived by pills and brandy.

Throughout all this activity Alex Burnside remained immured in the back bedroom with his wife's remains.

Alison seated herself on the arm of her mother's chair by the fire and listened without much interest to her brothers' discussion.

'We'll have to let Uncle Willie know.'

'Aye. What about Bob in Newcastle?'

'Telegram, first thing tomorrow.'

'There's Dad's cousin Jeannie as well.'

'Ach, t' hell with her.'

'Dad'll want her informed.'

'But we haven't seen her in years.'

'No, she won't come – but she has to be told.'

'We'll have to lay something on, a meal, won't we?'

'What – here?'

'Either here or a spread at the City Bakeries.'

22

'It'll cost a fortune at the City Bakeries.'

'Not if we restrict it to immediate family.'

'It'll mean extra cars.'

'We could hire a bus.'

'A bus? Don't be bloody stupid.'

'Why not? They laid on a bus when Tommy Mackenzie died.'

'Aye, but he was buried in Ayrshire.'

'And the Masons paid for it.'

'How do you know?'

'Raymond told me. A right royal booze-up it was an' all.'

'Well, it won't be a booze-up on Tuesday.'

'Is that when it'll be – Tuesday?'

'I expect so, yes.'

'What about tomorrow? Do we go to work?'

'You three had better,' Henry said. 'I've got a couple of days in hand, so I'll be here to help the old man.'

Suddenly Bertie began to cry again. He removed his prim, rimless spectacles and wiped the lenses with the edge of the tablecloth.

'I never imagined she'd leave us so soon,' he sobbed. 'I don't know what I'll do. I don't know if I can manage without her.'

'You'll have to,' Henry said. 'We all will.'

At that moment the back bedroom door clicked open and Alison and her brothers, silent and somehow guilty, stared at their father.

Henry was the first to find his voice. 'Dad. Are you all right?'

'Fine, fine,' Alex Burnside answered vacantly. 'Alison, a minute of your time, darlin', please.'

Without hesitation, Alison got up and joined her father in the small back bedroom where her mother's body lay.

* * *

In the gloom his tan seemed darker than ever. He had dressed himself in a clean striped blue shirt and his one and only suit, a shiny black three-piece. He had put on his Sunday shoes, polished to a high gloss but showing like smiles creases across the uppers. The stringy black tie and black crape armband, dug up from heaven knows where, contrasted starkly with the handkerchief which protruded from his breast pocket like a little white sail.

'Come in, come in. There's nothin' to be frightened of, darlin',' he said. 'Your mam doesn't look any different. It's just as if she was sleepin'.'

The bedroom appeared to be packed with furniture. In fact it contained only a bed, a cane chair and a huge, old wardrobe which Mavis had refused to leave behind in Sutton Street. The wardrobe door was jammed against the bed-end, the deep drawer at its base open. Alison's first glimpse of her mother was as a reflection in the wardrobe mirror. Mavis seemed not so much asleep as aloof, head raised by a bolster, nose pointing to the ceiling. Her eyes and mouth were closed, the quilt across her bosom motionless. Alison looked quickly away.

Her father shuffled into the room. He moved with a strange hobbled gait, hunched over, the way he had five or six years ago when he had racked his back. He beckoned to Alison, inviting her to stand by him at the bedside. 'Is she not bonnie?' he said.

'Yes, Daddy.'

It wasn't true. Laughter-lines had vanished from about Mavis's eyes and the little curls of flesh at the corner of her mouth had flattened out, giving her face an uncharacteristic gravity. Alison's sense of unreality increased. She had expected something more lurid and definite than this quaint posturing.

'Well,' her father said with a sigh, 'she's at peace. We'll

not disturb her.' He clapped his hand to Alison's shoulder, making her start. 'Besides, we've got things to do, Ally, haven't we?'

'What – what sort of things?'

He dragged the cane chair away from the wall, seated himself and fished a piece of paper from his waistcoat pocket.

'I thought he might have made trouble for us,' Alex said, 'but he's a toff, is Dr Lawrence. He signed right on the dotted line. Have you ever seen a death certificate before?'

Alison shook her head and stared obediently at the paper. She could not understand why her father was so eager for her to study the official document with her mother's full name, Mavis Elizabeth Gilfillan Burnside, in fresh blue ink upon it.

'Brain haemorrhage,' Alex said. 'Dr Lawrence says if it hadn't killed her she'd have been crippled for life. She'd have hated that.' He gripped Alison's hand tightly. 'If you hear any sort of guff about it bein' our fault, you just tell them what the doctor said. All right?'

'All right, Dad.'

Mam's private box had been taken from the wardrobe and lay open on the bedspread. Now and then Alison had been permitted to peep into it but had found little of interest there, no photographs, no mementoes except two faded lace handkerchiefs and a batch of receipts going back twenty-five years. The box itself had once held two pounds of Golden Moments handmade chocolates, Mam's first present from Dad, and the pasteboard still retained the faint fragrance of the perfumed sweetmeats.

On the floor beside the bed were a glass ashtray filled with cigarette butts and a tumbler of whisky, nearly empty.

Alex plucked the death certificate from Alison's fingers. 'Our guarantee o' fifty pounds.' He winked slyly. 'So long as we've got this bit o' paper the buggers'll have to pay out.'

'Pay out?'

'Never trust insurance men.' He rummaged among the papers on the bed. 'There's more too. Penny policies paid from the year dot, kept up even when we had hardly enough in the house to buy a loaf o' bread.' He glanced at the corpse and winked. 'Always a careful manager, weren't you, honey?'

The bedroom seemed suddenly stifling and Alison was filled with faint disgust at her father's behaviour and longed to be back with her brothers in the living-room again. Alex pushed himself to his feet and began to pick the documents from the bed.

'Well,' he declared, 'since Mavis was the one who accumulated all this cash it's only right it's spent on her farewell.'

'You mean, like a wake?'

'No, no, lass. She wouldn't have appreciated one o' those.'

'What else is there?' said Alison.

'We can ask the undertakers to do her up, make her as pretty as a picture, lay her out in the wee church in Houston Street, then on Tuesday we'll have Mr Jarman down there to conduct a service before we go up to the cemetery. When that's done, back we'll all go for a feed at the City Bakeries' tearooms. How about that?'

'Dad, you can't.'

'If you've got the money, you can do anythin',' Alex said. 'What else am I goin' to do with the bloody stuff now she's gone an' left me?'

'Mam wouldn't have wanted to see the money wasted.'

'Wasted? How could it be wasted on the best wife a man

26

ever had?' He put a hand to his mouth then took it away again. 'Listen, the undertakers will be here any minute. I can't do this myself, Alison. She's just the way she was when we found her. Except the apron. Dr Lawrence took off the apron. She's got to be nice. She must be nice. I want you to sort out her best frock—'

'I won't put it on her.'

'No, the men'll do that,' Alex said. 'If you look everythin' out and put it in the case from the top o' the wardrobe, they'll attend to the rest of it. An' the next time we see her she'll be just like – like she was all those years – all those years ago.'

Hand to his face, he groped blindly for the chair.

'Daddy! Oh, Daddy!' Once she began to weep there was no stopping the flood of tears. She stood by the bed with elbows tucked into her stomach, fingers curled under her chin, and sobbed.

Alex looked up at her, frowning. At first he seemed surprised at her display of emotion, then gradually the dazed expression faded from his features and he reached out and drew her on to his knee. 'There now, Alison,' he said gently. 'There, there. Mam's away an' left us – but you've still got me. You'll always have me, darlin', come what may.' He kissed her brow tenderly and hugged her tightly to him while Alison, quite unabashed, wept at last as if her heart would break.

Conventional wisdom, as expounded by Granny Gilfillan, eventually won the day. Clad in her best brown velvet dress, lightly made up and with a fresh rose from Mr Wilson's garden resting on her bosom, Mavis Burnside was inexpensively laid out in the back bedroom of the family home in Flannery Park to be visited and viewed by relatives, friends and neighbours until ten o' clock on

27

Tuesday morning. At that hour, on the dot, the Co-op's new motorised hearse pulled up in front of 162 and Mavis was taken away to be interred beside a clutch of Gilfillans in the sprawling old cemetery at Hallwood on the green grassy braes which looked down upon Clydebank.

Granny Gilfillan had already buried two husbands, two sons and a daughter. When it came to proper behaviour at funerals there was simply no arguing with her wealth of experience. Escorted by Jimmie McIntosh, one of her sons-in-law, the waspish old woman had turned up hot on the heels of the undertaker on Sunday evening and had immediately taken charge. At that particular juncture the Burnsides had needed all the support they could muster to guide them through the vale of tears, and Granny Gilfillan was nothing if not authoritative. She was a tiny wren-like woman who, even at the age of eighty, was belligerent to the point of tyranny. Dry as gunpowder and just about as volatile, she'd brooked no new-fangled nonsense about expensive funerals from Alex Burnside. She'd never liked the man and had vigorously if unsuccessfully opposed Mavis's marriage to him.

On that Sunday night, it seemed, she was destined at long last to have her revenge. Granny, however, wasn't one to risk losing the initiative and on Monday evening she turned up again, flanked by two of her surviving daughters, Belle and Flora, Alison's aunts. They were big, buttery women, apparently passive. But Alex and his lads knew only too well that the pair had successfully tamed and trained their husbands and sons, had rendered them so timid and trouserless that one simple word of command had the poor down-trodden devils louping through hoops.

Alison was a little afraid of her grandmother and, having

28

endured a day and a night bereft of both consolation and sleep, she was initially too weak to stand up to the beady little woman and allowed herself to be pulled from the crowd in the living-room and drawn alone into the kitchen.

Whatever the circumstances Granny Gilfillan was not one to mince words. She closed the kitchen door and turned on Alison not to offer comfort or advice but, as was her way, to issue orders.

'You'll have to look after them now,' she said.

They were enveloped in the aroma of steak pies baking in the gas oven, pies that Jimmie McIntosh, who was Belle's husband, had lugged up from Clydebank early that evening. The strain of greeting visitors had taken its toll of Alison and she was filled with such a dread of tomorrow's ordeal that she felt almost stunned with exhaustion.

'What?' she said, stupidly. 'Who?'

'Your father and brothers,' Granny Gilfillan told her. 'It'll be up to you to take care of them now.'

'How can I? I've got school to go to.'

'Look at you.' Granny Gilfillan scowled up at her granddaughter who towered almost ten inches above her. 'Big lump that you are. School? What age are you?' Discounting Burnsides, Granny Gilfillan had seventeen grandchildren and a dozen great-grandchildren and was excused for being ill-informed on birthdays and ages.

'Sixteen.'

'Aye, well, you see? This'll be the end of school for you, m'dear. Not before time if you ask me. School at your age. Never heard such nonsense.'

'Mam wanted me to take my Leaving Certificate.'

'I know nothing about these things, of course,' Granny Gilfillan admitted magnanimously, 'but I do know that if Mavis had wanted a scholar in the family she'd have done better to see to her boys. Not one of them a foreman yet.'

'They're too young to be foremen.'

'Rubbish!' Granny Gilfillan said. 'Marion's lad was promoted foreman in Brown's before he was thirty.'

Alison was too upset to argue.

'You can leave school at the end of the week,' the old woman said with a curt little peck of the head. 'I'll tell your Dadda what we've decided.'

'We haven't decided anything. I don't want to—'

'It's not what you want, m'lady. It's what must be done to keep bread on the table. It'll not be up to you to change things just to satisfy your own selfish whims. Leaving Certificates, indeed!'

With sudden cold clarity Alison realised that this was not the voice of experience talking but some repressive echo from a past that was not her past, a past that had faded. She opened her eyes wide and focused upon the pugnacious little woman and for the very first time saw her grandmother not as a matriarch replete with female virtues but as a bully, plain and simple.

She said, 'Do you even know what a Leaving Certificate is?'

'Don't you talk to me in that tone of voice.'

'I'm just asking you a question, Granny. Do you?'

'What you get when you leave school.'

Perhaps being exhausted was like being drunk. Free of the need to please and protect her mother she took a tipsy pleasure in standing up for herself. 'Uh-huh,' she said. 'But there's an enormous difference between a Day School Certificate and Higher Leaving. Do you know what?'

Experience of births, deaths and marriages and an infinite knowledge of distinctions in social standing had given her grandmother an unchallenged platform down the years. But, Alison realised, whatever lay outside that narrow sphere was dismissed out of hand as having no worth or value at all. Her grandmother began to rock back and forth like a budgerigar which spies something threatening through the bars of its cage. 'Paper,' she cried, 'useless bits of paper, that's all these things are.'

'One useless bit of paper, Granny, will ensure me a very good job.'

'You're not needin' a job. You're needin' a husband.'

'Really?' Alison was temporarily diverted from the pain of not knowing quite where she stood. 'I thought you wanted me to be Daddy's servant.'

'Your Dadda earns the bread. He needs looked after.'

'Do I not need looked after?'

'A husband—'

'Where's the logic in that?' Alison was uncomfortably aware that she was beginning to sound like Henry. 'First you tell me I'm to look after Daddy and the boys. Next you tell me I've to find a husband to look after me.' She paused. 'What if I prefer to look after myself?'

'God, but you're impudent.'

'We have,' said Alison, 'an unresolved question. I think it's what's called a paradox. Can you help me solve it, Granny?'

She would never have spoken to her mother in such an arrogant manner. Mam would have been hurt by it. Mam would also have been hurt to learn that Alison had given up cheek to Granny Gilfillan. But she did not have to answer to her mother now and, besides, she wasn't sure it was cheek. Was she not entitled to have a mind of her own and, because she was young and her grandmother old, to express valid opinions?

Granny Gilfillan stared at her impassively for several seconds then, hardly moving her lips, said, 'The pies are burning.'

'No, the pies aren't burning. You just don't want to answer my question,' Alison said. 'What if I choose to look after myself?'

The old woman turned her back on the girl, stooped and peered at the cooker's painted dials as if nothing else mattered.

'Gas stoves,' she muttered. 'Wouldn't have one in the house.'

Alison watched the old woman fiddle with the oven's bakelite knob, twist it savagely left then right before setting it back precisely where it had been before, but with a smugness which suggested that things had been altered for the better by her intervention. Alison was inclined to walk away from the round little backside in its trim black skirt but kinship with Gilfillans, a share of their stubborn streak, prompted her to stay. She watched Granny Gilfillan straighten, take a teacloth from its hook and wipe her hands carefully, finger by finger as if she had just completed a piece of hard manual labour entirely unsuited to a woman of her years. She was, Alison realised, regrouping.

'Mavis was my youngest, you know,' Granny Gilfillan said at length. 'I gave her birth and I reared her. I think you forgot that when you spoke to me the way you did.'

'No, I didn't forget.' Alison might have continued if, at that moment, the door from the living-room hadn't opened to admit Aunt Belle.

Aunt Belle carried a teapot in one hand and three or four empty plates in the other. She still wore her hat, a clam-shaped object of green felt which clung to her frizzled grey hair at a raffish angle which suggested that she'd allowed herself to be pressed into consuming a glass of gin, or two. She was certainly unsteady and swayed hazardously in the doorway, giggling at her own ineptitude. There would be lots of heavy drinking after the funeral tomorrow, Alison guessed, laughter, jokes and, inevitably, debates which would turn into heated arguments. All family gatherings were very much the same, she'd learned, and she doubted if Mam would have wanted her funeral to be in any way different.

'Naughty me. Been at the bottle,' Belle said. 'Och, what the hell,' and listed ponderously towards her mother who, with an alacrity born of practice, caught the rattling teaplates just before they fell.

Cool night air sobered Aunt Belle. She clung to Davy more for warmth than support. Ungrudgingly he put an arm about her enormous waist and let her nuzzle flirtatiously against him while they waited at the bus stop by the shops for a scheduled single-decker to appear. At this hour on a Monday night, however, traffic was mostly from the other direction, flowing into, not out of Flannery Park, men and girls returning from pubs and picture palaces along Dumbarton Road, from the cafés and fish and chip shops to which the exiles of Glasgow's unexciting suburbs gravitated after the day's work was done.

Alison had accompanied Davy and Bertie, and the dog too, on the walk to the bus stop in the vague hope that she might repair the damage to her relationship with her grandmother, that the old woman might relent and offer an olive branch. It was not to be. Granny Gilfillan was thoroughly in the huff. She could barely bring herself to be civil to the boys, addressed not a word to Alison and hoisted herself crabbily on to the bus, Belle and Flora puffing in her wake, without saying goodnight to anyone. It was left to Belle to wave to the Burnsides and call out cheerily, 'See you all tomorrow then,' as if her sister's funeral was something to look forward to.

As soon as the bus had rumbled off, Davy said, 'The old

biddy's got a right bee in her bonnet. What did you say to her in the kitchen, Ally?'

'Oh, she was rattling on about her plans,' Alison answered.

'Plans?' said Bertie. 'What sort of plans?'

'According to Granny Gilfillan, I'll have to give up school and stay home to take care of you lot.'

'How did you react to that suggestion?' Bertie asked.

'It wasn't a suggestion. It was an order.'

'What did you tell her?' Davy said.

'More or less that it was none of her business.'

'Quite bloody right,' Davy said.

'You shouldn't have talked back to Granny,' Bertie said.

'I'm entitled to stand up for myself,' Alison said. 'Surely you don't think she's in the right?'

'Well, somebody has to take care of us,' Bertie said.

'Why should it be me?' said Alison. 'I've more important things to do than stay at home pressing your blessed trousers. Didn't it occur to you I might want a career of my own?'

'A career? Don't make me laugh.'

'All right, all right,' Davy interrupted. 'This isn't the time for squabblin' or for makin' decisions. Let's get tomorrow over and done with first.'

'Yes,' Alison said. 'I'm not looking forward to tomorrow. I wonder what it'll be like?'

And Bertie answered, 'Grim.'

TWO

Class Distinction

Having shelled out for the building of a fine new school, the
Education Board in its wisdom had immediately conferred
upon it all the advantages of Senior Secondary status. The
board's hope was that Mr Pallant and his staff would be
able to persuade the sons and daughters of Flannery Park's
hand-picked tenants to continue with education beyond the
age of fourteen and thus justify the employment of
specialist teachers. The establishment of a fifth and sixth
year was the staff's initial objective and, in the headmaster's not so humble opinion, quite enough to be going
on with.

Younger teachers like James Abbott had, however,
more vision.

They saw a future sparkling with college places and university degrees and were constantly on the lookout for the
smart boy, the dedicated scholar, a lad equipped by nature
to lead the school's unwashed hordes into the exalted
realms of higher education. It came then as a mild surprise
to Jim Abbott to discover, tucked modestly among the
inkwells, that one of the two pupils to whom the accolade of
'clever' could honestly be accorded was not male but
female.

Jim couldn't quite pinpoint the moment when he first

spotted Alison Burnside's potential. In the chaotic year after its opening Flannery Park had become the repository of such an accumulation of waifs and strays from other schools that only delinquents and star football players had acquired much individual identity. Suddenly, though, there she was – Alison Burnside, tall and leggy, and as pretty a girl as Mr Abbott had ever had in his charge. Apparently, she had transferred from Hamilton Crescent School at Easter. In August she had joined the academic trickle of eleven girls and twenty-one boys who had come forward into Jim Abbott's fifth year class.

Mr Pallant was gratified with the intake. He had arranged the curriculum with as much flexibility as the Inspectorate would allow to stimulate those parents who sensed stagnation in industry and saw a career in banking, teaching or clerking as the only way forward for their daughters and sons. Jim was content to leave social speculation to the head. He had quite enough to do coping with a fifth year in whom resentment was never far from the surface and in whose cells rang the piping of primitive messages so shrill that no adult ear could catch let alone interpret them.

Flannery Park, with its undercurrent of middle-class pretension, was a far cry from Masterton, the small-town school in Stirlingshire where Jim had started his career. There every boy was destined to work in the pits, and every girl to labour in the mills until marriage or pregnancy carried her into oblivion. In Masterton's industrial parishes rickets and headlice stood higher on the agenda than Latin roots and Lakeland poets, and poverty not puberty was the pressing problem for the young. In Flannery Park, however, the heirs of Glasgow Corporation's specially selected tenants were clean, well nourished and probably educable. Yet all Jim Abbott could see out there were spots and whiskers and alarmingly well-developed bosoms; all he could hear were broken voices and sniggering giggles, the discordant rhapsody of sexual awakening and the curious sufferings that accompanied it.

'McLeod.'

'Aye, sir.'

'What have you got there?'

'Nothin', Mr Abbott.'

'No, don't try to hide it. Bring it here, McLeod.'

'But, sir—'

Jim would take the crumpled sheet of paper from a hand larger and more powerful than his own, would scowl at the culprit who, with cheeks aflame and every pimple puce, would hang his shaggy head and shuffle his feet in embarrassment while Mr Abbott, still an unknown quantity, would unfold the grubby sheet and glance at it. 'What is this, McLeod?'

'Just – just a drawin', Mr Abbott.'

'Is this the art class?'

'No, Mr Abbott.'

Jim would angle the crude pencil sketch this way and that as if he could not make head or tail of it, would make poor McLeod sweat for the next question, one that would surely lead to discussion of the scribble and the sort of public humiliation that boys feared more than physical punishment. What silly drawings they were too, banal to the point of despair, exaggerated, anatomically inaccurate and usually more concerned with urination and defecation than natural sexual congress.

Jim sometimes wondered how the callow lads of Flannery Park would react to the sort of pictures which had circulated in the trenches and had infested the camps where he had received his initiation into sexual matters,

37

propaganda whose printed images remained indelibly in his mind, mingled with scenes of carnage so revolting that the young bucks of Class 5A could not have imagined them let alone given them shape and form. At length he would crumple the paper in his fist and lob it scornfully into the wastepaper bucket. 'It's as well for you this isn't the art class, McLeod,' he would say, 'otherwise you'd be thrown out on your lug. What do you think I should do with you?'

'Belt me, sir.'

'How many do you think you deserve?'

'Six.'

'Perhaps I should send you to Mr Pallant.'

'Christ – I mean, no, Mr Abbott. Just belt me, eh?'

'Oh, very well. If you insist.'

Out would come the tawse, a thin, hard leather strap which reposed like a snake in the top drawer of Jim's desk. With the strap tucked into his armpit, Jim would arrange the boy's wrists across the desk edge, would withdraw the strap, snap it once or twice then – without any pleasure – would administer six quick blows to the young man's quailing palms.

'No more of this scribbling nonsense, McLeod, you hear?'

'Aye, sir.'

'Go back to your seat.'

Jim Abbott would turn away, invariably confused by the class's reaction to punishment, by the girls' smirking faces, the ugly resentment of the boys. One-handed, he would coil up the strap and lock it away in the drawer before swinging round to face them once more.

'Well?' he would shout, expecting no answer.

It was in the wake of one such incident that he first really noticed Alison Burnside and detected her quality. He had remarked her capacity to grasp salient facts in both English and history and regurgitate them almost verbatim, but a quick, acquisitive mind did not necessarily signify intelligence and he had paid her no particular attention.

Jim had turned from the desk while the culprit of the hour sloped back to his seat, blowing on his fingers and fighting tears. It was then that Jim had noticed a gap at the rear of the classroom next to fat little Brenda McColl.

'Alison?'

She stretched up abruptly and gave her hair a shake in a gesture that was unintentionally coquettish.

'Alison, are you with us?'

'Yes, Mr Abbott.'

'Good.' He glanced at the textbook open on his desk. 'Now, can anyone tell me what important event took place in 1745?'

Silence. Resentment or ignorance? It could hardly be the latter. The fifth year course of study had an unrealistic bias towards Highland oppression in which the so-called romantic figure of Bonnie Prince Charlie featured prominently.

'Come on, that's an easy one,' Jim Abbott urged.

More silence, unmistakably dour. Yes, the wee devils were defying him. He plucked a stalk of chalk from the box on his desk and slashed at the blackboard with it, numerals fair flying on to the painted slate.

'All right,' he said. 'Alison, you tell me.'

The girl glanced round the classroom in the hope that someone else might break the deadlock. No takers.

Resigned, she said, 'Second Jacobite Rebellion.'

'More.'

'Suppression of the Stuarts by the Hanoverians.'

She seemed less than eager to display her knowledge and

39

imparted the information as flatly as if the question was too basic to be other than tedious. Jim yielded to impulse and pressed her for an interpretation.

'Surely,' he said, 'there were more complex issues at stake?'

'Yes,' Alison said. 'Repercussion.'

'Give me an example of repercussion.'

She fired off an explanation without pause.

'There were lots of Scots, including Highlanders, in Cumberland's army and three complete Scottish regiments fought on the English side at Culloden,' the girl said. 'If Cumberland was really the butcher we're told he was then he had plenty of Lowland Scots to help him in his bloody work.'

Jim advanced up the aisle between the wood and iron desks, struggling to hide his surprise. 'You didn't find that in the textbook, Alison.'

She was embarrassed by his attention. 'No, Mr Abbott.'

'But you still haven't answered my question about repercussion,' he said. 'What was the real significance of the suppression of the Jacobite Rising on Scottish history?'

'It marked the absolute death of the Stuart cause,' Alison answered promptly. 'Legislation was introduced soon after Culloden to put an end to the feudal powers of the Highland chieftains.'

'What was the nature of the legislation?'

'For one thing,' she said, 'the Highland clansmen were forbidden to wear the tartan and they were, under law, disarmed.'

Fusty old Highland chieftains were not the only ones to be disarmed. Jim clapped his hand against his thigh and muttered, 'Well done.' He was close to her now and said in a quiet voice that few in the class could hear, 'Where did you acquire so much information, Alison?'

'My brother Henry has some books on the subject.'

'Your family's not from the Highlands, is it?'

'No, from Partick.'

Jim said nothing for a moment. He sensed that she had a question of her own and that she was debating the wisdom of putting it to him. At length, he prompted her. 'What?'

'If I was from a Highland family I wouldn't be allowed to spout all that stuff about Lowland officers, would I, Mr Abbott?'

'No, you wouldn't,' Jim said. 'Did your brother teach you that too?'

'Not really,' Alison said. 'My brother thinks all history is relative.'

'Do you know what he means by that?'

She nodded. 'The English regard Culloden as a famous victory. We regard it as a tragic defeat. Same battle, different perspectives. Henry says we make up much of our history to suit our own national prejudices.'

'Do you agree with your brother?'

'Yes, I think I do.'

He was fascinated by his discussion with this well-informed girl and would have continued for the remainder of the period if the class had not been growing restive behind him. And Alison's chum, Brenda McColl, wore a deep crimson blush upon her chubby cheeks as if the loitering proximity of the teacher was somehow embarrassing.

Jim cleared his throat, gave Alison a nod of approval and tramped back to his desk, shouting, 'All right, all right. Back to work. Page eighteen in *Hasting's* History. You, boy, read from the top of the page.'

'Me, sir?'

'Yes, McNeillage. You, sir.'

When Jim eventually risked a glance towards the back of

41

the class he saw that Alison Burnside was not, alas, gazing at him but appeared to be rapt in contemplation of the gloomy clouds that scuttled over the river beyond the plate-glass windows.

'Alison?'

'Yes, Mr Abbott.'

'Pay attention.'

'Yes, Mr Abbott,' Alison said, sitting up and squaring her shoulders as if to acknowledge that she still had much to learn and that he, in class at least, was the man best placed to teach it to her.

Mr Pallant was always impeccably groomed. His fine silvery hair was brushed back in a coif that not even the half gale that whistled perpetually along the school's open verandahs seemed able to displace. He was very smooth-skinned and pale, as if he had been plucked at a tender age and, like a chicken breast, preserved in aspic. He had been teaching since 1897, the very year in which Jim Abbott had been born, and had entered the profession out of conviction and not financial necessity. Why Ronald Pallant, so obviously a gentleman, had remained entrenched in public education for over thirty years was a mystery that Jim and his colleagues had often discussed without reaching any very satisfactory conclusion. No one, of course, had had the temerity to ask the head to explain himself for Mr Pallant, while not exactly a dictator, represented power and authority, qualities which were at that time still much admired.

'May I be of assistance, Mr Abbott?' the head enquired from the half-open door of the cubicle where Mrs Grainger, the school's part-time secretary, worked four mornings each week.

Jim jumped a foot in the air at the sound of Mr Pallant's

voice. There was nothing to prevent him consulting the Pupil Register yet at that moment he felt like a pimply adolescent caught out in mischief.

'I – I'm just checking the fifth year cards, Mr Pallant. Shan't be a minute.'

'Take your time,' Mr Pallant said. 'Are you searching for some name in particular?'

Unfortunately Jim was incapable of riffling through the index cards at great speed. He cursed the fact that he had only one hand to work with. Practice had taught him to cope with shoelaces, buttons, knives and forks, even to knot his necktie, but now and then a simple manual task, like pulling a file, would catch him out and he would experience a little spark of anger at the German shell which had ripped away his left hand and arm.

'Do allow me to assist you,' said Mr Pallant.

Jim fumed. Why didn't the nosy old beggar mind his own business and toddle off to his study to smoke an afternoon pipe. Mr Pallant peered over his shoulder at the card in Jim's hand. 'Ah! It's McLeod,' said Mr Pallant. 'Is that miscreant making trouble again, Mr Abbott?'

'What? No, not exactly.'

'He's a blackguard, that one,' said Mr Pallant, 'a born mischief-maker. Personally I won't be surprised if he winds up behind bars.'

Jim hadn't a clue what poor McLeod had done to deserve such condemnation. He had no opportunity to defend the lad, however, for at that moment the telephone in Mr Pallant's study rang and the head sloped off to answer it, closing the connecting door behind him.

Jim heaved a sigh of relief, returned McLeod's card to the packed drawer, glanced nervously over his shoulder then whipped out the card marked Burnside, Alison G. He wondered what the G stood for. Gwendoline, Guinevere, Grace perhaps? Grace was very nice, very fitting.

He cupped the card in his palm and scanned it rapidly.

Father's name: Alexander. Father's occupation: Riveter. Place of Employment: Ransome's. Home address: 162 Wingfield Drive. He also discovered that Alison had four brothers, a piece of information that, for some reason, made him feel uncomfortable. But her academic record cheered him. She had emerged from Hamilton Crescent School with the sort of class marks that would have singled her out as a high flyer in any fee-paying school in Scotland. His next move would be to have a quiet word with science teacher Norman Borland, known colloquially as Big Boris, and maths teacher Charlie Hammond to discover what they thought of Alison Burnside. If they too had singled her out as a pupil of exceptional ability he would certainly make time to discuss with Alison her family's plans for her career.

He returned the file to its place, closed the drawer and slipped out of the office before Mr Pallant could nab him again. As he walked along the verandah he could not put Alison's dark brown eyes and soft oval face out of his mind and just for a moment he felt as if he were walking on air.

Four days later the poor girl's mother dropped down dead and that, Jim Abbott assumed, was that as far as Alison Burnside's future was concerned.

Cold grey wind, running before rain clouds, snapped at the washing in the gardens and drove a litter of leaves down Wingfield Drive. For the first time in months Brenda found it necessary to pull up the hood of her old green raincoat as Alison and she legged it home for dinner at half past noon.

Alison was more depressed than she'd been since Mam's funeral a week ago, so down in fact that she was near to tears. She knew that she would find no comfort at home. A small electric radiator was no substitute for a blazing coal fire. Pots and breakfast dishes piled unwashed in the kitchen gave the house an unfamiliar staleness that emphasised its emptiness.

Davy, who also came home for midday dinner, would have led the dog out for a short walk. Pete too had become surly and would snap without warning. He hated being cooped up all day alone in the house without Mam for company. Alison would take him with her when she went shopping late in the afternoon but she was so swamped by household duties that she had no inclination now to romp with poor old Pete. The boys had vowed to pitch in with the chores. In practice that meant they made their own beds, squabbled about whose turn it was to wash the supper dishes, and left the rest to Alison. She felt as if she was being buried in a landslide of grubby shirts, undarned socks and sheets that would not dry, but she did not complain and did her best to fit schoolwork into the new, domestic routine. Evenings at home were no longer cosy. The boys spent as little time as possible in the living-room and her father had taken to coming home reeking of beer. After he had eaten whatever Alison put before him he would slump into the smoker's chair by the fire and fall asleep, snoring like an old, old man.

The bleak grey day emphasised her sense of isolation. She had not supposed that grief would be so quickly swallowed up by frustration and harassment, trivialised by housework. In daylight hours she was consumed less by sorrow than by resentment at the legacy of confusion that Mam had left behind; guilt and disloyalty only added to her burden. There would be no hot dinner for Davy today. She had forgotten to steep lentils for the soup pot last night and nobody in the household had thought to remind her. Davy would just have to make do with sardines.

She had been upset all morning and had very nearly burst into tears when Boris had wigged her for shoddy homework.

Brenda said, 'You're fair down in the mouth.'

'It's the miserable weather, that's all.'

'Old Boris—'

'I don't care about Boris,' Alison snapped.

'Sorry I spoke,' said Brenda.

'It's not your fault.'

'It'll be, you know, reaction,' Brenda told her. 'At least that's what Mum says. She says it takes a while for that sort of thing to sink in.' She shivered and plucked at the coat's hood, drawing it over her ears. 'God, but it's freezin'. Winter woollies tomorrow if this keeps up.'

The girls neared the patch of grass and staked saplings which sent Foxhill Crescent curving gracefully away from the long straight of Wingfield Drive. The smell of coal smoke and cooking was thick in the air and the brawling wind carried the clatter of Clydeside's industries deep into the suburbs. Alison peered across the corner of the park to 162. No lights, no warmth, no sign of welcome. She rubbed her nose with the sleeve of her cardigan, and was on the point of separating from Brenda to cross the road when Brenda said, 'Look, there's Mum. I wonder what she's doin' at the gate.'

In her present frame of mind any minor deviation from the norm sent tremors of anxiety through Alison. She stopped and stared at Mrs McColl who, smiling, did not seem to offer any sort of threat. The woman wore a floral apron over a frilly imitation-silk blouse and her hair was bobbed in a style that made her look vaguely American. Opening the iron gate, Ruby McColl beckoned. 'Come into our house, Alison. Have your dinner with us.'

'That's very kind, Mrs McColl,' Alison said, 'but I've got to make something for our Davy.'

'Davy's upstairs,' Mrs McColl said, 'tucking in.'

'What about Pete, he—'

'The mutt too,' Ruby McColl assured her. 'Come on, dear, a big plate of mince and tatties will do you the world of good.'

In the McColls' living-room Alison could make out the flicker of a coal fire and see her brother Davy seated at the table close to the window with, of all things, a napkin tucked into the bib of his bricklayer's overall. Spotting Alison, he gave a broad grin and beckoned her to join him.

'Thank you, Mrs McColl,' Alison said. 'That would be very nice.'

'My pleasure,' said Ruby magnanimously and putting an arm about Alison's waist led her up the garden path while Brenda, neglected, trailed sulkily on behind.

'I don't know why you did it,' Brenda said.

'Because she's a poor thing,' said Ruby.

'Aye, but why did we need to have him here too?'

'Davy's a nice lad.'

Slouched in the knobbly leather armchair which had once belonged to her grandfather, Brenda wriggled her bare toes towards the fire, squinted at her mother and grumbled, 'He ate enough, I'll say that for him.'

'He probably hasn't had a decent meal in a week.'

'Aye, well, as long as we don't, you know, make a habit of it.'

'You're not very charitable, Brenda. I thought Alison was your chum.'

'She is, but I just don't want . . .' Finding no end to the sentence Brenda let her protest dwindle into silence.

Ruby was fussing before the ornamental mirror in the living-room. She was dressed in the same white blouse and black skirt she had worn at dinnertime and in accordance with nightly ritual was busy decorating herself with rings, earrings and bangles.

'When did you get your hair done?' Brenda asked.

'This morning, first thing.' Ruby titivated the big flat waves that covered the tops of her ears. 'Took the bus to Clydebank specially. Like it?'

'I liked it better the way it was.'

'Well,' Ruby reached for her hat, 'I felt it was time for a change.'

Brenda leaned an elbow on the chair's worn wooden arm and rested her chin on her knuckles. 'Where's all the money comin' from?'

'Money? What money?'

'New hair-do, new apron,' Brenda said, 'not to mention what it cost for the feedin' o' the five thousand.'

Hat in hand, Ruby swooped upon her daughter.

'What's wrong with you these days?' she demanded. 'You never worried about how much we spent before. Well, it's my hard-earned cash, Brenda. I'll spend it as I see fit.' She drew back and, less forcefully, said, 'I performed a wee kindness today, that's all. I'll do it again if and when I feel like it – have Alison in for her dinner, I mean.'

'Him too?'

'For all it costs for an extra dollop of mince.'

'You're up to somethin',' Brenda said.

Unfazed by her daughter's accusation, Ruby assumed an expression of incomprehension. 'I provide your chum and her brother with a hot meal on a cold day and the next thing you know I'm Mata Hari.' She returned to the mirror, put on and adjusted her hat. 'Anyway, what could I possibly be up to?'

Brenda was not mature enough to discuss delicate matters without a degree of embarrassment. She wriggled in the armchair and stretched her bare legs to the fire. It had come on to rain in mid-afternoon and her shoes and stockings had been wet when she'd got home. The shoes were steaming by the hearthstone, her stockings drying on the wire fireguard. She curled her toes towards the fire and blurted out, 'I just hope you're not tryin', you know, to marry me off to Davy Burnside.'

Ruby's mouth opened in amazement and, before she could help herself, laughed aloud. 'Marry you off? For God's sake, Brenda, you're only sixteen years old.'

'Well, I just thought – you know—'

'That I want rid of you?' Ruby said. 'Well, I don't, so you can stop frettin' about bein' sold into bondage against your will.' She went into the little hall and returned a moment later, buttoning her overcoat. 'Mark you, you could do worse by way of a husband than Davy Burnside.'

'He's only a brickie.'

'And what's wrong with marrying a brickie? Take it from me, slump or no slump, brickies are seldom out of work.'

'Is that all you ever think about – work?'

Ruby turned up her coat collar, gave a final tweak to the brim of her hat. 'I'd better think about gettin' to *my* work or I'll be late for the third time this week.'

She stooped, kissed her daughter on the forehead and, with a casual scatter of last-minute instructions, hurried out into the hall and was gone. For two or three minutes after the outside door clattered shut Brenda remained motionless. She could hear the clock on the sideboard ticking, the fire crackling, the wind flinging rain against the window-panes, but warmth and comfort were no longer enough to soothe the grinding panic she'd nursed since she'd seen Davy and Alison Burnside with their feet under her table.

Anger swelled within her. She shot to her feet and shouted aloud, 'What about *my* tea then? Who's goin' to serve *my* tea?'

There was, of course, no answer, only a plate of salad and sardines left under a bowl in the kitchen to stimulate poor Brenda's appetite and keep her appeased until morning.

Jim Abbott knew better than to accost a full-grown female pupil in the street. He might give older girls and boys a nod of recognition if he happened to encounter them outwith the bounds of school but he did not pause to pass the time of day with them. Master-pupil relationships had, however, changed for the better since Jim had cowered behind a school desk fifteen years ago. In his day all sorts of tragedies might befall pupils without word ever reaching the teaching staff. Now it was no longer considered treachery for a pupil to impart the odd bit of information to a teacher nor was it necessary for a teacher to pretend that the real world ended at the school gates.

Since transferring from Masterton to Flannery Park Jim Abbott had developed a crafty method of finding out about his pupils' personal lives. He would button-hole a chum or close associate and casually enquire what was wrong with so-and-so today. He seldom failed to receive an honest answer, though some of the answers were so dashed odd that they might almost have been little white lies.

'What's wrong with Doris?'

'The cat ate her budgie.'

'What's wrong with Colin?'

'His granny hit him with a chip pan.'

Other less transient events also marred the lives of his charges, however. Jim Abbott would listen and nod and at some point later in the day would have a quiet word with the pupil in question and do what he could to salve the hurt with sympathy and understanding.

'Johnny?'

'Father laid off.'

'Isobel?'

'Wee sister in hospital.'

'Peter?'

'Brother nicked by the polis.'

'Alison?'

'Mother died.'

'Suddenly?'

'Aye, dropped dead at the sink, Mr Abbott,' Brenda had told him. 'Here today an' gone tomorrow. Just shows, you never know the minute, eh?'

'Thank you, Brenda,' he had said, rattled.

Alison had returned to school on Wednesday, the day after the funeral. He had been a little bit surprised to see her back so soon and there was the smack of callousness in it, but also of practicality. She'd been dry-eyed and tight-lipped but with a cloudiness in her brown eyes which worried Jim Abbott considerably. Experience had taught him just what damage could be done by stiffening the upper lip and struggling to hide one's emotions. He had spoken with Alison at her desk. He had risked putting a consoling hand on her arm.

For an instant he had felt a slight easing of the tension that kept her shoulders rigid and had fancied that he saw her bottom lip wobble. He had almost succumbed to the fatal temptation to put an arm about her. Instead he had sensibly contented himself with giving her a gentle pat on the back and then, in the uncomfortable silence which had enveloped the class, he'd walked back to his desk and plunged gruffly into the morning's lesson.

Three weeks passed before he had an opportunity to talk to Alison alone. The day, like many that month, was so dark that by mid-morning most classrooms were already lit by electric lights which were reflected in crayon-like scribbles in the playground's puddles. October rains swept over the school's rooftops and the back playground, tucked into a horseshoe of buildings, was slick with floodwater. Jim was two or three minutes late for his fifth year English class. He had been detained by Mr Pallant who had received notification of a visit from the Inspectors and wished to ensure himself Jim's classes would be tuned up to face the ordeal. Empty left sleeve flapping against his ribs, Jim walked at high speed across the little playground, heading for the stairs at the end of the verandah. He would have put decorum aside and dashed the last few yards to shelter if he had not caught sight of Alison Burnside emerging from the open-roofed lavatories. Jim skidded to a halt.

In an adjacent classroom Mr Watson, the music teacher, was hammering out chords on a piano, the class raggedly chanting '*Doh Me So-oh So-oh*,' over and over again, Mr Watson shouting with angry enthusiasm, '*Doh Me Soh-Soh*. Blast it! *Doh Me Soh-Soh*.'

Jim said, 'Alison?'

Startled, she looked up. She was red-eyed and her cheeks were wet with something other than rain. Jim wondered how long she'd been hiding in the lavatory, all during playtime probably, too distraught to come out even when the bell rang. She glanced towards the stairs as if considering a sprint for the safety of the crowded classroom.

'Go on, Alison,' Jim Abbott said, grinning. 'I'll race you for it.'

'I'm – I'm sorry, Mr Abbott.'

'Sorry for what?'

'For being late.'

'I'm late myself as you can see,' Jim said. 'Tell you what, we'll walk sedately upstairs together and you can nip into class ahead of me.'

'F – fine, Mr Abbott. Thanks.'

The tremble in her voice indicated that she'd been crying for some time. In a baggy green cardigan and damp grey skirt, left stocking wrinkled and one shoelace undone, she looked quite pathetic.

As he ushered her towards the staircase, Jim Abbott said gently, 'You must miss your mother dreadfully.'

'Oh, yes I do, but—'

'But?'

'I haven't had time to think about her much.'

'Are you looking after the house?'

'I'm trying to.'

'Did it catch up with you, Alison?' He touched her very lightly on the elbow and halted her under the lofty first landing window. 'Just now, I mean?'

She was too intelligent to prevaricate. 'Yes, it did.'

'Is that why you were crying?'

'Yes.'

'How do you feel now?'

'A bit better.'

'How many brothers do you have at home?'

'Four.'

'All older than you?'

Alison nodded.

Jim Abbott said, 'Don't they cry?'

'No.'

'I'll bet they do,' Jim said, 'when nobody's watching.'

'Well,' Alison admitted, 'Bertie might.'

The big windowpane was rivered with driving rain whose shadows freckled the girl's pale face. Jim said, 'Will you leave at the end of term?'

'I expect so, yes.'

It came as no surprise. Even so, a strange sadness stole over him, a sense almost of loss. Once the girl left school she would soon become just one more faceless factory worker, shop assistant or office clerk, intellect smothered, talents wasted. 'Is there no possibility you might remain at school long enough to attain the Higher Certificate?'

'I doubt it.'

'And university?'

'My father wouldn't understand about university.'

'Couldn't you explain to him?'

She seemed surprised by his naïvety. 'He's my father. I can't explain anything to him. Besides, I'm needed at home now my mother's gone.'

'Is that what you'll do – stay at home?'

'I really don't know, Mr Abbott.'

He knew only too well what that meant. She would leave school at Christmas; *fait accompli*. If by chance he encountered Alison again she would probably be hanging on the arm of some cocky young platelayer or trailing about the shops with a couple of bairns tagged to her skirts and not a thought in her head except how to make ends meet. The prospect, the inevitability of it, saddened Jim Abbott but there was not one damned thing he could do about it.

He sighed. 'All right, Alison. I realise how difficult things are for you right now. If there's ever anything I can do to help you know where to find me.' He sighed again.

'Perhaps you'd better cut along to class now. Go on with you.'

'Yes, Mr Abbott,' she said. 'And thanks.'

'For what?'

'For trying.'

He watched her mount the stairs ahead of him, all legs and optimism.

At least he'd cheered her up a little. But that, it seemed, would be all he would be able to do for Alison Burnside who, by Christmas, would slip out of his life and be lost to his influence for ever.

THREE

Secret Lives

Each day from eight to five Henry Burnside was indistin-
guishable from his workmates in Ransome's shipyard. He
wore the same brown cotton overalls as they did, the same
studded boots, a cloth cap mottled by sweat and weather
and, in winter months, a grey woollen muffler to protect his
neck and chest from sleet and driving rain. What Henry
did, day in and day out, to earn his bread was drill holes in
hull plates. He spent most of the forty-five-hour working
week stooped over lengths of metal atop a low wooden
platform or, when the job required it, hunkered on his
heels on a carpet of shiny steel flakes amid a tangle of heavy
rubber air hoses. He was clever with the drill bits but it was
not the sort of job in which a man could take much pride.
Henry did it, was paid for it and wisely left it all behind him
the minute the five o'clock whistle sounded.

You wouldn't find Henry propped against the bar in the
Queen of the Clyde public house where, oiled by whisky
and beer chasers, his cohorts bragged about an industry
which, in Henry's unvoiced opinion, was sinking faster
than the bloody *Titanic*. He had never been a taproom
vigilante hunting the scalps of bosses and owners. And he
didn't subscribe to the belief that a return to power of a
Labour government would bring the dawning of a New Age
and fulfil the Utopian ideal of fair shares for all. All in all,

Henry didn't much care what happened on the Clyde and what other men put down as cynicism Henry regarded as plain common sense.

By the time he was six Henry had had three siblings to contend with. By the time he was ten, four of the same. By the time he'd reached the ripe old age of fourteen he had been forced to bow to the sad economic fact that there was no money to advance his education. He was articled to Ransome's as an apprentice before you could say 'Knife' and, about the same time, consciously decided to dedicate himself to one cause only, namely his own material welfare and advancement.

In the course of the next ten years young Henry developed a system for dealing with adversity, a system he kept dark from the folks at home.

Where Henry went and how Henry spent his leisure hours were mysteries never solved by his family. Now and then Alex would pop his head out from behind the *Evening Citizen*, glower round Sutton Street's kitchen cum living-room and tendentiously enquire, 'Where the hell's our Henry?' And every time he did so he would receive the same reply. 'God knows!' Eventually Henry's absences came to be seen as a normal part of Burnside family life. If, however, Mam or Dad had ever uncovered exactly what Henry was up to they'd have turned white with anxiety and red with shame, for Henry, like Dr Jekyll, enjoyed not one but several distinct and separate existences.

Being something of a cold fish, Henry had made few real friends in the course of his climb up the ladder of success. In fact only two people seemed willing to endure his company for long, and wee Eddie Ruff was one of them. Eddie and Henry had shared a desk in primary school, had skulked about Partick's closes and lanes together and had left Hammy on precisely the same day. Thereafter their ways had tended to part until Eddie's chequered career as a jobbing printer, not to mention his devotion to radical politics, eventually brought Henry and he together again.

Home for Eddie was a cold-water flat in the warren of halls and workshops that made up the Caledonia Institute in Horseferry Road in the nether ward of Partick. The Cally had been there from time immemorial and at one stage in its history had been considered very classy. What remained, sandwiched between crumbling tenements, was an ugly, four-storey building so badly in need of repair that the owners were happy enough to lease it to the Scottish People's Party who somehow, God knows how, managed to make it pay.

At pavement level were small scrofulous offices and workshops, sub-leased by the SPP to dedicated entrepreneurs who did wondrous things with wireless sets or motorcycle parts or conducted furtive agencies in imported rubber goods and the sort of photographic magazines that respectable wholesalers refused to stock. On the first floor, at the top of a narrow staircase, was the Cally Hall itself. The hall's place in legend had been established not by the SPP's lectures or dreary concerts in aid of starving Bolsheviks but by the Saturday Night Dance. As these things go the Cally's dances were regarded as hot-beds of iniquity, which meant, of course, that they drew large crowds of daft and daring young men and women all too eager to sample the delights of depravity.

Dance-hall takings paid most of the SPP's bills and kept Eddie Ruff in employment. Members of the Central Committee might have been political fanatics but they weren't exactly naïve in financial matters and not a whiff of proselytising rose above the strains of 'Everybody's Doin' It', or 'Oh, How I Miss You Tonight'. Henry, however, was conspicuously absent from the Cally Hall on Saturday nights. To Henry the Cally was a place of work, not entertainment.

On the building's fourth floor, well above the dance-hall, snuggled the SPP's printing house where Eddie Ruff laboured long and hard and Henry rented a dank oblong room which he used as an office and general retreat. Also on this floor was Eddie's one-roomed flat, for Eddie was not only the SPP's official printer but also its watchdog, enjoined to guard the property against the hirelings of capitalist swine who, Red Eddie liked to believe, felt their power imperilled by the Cally's very existence. In actual fact the capitalist swine couldn't have cared less about Eddie, the Cally or the SPP, a party too humourless and narrow of view to carry much weight even within the ranks of the Scottish Labour Movement.

Henry came up Horseferry Road from the direction of the riverside. He had learned the habit of caution in the years before the family had flitted out to Flannery Park and he found it hard to break. He slipped into the building by a side door and ascended to the fourth floor via the steep back stairs. Vibration and noise told him that Eddie was engaged in printing out the weekly issue of the *Workers' Banner* on the ancient press that the pair of them kept in working order with string, spit and baling wire.

Henry had not seen Eddie for almost three weeks, not since the day of Mam's funeral at Hallwood cemetery. Eddie had stood off by himself under the elms which protected the site from the north wind. Henry had been touched by Eddie's gesture but had not had an opportunity to shake the wee man's hand or thank him for turning out to pay his respects for Henry, even Henry, had been too distressed to carry on as if nothing at all had happened.

He entered the long, low-roofed room and yelled above the clatter of the press, 'Eddie! Hoi, Eddie! It's me.'

Eddie started, spun round and peered through the gloom.

The nickname 'Red' derived not from the colour of Eddie's hair, which in fact had the hue and nap of moleskin, but from his extreme political convictions. He had jet black eyes and the myopic habit of peering so hard at you that he seemed to be permanently belligerent. Like the majority of his brethren in the SPP, Eddie had no sense of humour and not an awful lot of brain. He was a gentle soul at heart, though, and an ideal servant to the party.

'Only me.' Henry waved.

'Henry!' Eddie raised an ink-stained hand in greeting. 'Ach, man, am I glad t' see you. I thought you'd deserted us for good.'

'Now why would I do that?'

Eddie frowned. He was plastered with treacly ink, his canvas apron stiff with it. If Henry's characteristic neatness was offended by the mess he gave no sign of it but fashioned a handshake in the air without actually touching Eddie's saturated fingers.

'I mean,' Eddie said, 'I was at the funeral.'

'I saw you,' Henry said. 'Thanks for turning out.'

'I thought, I mean, you wouldn't mind.'

'Of course I didn't mind. Mam was always fond of you, Eddie, you know that,' Henry lied.

Mavis had not been fond of Eddie at all; not even his pathetic eagerness to please had been able to soften her heart towards the boy. To be fair, though, she had fed him, let him warm himself at her hearth and had even washed his shirt now and then when Eddie's parents were too drunk to care whether their son lived or died.

'Was she? I mean, aye, she was. I was sorry to hear she'd gone.' Eddie scowled sympathetically. 'It must've been a sore time for you, Henry.'

Henry shrugged. 'The work must go on.'

'Right you are.' Eddie seemed relieved that he would not be called upon to ransack his stock of clichés for further expressions of condolence. 'Are you here for the writin'?'

'What else?' said Henry.

'By God, man, we could do wi' some o' your stuff. Mr Ormskirk was askin' where you were. He done all the copy himself when you were away. It wasn't up t' your high standards.'

Ormskirk, Niven and Margaret Chancellor were the leading lights in the West of Scotland branch of the party to which Henry paid lip service, the persons who employed him to stuff the columns of the *Banner* with uncredited propaganda.

'How could it be?' said Henry.

'I mean, Mr Ormskirk's a very edu-kated chap an' all that but, I mean, he just doesn't have your gift.'

'I'll make up for it,' Henry promised.

He had no need to be modest with Eddie or, for that matter, with Jock Ormskirk and his gang. He was well aware that his talent was unique and individual. Complete lack of interest in the truth behind the issues which he exposed upon the *Banner*'s narrow front page was an asset not an impediment. He had a way with words and absolutely no scruples, which put him two points up on his paymasters for starters.

'How's circulation?' he enquired.

'Down.'

'How far down?'

'Three hundred.'

'Hell's bells! I've only been gone three weeks,' Henry said. 'What did Ormskirk write about?'

'The Millport conference.'

'What?'

'Two issues.'

'Were you there, Eddie, at the conference?'

'Nah, I couldn't be spared here.'

'Let me see what Jock wrote.'

'Did y' not, I mean, read the latest editions?'

'Couldn't find the time,' Henry said, lying again.

During his absence Henry had made no effort at all to keep up with the *Banner*'s notion of hot news. He hadn't even bothered to pick up one of the crumpled sheets which blew freely about Ransome's yard, particularly in the vicinity of the lavatories.

'I'll fish them out for you,' Eddie said.

'Please,' said Henry, then added, 'How much do you have to do here? What's the run?'

'One thousand copies, front an' back.'

'Let me see tomorrow's copy as well then.'

'Aw, here, listen, I mean, you're no' thinkin' o' changin' this issue, are you, Henry?'

'It depends how bad Jock's stuff really is.'

Eddie opened his mouth to complain but thought better of it.

'Have you had anythin' to eat yet?' Henry asked.

'Naw.'

'Tell you what, I'll get wired in at the writing, you clean yourself up and I'll stand you a hot supper.'

'I could fair do wi' a pint,' Eddie admitted.

'Food,' said Henry, sternly. 'No booze.'

'An' then what?'

'If necessary I'll help you re-set.'

'Och, Henry, it'll take all bloody night.'

'I've got all night. Most of it, anyway. Remember, Eddie, it's for the good of the cause.'

'Aye, but will it, I mean, be better?'

'Than Ormskirk's rubbish? Of course it will.'

'Okay then.' Eddie capitulated with an ease born of much practice. 'You're on.'

Henry unlocked the padlock that secured his rented office. He entered the room, closed the door, and groped for the length of string that dangled in the darkness. He gave it a tug and a ceiling bulb flickered on.

The room was stark but clean. The skylight was covered by a hessian sack nailed to the frame and a single-bar electrical heater stood by a scarred old dining table against which was propped a kitchen chair. Shelves supported a weight of books and a couple of metal lockers, also padlocked, narrowed the space still further. At the room's nether end was a canvas curtain behind which lay a stone sink, a cold water tap, a workbench and a wooden cupboard in which Henry kept clean shirts, shoes, flannels and one decent sports jacket.

From his raincoat pocket Henry removed a bulky manilla envelope which he placed upon the table next to the room's most valuable asset, a telephone. He took off his raincoat, draped it from a hook on the back of the door, bent over the table and opened the manilla envelope.

From it he extracted a thick wad of press cuttings. Westminster speeches, parliamentary reports, editorial diatribes, industrial forecasts and a smattering of minor items of local interest clipped from the pages of national and provincial newspapers would provide the grist for Henry's mill. In an hour or two of demonically hard work he would plunder the printed columns and hack from them a sensational front-page article for the *Banner*'s next issue.

Henry had been the *Banner*'s feature writer for almost three years now. In that time he had developed a flair for radical jargon and for spinning fantasies out of facts. It mattered not to Henry that the pieces appeared anonymously, that those who believed themselves to be in the know assumed that Margaret Chancellor, a forthright speaker for the SPP, was behind 'the screamers'. Henry had taught himself to write prose pitched at Lanarkshire miners, locomotive operatives, iron workers, factory hands and, of course, at the disgruntled masses who laboured as he did in shipyards all along the Clyde. He was particularly adept at devising eye-catching headlines. He took pride in his work, even if he did not believe a word of it, and, most important of all, he was paid for it.

He opened one of the lockers, took out a newish Underwood typewriter and transferred it to the table. He was eager to begin, for his headline – RENT STRIKE THREAT – and the substance of the article were running vividly through his mind. When he turned to fetch paper from the shelf, however, he was brought up short by a couple of photographs thumb-tacked to the inside of the locker door.

One was a studio photograph which showed a beautiful woman with silky blonde hair, clad in an evening gown and artistically posed against a granular snow-white background.

The second photograph was much older and quite faded. It showed a young boy and a young woman awkwardly posed before a tenement close: Henry and Mam caught by a hawker with a tripod camera in Sutton Street some fifteen years ago, the one and only family snapshot in which Mavis was alone with Henry and in which he seemed to be her exclusive property, her favourite son. Until that moment Henry had regarded the photograph as a bit of sentimental indulgence. Now, suddenly, it seemed very precious indeed. He felt his throat grow thick. He leaned his brow against the door's edge and studied the photograph as if he had never seen it before, then, yielding, touched his finger to his lips and transferred a kiss to the snapshot's surface, to Mam's wan and distant cheek.

Then he slammed the locker door, lit a cigarette, seated himself at the table and began, furiously, to type.

'I really don't know what we're doing here,' Alison said. 'You told me we were going to the pictures.'

'There's nothin' much on, you know, worth payin' good money for,' Brenda said. 'I thought we'd go for a walk instead. It beats stayin' at home.'

'It's all right for you, Bren,' Alison said, 'but I've a pile of ironing to get through, as well as the extra chemistry homework old Boris dished out.'

'All work an' no play,' said Brenda. 'You're gettin' far too fond of skulkin' indoors every night of the week.'

'I've no choice. Somebody's got to do the housework,' Alison said. 'Besides, I can't say I find it all that thrilling to charge along Dumbarton Road in pouring rain.'

'The rain's off,' said Brenda. 'I mean, nearly.'

'Where are we going anyway?'

Brenda had no definite plan in mind. She was bored and restless. Flannery Park's avenues and crescents all seemed the same after dark, with shops closed and nobody out there, no boys. She was driven by a longing for companionship, for novelty, but didn't yet have the confidence to search for adventure on her own.

She'd popped over to 162 in the hope that she might encounter Jack or Henry. Fat chance! The Burnsides' house was as gloomy as a morgue, with Bertie reading a

Western by the fire, Mr Burnside snoring in his chair and Alison ironing in the back bedroom. It had taken all her wiles, and a deliberate lie, to coax Alison to come out for a couple of hours.

Brenda could not explain the buzzing little impulse that lured her into the rain-wet streets. Back in Partick there had always been something to do, something to see, the chance of an interesting encounter. If the worst came to the worst you could drift from shop to shop and dream about buying the things that glittered in the windows. Alison and she had done that many a night and had never noticed time slipping past. In Flannery Park if you didn't belong to the Church Guild or the Girl Guides or some such organisation you were up the proverbial creek, and Brenda for one resented it.

'If we're really not going to the pictures,' Alison said, 'I'm not staying out long.'

'We could take the bus to Partick.'

'What for?'

'To look at the shops.'

'I don't particularly want to look at the shops.'

'God, Ally,' Brenda said, 'you're turnin' into a right stick-in-the mud.'

Alison had been aware for some months that her friendship with Brenda was disintegrating. Once it had been fun to stroll aimlessly about the streets together but, even before Mam had died, Brenda's lack of purpose had begun to wear thin and Alison had found herself bored both by the girl's bounciness and her lack of centre. Brenda was also jealous of the attention that had come Alison's way, particularly from Mr Abbott. She had taken to calling Mr Abbott 'Wingy' and making remarks about his empty sleeve, remarks which Alison thought cruel and unnecessary.

'Tell you what,' Brenda said, 'why don't we nip down to Ferraro's for a bag of chips or an ice-cream?'

'I'm not that hungry.'

'You're always hungry enough at dinnertime.'

The fact that Mrs McColl provided Davy and Alison with a midday meal two or three times a week had become another sore point with Brenda. The way she chanted on about it you'd have thought they were taking the food right out of her mouth.

'All right.' Alison capitulated. 'Ferraro's.'

'We'll sit in the café an' have an ice-cream.'

'If that's what you want,' said Alison.

'Have you any money?'

'Only the shillin' Bertie gave me.'

'That'll do.' Brenda seemed satisfied that she had obtained her own way, that her will, even in such petty matters, had proved stronger than Alison's. 'Ferraro's it is then.' She took Alison's arm. 'I wonder who'll be there tonight?'

'What?'

'You know – chaps.'

'Oh!' said Alison, unimpressed.

Cowpokes, gunslingers, rustlers and redskins held no special appeal for Bertie. He read Western fiction with the same pallid appetite as he read detective novels, because it was an activity as effortless as eating sherbet, and because the Post Office circulating library stocked very little else, except romances, which didn't interest Bertie in the slightest. He read at every opportunity, at work, on buses and trams, at mealtimes, in picture-house queues, anywhere that necessitated protection against being drawn into conversation. For Bertie a book was a defensive weapon, something you could stick in front of your face and hide behind. Strangers and workmates would accost you without qualm if you had a newspaper in front of you but few dared interrupt a man who was actually reading a book.

Printed fiction was, however, just a poor substitute for Bertie's real passion, an addiction to moving pictures. When not at work or at home, Bertie could usually be found slumped in the stalls of the Toledo or the Astoria with steely-grey images flickering across his glasses and the strains of a pit organ drumming in his ears. Bertie was, therefore, a soft mark when it came to shelling out a shilling to provide Alison with the price of a cinema ticket provided she did not try to discuss the programmes with him afterwards, for he was afraid she would find fault with films that he had uncritically enjoyed.

Over the rim of the latest Zane Grey, Bertie watched his father stir, stretch, yawn and peer blearily about him as if he did not quite know where he was. Bertie did not comprehend the mechanics of the cat nap or understand why since Mam had died his father's forty winks had expanded into an hour of deep, trance-like sleep. Once, about a week ago, his father had wakened suddenly and had shot out of the chair, crying, 'Mavis, Mavis, wait for me,' an incident which had alarmed Bertie so much that he'd had to go upstairs to the bathroom, take two aspirin and have himself a weep.

The old man groped a hand to the mantelpiece for his cigarette packet and asked, stickily, 'Where's Alison?'

'Gone to the pictures.'

'Why didn't you go with her?'

'I've seen it.'

'She's not on her own, is she?'

'No, with Brenda.'

Alex lit a cigarette, inhaled deeply, coughed raspingly and sat forward. 'When did Brenda arrive?'

'About an hour ago.'

'I must've been dead to the world.'

'You were,' Bertie said. 'I'm surprised you didn't waken up, though, the racket she makes.'

Bathed in cigarette smoke and still dazed, Alex stared into the fire.

Bertie said, 'It's high time she was married.'

'Who?' Alex gave himself a shake. 'Alison?'

'No, Brenda McColl.'

Alex cocked his head and squinted at his son.

'What makes you say that?'

'Huh! You just have to look at her to know what she's needin'.'

Hiding a grin with his cigarette, Alex said, 'Now you mention it, I suppose wee Brenda has filled out. She's still a bit on the young side, though. I reckon you'll have to bide your time there, Bertie.'

Bertie blinked and lowered the book. 'Me?'

Alex clicked his tongue and winked. 'You could do a lot worse than hitch up with wee Brenda. She'd soon teach you what was what.'

'Brenda McColl! My God!'

The horror in Bertie's voice left Alex in no doubt that he was barking up the wrong tree. He retreated into silence, sprawled back in the smoker and watched Bertie pretend to read for a while.

'What about her mother then?' Alex said at length.

'Can't stand her either.'

Bertie had been reading about two young cowpokes who had trailed a band of desperadoes across the edge of the Painted Desert for three days. Having finally stumbled on a creek the cowboys had stripped off their dusty clothing and had thrown themselves into the water where, like bear cubs, they splashed and cavorted and wrestled gaily.

In spite of his fleeting engagement with the fiction Bertie didn't lose the thread of conversation with his father. Without raising his eyes from the page he said, 'Ruby McColl's a cow.'

'Here, here, that's a bit strong, son,' Alex said. 'Anyway, I don't see what you've got against her. Your mother always got on fine with Ruby, an' she's been very kind to Alison an' Davy since – since it happened. Which is more than you can say for the bloody Gilfillans.'

'Granny Gilfillan's in the huff.'

'I guessed as much,' said Alex. 'Still, we don't need the likes o' them, do we, son? We're managing fine without them.' He hesitated. 'It won't be long until you an' your brothers have wives an' families of your own.'

Bertie did not respond.

Alex said, 'Won't it?'

'What'll you do then?'

'Ally'll look after me.'

'What if she wants to get married?'

It was Alex's turn to say nothing.

Bertie said, 'Wouldn't you consider marrying again?'

'Nah, nah, nah,' Alex said, and added, 'Who the hell would take on an old josser like me?'

Bertie sensed that his father wanted to be reassured that if he wished to do so he could still attract a mate, and he had a queasy feeling that his father might already have begun to size up candidates for the post.

He studied the old man over the tops of his glasses for a moment or two then said, 'Nobody in their right mind.'

'Eh?'

'At your age,' Bertie blinked, 'the very idea's disgusting.'

'Well, I wouldn't go that far,' Alex said.

'Disgusting,' Bertie repeated and, purse-lipped, returned to reading about cowpokes wrestling bare-naked in the creek.

'Well, well, well,' said Brenda. 'Look who's here.'

Through the rails of the gallery of Ferraro's Cafe Henry peered glumly down at the girls below, a forkful of soft white fish flakes poised short of his mouth. As Brenda clumped up the little staircase he thrust the fork into his mouth and chewed frantically. He did not turn to greet the girl as she emerged on to the upper level but looked across the checkered tablecloth, over sauce and vinegar bottles, at Red Eddie and pulled a face in mute apology for the unexpected intrusion.

Eddie did not seem particularly dismayed at the appearance of two young bits of fluff. He was a lot less reluctant than Henry imagined him to be to interrupt an intense discussion on the topic of short-time working versus universal unemployment.

'Fancy meetin' you here.' Brenda reached the table. 'What's wrong, Mr Ruff? Don't you remember me?'

Eddie scratched an earlobe with an ink-ingrained finger, and blushed. 'Can't honestly say I do, hen.'

'You once bought me a coconut from old Mrs McCluskie's shop in Muirpark Street,' Brenda urged. 'Remember?'

Obviously Eddie could recall no such act of youthful generosity. Embarrassed, he switched his gaze from the girl to Henry who, toying with his fork, explained, 'She's Brenda McColl. Ruby's daughter.'

'Oh, I remember Ruby all right,' said Eddie with the merest trace of lasciviousness. 'She used to – eh – live in Sutton Street too.'

'Well, I'm her daughter.' Wrapped in a heavy tweed coat and flannel skirt Brenda looked less like a *femme fatale*

72

than something cranked out of the hold of a cargo boat. 'Do you not think I'm like her?'

'I suppose so – I mean, a bit,' said Eddie gallantly. 'Does your mammy still – eh – is she still resident in Partick?'

'We live in Flannery Park now. If you can call it livin',' Brenda replied. 'Across the road from Henry.'

Eddie let his glance wander from Brenda to the tall, good-looking girl who hovered nervously at the top of the steps. 'Who's your friend?'

'My sister,' Henry put in before Eddie could blurt out something that might, in the circumstances, prove offensive.

'Surely that's never your wee Ally?' said Eddie. 'By Jings, she grew up quick.'

'We've all, you know, grown up,' said Brenda. 'Aren't you goin' to invite us to sit down?'

'No,' Henry said.

'Huh! An' I always thought you were a gentleman.'

'Can't you see we're busy?' Henry said.

'You don't look very busy to me,' said Brenda.

Henry leaned his elbow on the chair back and addressed himself to Alison. 'What are you doing here, anyhow?'

Alison was embarrassed by Brenda's precocious behaviour and, if it had been possible, would have dragged her chum away without more ado.

'I'm sorry, Henry. We came down for ice-cream,' she said. 'How was I to know you'd be here?'

Henry was inclined to order her to buzz off but in a disconcerting flash he suddenly saw Brenda and Alison through Eddie's eyes, no longer children. At the same moment he experienced a wave of sympathy for his sister, caught, motherless, between puberty and maturity.

'All right,' he said. 'Now you're here I suppose you'd

better stay. One dish of ice-cream, though, and you'll have to scoot. Eddie and I do have business to discuss.' To Eddie he said, 'You don't mind, do you?'

'Not me,' said Red Eddie Ruff and nipped away to fetch a couple of extra chairs before Henry could change his mind.

Stupid, really, to come this far west just for a hot supper; Henry cursed himself for his carelessness. Ferraro's, however, occupied a place in the scheme of things mid-way between the greasy eating houses of Finnieston, which wouldn't suit him, and the city's high-toned restaurants, which wouldn't suit Eddie. A tram ride out to Ferraro's had seemed like the perfect solution. He hadn't, of course, expected to bump into Alison and Brenda McColl and for the ensuing hour had had to live with his mistake and make the best of it.

It was after nine o'clock before they left the restaurant. A queue had formed at the fish and chip shop which adjoined the café and a heavy drizzle veiled the big yellow streetlamps of Scotstoun junction. To Henry's relief Brenda had attached herself to Eddie. She clung to his arm, playfully rather than possessively, while Eddie scouted for a tram to carry him back to his natural habitat.

Henry drew Alison into the shelter of a close-mouth.

'You go straight home now, you hear?'

'Aren't you coming with us?' Alison said.

'I'm going back to Eddie's place for a while.'

'Eddie's place?'

'In Partick. For a wee dram,' Henry lied.

'But you don't drink.'

'Sometimes I do.'

'It's awfully late.'

'Not for me it isn't,' Henry said. 'Listen, the old man doesn't like Eddie so I'd be obliged if you wouldn't mention you saw me tonight.'

'What about Brenda? She's bound to say something.'

'Try to persuade her not to.'

'What are you up to, Henry?'

'Nothing. I just don't like folk knowing my business when they don't have to, that's all.' He managed a sheepish grin. 'I haven't become a cat-burglar, if that's what you're thinking.'

'No, somehow I can't see you halfway up a drainpipe,' Alison said. 'I won't say a word, I promise.'

'And you'll talk to Brenda?'

'If I can get a word in edgeways.'

Two or three minutes later Alison waved goodbye to her brother and his friend and watched the Partick tramcar carry the men off along Dumbarton Road. She suspected that Brenda might want to return to Ferraro's for there were other young men there now. But Brenda had had enough adventure for one evening and led the way across the tramlines towards Shackleton Avenue. They walked quickly through thickening drizzle, Brenda skipping now and then to keep up with long-legged Alison.

'Here, that was great, wasn't it?' Brenda said. 'He's awful nice when you get to know him.'

'Who – Eddie?'

'Henry, I mean. Your brother.'

'I thought you liked Jack best?'

Brenda laughed and skipped again. 'I could be persuaded to change my – what's the word, Ally?'

'Allegiance.'

'That's the feller.'

'In that case,' said Alison carefully, 'I wouldn't go telling anyone what happened. About meeting Henry.'

'Why ever not?'

'In case anyone thinks we met Henry by arrangement,' Alison said. 'You wouldn't want your mother latchin' on to the wrong idea, would you?'

'Here,' Brenda said, with a touch of alarm, 'I see what you mean. I never, you know, thought of that.'

'Our secret then?' said Alison.

'Our secret,' Brenda agreed.

'Henry! What a pleasant surprise.'

'I hope I didn't wake you?'

'Not at all. I am in my bedroom but I am not asleep.'

'Are you alone?'

'In my bedroom? I am alone, of course.'

'I didn't mean – I meant, are you free to talk?'

'Completely.'

'I'm sorry I haven't been in touch, Trudi, but things have been a bit hectic at home lately. Perhaps you heard?'

'I hear how your poor mother is deceased,' Trudi said. 'I thought to send you a letter of condolences but, when I considered it, it did not seem advisable.'

'You could have sent it here,' Henry said.

'But you were not there, were you?'

'No.' Henry paused, then asked, 'How did you know that?'

'I called by telephone.'

'Did you now?' said Henry.

'Again and again. There! Are you not flattered?'

'Very,' said Henry. 'I'm just sorry I wasn't around to talk to you.'

'Are you very sad?' the woman asked.

Henry said. 'It's been difficult, what with the family an' all.'

'I ask about you, Henry, not about the family.'

'Yes, I was upset. Sad. Yes.'

'I could make you cheerful.'

'I'll bet you could,' said Henry.

'Are you with the printing?'

'Yes, Trudi, I'm with the printing.'

'By foot you could be with me in a quarter hour, Henry, or catch the taxi and arrive before I have time to set down the speaking piece.'

'What would Georgette have to say to that?'

'Georgette is fast sleeping. I will come down to the side door.'

'It's a thought.'

'For a boy like you to translate thought to deed would be a very simple matter,' the woman said. 'Will you not come to visit me, Henry?'

Beggaring the question, Henry said, 'What are you wearing?'

She laughed softly. 'Silk.'

'Peach silk.'

She laughed again. 'How naughty you are to remember.'

'Forgetting's the problem.'

'Come to my apartment. We will discover how much you have not forgotten.' For several seconds there was silence on the line. 'Henry?'

'I'm wrestlin' with my conscience.'

'You have no conscience, my boy.'

'Aye, but I do, Trudi,' Henry said. 'Fact is, I've got to work tonight.'

'Another girl, a young girl, is that how you work?'

'Don't be daft. I really do have to work. I promised the printer I'd help him set up. He'll be stuck otherwise.'

'I am not to be stuck – otherwise?'

'How about Sunday?' Henry said. 'If you're free?'

'I do not think you want to see me.'

'I do, I do, Trudi, for God's sake. How about it?'

She kept him on a string for what seemed like minutes. He could hear her breathe. He could almost smell her perfume, catch the whisper of her peach silk pyjamas. 'Sunday?' she said, still pouting.

'Yes,' said Henry. 'The usual arrangement?'

'Are you sure you can spare me the time?' said Mrs Trudi Coventry and, before Henry could assure her of his undying devotion, hung up on her youthful lover.

Alex Burnside was not the sort of chap to wear his heart on his sleeve. He did not confide his inner feelings to his sons, his daughter or his workmates. Although he had always been a model husband, he had been born with a fair share of masculine pride and, as far as emotions went, had kept himself to himself, even from Mavis.

It would have come as a great surprise to the boys to learn that their father did not miss their mother all that very much in the late hours of the night. The fact was that Alex rather liked having the bed to himself, with room to stretch and wallow. In recent years Mavis had grown heavy and, while he had been careful to coddle her, he had actually found her weight objectionable. He'd needed no counsellor to instruct him how to please his wife, however, how to keep her happy.

He had assumed that he was growing old and his powers diminishing, and he didn't need any of Henry's half-baked psychological mumbo-jumbo to complicate the issue. But it came as something of a shock to Alex when, at the august age of forty-seven and hardly more than a month a widower, he suddenly began to be teased by a restlessness that even he recognised as sexual. There was something indecent about it, something horribly disloyal to the memory of a good woman, now deceased.

Deceased, in fact, was a word that acquired a lot more meaning in the cold light of day than in the dark, sensitive hours of the night, for the time when Alex missed Mavis most was when he opened the lid of his dinner pail.

'Whassat?' Jerry, the apprentice, would say.

'What does it bloody look like?'

'A dog's breakfast.'

'Watch your lip, son.' Even allowing for his youth Jerry was far too impudent for Alex's liking. 'Can ye not see it's a fried egg?'

Jerry would peer at the object in the bottom of the tin dinner pail and snigger, and Billy Strong, the hammerman, would smother a guffaw.

Alex's workmates were entitled to mock his culinary efforts. No matter how careful he was in the kitchen at a quarter past seven in the morning, the fine art of sandwich-making eluded him. Eggs were either runny as jelly or burned like black lace at the edges, and when he slipped one out of the pan and on to a bread roll – well, all sorts of disastrous transformations occurred. Daily at noon, therefore, he was condemned to hunch over a brazier in the shelter of the cold steel plates, gaze at the sorry offering in the pail and mourn for Mavis and all she had meant to him.

Sandy Simpson and Alex Burnside had been apprentices together and had spent all their working lives in Ransome's. Sandy was a hulking great chap with a lantern jaw and a walrus moustache. His brutal appearance was deceptive, however, and he was as soft as butter inside.

He would sit on the plank bench with Alex and share dinner. He would even bring an extra bit of pie or a fresh baked scone for the widower and would slip Alex the titbit stealthily so that the rest of the gang did not notice charity being given and received.

Although he had been hearing about Sandy's wife Peggie

for years Alex had in fact never met the woman. He knew her only from her floury scones, mincemeat pies and rich dumpling slices, and from a wealth of small details about her that Sandy had imparted over the course of the years.

In Sandy's wife Alex now saw a mirror image of Mavis and reflections of his own marriage. The tragedy was that he had not known he was happy, had not realised that the years of struggle were the whole score, that there was nothing more. He would have given anything to have had those years back again, and Mavis with them. But in the meantime, God help us, he was jealous of big Sandy and lusted after Peggie Simpson, a woman upon whom he had never clapped an eye.

Four or five years ago McCandlish, a foreman, had lost his wife to puerperal fever and at the time Alex and Sandy had discussed the tragedy at some length. 'If, God forbid, Peggie were took like that,' Alex had asked, 'would you marry again?'

'Naw, naw.' Sandy had been aghast at the very idea. 'Nobody could ever replace ma Peggie.'

It had been an easy and proper answer to give since the question had been hypothetical and loyalty, like love, was blind to changing circumstance. Now, though, Alex was less sure. It was all very well for Sandy, who still had Peggie to minister to his needs. He had nobody, unless you counted Alison, which he did not.

'Are you gonna eat that, Mr Burnside?' Jerry asked.

Alex stared mournfully down at the greasy bread roll, the leathery egg, and answered, 'Naw.'

'Give's it here then,' Jerry said and in spite of his initial scorn gulped the sandwich down like a heron swallowing fish, and left poor Mr Burnside hungrier than ever before.

Something very odd was happening at school. For a couple

of weeks in November Alison wondered if it was her imagination which made her suppose she was being bullied.

The culprits were not her schoolmates, not even the hulking brutes in third year who were only playing out time and had nothing to lose by enjoying themselves. The attacks were more subtle than a hand thrust up her skirt or a wet apple core stuffed down the neck of her blouse. It took Alison some weeks to realise that, in fact, she was being put upon by her teachers.

It wasn't that the teachers roared at her in class – Boris roared at everyone, of course – but that they were unfairly piling on to her shoulders extra homework assignments which she was expected to complete in short order. She was already working on sections of textbooks which the class would not be obliged to study until summer term and there seemed to be no reason for Mr Hammond and Mr Borland to push her so hard unless Mr Abbott had put them up to it. If she had liked Mr Abbott less she might have demanded to be told why she was being punished. As it was, she completed the assignments to the best of her ability and said nothing.

If she had not been so self-absorbed she might have noticed that she was not quite the only pupil who was being singled out for unwarranted punishment. At lessons' end Walter Giffard was also summoned to wait in front of Boris's desk or Mr Hammond's table to be treated to a brief thesis on new and unfamiliar material before being dismissed with the injunction to have the relevant exercises completed by Monday. It was mid-November before Alison realised that Walter and she were afloat in the same small boat. Until then she had given Walter Giffard hardly a second glance for Walter had always struck her as being definitely and irredeemably weird.

The Giffards had been among the first council tenants to

settle in Flannery Park. Walter had been a pupil at Mr Pallant's school for almost two years. In that time he had made few friends, in spite of the fact that many of the girls, Alison not included, thought he was scrumptious. He was exceedingly scruffy, had hair that the teaching staff found offensively long and dressed in baggy tweeds that made him look more like a Victorian farmworker than a twentieth-century teenager. What made Wattie attractive to impressionable females, though, was his overwhelming indifference to their very existence, that, and a lazy eye, a drooping lid which gave him a supercilious air which some girls apparently found irresistible.

Brenda was not immune to Wattie's charms, however. She waxed lyrical about him from time to time, indulged in longing sighs and laid speculative plans to bring young Walter to heel. Walter Giffard may have been a great original but he certainly wasn't daft. He treated Brenda with the same disdain with which he treated every other girl and her flirtatious advances had no more effect upon him than spray upon granite.

Alison was, therefore, surprised to find no less a person than Walter Giffard waiting for her outside Mr Hammond's classroom on a bitterly cold November afternoon at the end of the last period.

Walter's first words were, 'Where's your friend?'

'Brenda?' Alison said. 'Waiting for me at the front gate, probably.'

'Where do you live?'

By now it was ten past four and echoes of the bell had died along the verandahs. Mr Williamson, head janitor, was hosing out the boys' toilets and two or three of the women who cleaned classrooms were clanking pails and mops in the storeroom at the head of the stairs.

'Wingfield Drive.'

'Very nice,' said Walter.

Like Alison, Walter carried his textbooks in a briefcase, not a schoolbag. He slung the tattered case over his shoulder by a handle bound with cord and ambled beside Alison as she drifted, still puzzled, towards the head of the staircase which led to the playground.

'You don't even know what's happenin', do you?'

'Pardon?' Alison said.

'You an' me,' Walter went on, 'you don't know what Abbott's got in store for us, do you?'

'Sorry,' Alison said. 'I'm not with you.'

'Oh, but you are,' Walter told her. 'That's what those crafty beggars have in mind. Big things for you and me.' He saw that she was still bewildered, sighed and asked, 'What do you think all this extra work's in aid of? Don't tell me you thought it was punishment?'

'It had crossed my mind.'

'Blow me, an' you're supposed to be smart.'

'I did better than you in the last English exam.'

'Oh, grow up,' Walter said, scathingly. 'Test marks don't mean a thing for the likes of us. We're not being punished, we're being pushed.'

Alison frowned. Further questions were unnecessary. She nodded. 'Of course. You're absolutely right.'

'I've seen how old Abbott fusses over you like a mother hen. Boris does the same sort of thing with me. He wants me to smarten myself up. The bastard even chinned me about my slovenly Glasgow accent.'

'You can't help that.'

'Boris thinks I can.'

'What? Elocution lessons?'

'That's not even funny,' Walter said.

Through the railings by the main gate Alison caught a glimpse of Brenda who was lying in wait with three fourth year girls. Walter had seen the group too and as if by tacit agreement the young man and the girl turned right at the bottom of the staircase and headed along the lane that led to the school's back gate. As Walter and she passed out of sight of Brenda's crowd Alison had a sudden desire to giggle.

Walter said, 'She's not going to like it, is she?'

'What?'

'You going off with me.'

'No, she's not,' Alison admitted.

'If you'd rather be with her—'

'No, I'd rather be – No, this is fine.'

She had not wished it, willed it or even considered it but now that it had happened she found that she was flattered to be singled out by reclusive Walter Giffard. More to the point, he had removed all her guilt and grievance with a word or two of explanation. She felt suddenly confident, almost cocky.

'Has Abbott mentioned bursaries yet?' Walter asked.

'No, not yet.'

'Boris is pressing me to sit all kinds of exams so I can cruise into university without financial worries,' Walter said. 'He also keeps assurin' me we're just as good as they are.'

'They?'

'Toffs. Academicals an' High School boys,' Wattie said. 'I suppose he's right an' all.'

'Of course he is,' said Alison staunchly. 'You're every bit as good as they are.'

''Cept I don't tawk praw-pah.'

'That's something you'll learn by imitative acquisition,' Alison said.

'Yeah, I wonder what else we'll learn by imitation?'

'Anythin' we want to.'

It occurred to her that she had adopted the pronoun of the first person plural nominative and Walter had put up no complaint.

He said, 'What about things we don't want to learn?'

Alison said, 'Ignore them.'

'Might not be so easy.'

They had reached the steps that dropped steeply down to the school's back gate. Council houses were spread out below, a long quiet curving backwater of black slate roofs, dun-coloured gardens and net-curtained windows. As Alison and Walter approached, the glass globes at the top of the steps flickered and lit, darkening the landscape below.

Walter opened the iron gate and let Alison pass through.

'Actually,' Alison said. 'I don't think it'll matter much since I won't be staying on at school.'

Walter paused. 'What age are you?'

'Sixteen.'

'Will you leave without the Certificates?'

'My mother died, you see.'

'Yeah, I heard,' Walter said. 'Pity. Money's tight, I suppose?'

'No, we're not short on shillings,' Alison said. 'It's just that nobody at home seems to care what happens to me.'

'Buggered if I'd let that stop me.'

At the corner of Summerston Street two or three boys were raucously chasing a rubber ball and a youngster, hardly older than ten, swung from the arm of a lamppost like a gibbon. Alison doubted if there had been much horseplay for Walter Giffard. She could not imagine him ever squandering energy on childish pursuits. He reminded her of Henry and, like Henry, he seemed older than his years.

Chatting casually and oblivious to the cold, the couple

drifted towards Summerston Street. 'Can you dance?'
Wattie asked.

'Yes.'

'I don't mean the Pride of Erin. I mean ballroom.'

'In that case, no,' Alison admitted.

'I was sent to dancin' classes by my mother.'

'What for?'

'Search me,' said Wattie. 'Ten years old, I'm away every
Saturday mornin' to McKennoway's Academy to stand
about among the girls.'

'I bet you loved it.'

'Didn't then, do now.'

'Are you good at it?'

'Great. Silver Medal class,' Walter said. 'I'll take you to
the Cally some Saturday night an' you can judge for
yourself.'

'I'd like that,' Alison said, 'But I'm not sure if my Dad
would let me go to the Cally.'

'Don't tell him then.'

'Oh, I couldn't . . .' Alison began just as Mr Abbott
appeared out of the gloaming behind her.

The teacher came quickly around the corner from Cairns
Road, a satchel tucked under the sleeve of his left arm, a
square cardboard document case clutched in his fist.
Harassed and distracted, he did not seem to notice Alison
and Walter until he was almost upon them.

'Hullo, Mr Abbott,' Walter said.

'Hello,' said Mr Abbott gruffly and, tucking his chin into
his scarf, side-stepped the couple and sped away across
Summerston Street without looking back. Alison watched
the man vanish into shadows then reappear in pools of light
from streetlamps, growing smaller and smaller as he
receded into the dusk. 'He's all right, is old Abbott,' Wattie
said.

Alison was suddenly and unaccountably embarrassed and did not wish to discuss the teacher with a pupil who seemed rather too wise in the ways of the world.

A moment later she made an excuse to part from Walter Giffard and hurried home to 162 to press on with her evening chores.

By the time he reached the row of shops at the end of Summerston Street Jim Abbott was seriously winded.

As always, several pupils milled about the tobacconist cum sweet shop at the end of the row. Jim ignored the sly glances and half-baked nods directed towards him when he stopped outside the window of Snapes' Provision Merchants. He put down the cumbersome satchel and case, fumbled in his pocket for the shopping list his sister had given him and squinted at Winifred's neat script in slanting light from the window. His hand, he noticed, was trembling.

He drew in a long deep breath, tasted the faint foul fog from river ships, forges and factory stacks which had already crystallised in November's first frost. He could also smell the rich aroma of ground coffee, cheeses and smoked hams that seeped enticingly from Snapes' doorway. He stuffed the shopping list into his pocket, dug out a Player's, struck a match with his thumbnail and with the flame cupped in the palm of his hand, lit the cigarette.

He had been shocked – no other word for it – to bump into Alison and Walter Giffard loitering at the corner. He could spot the beginnings of a romance a mile away. He was infuriated and at the same time gratified that Alison had been drawn to Wattie Giffard and not some brainless lout like McNeillage. Even so, he was more upset than he had any right to be.

'Hullo, Mr Abbott. Cold night, i'n't it?'

'Yes – yes, Beryl, it is.'

Deliberately turning his back he pretended to study the display of spiced sausages, tinned biscuits, kippers and teas with which Snapes dressed the window. He did not take in any of it. He remembered how winsome Alison had looked in the light of the streetlamp. She was undoubtedly stimulated by Walter's attentions; Walter Giffard, a boy with everything before him, a boy with two good arms and precisely half his age.

It had been folly to assume that anything could ever come of his infatuation with Alison Burnside. She was hardly more than a child and he was a wounded veteran, too stolid and mature to moon after the impossible. Even if he did persuade her to sign on at school for another four or five terms, even if he did promote her into advanced education – what point would be served? Sooner or later she would meet someone of her own age and, as girls will, fall head over heels in love. Walter Giffard? She could do a lot worse, Jim told himself.

He had never been head over heels in love. He had been too busy fighting a war, too busy recovering from his wounds, too busy finding a job, too busy caring for his widowed sister to indulge in courtships. One day, he had supposed, he would stumble across a soulmate, but not in his wildest dreams had he reckoned on falling for a sixteen-year-old schoolgirl.

Taking a grip of himself he stuck the cigarette in his mouth and fished the shopping list from his pocket again. Kippers, Ceylon tea, cube sugar, marmalade, a seed cake, shelled walnuts, a half pound of fresh butter. His brain still dimmed by longing and disappointment, he stepped into the shop and joined the queue of women who waited at the counter.

'Mr Abbott, Mr Abbott?' The drawl was unmistakable.

Jim swung, blinking, towards the open door, possessed by the ridiculous fear that Walter Giffard had mind-read his dishonourable intentions and had come to have it out with him.

Grinning, the young man held up the satchel and the case which Jim had negligently left outside on the pavement. He lofted one in each hand like Samson showing off his muscles and gave them a little shake.

'Yours, Mr Abbott?'

Jim heard himself say, 'Yes, Walter. Mine.'

The young man brought them into the shop and waited patiently while Jim negotiated their retrieval.

'Did you mean to leave them out there, Mr Abbott?'

'No, Walter,' Jim Abbott answered. 'I just forgot I had them with me.'

'My mother's a bit like that,' Walter said. 'Forget her head if it wasn't sewn on. Beginnin' of the end, she says.'

Jim scrutinised the young man's face for an indication that the remark was intended to be insolent and was not merely ingenuous. Wattie's lazy eye was implacable, however, touched only by that knowingness which was the trademark of all teenage boys, and signified nothing.

'Got them safe now, sir?' Walter said.

'I've got them, thanks.'

'Well – take it easy, Mr Abbott.'

'I will, Walter,' Jim Abbott promised and, oddly pacified, watched the young man stroll off towards his home in Dunsinane Street.

Since the move from Partick Alison had inherited a big double bed which, in the bad old days in Sutton Street when space was at a premium, had once provided a place of repose for three of her brothers.

When she had been very young Alison had simply slept

89

where she'd been put, sharing first a bedroom with Bertie, then the hole-in-the-wall kitchen bed with her mother while her father made do with a single in what had become known as Bertie's room. In Wingfield Drive, however, everyone had a bed of their own, though the boys still had to share rooms. Alison had the front room at the top of the stairs all to herself, which would have been absolutely perfect if only the household budget could have been stretched to the purchase of a single bed.

The old double, with a spongy mattress and melodic springs, was crammed against the wall and barely left space for a quilted stool and the neat wooden dressing-table which Jack and Davy had carpentered into the slot by the window. Alison's clothes were stored in two hampers which lived under the bed and each evening, cursing the inconvenience, she was obliged to kneel and stretch to fish out what she required to wear to school next day.

Big though it was, the bed was easily managed. In winter Alison would build a nest in the warm patch in the middle, sink into it and haul the blankets over her head. For hot summer nights she discovered a position close to the wall which, with its faint odours of new plaster and wallpaper paste, seemed cool. The quilt was an old patchwork, a gift from Auntie Flora in the dim and distant, and its stains, both pale and dark, seemed to add history to Alison's use of it. Best of all, the bed provided a workplace and Alison had passed many a contented hour sprawled upon it, reading and writing by the light of the bracket lamp that Dad had rigged up for her.

That dark autumn she had been glad of the bedroom's privacy, for it had offered a place where she might let the tears flow without embarrassing her brothers. She had cried less frequently these past weeks, however, for she had too much to do to brood for long. As she drudged through housework and prepared meals her mind was filled with the formulae and equations that Boris and Mr Hammond had dished out and now that Walter Giffard had explained its real purpose she devoted time ungrudgingly to homework.

On that cold night Alison went early to bed. All the boys, except Henry, were at home but the living-room had seemed empty rather than crowded and she was afraid she might begin to pine for her mother again and not be able to concentrate on necessary reading.

She undressed rapidly, put on her flannel nightgown and paused for just a moment at the window to inspect the state of the weather. It was glitteringly cold, not hazy. Frost dusted the lawns and hedges like icing sugar and the sky above the streetlamps had a depthless quality, like a dark ocean. Very clearly she could hear the squeal of bus brakes from Shackleton Avenue and the long piercing whistle of a train from the tracks below Summerston Street. Lights in the McColls' house reminded her she hadn't seen Brenda at all that afternoon or evening. She was surprised Brenda hadn't come galloping over to enquire where she'd been at four o'clock. Part of her looked forward to confessing that she'd been with Walter Giffard, to Brenda's chagrin and the gossip that was bound to ensue. Another part of her wanted to keep her conversation with Wattie secret, something to mull over and selfishly enjoy.

She plucked a volume of the Arden Shakespeare from the bundle of books on the dressing-table and with a sudden almost joyful surge of energy hopped into the big bed and thrust herself under the clothes.

She settled against the pillows to study *Twelfth Night* with an enthusiasm which Mr Abbott would have found gratifying. She was fascinated more by the substance of the play than by its poetry and scanned with interest the edition's copious footnotes. Part of her mind remained occupied with fretting about her future, however, and another small part lingered inexplicably on the image of poor old Mr Abbott hurrying away in the half dark. Under the bedclothes her body was warm but her nose, lips and the tips of her ears were like ice and *Twelfth Night* lay steepled against her chin.

She opened her eyes.

Apparently she had dozed off. It took her a moment to realise that house and street were silent and that she must have been asleep for some time. She put the book upon the floor, switched out the light, snuggled on to her side and folded her arms across her breasts, knuckles cold even through her nightgown. Then she raised her head from the pillow and frowned at the sounds which filtered through the wall from the Rooneys' bedroom.

Although they lived directly next door Alison had been inside the Rooneys' house only once or twice. She'd found the religious statues and framed prints of Jesus mysterious and rather frightening for she had inherited from her father and brothers an irrational prejudice against Catholics, even though Mrs Rooney and her husband seemed to be perfectly nice people in other respects. Sometimes she heard noises from next door, children crying, Mr Rooney yawning, music echoing from the wireless set which Mr Rooney had recently bought. But she'd never heard sounds like this before. She was both intrigued and a little alarmed by them. Yielding to inquisitiveness she slid into the cold quarter of the bed, close to the dividing wall, and listened unabashed.

There was a threnodic quality to the sound and it took Alison a moment or two to separate individual strands in the primitive rhythm, to recognise Mrs Rooney's panting, Mr Rooney's grunting, the bedsprings groaning. The woman gave out a soft, saturated cry, the man a throaty shout, then for two or three seconds there was no sound at all.

Alison's hands cupped her breasts. Suddenly she seemed to be acutely aware of every wrinkle in the bedsheets, every dimple in the mattress beneath her. Mam, red-faced, had vaguely explained what men did to women to help make babies. But, until that moment, Alison's knowledge of sexual matters had remained unconnected with reality. Now she felt as if she had been thrust into bed with a married couple, forced to lie there like a ghostly presence side by side with pretty Mrs Rooney while the woman endured – what?

Mr Rooney spoke. Alison hugged herself tensely, not daring to move. The words were unintelligible but the tone was rueful, almost jocular. Mrs Rooney laughed as if the awful act was more pleasing, more ordinary than it had sounded.

When Mr Rooney spoke again, Alison was suddenly deeply ashamed of her furtive eavesdropping and flung herself back from the dividing wall.

She lay on her back, gasping, hands clapped to her ears for several minutes then gradually curled into a ball beneath the bedclothes and, in that tense foetal position, eventually fell asleep.

FOUR

Council of War

Come December the melancholy shadow of Christmas leaned rather heavily upon the Burnsides. It was not all gloom, however. Jack's book of musical engagements was full and Davy had been invited to run for Flannery Park Harriers in a prestigious cross-country event. Henry – well, nobody knew how Henry planned to spend the festive season, which was not in the least unusual. Before his sons could prance off for fun and frolic, however, Alex managed to muster them all together for a Sunday visit to Hallwood cemetery to view the newly erected headstone for which he had at last received an invoice. So, clutching limp posies and bouquets and dressed in sober Sunday best, Dad, Alison and the boys set off in column of route about a quarter past noon to catch the twelve twenty bus which, as it happened, was late and did not deposit them at Hallwood until ten past one o'clock.

Chilled, depressed, and lightly sprinkled with ash from too many cigarettes, the Burnsides set off in pairs up the winding avenue towards the section of the cemetery where Mam had been put to rest.

It was Alison's first visit to Hallwood. It was not as she had imagined it would be. In brittle winter light the Clyde bent away into the distance like a glacier and the lawns

95

were bleached by frost, the ornamental trees stark against the outline of the Old Kilpatrick hills. Alison, like her brothers, was no longer spongy with grief and was impatient to have this hollow, sentimental ceremony over and done with. Even Alex had the uncertain stoop of a man who was not entirely sure what he was supposed to be doing. He held a bunch of flowers out ahead of him like a talisman and glanced up now and then at Henry who, being a natural poseur, could emulate solemnity while standing on his head.

'I can think o' better places,' Davy muttered, 'to spend a Sunday afternoon.'

'Dad won't expect us to say a prayer, will he?' Alison whispered.

'God, no,' Davy answered. 'It won't even occur to the old devil to do a bit of the religious. He'll have to tidy up the grave, check the letters on the headstone against the masons' invoice to make sure we're not bein' diddled then, I suppose, we'll just mooch around until it's time to go home.'

'I imagine Dad feels he has to do something to show his respect,' Alison said. 'After all, Mam would have come to see him, his grave I mean?'

'Aye, but that's women for you,' Davy said. 'They really enjoy a bit of sufferin' in their lives.'

'I don't believe it!' Alison exclaimed.

'I'm tellin' you, women enjoy—'

'Look over there.' Alison pointed.

'Jeeze!' said Davy. 'What are *they* doin' here?'

'Bringing flowers by the look of it,' said Alison.

'Jeeze!' said Davy again.

The group gathered at Mavis's graveside consisted of Granny Gilfillan, black as a crow in twill and bombazine, fat Aunt Belle and her sisters Flora and Marion.

'Do you think Dad knew they'd be here today?' said Alison.

'Are you kiddin'?' Davy replied. 'It's just lousy co-incidence.'

Granny and her daughters had turned to face the pathway where Alex and Henry, stopped in their tracks, conferred in whispers as if it was in their minds to beat a tactical retreat. They knew that they were trapped, however, and that common decency would have to prevail. With an audible groan Alex advanced towards the Gilfillans, the family trailing in his wake.

'How did *you* get here?' Alex asked.

'Took the tramcar,' Belle answered.

'We were here last week too,' said Flora.

'And the week before,' put in Marion.

'What for?' Jack said.

'Somebody has to look after her,' said Flora.

'Aye, you're the last person I expected to meet here, Alex Burnside,' said Granny Gilfillan. 'I see there's a gravestone. It's paid for, I hope.'

Pouring oil on troubled waters, Henry temporarily silenced his grandmother by giving her a kiss upon the cheek. He had to stoop to do it and placed a hand behind the little woman's shoulders lest the unexpected gesture bowl her over completely. 'Well,' he said, 'it's nice we're all here together. Mother would have liked that. Bertie, aren't you going to give your Gran a kiss?'

One by one each of Alex Burnside's brood sidled forward to peck Gran's wizened cheek. She appeared more offended than mollified by this show of respect and, as if her moral integrity had been challenged by it, stepped quickly back to hide between her daughters.

'What about me?' said Belle. 'Don't I get any kisses?'

Davy gave a spluttering chuckle. Bertie flinched. It fell to

Henry to explain to their largest aunt that snogging in graveyards was not the done thing. Belle, always one to see a joke, laughed. Her sisters did not.

Alison was quite shocked by Marion's gaunt appearance. She had not seen the woman for many months and Marion looked so worn out that it seemed unjust that she was still alive and Mam was not. While Dad and the boys arranged their floral tributes upon the grave, Alison gravitated towards her aunt and asked solicitously, 'Have you not been well then?'

Marion's reply was so surgically detailed and prolonged that Alison began to wonder if she was in the presence of a medical miracle. Auntie Marion, it seemed, had had almost everything 'downstairs' removed, and several other organs 'interfered' with as well. But she sounded proud of her suffering, as if she had gained status not from stoical forbearance but from her sheer durability.

The solemn gathering soon dissolved into comedy.

Alex planted himself astride his wife's grave and moved his lips not in silent prayer but as an aid to arithmetic as, letter by letter, he checked the charge for the inscription against the invoice. Bertie knelt on a newspaper and arranged the various sprays across the mound while Granny nagged him from the rear, her brittle little finger wagging like a metronome. Jack and Davy chatted with Flora and Belle and enquired about the health and welfare of their pretty girl cousins. Only Henry stood alone. Arms folded and chin tilted, he seemed to be scanning the sky for signs of snow. From the corner of her eye Alison saw him dab his eyes with a clean white pocket handkerchief then blow his nose. Deliberately she looked away, not wishing to embarrass him. Within minutes, though, Henry had restored himself to equilibrium and had coaxed both Burnsides and Gilfillans away from the graveside and led them at no great pace in the direction of the gates.

Alison lagged behind and took one last long look at her mother's grave. She had a feeling that it might be some time before she returned to Hallwood. Try as she might she could not associate the raw headstone with memories of her Mam or foster even a trace of morbid sentimentality in this depressing place. Turning away, she quickly caught up with her father and grandmother at the back of the column. They ignored her and continued with their conversation as if she was not there at all.

'I hear a rumour Singer's have vacancies for girls,' Granny Gilfillan said. The Singer Manufacturing Company's Clydebank plant covered over a hundred acres and was reputed to be the largest factory in Europe.

'On the shop floor?' said Alex.

'For work in the offices.'

'If we were lookin' for employment for her,' Alex said, 'I suppose office work might suit. She fair likes her books.'

'She's too old to still be at school.'

'She's happy there, an' a bit of extra education will do her no harm.'

'Girls don't need educatin',' Gran said. 'Education gives them ideas above their station.'

'Are you talking about me?' Alison said.

'Aye,' Alex admitted. 'Granny tells me Singer's are employin' clerks.'

'But I don't want to work in Singer's.'

'Well, you might have to,' said Gran smugly.

'Why?'

'When Ransome's closes there'll be no money for falderals.'

'Ransome's isn't goin' to close,' Alex said.

'That's not what I've heard,' Gran said.

'Where in God's name do you pick up these wild rumours?'

'From Flora's boy, from Georgie.'

'An' that's your idea of Gospel truth?'

'Georgie hears things that never reach the likes of you.'

Ransome's specialised in building tramp ships and cargo vessels to high specification, and had so far weathered the downturn in trade. But closures were taking place every week on Clydeside and even famous old firms were going to the wall. A man could be in work one day and in the dole queue the next. Alison sensed her father's anxiety and knew that her grandmother's jibe had found its mark. Pouches of loose skin tightened about the old woman's mouth and her faded grey eyes glittered, for she took pleasure in taunting her son-in-law.

'I don't see what this has to do with Alison,' Alex said.

'You, Henry, Jack – three wages,' Gran said, 'gone like a puff o' smoke. You'll not be able to treat this one like a lady then, will you, eh?'

'Maybe not,' said Alex. 'But since we're all still in work I can treat "this one" how I damned well please.'

'She should be earnin' a wage like other decent girls her age,' said Gran. 'Maybe then she'd learn to respect her elders an' betters.'

Although her intention seemed spiteful there was some truth in what Gran said. Education was expensive and if Ransome's did lock its gates then two wage packets would hardly pay the rent and keep the family fed. She, Alison, would be obliged to find employment quickly and, she supposed, there were worse places to work than Singer's factory.

'Listen,' she heard her father say, 'if I decide to keep Ally on at school then it's my business, not yours. I hear she's got brains, so perhaps I'll decide to give her the chance Mavis never got.'

'Mavis could have been—'

'Go on, tell me what could Mavis have been.'

'She could have married a better man than you.'

'I don't doubt it,' Alex said.

'She was clever at school,' Granny Gilfillan said.

'So why didn't you do somethin' about it?' Alex said. 'Put her to college instead of stickin' her behind the counter in Farrell's Dairy as soon as she was old enough to tie on a bloody apron?'

'We didn't have money to burn.'

The old woman was almost trotting now, anxious to reach the group which gathered on the pavement by the gates and to enlist the loyal support of her daughters.

'Do you think it was any easier for me?' Alex said. 'I'll tell you this, I did all right by your Mavis. She never went hungry, never went cold. She always had a bed to sleep in an' a chair to park her backside on. What's more, I'm going to do even better by this one if I possibly can.' He tossed away his cigarette and wrapped an arm about Alison's shoulder and, at that moment, she was proud of her father's stubbornness. 'Whatever she decides to do she'll have my support.'

'Alex Burnside, I think you're a fool.'

'What about you, Ally? Do you think I'm a fool?'

She caught her father's frown and the little shake of his head and said stoutly, 'No, Dad.'

'Hah! You're as bad as each other,' Gran snapped and scuttling the last few yards hid herself behind the skirts of Flora's overcoat and, like a spoiled child, refused to say another word until the tramcar came to carry them off to Clydebank.

* * *

The journey back to Flannery Park seemed interminable. Alison did not feel entirely well. The smoky atmosphere inside the bus brought a stuffy congestion to her nose and made her throat feel raw. She'd planned on attending evening service at the Congregational church but she didn't think she'd be up to it now. Her brothers were also depressed, thinking perhaps of the empty house, unwashed dishes, an unlighted fire, of Pete whining to be taken for a walk.

The bus deposited them on Shackleton Avenue.

They trudged silently along Wingfield Drive until 162 came into view and Henry, rearing up, exclaimed, 'What the hell!' and began to run.

The house, however, was not on fire.

What had alarmed Henry was the reflection of firelight on the window glass. That in itself was disturbing, though, for Alison had been last to leave and could have sworn that there had been nothing in the grate but ashes.

While Henry fumbled with the front door key Alison, her father and brothers piled up by the step and squinted through the bay window.

'Good God!' said Jack. 'Somebody's in there.'

'Goldilocks?' Davy suggested.

'Well, I hope she's sleepin' in my bed,' Jack said.

'Mind your mouth, son.'

Alex hopped from foot to foot, more concerned with answering nature's call than solving the riddle of the intruder. Tentatively Henry pushed the door open and called out, 'Who's there?'

The only answer was an inquisitive *wuff* from Pete who had padded to the open door of the living-room to see what all the fuss was about. Davy found the light switch just as Alex rushed past him and shot upstairs to the bathroom, Bertie hard on his father's heels.

Alison could see firelight dancing in the mirror, smell hot scones, hambone soup, sausage rolls and, lingering in the little hall, the faint whiff of a familiar perfume. She ducked under Jack's protecting arm and looked about the living-room. Someone had cleaned the grate, lighted a fire, had set the table with a fresh linen cloth and covered it with fine net muslin.

'There's hot soup in a pot and sausage rolls in the oven,' Davy called from the kitchen. 'Who the hell's been in here?'

'Can't you guess?' Alison murmured as the lavatory flushed upstairs.

A second later Alex burst into the living-room, shouting, 'What's all this then? What's all this?'

'Suppose you tell us.' Henry whisked the net muslin from off the table. Davy's eyes popped at the sight of teabreads, scones, cream cakes and a mound of freshly cut gammon sandwiches. 'Dear God!'

'Who's responsible for this?' Jack said.

Henry threw the muslin across a chair and, leaning, plucked up a square of white cardboard which had been placed against the milk jug. He glanced at it, scowled, then passed it without comment to his father.

'What does it say, Dad?' Jack asked.

Squinting at the card's pencilled message, Alex laughed. '"A wee surprise for you and yours."' He glanced up. 'It's from Ruby McColl. Now isn't that nice of her?'

'How did she get in?' Jack said.

'Somebody gave her a key,' said Henry. 'Right, Dad?'

'Aye.' Alex turned the card over and over in his fingers and grinned sheepishly. 'I did.'

'I knew it,' Henry exploded. 'I knew it was only a matter of time.'

'Henry, where the hell are you goin'?' Davy said.

'Out,' came Henry's answer a split second before the front door slammed behind him.

'Well, what's got into him?' Jack said.

'I don't think he likes Mrs McColl,' said Alison.

'Why not?' said Davy. 'Old Ruby's a bit of all right.'

'I couldn't agree more, son,' Alex said enthusiastically, and peeling off his overcoat helped himself to a plump gammon sandwich from Ruby's floral plate.

'You don't half look rough,' Brenda said. 'Don't you think she looks rough, Walter?'

'It's ond-ly a head code,' said Alison.

'Your eyes are all pink,' said Brenda.

'I doh that,' said Alison.

'Must admit,' said Walter Giffard, 'Brenda has a point. Are you sure you're well enough to be at school?'

'Here dow, may as weld stay.'

'If you're goin' to stay,' said Brenda, 'do you mind wipin' your nose?'

Alison sniffed and dabbed at her nose with a balled-up handkerchief. She was all too conscious of how awful she looked without Brenda's graphic commentary.

'English next,' Walter reminded her. 'Tell Abbott you feel rotten. He'll send you home.'

'No, he won't,' said Brenda. 'He'll send you to the nurse first.'

'It's Tuesday. Nurse isn't here today,' said Walter. 'Listen, Alison, you shouldn't be out in this lousy weather. Are your bones sore?'

'A bit.'

'Headache?'

'What're you then,' said Brenda, 'a doctor? Watch out for him, Ally. He'll be askin' you to take your clothes off, you know, in a minute.'

'Shut it, Brenda,' Walter said mildly.

It was playtime, about ten past eleven. Alison could not believe that a schoolday could seem so long. The first two periods of the morning – algebra – had taxed her concentration to the limit. She could think of nothing except the throbbing in her head, the ache in the small of her back and the shooting pains in her joints. Her throat felt as if it was being hosed with a blowtorch and the little fleshy bell behind her tongue was swollen.

And her nose was running.

She dabbed it with the damp handkerchief and shivered.

The three of them were seated on a low brick wall beneath the shelter of the eaves at the verandah's end, a fairly private spot in spite of the babble of infants just around the corner and the clatter of seniors on the main stairs. Alison could not be quite sure when it was that Brenda had attached herself to them. Two had become three without plan or invitation. Wherever Alison went Brenda, like Mary's little lamb, was sure to follow. Walter, though, did not seem to resent Brenda's presence and gave no indication that he would have preferred to have Alison to himself.

Alison bleakly contemplated the rain that fell from a lid of blue-black cloud. She could feel the dampness in her bones and shivered again.

'Nah, nah, this won't do.' Wattie put his arm about her and helped her to her feet. 'Come on. I'll take you to see Mr Abbott right now.'

'You can't do that.' Brenda's contempt for teachers was tempered by her fear of authority.

'Wanna bet?' With an arm securely about Alison's waist, Walter led her towards the main staircase and left Brenda, gawping, behind.

* * *

By nature Jim Abbott was not gregarious. One of the main hardships of army service had been the inescapable intimacy of camp and barrack life. Although he had been younger and more resilient in those days he had shied away from rowdy games and boisterous drinking bouts, the camaraderie upon which so many young men seemed to thrive and which, in retrospect, had made the years of the Great War the happiest time of their lives. At the Front in the trenches there was no privacy at all. He had taken refuge in foxholes and redoubts and had cultivated his streak of fatalistic pessimism to the point where he almost wished for death and the blissful solitude of the grave.

The staffroom of Flannery Park School was hardly the equivalent of Mons, or even Chapelton Barracks. But smoke, chatter and odours of chalk, floor polish and hair oil still unnerved him somewhat. For this reason he usually took his morning break alone in a classroom where he would sip black coffee from a Thermos flask and browse over the agony columns of the *Herald* or the share prices in *The Times*. Lately, though, the newspapers had remained unread as Jim sipped coffee and puffed a Player's and speculated on how rapidly the years were slipping past and life was passing him by. His foolish yearning for Alison Burnside was no doubt at the root of it.

He had his heels on the desk and the cigarette in his mouth when he realised that somebody was approaching. Hastily he swung his feet to the floor and ground out the gasper in a tobacco-tin ashtray in the strap drawer. He rattled the drawer shut just as someone knocked on the door.

'Who is it?'

'Giffard, sir.'

'Giffard? Come in.'

To Jim's surprise Giffard was not alone.

Alison clung to the young man's arm as if Walter intended to spirit her bodily away. Jim pushed back his chair. 'What's wrong?'

'Alison's not well, Mr Abbott.'

'Code,' Alison mumbled.

'I reckon she should be at home,' Walter said, 'in bed.'

Jim placed the back of his wrist against Alison's brow. She offered her face up to him, eyes half closed as if his touch brought ecstasy. Nothing of the sort, of course. Her eyes were rheumy, nose runny, temperature high.

'Yes.' Jim stepped back. 'Home at once. Will there be anybody there to take care of you?'

'Sub-body,' Alison croaked.

He felt an appalling wave of pity for her, all desire erased. He would have felt something of the same emotion for any suffering child.

'I'll go with her,' said Walter. 'If that's all right?'

Jim frowned. He had a sudden vision of a four-bedroomed house with five or six empty beds in it, Alison and Walter Giffard all alone with temptation and opportunity. Lord above, if he could not trust his two most intelligent and responsible pupils who could he trust?

'It's not really all right, Walter,' he said. 'But, yes, you'd better. See her safely into the house then fetch a neighbour to help her to bed. You understand?'

'Yes, Mr Abbott.'

'When will your family be home, Alison?'

'Davy ad dinner dime.'

'Then he'd best send out for the doctor,' said Jim Abbott. 'Cut along then, both of you. And Walter—'

'Yes, Mr Abbott.'

'Report back to me in thirty minutes.'

'But what if—'

'Half an hour, not one minute longer.'

Walter nodded. He understood that he was being treated fairly, as an adult, but that compromise was none the less necessary.

He wrapped an arm tightly around Alison and, with a gesture that Jim Abbott could do nothing but envy, touched her soft cheek and without a blush told her, 'Cheer up, Ally-Pally, I'll soon have you home in bed.'

It was a very strange time for Alison. Later she wished she'd been in a fit state to enjoy its novelties and the cossetting which illness occasioned.

It began with the odd experience of floating down Wingfield Drive in teeming rain with Walter's arm around her – then the even odder experience of seeing Walter and Mrs Rooney together in the living-room of 162 – Pete barking, Wattie hunkering down to pet the dog, Mrs Rooney in the kitchen filling a hot-water bottle – a warm drink which tasted of cinnamon and honey.

Walter faded away.

She was alone in her bedroom with Mrs Rooney, being helped out of her wet school clothes and into her nightie. Waves of guilt at the eaves-dropping episode washed over her. 'I'm soddy, I'm soddy,' she cried – and Mrs Rooney assured her she'd nothing to be sorry about, anyone could come down with the flu, not her fault, poor lamb. Vague recollections of calling for Mam – then it was all bits and pieces, jumbled and dream-like, with voices and faces appearing and receding, and no sense of time at all.

Mrs Rooney – Mrs McColl – Davy – Dr Lawrence in his fine blue suit taking her pulse, sounding her bare chest with a cold stethoscope, his presence in the bedroom so light as to be almost ethereal – then it was dark and she slept, waking once to see Pete, paws on the patchwork, blinking at her balefully – Dad and her brothers, one by one. Bertie held a camphorated handkerchief to his nose. Henry brought her a milky drink and told her a great deal she didn't want to know about the effects of epidemic diseases on industrial enclaves; and she fell asleep with her head resting on Henry's forearm.

She wakened once in the night, drenched with perspiration, shuffled and shivered across the darkened landing to the bathroom while heads popped out of doors and various brothers anxiously enquired if she was in need of nursing attention.

In three days Alison was on the mend.

Propped up in bed, shaken and skinny, she was sufficiently recovered to revel in the extra attention and enjoy the gifts of magazines, oranges and peppermints which her brothers showered upon her. Ruby McColl had usurped Mrs Rooney as nurse-in-chief. She was in and out of 162 a great deal in the course of Alison's ten-day convalescence, bearing soup and fish-in-milk and other light, nourishing dishes to tempt the invalid's appetite.

It was left to Brenda to bring Alison news from school, not about lessons but about Walter Giffard, who seemed, by appropriation, to have become Brenda's boyfriend too.

'Did Walter ask about me today?'

'Oh, aye.'

'What did he say?'

'He said, "How's Alison?"'

'What did you tell him?'

'I told him you were fine.'

'Tell him – tell him I'll be seeing him soon.'

'I could ask him to come an' visit.'

'That wouldn't be proper.'

'He could pop in at four o'clock,' Brenda suggested,

'when there's nobody else here. I could tell him you want him to come an' kiss you all better.'

'Don't you dare.'

On Friday forenoon Dr Lawrence called for a second time. He seemed satisfied with Alison's progress, prescribed tonic medicine and told her that she could get up for a little while, provided she didn't tax her strength. When pressed, he predicted that she would probably be fit to return to school on Monday week, the day on which the pre-Christmas examinations began. Alison wasn't apprehensive about the half-yearly tests. Everything she needed to know to complete the papers was already laid out plainly in her mind. She had not, though, dared raise the subject of her future career with her father who, she suspected, might not approve of her scholastic ambitions when it came right down to it.

On Sunday afternoon, however, while Alison slept, Alex Burnside received an unexpected call as a result of which young Alison's life was swung about and changed for ever.

It would have been a simple matter for Mrs Trudi Coventry to send a servant around the corner from her house in Astor Gardens to fetch her motorcar from the garage in Maidmont Lane. Nothing that Mrs Coventry did was simple, however, and she chose to conduct her affair with Henry Burnside with a deviousness which was both calculating and stimulating, and which did not involve too obvious a display of wealth.

To maintain a pretence that her servants did not realise what was going on, Mrs Coventry would personally telephone for a taxi-cab to transport her to the railway station on Sunday afternoons. At Queen Street station she would enter a first-class compartment in the non-corridor coach and settle down with a magazine to while away the five or six minutes it took the train to reach the grubby little station at Wharf Street where, hidden in the shadows, Henry would be waiting. He would scan the carriage windows until he caught sight of her behind the grimy glass then he would dart across the platform, fling open the compartment door and clamber quickly inside.

Pressed into the corner against the plush, Mrs Coventry would stare at him in apparent alarm, her blue eyes wide and frightened.

'Why, sir,' she would say, 'do you not see that this compartment is occupied? I trust that you do not intend to take advantage of my situation?'

Now and then, depending on her mood, she might address her questions to the intruder in French or German, her tiny childlike voice making use of all the subtleties that the chosen language offered. Henry, bless him, ignored her pretensions and her protests in all tongues. He would snap up the strap to seal the window and, casually lighting a cigarette, would seat himself opposite her and eye her up and down without a word while the train steamed slowly into the gloom of the Wharf Street tunnel.

Sometimes they would be unlucky and a portly gentleman or a pair of snooty spinsters would invade their privacy. Henry would pretend not to know her and she would modestly avert her gaze and diffidently study the wintry hills or the foam-flecked Clyde, her curly-lamb collar turned up, the brim of her hat pulled down, knees primly squeezed together. Only Henry would be aware that beneath the lady's expensive black skirt, between the edges of her corselet and her gartered stockings Mrs Trudi Coventry wore absolutely nothing at all.

Winter was the best time for railway games. In early dusk Helensburgh's seafront promenade would be almost deserted and Henry and Mrs Coventry would walk its length arm in arm until, out of range of the streetlamps, Henry would kiss her and crush her body against his own – after which exercise they would repair to the Victoria Hotel to partake of a high tea preparatory to the long ride home.

Henry Burnside was by far the best travelling companion Trudi Coventry had ever had. Once upon a time she had considered her husband, Clive, to be the epitome of masculinity but Clive, in spite of a genteel upbringing, had been greedy and brutal in a way that the young Clydeside shipwright was not. She had first met Henry twenty-one months ago at a British Union lecture in the Barbour Institute in Stockwell Street. She had been attracted there less by the subject – Fascism and the Corporate State – than by the speaker, Charles Ross, an Italian-American industrialist who was currently acting adviser to Benito Mussolini but had, at one time, been a nodding acquaintance of her father.

Trudi had recalled Señor Ross as a compact, virile man whose ugliness was redeemed by a sparkling white smile and a great deal of plausible charm. He had been a frequent visitor to the hotel-restaurant which her father had managed and she had become quite excited at the discovery of a fragment of her cosmopolitan childhood here in smoky old Glasgow. But, to her disappointment, Charles Ross had not been at all as she had remembered him and the white smile had vanished into sullen grooves which bracketed his mouth like scars. The lecture had been clever and persuasive but, during the course of it, she had lost all inclination to reintroduce herself to Señor Ross and to remind him of his visits to her father's discreet little hotel in Paris in the golden age before the war.

So that the evening would not be entirely wasted, however, Trudi had inclined for consolation towards the young man who had been gazing at her with such intensity during the lecture. She had approached Henry in the lofty, marble-floored foyer of the Barbour Institute and had asked him point blank if he would care to take her to supper. Sometimes her directness frightened young men off, particularly those who wore off-the-peg suits and carried raincoats draped over their arms. But not this fellow. This fellow was well able to take care of himself.

'I'd love to, sure,' he'd said, 'but I can't afford it.'

'It will be my treat.'

'That's not what I meant.'

'Explain, please.'

'I mean I can't afford to tangle with the likes of you.'

'Tangle? I do not understand "tangle".'

'Become involved.'

'I only ask you to eat with me.'

Henry had said, 'How long have you lived in Glasgow?'

'A long time.'

'In that case,' Henry had said, 'you'll know what I mean when I say I didn't come up the Clyde in a kipper box.'

'You mean you are not ingenuous.'

'Too true,' Henry had said. 'I'm obviously a shipyard worker and women like you don't suddenly latch on to shipyard workers unless they want somethin' from them. An' I don't just mean the time of day.'

'I know what time of day it is,' Trudi had said. 'I wish only to discuss what Señor Ross had to say with a serious-minded young man.'

'Señor Ross?' Henry had grinned. 'So you know the old buzzard from way back, do you? Are you Italian?'

'I am Swiss,' Trudi had lied. 'Why did you stare at me?' She had wagged a finger in warning. 'Do not deny it.'

'Half the blokes in the audience were staring at you. Are you goin' to invite them all to supper?'

'No, I only invite you. If you will come.'

113

'Sure, I'll come,' Henry had said. 'But before I do, answer me one question – are you married?'

'Does it make a difference if I am?'

'None at all,' Henry had said and, even before she had learned his name, Mrs Trudi Coventry had instinctively known that at last she had found a man to suit her purposes.

Alison was asleep upstairs, the boys were all out, and Alex was doing nothing in particular when the visitor arrived.

Since Mavis had died Alex had lost all desire to maintain the fabric of the house or improve its habitability. He was vaguely aware that the place was deteriorating into a pig-sty but had managed to convince himself that untidiness equated with comfort and that laziness was a widower's prerogative. He had considered polishing his boots or repairing the carpet sweeper but had thought better of it and had remained slumped in his chair by the fire, puffing on one cigarette after another. He did not even have the prospect of a visit from Ruby McColl to cheer him up for Ruby was at work that afternoon, and he was both relieved and annoyed when the doorbell rang. 'Hullo, who's this then?' he said aloud. He hoisted himself out of the chair, crossed to the hall and opened the front door before the visitor could ring a second time.

The stranger wore a neat black overcoat and bowler hat. If it hadn't been Sunday Alex might have taken him for an insurance salesman. He was faintly disappointed that it wasn't some member of his own unsociable family who had taken a notion to make a rare and unexpected call, for he did not at first see in the stranger much hope of diversion.

114

'Yes?'

'I'm sorry to disturb you, Mr Burnside. I – I was just passing and I thought . . . How's Alison?'

'Alison?'

'I'm James Abbott – Alison's English teacher.'

The man offered his hand which Alex, still puzzled, shook.

'Has she been up to mischief at the school?' Alex said.

'No, no, nothing like that.'

Alex had a notion that there was something off-key about a male school teacher visiting the home of a female pupil but he could not bring the word 'impropriety' to mind. 'Alison's sleepin'. She hasn't been well.'

'I know, Mr Burnside. As a matter of fact, it's you I came to see.'

'In that case, I suppose you'd better come in.'

'It's not inconvenient, is it?'

'Nah, nah.' Alex allowed the teacher to enter the hallway.

The man glanced upstairs into the gloom of the landing and asked, 'Is she all right?'

'On the mend,' Alex answered. 'The living-room's this way. 'Scuse the mess. I lost my wife recently.'

A minute or so later Mr Abbott was seated on the edge of an upright chair with a dram of whisky and a lighted cigarette in his one good hand, his bowler hat and glove on the carpet by his feet.

Now that he had played the host, Alex did not know what to do next. He said, 'Do you want to take off your coat?'

'No, I shan't stay long, thanks.' Mr Abbott lifted his glass. 'Well, here's to Alison's recovery – and to her future.'

'Her future?'

'Yes,' Mr Abbott said. 'In fact, Mr Burnside, I'm rather

glad Alison's asleep. It gives me an opportunity to talk to you about your plans for the girl.'

'Plans?' Alex sipped whisky then put the little glass on the mantelpiece. 'What plans?'

'She's a highly intelligent young lady, you know.'

'Aye, I know.'

'She deserves the best you can give her.'

'She gets that already,' Alex said. 'Anyway, what's Alison's future got to do wi' you?'

'I believe Alison has a brilliant career ahead of her,' James Abbott did not meet the riveter's eye, 'if you're willing to give her the chance.'

'What's Ally – Alison been tellin' you?'

'Nothing,' Jim Abbott said. 'I expect she would be embarrassed if she even knew I was here.'

'So she hasn't been complainin' about me then?'

'Come now, Mr Burnside. Alison isn't that sort of girl,' Jim Abbott said. 'She isn't in the least rebellious, is she? By which I mean she'll be guided by your instruction and advice.'

'She'll do what I tell her to, aye.'

'Then leave her where she is,' said Jim Abbott.

'Keep her on at school you mean?'

'For a start.'

'University?'

'That is what I had in mind.'

'To become a teacher, like you?'

'I think Alison may be capable of better things than being a teacher.'

Alex stroked his wiry hair thoughtfully with the palm of his hand. 'Could she be – a doctor, for instance?'

'I don't see why not.'

'Never been a doctor in our family,' Alex said and then to Jim Abbott's astonishment suddenly doubled over and began to weep. 'Her mother always said – Och, this's terrible, bubblin' like a bairn. I'm sorry, sir.'

'I understand.' Jim Abbott put his hand on Alex's shoulder.

'Mavis always had such high hopes for the lass. Hopes she'll never see fulfilled.' Alex rubbed his nose and looked up, wet-eyed. 'I wish you could have met my wife, Mr Abbott. She was the clever one. Ally got her brains from her mother, not from me.' He forced a moist self-deprecating laugh. 'You just have to look at me to know that. Takes no brains to be a bloody riveter.'

'It takes other qualities, Mr Burnside.'

'I wish I could think o' them.'

'Toughness, determination, strength of character.'

'Maybe you're right,' Alex said, nodding.

'Qualities Alison would also require if she's to survive six years of medical training.'

'Six years?'

'Eighteen months of schooling, followed by five years at university.'

'Six years! God, I'll be an old man by then.'

'She will, of course, receive assistance.'

'What do you mean "assistance"?'

'A bursary.'

'Charity? I'm not takin' charity.'

'It isn't charity, Mr Burnside. Eighty per cent of all students receive financial assistance from the Carnegie Trust.'

'Carnegie, the millionaire?'

'Yes.'

'He was Scottish, you know,' said Alex.

'I know. That's the reason—'

'Well, if the money comes from him, he can well afford it.' Alex frowned. 'I thought he was dead, but.'

'He is,' Jim Abbott said. 'But he left money in trust to assist with education for less privi – for promising Scottish students.'

'Good for the old boy,' Alex said. 'Well, I wouldn't object to that, not if everybody else is gettin' it. Our Alison's as deservin' as anyone. Right?'

'Even so, it won't be easy,' Jim Abbott said. 'Financially, I mean.'

'I'm in work. I've always been in work. Never had a day off in my life,' Alex said. 'Aye, I know times are hard on Clydeside but Ransome's will weather the storm. We'll be all right about the money. Her brothers'll pitch in.'

Prudently Jim Abbott kept his doubts on that score to himself. He said, 'The first thing that has to be done is to make certain Alison's willing to undertake such an arduous course of study.'

'Willin'? She'll be as keen as mustard.'

'What if – I mean, she may prefer to get married,' Jim suggested.

'She's near the age for it, right enough. It's what her old granny thinks she should be doin',' Alex said. 'But we know better, don't we?'

Jim nodded soberly.

'Time enough for marriage when she's got her degree an' hung up her brass plate,' Alex went on. 'I'll bet there's some fine, rich young doctors hangin' on the bough, the sort who'd fall for the likes of our Alison.'

A similar thought had occurred to Jim Abbott who, changing tack, said, 'There is one small obstacle to all of this, Mr Burnside.'

'What's that?'

'The University Entrance Board requires applicants to have a Lower Leaving Certificate in Latin.'

To Jim's surprise the riveter seemed to grasp this point immediately. 'An' Ally hasn't?'

'Alison has had no Latin at all,' Jim said. 'Latin isn't yet part of the curriculum at Flannery Park.'

'Aye, that's a poser,' Alex said. 'I'm stumped on that one, Mr Abbott.'

Jim cleared his throat. 'I would be willing to tutor Alison in Latin.'

'Like, extra classes?'

'Yes, after school.'

'What would that cost me?'

Jim was taken aback. 'Cost you? Lord, no, I wouldn't charge for tutoring Alison.'

'What would you get out of it then?'

'The satisfaction of helping Alison become Flannery Park's first graduate.'

'Like a feather in your cap?'

'Exactly.'

'Somethin' for everyone, in other words.' Alex laughed and got to his feet. 'Look, why don't you nip upstairs an' ask Alison what she thinks of all this?'

'Isn't she in bed?'

'Aye, but it's time she was up,' Alex said. 'She'll be fair pleased to see you.'

Jim fought the temptation to exploit the father's trust. 'Perhaps it would be better if you told her.'

'I'll waken her then.'

'No, let her sleep. She probably needs it.' Jim glanced at his wristlet watch. 'Besides, it's time I was pushing along.'

'Not a bit of it.' Alex brought the whisky bottle from the sideboard. 'You'll have another dram before you go.'

Jim was disappointed at not having seen Alison. None the less his boldness had paid marvellous dividends. He would have Alison near him for another eighteen or twenty months, and all to himself for four hours a week. The only fly in the ointment was Walter Giffard – and he could leave the solution of that little problem to another day.

Smiling, he held out his empty glass.

'Why not, Mr Burnside?' he said.

Quite out of the blue Trudi Coventry said, 'I am so sorry to learn of the death of your mother.'

Henry was wiring into a dish of the Victoria Hotel's salmon au gratin accompanied by slices of Hovis spread with fresh farm butter. In appeasing one appetite he had managed to put the other into store for a time. One of the things he liked about Trudi was that she was constantly engaged in sensual and intellectual manipulations and he had to be damned fast to keep up with her. 'Oh,' he said, 'I thought you'd forgotten.'

'I do not speak before because it does not seem appropriate.' Trudi put down her fork and touched the back of his hand. 'It is such a sad thing to lose one's mamma. It is especially sad for boys. No other woman can ever again take her place.'

'Yeah,' said Henry, solemnly.

'What do you do at home now she is gone?'

'Muddle along as best we can.'

'Your papa, he will remarry?'

'Give him a chance,' said Henry.

'He does not like girls?'

'I doubt if he pays them much attention.'

'Now he will, you bet.'

'He's Scottish, Trudi, not French.'

'He is a man, no?'

'Oh, he's that all right.'

'You will see. He will take after you.'

'Other way round,' said Henry.

'Ah – get it correct – you take after him, no?'

She had a habit of finding soft spots in his character and dabbing away at them the way a child will at a snail.

'I don't think I do, really,' Henry said.

'Your sister is sad too?'

'Of course she is.'

'Do you sleep with her?'

'Trudi! For Christ's sake!'

She shocked him more often than he cared to admit, less by what she did than by what she said. She would pretend that her tactlessness was a fault of her English but she seldom apologised and would often persist, in that tinkling, Swiss-made voice of hers, in teasing him about his Presbyterian attitudes and lack of *joie de vivre*.

'I mean for you to give her comfort.'

'I don't have to sleep with her to do that.'

'How do you do it?'

'Do what?'

'Comfort her.'

'I don't know,' said Henry. 'I just do, that's all.'

Even on a cold winter's night the Victoria Hotel's dining-room seemed stuffy. From the huge uncurtained windows Henry could look out at the river, at the riding lights of little boats in the bay and cargo ships behind the buoys that marked the channel. He fancied he could hear the pulse of waves on the shingle shore and the tolling of a kirk bell summoning the faithful to worship.

'Do you hug her?' Trudi said.

'No,' said Henry. 'In this country you don't hug your sister.'

Beneath the table Trudi stretched out her leg and rubbed the toe of her shoe against his shin. 'Not even if she needs your arms?'

'I wish you'd cut this out,' Henry said.

'I am interested.'

'Well, I'm not.'

He scooped what remained of the salmon into his mouth and, chewing, reached for the heavy silver-plated teapot. All about him kirk-goers, fed in body, were rising to pay their bills. Soon they would be off into the streets in search of spiritual recreation. Fleetingly Henry envied them their dreary rituals, their security and self-satisfaction.

'What are you interested in, Henry?'

'You,' he answered, almost too quickly.

He sensed exactly what stage the game had reached. Trudi was deliberately annoying him so that he would enter the train to Glasgow ready to take revenge, for she knew that his man-of-the-world *hauteur* was no more than pose, as fragile as eggshell.

'Does she not cry, your sister?' Trudi persisted.

'We all cry.'

'You too, Henry?'

'Yes, me too.'

'It is difficult to imagine your tears.'

'I'm not going to cry just to please you.'

'I do not want to make you cry.'

'Pleased to hear it,' Henry said.

'If I told you you would not have employment after the month of March,' Trudi said, 'would you cry then?'

'What the hell are you on about now?'

'I believe how some men who are put on to the dole shed copious tears,' Trudi said. 'Men to whom work means everything.'

She had been stroking her ankle against his calf but suddenly stopped as if to indicate that her mood had turned serious. Henry munched a crust of brown bread, drank tea which had already gone cool in the cup, and tried to appear as nonchalant as possible. 'What have you heard, Trudi?'

'Ransome's will close in the spring.'

'Are you sure? We've been told there are new contracts coming through,' Henry said.

Trudi shook her head. 'It is not Peter Ransome who will padlock the gates. It is the company to whom he sold controlling interest.'

'Whitton Engineering?'

'Yes, they are already selling assets to keep solvent.'

Henry clicked his tongue and frowned. He didn't doubt that Trudi was telling him the truth. Clive Coventry had been, and still was, a businessman of considerable repute. Without doubt dainty little Mrs Coventry had access to market secrets worth their weight in gold.

'Whitton's will not bring contracts to the Clyde. They will put all the pieces of work to the home yard in Newcastle after the month of April.'

'Bloody hell!' Henry exclaimed softly.

Ransome's had been established back in the 1870s but had not been a family-owned firm for the best part of a decade. With holdings in Newcastle and Belfast as well as Clydeside, the Whitton Engineering Company had acquired a majority interest in Ransome's soon after the war. Although Peter Ransome had remained as managing director, he was no more than a figurehead. When push came to shove young Peter would be in no position to stand behind the workforce as his father and grandfather had done.

'Just how imminent is closure?' He watched Trudi dissect a meringue with surgical precision. She had an unwholesome partiality for anything which oozed cream. 'Trudi?'

'When will the last vessel be launched?' she asked.

'March,' Henry said. 'Early March.'

'They will lay away men soon after that.'

Trudi seemed remarkably unconcerned at the effect her

news might have on him. Why should she be concerned? If she had ever held stock in Whitton's she had probably sold it months ago and shrewdly cut her losses. Women like Trudi Coventry knew nothing about the despair and desperation that accompanied unemployment.

'What will you do, Henry?' Trudi asked.

Dole would provide a frugal income. Few families would actually starve, but the prospect of a long spell out of work would drag many a man into the gutter and even in a model community like Flannery Park the spectre of poverty would loom large. Henry watched the woman's small, even teeth snip meringue from the fork. At that moment he realised how easy it would be to detest everything she represented – and yet she looked more elegant and desirable than ever, almost as if she had been created just for him.

'Henry, answer me.'

In a phrase his father would have recognised, Henry said, 'We'll manage.'

'Will you not write more for the *Banner*?'

'What the *Banner* pays is pocket money. As a living – not enough.'

'Find a better job. You are an educated man.'

'I wish to God I was.'

'I can help, if you will allow it.'

She would not be so crass as to offer him money but he suspected that she had contacts in all sorts of unexpected places. In spite of the fact that she was no longer married to Clive Coventry she seemed to have retained the goodwill of half the power brokers in Glasgow.

If and when it came to the bit, he would not be stubborn.

'You have not eaten your scone, Henry.'

'I seem to have lost my appetite.'

'Scone before cake, *n'est-ce pas*?'

'I don't want the cake either.'

124

'I have angered you with my news?'

'What did you expect – cartwheels?'

'You must not worry, Henry,' Trudi said. 'If you have no work to go to, you will have more time for me.'

'And no money.'

'Money? Pooh!' she said. 'If it is just money that you want you can have it by marrying me.'

Henry tried to remain impassive but did not quite succeed. 'Are you kidding?'

She gave a little laugh which tinkled like a cow-bell. 'Of course, I am kidding with you, of course.' She glanced up with an expression that Henry could not read at all. 'Do you think I would be serious about such a subject?'

'No, I don't suppose you would.'

'Do you not wish to eat your eclair?'

'No, Trudi,' Henry said. 'Feel free to help yourself.'

A half hour later Henry Burnside and Mrs Coventry were alone in the first class compartment of the 7.22 train as it steamed out of Helensburgh station. As usual Trudi had suggested that he return to Astor Gardens and spend the night with her. As usual Henry had made a plausible excuse and had gently refused. He had been to her vast mansion house only three times and had made love to her there only once. He was intimidated by her habitat and resentful of the scale on which she lived. On moving trains, in the back seat of her magnificent motorcar, on plaid rugs in deep woods, everything between them meshed and functioned. But in Astor Gardens he was too obviously an intruder. He imagined he heard her snooty servants whispering behind the peacock wallpaper, sniggering at the youth and gaucheness of madam's latest conquest.

Hardly had the train cleared the platform than Trudi began to taunt him. She flung off her hat, unbuttoned her coat and sprawled upon the seat like a tart. She braced her shoulders against the cushion, stretched out her legs and planted a foot on each side of Henry's thighs. She slid forward, raising her knees until Henry could see her stocking tops and catch a glimpse of milky flesh. She cocked her head. Ash blonde hair spilled across her neck. She smiled, defying him to look away while she unbuttoned her blouse and, just as the train pulled into Craigendoran and rocked to a halt, placed the heel of her shoe in Henry's lap.

Impassively Henry listened to the hiss of steam, the clash of milk churns, raised voices. He saw a face, fuzzy as a flannelgraph, appear briefly at the compartment window. Henry kept his nerve. Cupping Trudi's calf with one hand he stroked her stocking with his middle finger, working it gradually upwards into the little wrinkled fold behind her knee. Out of the corner of his eye he glimpsed a porter's alarmed expression just as the whistle shrilled and, in the nick of time, the train steamed out.

'Please, Henry, please.' No laughter in her voice now, no teasing in that tiny, little-girl tinkle. He had wrung something from her, something valuable and out of the ordinary, yet he experienced no sense of triumph.

Turning her towards him he pushed up her skirt, slipped his hands around her waist and pulled her down across his knees. Trudi let her head loll backwards, cheek against his cheek. She murmured something in French.

Henry's fingers brushed moist and springy little curls, caressed them gently. She rolled against him, panting. Henry hesitated. In the light of the compartment lamp he could not fail to notice the tiny tracks of skin at the corners of her eyes, the slight creasing on her slender neck and for the first time he realised just what it meant to Mrs Trudi Coventry to be almost forty years old.

'Do you love me, Henry?' she whispered.

'Of course I do,' Henry answered flatly and, without passion, kissed her softly on breast and brow and throat.

'I don't know what all this is about, Dad,' Henry said, 'but I'd be grateful if you'd make it quick. It's late and I want to get to bed.'

'What have you been up to then?' Davy said.

'Taxin' his strength with women, I expect,' Jack said. 'Look at the puss on him. Jeeze, he looks knackered.'

'He always looks knackered,' Bertie said, without glancing up from the Puzzle Page of the *Mail*.

Henry ignored his brothers' jibes. He slumped on to one of the chairs at the dining table and lit a cigarette. The table was littered with an odd assortment of foodstuffs. Dates vied for space with cheese, raspberry jam with fish paste, bananas with Marmite, bread rolls with sponge cakes.

'No squabblin', lads,' Alex called from the kitchen. 'I don't want Ally wakened.'

'What's going on?' Henry asked. 'Why the big palaver?'

'God knows!' Davy answered.

'The old man's been struttin' about all night,' Jack said.

'He had a visitor this afternoon,' Bertie said.

'Who?'

'He wouldn't tell me.'

'Maybe it was Ruby,' Jack suggested.

'Here,' said Davy, 'you don't suppose he's done anythin' daft?'

'At his age it's not very likely,' said Jack.

'He's not so old,' said Davy.

'Forty-seven,' said Henry.

'I can hear every word o' this conversation, by the way,' Alex shouted. 'Be patient.' A few moments later he appeared with a teapot which he set down upon the mat on the table. 'Gentlemen,' he said, 'be seated.'

127

Henry slipped a cracker and cheese into his mouth and demanded to be told what all the secrecy was about.

'Alison,' Alex answered.

The brothers exchanged bewildered glances.

'I'll bet she's got herself in trouble,' Bertie said.

'What d'you mean – trouble?' Davy said.

'I mean, with a boy.'

'How could she?' Jack said. 'She's only a wee lassie.'

'She's old enough,' said Bertie. 'Have you not seen how she—'

'Enough o' your lip, Bertie,' Alex said. 'Alison's not in any trouble.'

'Come on, Dad,' Henry said. 'Spit it out.'

'Her teacher called to see me this afternoon. Mr Abbott. Real nice chap. He thinks we should send Alison to the university.'

Bertie broke the silence. 'To do what?'

'To become a doctor.'

'Our Ally?'

'Why not our Ally?' Alex said. 'Mr Abbott seems to think she'd scoosh the examinations.'

'What does he know?' Bertie said.

'He's her bloody teacher,' Jack said. 'If he doesn't know, who does?'

'Huh!' said Davy, wistfully. 'Imagine our Ally a doctor.'

'How long will it take?' said Jack.

'Four or five years, apparently.'

'More like six or seven,' Henry said. 'Any idea what it'll cost?'

'A flamin' fortune,' Bertie said. 'Money wasted.'

'Andrew Carnegie pays for the studies,' Alex said.

'Who's he?' said Davy.

'The millionaire,' said Jack.

'I thought he was dead,' Davy said.

'He is,' said Henry. 'I imagine Abbott's referrin' to the Carnegie Trust Fund.'

'It's not charity,' Alex said. 'Everybody who applies for help, gets it.'

'Is that true, Henry?' Jack said.

'Near enough,' Henry answered. 'Costing tuition won't be the problem. Paying for her clothes, books, fares, lunches, will.'

'She can work in the holidays,' Davy suggested.

'Doin' what?' said Bertie. 'Layin' bricks?'

Henry propped his elbows on the tablecloth and stroked his upper lip thoughtfully with his forefinger. 'Tell me, Dad, why are you so keen to give Alison a university education?'

Alex shrugged. 'It's what your mother always wanted.'

'I knew he'd put the blame on Mother,' Bertie said.

'We talked about it often,' Alex said. 'In fact, it was her dyin' wish.'

'Then why are you only tellin' us now?' said Davy.

'Because he expects us to pay for it,' Bertie said.

'Well, hell, I can hardly do it all myself,' said Alex. 'I thought you lot might be willin' to pitch in. She is your sister, after all.'

'What does Alison have to say about it?' Henry asked.

'I haven't told her yet,' Alex said. 'She was asleep when Mr Abbott dropped by so I kept mum about his visit. I thought I'd discuss it with you before I said anythin' to Ally.'

'That's a relief,' Bertie said. 'At least she won't be disappointed.'

'What d'you mean?' said Davy.

'We can't afford it, that's what I mean,' Bertie said.

Davy said, 'Nobody expects you to help.'

'*He* does,' Bertie pointed at his father. 'He expects us to volunteer for short commons just so his precious daughter can go swankin' up University Avenue like a middle-class tart.'

'Shut it, Bertie,' Davy warned.

'Sendin' a girl to university's like tossin' pound notes into the canal,' Bertie went on. 'She'll be there ten minutes and she'll decide she wants to get married, and that'll be that.'

'He's got a point, Dad,' Jack admitted.

Alex thumped his hand upon the table. 'You don't think Alison's good enough, do you?' he snapped. 'By God, I tell you she's as good as any of those toffs at Gilmorehill.'

'Aren't we puttin' the cart before the horse?' Jack said. 'After all, Alison might not fancy bein' a doctor. I mean, you wouldn't catch me porin' over books, never mind cuttin' up dead bodies, for five or six years.'

'Alison will leap at the chance,' said Henry.

'How do you know?' Bertie said.

'Because she's smart,' Henry said, 'too smart to turn down the opportunity of making something of herself. No, it's up to us to make the decision. If we go along with Dad on this it'll mean considerable financial sacrifice from each and every one of us.'

'I reckon we can afford it,' Jack said. 'We're all workin', after all.'

'But for how long?' said Henry.

'Ransome's won't close,' Alex said.

Henry did not condone his father's stubborn refusal to face facts. On the other hand he did not to wish to undermine his optimism.

'Suppose it does, though,' he said. 'Suppose we promise to see Alison through then Ransome's locks its gates?'

'With three of us on the dole,' Jack said, 'we wouldn't have anythin' to spare for educatin' Alison.'

'I'd still be earnin',' said Davy. 'Bertie too.'

'Huh!' Bertie snorted.

'It's all very well making sentimental decisions here and now,' Henry said, 'but circumstances can change in six months, never mind six years. What if next year or the year after I meet somebody I want to marry? I'd need every red cent to set up a house. Same goes for Jack, Davy, even Bertie.'

Bertie snorted again.

'I see what you're drivin' at,' Jack said.

'Listen,' Henry said, 'the worse thing we can do for Alison is to make her a promise that we can't keep.'

'We'd never do that,' Davy said. 'Would we?'

Jack filled his chest with air and let it out in a sigh. 'I dunno. Henry's right. Six years is a long time.'

'Make up your mind,' said Henry.

Jack scratched his ear, frowning. 'I mean, it's not really up to me, is it? We're not going to be able to manage without you behind us, Henry, an' you're obviously set against the idea.'

'Who says I am?'

'By the way you're rattlin' on, I thought—'

'I just want you to be clear what you're getting yourselves into,' Henry said. 'Personally I think we should give Alison the chance.'

Davy rocked in his chair. 'If Mam was alive we wouldn't be thinkin' twice about it, would we? We know what she'd want us to do.'

'Forget Mam,' Henry said. 'Mam's dead. What we're doing now is considering Alison's future.'

'And our own,' Jack reminded him.

'Is she, or is she not, our responsibility?' said Henry.

'Vote on it,' Alex suggested.

'Yeah,' Jack said. 'Let's have a show of hands.'

'Why bother?' Bertie said. 'We all know how the flamin' vote will go.'

'Make it unanimous then, Bert,' said Davy.

'Blowed if I will,' said Bertie and, rising, minced into the kitchen and closed the door behind him.

'Are there any more dissenters?' Henry said.

'Speak now,' said Alex, 'or for ever hold your peace.'

'Count me in,' said Jack.

'Me too,' said Davy. 'How about you, Henry?'

'Oh, I'm for it.' Henry nodded.

'I take it that's it settled then?' said Alex.

'Now what do we do?' Davy asked.

'Tell Alison,' Henry said.

'When? Tomorrow?'

'Hell, no,' said Jack. 'Wake her an' tell her now.'

'Dad?'

'No time like the present, son,' Alex answered and eagerly led his boys upstairs.

FIVE

Winds of Change

Jim Abbott's professional responsibility prodded him into treating Alison and Walter Giffard to equal shares of his time. It would have been simpler to tutor them in tandem but he was just selfish enough to keep girl and boy separate and for four evenings a week throughout the winter bound himself to the living-room and banished his sister Winnie to the kitchen.

He started his pupils off together and observed their progress with interest. Wattie was quicker but inclined to show off his mental agility to the detriment of accuracy. Alison, on the other hand, had a logical approach to learning which was ideally suited to assimilating the precise grammatical constructions of a classical language. Try as he would to be even-handed Jim could not help but favour the girl over the boy.

For four hours each week he had Alison all to himself, though his sister Winnie lurked close by and regulated the length of the lesson with cocoa and hot buttered toast. Supper was served on the stroke of nine o'clock and the pupil, like it or lump it, would be nudged out on to the path by a quarter past the hour.

'You're sweet on that girl, aren't you?' Winnie asked her brother a week or two after Christmas; to which Jim replied, as honestly as he dared, 'Of course I am.' He

133

expected his sister to remind him of the dreadful fate that lay in store for teachers who became infatuated with pupils but Winnie knew him too well to suspect him of serious indiscretion and said no more about it.

Jim was careful not to let Latin studies interfere with Alison's school work. He gathered that she was learning to cope with running a household and that a neighbour, Brenda McColl's mother, was lending a helping hand. Even so, he could not help but imagine what a noble thing it would be to rescue Alison from the cluttered male-dominated household.

Monday and Wednesday evenings, right after tea, he would loiter by the window of his council-owned semi-detached and watch Alison pedal up the Kingsway into Macarthur Drive and approach the Abbott residence. By its spacious and lofty position on the summit of the hill Jim's house seemed raised in stature above the villas which surrounded it as if white-collar workers deserved something a little better than artisans and labourers. When Alison swung off her bicycle and arranged her skirts decently over her wonderfully long legs and tugged, less decently, at her stockings before she rang the doorbell, Jim felt a strange self-satisfied glow, as if he was about to welcome her not just to his home but on to a different plane of existence.

Walter was not impressed by Macarthur Drive's marginally elevated position, nor by Jim Abbott's free lessons. Face to face, Master Giffard was polite if not exactly obsequious, his diffident air a rebellious indication that he would yield ground to nobody. There was something admirable as well as irritating in the young man's attitude and Jim did not grudge him it.

He would have been much less forgiving, though, if he had known what went on every Monday and Wednesday night when Walter Giffard led Alison into the shadows of the school's back gate for a purpose that smacked less of courtship than seduction.

In the early months of the New Year Alison was unusually sensitive and unsettled. She felt divided within herself, split between awareness of her intellectual ability and a distressingly sloppy emotionalism.

The prospect of becoming a medical student did not daunt her, however. One afternoon, two or three days after Daddy had made his announcement, she had ridden up University Avenue on the bus, had disembarked in Gibson Street and had walked back over the avenue to mingle with the students who milled about the gates. Collectively they were not in the least intimidating. Some of the males were obviously harassed, others were show-offs, while the female students, numerically scant, clustered in groups, confident and companionable in spite of the drizzle.

Alison had told no one of her family's plans for her future, no one except Walter and she'd sworn him to secrecy. It had been daft to suppose she could keep it secret for long, though. Davy had confided in Mrs McColl and Mrs McColl had confided in Brenda, and Brenda had gone up in a wee blue light. Apparently she had screamed, shouted and raged, had demanded that she too be sent to be a lady doctor. When the sheer impracticality of that course of action had been pointed out to her she had taken refuge in a sulk so sullen and prolonged that Ruby had threatened to take a strap to her if she did not snap out of it. All very embarrassing for Alison and Davy. Even poor old Pete suffered from Brenda's jealous rages and had been kicked more than once under the table so that he hid himself, whining, behind Davy's legs as soon as the girl appeared. Tantrums, jibes and malicious threats were all to no avail, however. Brenda knew that come Easter she was destined for Singer's Manufactory – and that, Ruby indicated, was that.

Meanwhile Alison continued to ride up to Mr Abbott's house two evenings in the week and sit in the living-room – which Mr Abbott's sister called 'the parlour' – and enjoy the genteel air of primness and calm which, at that time, she believed to be hallmarks of the middle class.

'Baloney!' Walter said. 'It's only a council house.'

'But it's so nice, so clean.'

'That's because there aren't any kiddies to grub it up.'

'What about the antiques?'

'Old furniture, you mean. Inherited, most of it, from her husband.'

'I wonder what he was like, her husband?'

'He wasn't an officer, only a staff sergeant.'

'How do you know?'

'He's in the photograph on the table behind the armchair,' Walter told her. 'Staffie, Gordon Highlanders. Big moustache, big chin.'

'Whatever he was, I think she's nice.'

'Well,' said Walter, 'she doesn't think much of us.'

'Oh, Wattie, you're imagining things.'

'Look at her eyes next time you're there,' Walter said. 'She's suspicious of scruffs like you an' me, take my word for it.'

'Why doesn't she like us?'

'For one thing, she thinks I'm vulgar,' Wattie answered.

'Vulgar? You're not vulgar.'

'Aye, but I am, you know,' Wattie said.

'In that case I am too.'

'And proud of it, I suppose?'

'Not particularly,' Alison said. 'On the other hand I'm not ashamed of comin' from working-class stock.'

'But you have ambitions?'

'What's wrong with that?'

'Not a sausage,' Wattie said.

'Don't you have ambitions?'

'Sure I do, but I'm not tellin' you what they are.'

'Oh, go on.'

'Nah. You'd only laugh.'

'No, I wouldn't.'

'You would,' Walter said. 'Anyway, I'm not gonna risk it.'

'I thought we were friends.'

'Just because I kiss you doesn't mean to say we're friends.'

'If we weren't friends I wouldn't let you kiss me,' Alison said.

'Even though you like it.'

'How do you know I like it?'

'Because you never tell me to stop.'

'I would, though, if you – if you went too far.'

'Which,' said Walter Giffard, 'is why I never do.'

Mondays and Wednesdays, hail, rain or moonshine, Walter and Alison would slip into the slot of red brick that partitioned the school's steep back stairs and there, leaning against the locked iron gates, he would kiss her.

What Walter said was true. He never did 'go too far'. In fact, now that she had recovered from the first electrifying uncertainty of being held in a man's arms, Alison was disconcerted by his apparent lack of passion and kisses that seemed rather too expert, as if they'd been deliberately rehearsed with other, more accommodating girls. He did not prolong contact for more than a minute or two and his one and only liberty, installed into the procedure from the first, was to slide his right hand between the buttons of Alison's overcoat and place it lightly just beneath her breast.

Three or four layers of winter clothing protected Alison's modesty and she was rather put out by the fact that he did nothing more, nothing persuasive or impulsive to which she could respond or, if she chose, resist.

At all other times, in school and out of it, Walter's attitude towards her was casual, almost fraternal. Alison was understandably confused, rendered tense by the suspicion that Walter had somehow gained control over her in a way that was less than respectable, less than honest.

Even so, as winter eased into spring she began to wonder if she was falling in love with him. When she saw him waiting in the lee of the hedge at the old mansion house corner her heart would give a sort of sigh and, much as she hated it, her breasts would tingle, all the hard-learned Latin verbs would drain away and a kind of vacuous longing would possess her. They would kiss in the spring-night air, stroll home under the street lamps and discuss the Laws of Metre or Boris's latest injustice or, now and then, Brenda's pique. But Walter would never talk of love or shared affection, as if he considered her above such trivialities. How scornful he would have been if he could have seen her practising kisses before her bedroom mirror or hear her muttering to herself, 'Scio eum amare. Scio eum amare' – 'I know that he is loving. I know that he is loving' – with no one to correct her or assure her, in Latin or her mother tongue, that there was no disgrace to falling in love at the age of sweet sixteen.

Unlike his sister, Henry had never consciously applied

himself to any particular course of study. An ambitious nature and natural inquisitiveness had, however, combined to soak up much useful information on a wide variety of topics. To most folks, the family included, the things that Henry knew were merely unrelated snippets of data with which he demonstrated his superiority. Henry himself didn't have a clue what fascinating facts were stored in his head until he was seated at his desk in the loft of the Cally with his fingers resting on the typewriter keys. Only then would his brain click into high gear and all sorts of surprising stuff come out. Indeed, there were times when Henry felt that his most enduring relationship was not with his father, brothers or sister – and certainly not with Mrs Trudi Coventry – but with that bloody Underwood typewriter.

If the order books at Ransome's had been full Henry would not have forgotten that he was more shipwright than journalist. But the yard was on the short drop into oblivion and the launching of the last ship likely to leave the slipways in the foreseeable future was too good an opportunity for Henry to pass up. The launch was attended by all the usual formalities as if it was a huge Cunarder that was about to enter the Clyde and not merely another cargo vessel for the Argentine Navigation Company. The enthusiasm of the workmen might have been dampened by uncertainty but there was no hint of lost confidence among the members of the launching party. They were as upright, arrogant and formal as usual and betrayed not a sign of poignancy for the moment when the mass of steel became a floating ship or awareness that more than the *Rosario*'s keelblocks were being knocked away that gusty March forenoon.

Lady Elvira McCaine, the English-born wife of an Argentine shipowner, did the honours. Fur-decked and gorgeous she disdained to acknowledge the cheers of the men who packed the area behind the standing way and swarmed around the flag-draped platform, and she held a handkerchief to her nose when fifteen hundred tons of inert metal sloped into the narrow river and slid away through its crushing-slips, dragging a tangle of rusty chains behind it. To his astonishment, Henry heard himself cry out with the rest. It was no cheer, though, no romantic hurrah at the realisation that the plates which he had drilled would, in six months time, be cleaving the green waters of the Rio Plata or holding out the tidal surges of the Uruguay but an anguished growl for what was being lost.

He focused his attention entirely on Lady McCaine, a thoroughbred with a high-bridged nose and puckered rosebud mouth and when she held the handkerchief to her mouth he could have sworn he saw her shudder as if the smell of working men *en masse* was just too much for her to bear.

That was the image that he carried back to the Cally, the picture that burned in his memory when his fingers touched the keys. Within seconds Henry was hammering the typewriter with a fervour that amounted to fury.

The headline ran on to the page unbidden: RANSOME OF THE CLYDE. It was followed by a scathing pen portrait of Lady McCaine; and continued:

Do you like our fashion plate? What do you say to it? Do you say that it is wasteful and vulgar? Yes, you would be right. But what could be more wasteful and vulgar than a rich and worthless woman flaunting her wealth before a mass of ordinary working men upon whom, in short order, the axe of poverty and degradation will inevitably fall? Ransome's is to close. Make no mistake about it. It awaits but the signature upon the gate to make it official. Yet we, like fools, swallowed the lies and cheered the last

*vessel out. Would we have cheered so loudly if we had
been able to see into the future and view our wives or
daughters sunk to the level of beggars in the streets? Why,
you must ask yourself, should one man or woman lie soft
and suck the sweets of life while others endure hardships
not of their own making? Why should one woman, or one
man, waste wealth in peacock display while others have to
practise the most rigid economy? Why? Well, I will tell
you why.*

Henry paused to light a cigarette, loosen his necktie and
read over what he had written. He was pleased with his
oratorical outburst and did not for a moment consider that
he might have laid it on a bit too thick.

Scowling, he attacked the keys once more and was well
into the core of the article when the telephone rang. Still
typing with one hand, Henry snatched up the receiver and
growled, 'Yes.'

'Henry?'

'Yes, Trudi.'

'Where have you been?'

'Busy.'

He had seen Mrs Trudi Coventry only three times since
New Year. One chilly train ride to Helensburgh and two
late night dinners in a smoky basement restaurant had been
the extent of his involvement with her. Although he missed
the pleasure she gave him Henry had resolved to discon-
tinue the affair. Perhaps mention of marriage had scared
him off.

'Come tonight,' the woman said.

'Trudi, I—'

'Come tonight. Please.'

He removed his hand from the keys and squinted at his
watch. It was already twenty minutes to nine o'clock. He

had promised Eddie delivery of a finished article by half past and had even offered to help set up the page.

'Come to me, Henry, as soon as you are able.'

'All right,' he heard himself say. 'But it'll be late.'

'How late?'

'Eleven or half past.'

'Come to the house?'

'Yep,' said Henry, and angrily hung up.

Evenings off from labour behind the bar in the Argyll were precious but Ruby did not count time spent with Alex Burnside as wasted; nor did she expect him to feel privileged that she would abandon her own fireside – and Brenda – to cook him an evening meal, run an iron over his shirts or, when Alison was not about, do a bit of dusting and polishing. She was well aware that the boys resented her intrusions and took great care not to offend them by bossing them about.

Ruby's infiltration of the Burnsides' family circle may have seemed casual but Ruby was a strategist without equal when it came to dealing with men. She knew what they liked a woman to wear, what they liked her to say, even how they liked her to move. And she was absolutely convinced that what worked on hard-bitten commercial travellers would work even better on a middle-aged Clydeside riveter. She was also astute enough to recognise that matters must not be rushed and consequently went about her business with an air of effortless domestication that had 'wife' written all over it. Only when she was alone with Alex did her motherly façade slip somewhat and Alex was permitted a glimpse of her other attributes.

Ruby's wardrobe would hardly have done justice to the Duchess of Kent but all things considered it wasn't too bad for a working woman. Over the years she had expended whatever spare cash came her way on smart skirts and blouses and expensive shoes. She had kept her shape quite well and needed as a foundation garment only a light elasticated girdle with nothing over the bust.

That evening she wore a mid-length pleated skirt of fine brown wool and a mock-silk blouse in *café-au-lait* which exactly matched the shade of her stockings. Her shoes, which had cost her eighteen and sixpence in Bayne & Duckett's, were leather, strap-over-instep style and her hair had been coiffed and bobbed in a not-too-severe French swirl which was easy to keep shipshape with a couple of steel combs. Cost and effort were invisible to Alex Burnside, of course. All he saw was what he was supposed to see, an end product which he fondly imagined represented the 'real' Ruby McColl, as if females of the species came endowed by nature in the likeness of a Grafton's mannequin.

Seated in a fireside armchair Ruby was doing a little mending, buttons and cuffs mostly, the garment tucked under her elbow like a deflated bagpipe. It was quiet in the house and there was hardly a whisper of traffic from the streets, only the crackle of the coals in the grate to break the companionable silence. Jack had gone off to band practice, Bert to the pictures and Davy, toting vest, shorts and pumps in a haversack, had jogged away to the Scout Hall for a training session. Henry had not shown up at all and Alison, having washed the tea dishes, had vanished upstairs to apply herself to homework.

'She's a hard worker,' Ruby said.

'What?'

He had been watching her fingers push the needle through the cotton and pull it away again. Now and then she would lift the shirt sleeve and snip off a thread-end with her teeth. She had very good teeth, with one small filling of

143

pure gold against the gum of the left incisor. When she glanced up at him and smiled, Alex wriggled and cleared his throat.

'Alison,' Ruby said. 'She's a hard worker.'

Alex lit another cigarette from the butt of its predecessor, sat back in the smoker and raised his eyes to the ceiling as if to observe his daughter's industry from the underside.

'She has to be,' he said. 'She knows she's got the chance to better herself an' she's sensible enough not to waste it.'

Ruby wetted the tip of a fresh length of thread with her tongue. 'More than any of us ever had – the chance, I mean.'

Alex watched, covertly.

Ruby said, 'What are you lookin' at?'

Any one of thirty commercial gentlemen of her acquaintance would have been ready with an answer that would have led the conversation in a less than respectable direction, but Alex was no smooth talker. Innocence and naïvety were part of his charm. 'You're – you're awful good wi' a needle.'

'I went to a good school.'

'I thought you went t' Hammie?'

'I did, but not when you were there.'

'Did they teach you buttons at Hammie?'

'Domestic science,' Ruby said. 'But I learned more from my Mammy.'

'Mammy? You've never mentioned her before.'

'Been dead for years.'

Ruby tactfully did not mention that her father was still alive and wreaking havoc in the dockland pubs of Tyneside or that she had six stepbrothers and sisters upon whom she had never so much as clapped an eye. She had been alone since she was sixteen years old. She had stubbornly stood her ground and allowed the old man and her brothers to decamp to Newcastle while she'd stayed behind in Partick, living in shabby lodgings and toiling in Skidmore's rope-works, in the hope that one day Ernest McColl would notice her and marry her, which unfortunately he did.

After Ernie had been killed in the war she had vowed that she would never marry again. Now that she was growing older, though, she found the prospect of ending her days behind the bar in the Argyll less than pleasing. There was Brenda to think about too, Brenda's future.

'I suppose you'll be givin' some thought to Brenda's future?' Alex said, as if he had read her mind.

'Since she's my one an' only,' Ruby said, 'I'd like to see her settled.'

'Singer's, maybe?'

'Singer's would suit her – if there's a vacancy.'

'What does Brenda think o' that idea?'

'Heaven knows what goes on in Brenda's head these days.'

'What did you think about when you were her age?'

Ruby recrossed her legs beneath the mid-length skirt and considered the question.

'It must be a fair long time,' Alex said, 'since you had – I mean, did – did it.'

'Alex Burnside! What a thing to say.'

'Oh here, no. I didn't mean that.'

'What did you mean then?'

'I meant – since you were Brenda's age.'

'Not that long.' Ruby stuck the needle into the arm of the chair and ran both hands flatly down her ribs, smoothing her blouse so that one deep breath made it go taut. 'I don't look like an old biddy yet, do I? I've still got a long way to go before I lose my figure, don't you think?'

'A long way,' Alex agreed. 'You're in great cond – you look fine to me.'

'It's not elastic either. I'm still quite firm.'

'Aye, I can see that.'

Amusement wrinkled the corners of Ruby's eyelids as she plucked up the needle and, head down, began to sew again.

Alex lit another cigarette and puffed at it as if he'd been starved of tobacco for weeks. He cleared his throat loudly. 'Want one?'

Ruby cocked her head. 'Why not? Tell you what, though, I'll make us a cup of tea first. Time I had a break. Okay?'

'Oh, okay.'

She got up and stretched, put the mending down on the chair behind her and started towards the kitchen. Alex rose to follow her, and at that inopportune moment the doorbell rang.

Muffled in a heavy black overcoat with a fur collar, Granny Gilfillan stood on the doorstep. She glared up at her son-in-law and he glared down at her until she gave him a nudge in the belly with her umbrella and snapped, 'Are you goin' to keep me waitin' here all night, Alex Burnside?'

'I suppose not. You'd better come in.' He let her pass under his outstretched arm then peered out into the lamplit road in search of the old woman's escort. 'Are you on your own?'

'Belle's vistin' Betty McDougall.' Alex had no notion who Betty McDougall was or where she resided. 'She'll drop by at ten o'clock to take me home. What's wrong with your face? Are you not pleased to see me?'

'I'm just surprised, that's all.'

'I want a word wi' you, Alex Burnside.'

'Aye, I was afraid o' that,' Alex muttered as he ushered his mother-in-law into the living-room.

'Mrs Gilfillan, is it?' Ruby said. 'You're just in time for a cuppa.'

'Who is this woman an' what's she doin' here?'

'We've met before,' Ruby said. 'Don't you remember? I'm Ruby McColl, from over the road.'

'Tell her to go,' the old woman said.

'I will bloody not,' said Alex.

'Alex, perhaps I should—'

'Stay right where you are, Ruby,' Alex said. 'You were invited. She wasn't.' He turned to his mother-in-law. 'Now, what's on your mind?'

'Is she your fancy woman?'

'What? With Alison upstairs? What do you take me for?'

'I'll wait in the kitchen,' Ruby said, 'while you sort this out.'

She was not entirely displeased by the fact that Alex had not renounced her. She gave a flounce and let the old woman have an eyeful of her shapely derrière as she went into the kitchen and closed the door.

'She's after you,' Granny Gilfillan said.

'She's only bein' neighbourly,' Alex said. 'Anyway, what if she is after me? She could do a lot worse.'

'She's just a trollop.'

Ear pressed to the kitchen door, Ruby snorted in consternation.

'Well, if she is a trollop,' Alex said, 'she's a better class o' trollop than I can afford.' The statement was so ambiguous that it reduced his mother-in-law to silence. Ruby covered her mouth with her hand to smother a chuckle at his ham-fisted attempt at gallantry.

147

'Since you're here, Gran, you'd better sit down.'

Granny Gilfillan picked the mended shirt from the chair with finger and thumb, held the garment at arm's length and dropped it on top of the work-basket. She brushed the seat with the back of her hand then lowered herself on to it. Her feet did not quite reach the carpet and her tiny boots swung forth and back like little brown pendulums. 'Well, where is she?'

'If you mean Alison,' Alex said, 'she's upstairs.'

'What's this I hear about you makin' her promises you can't keep.'

'Who's been fillin' your head wi' this nonsense?'

'Bertie met Belle in the street. Bertie says Alison's goin' to be a doctor.'

'That's true enough.'

'She'll never be a doctor.'

'Why not?'

'She's a girl.'

'Plenty lady doctors around,' said Alex. 'Ally's goin' to be one of them.'

'Years, it takes years.'

'Six years, thereabouts.'

'And money, it takes money.'

'We've got the money, me an' the boys between us.'

'That's not what Bertie told Belle.'

Alex discovered that he was no longer afraid of his mother-in-law and her waspish tongue. She, like poor Mavis, belonged to a past that was almost dead and gone. He shook his head. 'You'd think I was sendin' her to sea as a bloody stoker the way you're carryin' on. Alison's goin' to university to study for a medical diploma. An' that's that.'

'She'll have to cut up bodies, dead bodies.'

''Course she will. They all have to do that.'

'My granddaughter, cuttin' up the dead.' The little boots treadled at a furious rate. 'Men too – without their clothes on.'

'Well, they're hardly goin' to be lyin' there in three-piece suits an' bowler hats, are they?' Alex said.

'Mavis would turn in her grave.'

'Mavis, rest her soul, is long past turnin',' Alex said. 'But if she does happen to be lookin' down on us I'm sure she'd approve.'

'Let me talk to the girl.'

Alex hesitated. 'Why?'

'If she tells me to my face that she really wants to be a doctor then I'll not stand in her way.'

'That's very nice of you,' Alex said, then, tilting his face towards the ceiling, yelled at the top of his voice, 'Alison, dear, your grandma's here.'

Alison had raced through the homework which Mr Hammond had given her to do and had then turned her attention to preparing an essay on 'The Romantic Movement in Scottish Literature'. Some prize or other was being offered in open competition to Glasgow schools and it was really to please Mr Abbott that Alison had taken on the task. She had little or no interest in Henry Mackenzie's *The Man of Feeling* or *Confessions of a Justified Sinner* by James Hogg, which latter gentleman, Wattie and she were agreed, was really a bit of a nut-case, in spite of learned opinion to the contrary. She was not particularly sorry to be interrupted by her grandmother's arrival and hurried downstairs at once.

'Granny.' She kissed the old woman on the cheek. 'How are you?'

Through the kitchen's half-open door Alison caught a

glimpse of Mrs McColl, a cigarette in one hand, a slice of toast in the other.

'Granny's come 'specially to see *you*, Alison,' her father told her as he backed into the kitchen. 'So *I'll* make myself scarce.'

Granny Gilfillan wasted no time. 'Who *is* that woman?'

Bright, brittle and smiling, Alison seated herself on the edge of the smoker's chair. 'Brenda's mother. Brenda's my school friend. The McColls used to live in Partick. Mrs McColl remembers you very well.'

'Does she?' Granny Gilfillan said sourly.

'How's Aunt Marion?'

'As well as she'll ever be.'

'And Auntie Belle?'

'I didn't come here to chat.'

'No, I don't suppose you did,' said Alison. 'I expect you've heard I'm goin' to university and you've come to talk me out of it.'

Caught off guard by Alison's directness the old woman blinked and fidgeted and did not seem to know what to say next.

Alison said, 'Why don't you want me to be different?'

'What was good enough for me, girl, should be good enough for you.' She spoke without edge. 'I've seen what tryin' to be different can do to folk.'

'If I'd been a boy, a man, would you—'

'I wouldn't have interfered.'

'Oh, I think you would have,' Alison said. 'What's more I think you'd have behaved just the same way no matter what I decided to do.'

'It isn't just you, lass,' the old woman said. 'It's the others.'

'What others?'

'If all the young girls decide they want to go to university, to be doctors and lawyers and things then what'll happen to the men?'

'I don't see what the men have to do with it?'

'The men make the money. There isn't enough to go round.'

'Daddy's promised to see me through,' said Alison.

'If he does it properly,' Granny Gilfillan said, 'he'll lose you.'

'I don't understand.'

The old lady gave an indulgent smile. 'See, you don't know everythin'.'

'If you mean I'll become too snooty to want to have anythin' to do with my family then you're definitely wrong.'

'You'll change. You think you won't but you will, and not for the better.'

Alison thought of the books upstairs, of Latin texts she could read more easily than her aunts or cousins could read the *Mail* or the *Mercury*. She thought of mathematics, of scientific principles that rendered the world as a series of systems and equations. She wondered if her grandmother was afraid of knowledge itself, of that grand accumulation of practical know-how which was so much the mark of men. Was Gran afraid that she, Alison, might shake the monkey-puzzle tree and expose Bella's husband and Flora's sons and the men whom Gran had married for what they really were?

Alison spoke softly. 'What would you prefer me to do?'

'Be like your mother.'

'And marry a man like Daddy?'

'She could have done better for herself. She could have had her pick.'

'She took her pick. She chose Daddy.'

'Well, that's all over,' Granny Gilfillan said with a sigh. 'I suppose it shouldn't matter to me what you do since I won't be here to see it.'

Or influence it, Alison thought. But she couldn't deny that the Gilfillan influence was in her blood. Whether she liked it or not, she was inextricably linked to her grandmother and would remain so until she in turn died and the legacy gradually faded, like those old card-backed photographs from the eighties and nineties that Gran preserved and treasured.

'Don't you see what I'm tryin' to do?' said Alison.

For an instant Gran's eyes were bright as stars and her humped shoulders straightened like wings that might ruffle into flight.

'You're tryin' to leave them all behind,' she said. 'I wish I had.'

The temporary rapport between them was no gentle thing yet Alison was more troubled by it than by a conflict of wills. It was on the tip of her tongue to ask her grandmother to explain her last remark but she resisted and said, rather pretentiously, 'I just want to be a doctor so that I can help people.'

'You'll always have plenty o' work then,' Gran said. 'You'll earn plenty of money, too.'

'I won't become stuck-up, though.'

'No, I think you're maybe too sensible for that.'

It was the kindest thing Granny Gilfillan had ever said to her. She did not know how to respond. She was even more disconcerted when the old woman leaned forward and touched her cheek with the back of her hand.

'So they're not forcing you to do it?' Gran said.

'No, no. It's what I want to do. Absolutely.'

'In that case,' the old woman said, 'I'll help you if I can.'

* * *

It had not occurred to Ruby that a father's relationship with his daughter was much different from that of a mother's. But that March evening, while Alison and the old woman conversed in the living-room, Ruby's eyes were opened. She had never seen Alex so nervous and upset and when he had pressed his ear to the door she'd whispered, 'What are they sayin'?'

'Can't bloody hear.'

'Go in then,' Ruby had said. 'It's your house. You're her father.'

'Aye, but Ally has to learn to stand up for herself.'

He had drawn himself away from the inner door and, a moment or two later, had opened the back door to the garden. He had lighted a cigarette and had seated himself on the top step, back bowed and hands between his knees. There he remained while Ruby ate a piece of toast and speculated on how this minor family drama might affect her prospects.

From across the gardens drifted suburban sounds to which Alex seemed oblivious. He was as sunk in on himself as if his daughter was undergoing some dreadful rite which he was powerless to halt. For the first time it dawned on Ruby that while she knew a great deal about men and how to please them she was sadly lacking in experience of fathers.

'Hear it?' Alex said.

'What?'

'The wind.'

He hadn't turned round but he had raised his head a little and she could see the pin-prick of the cigarette glowing against the planes of grey and black beyond the range of the house lights.

He sighed. 'It'll be stormy tomorrow. Typical March,

153

neither one thing nor the other.' He paused, then said, 'I wonder if I'm doin' the right thing.'

'Of course you are,' said Ruby.

He glanced over his shoulder. 'Think so?'

'Sure so.'

Ruby went to the door and stood just behind him, not touching. She folded her arms and leaned against the doorpost, looking out at the postcards of light across the backs. March, right enough. Quite warm and promising one minute, chill and withdrawn the next.

Alex frowned up at her and asked, 'What?'

But Ruby had no opportunity to give an answer for at that moment Alison came into the kitchen in search of supper for her gran.

The cobbled lane which separated Trudi Coventry's town house from the mansions behind it was broad and uncluttered. In the old days, Henry supposed, the lane would have led not only to kitchens and servants' quarters but to stables and coach houses. But these days only one elderly occupant of Astor Gardens still kept horses in the mews. Henry could just make out the faint odour of manure, an acrid whiff that reminded him of his childhood in Partick when haulage had all been done by heavy horse. Here in Astor Gardens, though, such memories had no validity. Most of the mansions seemed not just aloof but deserted, as if the residents had reached an age when stillness and silence were their only defences against the debilitating pace of change.

Trudi was waiting for him in the little side door. In the half-light she looked furtive, as if he was an unwelcome lover, like L'Angelier whom Madeleine Smith had murdered, not so very far from here, on a blustery March night seventy-odd years ago. Henry glanced up and down the lane, observed nothing more sinister than a cat perched on top of a wall, and slipped past the woman into the narrow stone-floored passageway that led to the basement kitchens. Trudi closed the door behind him, dropped the latch and without so much as a candle to give light, guided him up a steep flight of stairs, through a gaslit corridor and into the main hallway.

Armour and aspidistras, paintings by Leighton and Millais, great chunks of carved woodwork, a Jacobean chest or two, a table with lion's-paw legs topped with enough marble to rebuild the Parthenon; this part of the house, like the drawing-room and library, remained exactly as it had been when Clive Coventry had taken possession, too dark and formidable to be transformed by Trudi's taste and, like the bedroom upstairs, given the Edelweiss treatment.

As soon as they entered the hall Trudi pulled her to him, pressed her slender body into his arms and kissed him upon the mouth. She wore a loose housecoat in crêpe-de-chine, gartered silk stockings, a pair of silver slippers as fine as fishskin, and, it seemed, not much else.

'Hey!' he said. 'What is all this?'

'I am so glad to see you, so glad.'

'I gathered that,' said Henry as she rubbed against him. 'But what's Georgette goin' to think if she catches us in a clinch?'

'Georgette has gone. They have all gone.' Trudi began to cry.

Henry separated himself from her as best he could and glanced towards the oak door behind which the servants usually lurked. When he looked back at Trudi he saw that his guess had been correct. There was nothing much below the housecoat, only skimpy silk knickers. Her hair had come loose from its ribbon. The style, though short, gave

her a wild appearance, as if the departing staff had taken
her composure with them.

Henry removed his soft hat, flung it across the hall
towards the marble-topped table and hugged the woman to
him once more. As she clung to him, sobbing, Henry
experienced a strange tingling surge of power.

'I am sorry, Henry. I am sorry.'

'What's there to be sorry for?' Henry said.

'I have nobody else to whom I can turn.'

He wondered what had happened to the multitude of
solicitors, accountants and brokers, to the friends in high
places that Trudi had bragged about, if not directly
certainly by implication. Where had *they* gone to? They
couldn't *all* be out of town. 'When did they leave? The
servants, I mean.'

'Two days ago.'

'What, packed up and walked out without warnin'?'

'They had not been paid.'

'Why didn't you pay them?'

'Clive pays them.'

'Ah!' Henry pushed her gently away. He lifted one of her
hands. The silk sleeve of the housecoat slithered, baring
her forearm to the elbow. He brought her hand to his face
and laid her palm against his cheek. 'My God, woman,' he
said, 'you're frozen.'

'I have not been well.'

'I'm not surprised.' He kissed her open palm brusquely.
'Are none of the rooms fired?'

She shook her head.

'When did you last eat? Properly, I mean.'

'I have no hunger.'

'That's no excuse,' Henry cupped his hands and rubbed
them briskly together. 'Right. You pop upstairs to bed. I'll
be with you in ten minutes. Where's the kitchen?'

'Down below stairs. There.'

'Okay then, hop it, and leave all the rest to good old Uncle Henry.'

'Darling—'

'No "darlings", Trude, just go,' which, shivering visibly, she did.

For the first time in Trudi's house – Clive Coventry's house, really – Henry did not feel like an intruder. He had not realised before just how much the servants had intimidated him. Completely alone with Trudi, however, he moved confidently through the apartments as if he belonged there by right. Paintings and antiques might suggest wealth but there was not a scrap of food in the larders, except four suspect eggs, a jug of curdled milk, one packet of tea and half a cottage loaf gone hard as a rock. Henry took out his wallet, fingered the single ten shilling note that he carried for emergencies then headed out the side door into the lane.

He was back inside fifteen minutes. He laid out the feast of fish and chips on big round plates and uncorked the bottle of Sauterne which he'd bought from the St George's Vaults, arranged the lot with glasses and cutlery on a breakfast tray and carried it carefully upstairs to Trudi's bedroom.

Trudi was propped up in bed. She wore a nightgown and a lacy jacket and, Henry noted, had combed her hair and touched up her face with powder. She looked as fragile as a Burne-Jones pencil drawing, a fact which made her eagerness seem all the more cloying.

'I thought that you had also abandoned me.'

'Not I,' Henry said. 'Now sit up like a good girl.'

He leaned over her, set the tray across her knees.

'You have been outside?'

'I didn't find this lot in your kitchen, that's for sure.'

157

Henry speared a chip with a silver fork and held it out to her. She tasted it with her tongue then snapped it up with her teeth, nodding. He gave her the fork. 'What the hell happened, Trude?'

She held the fork between finger and thumb. 'What is this?'

'Peas, mushy variety.'

'And this?'

'A pickled onion,' said Henry. 'For God's sake, Trudi, just eat the damned stuff and never mind the definitions.'

Obediently she broke off a piece of haddock with her fork, added three long chips to the load and, opening her mouth wide, popped the lot inside.

She chewed, nodding, 'Good, it is very good.'

Henry poured wine into a glass, put the bottle on the floor, lifted his own plate and cutlery from the tray and retired to a tub chair in the corner.

'How sick have you been?' he asked.

'It is nerves,' she said, with a shrug. 'It is nothing to be worried about.'

'Tell me what is to be worried about.'

'I have not seen you for so long.'

'Well, you're seein' me now.'

'Will you stay tonight?'

'Yes. Tell me.'

'He came and took everything away from me.'

'Who did? Clive?'

'Three days ago. He came to make a settlement with the servants,' Trudi said. 'But they were not content with Clive's arrangement and left the following morning. They were gone before I wakened.'

'How long had they been with you?'

'Georgette – eight years.'

'Never mind,' Henry said. 'You'll just have to employ a new batch. Scottish this time, none of your Continentals.'

'I cannot employ anyone.'

'Why not?'

'I have no money.'

Henry swallowed and, gripping the plate in both hands, leaned forward, frowning. '*What?*'

'No money at all,' Trudi told him while Henry, dumbstruck, stared at her in disbelief.

It was always a treat for Jack to play the Cally. He had Kenny Cooper to thank for the engagement. Kenny's regular trumpet-player had gone down with a quinsy throat and Jack had been only too pleased to step into the breach at the last minute.

Kenny was an old sweat at the entertainment game. Fifty if he was a day, fat as a hogshead, with a dapper little black moustache and a pair of long black-dyed sideburns, he had played with some of London's top ballroom orchestras back in the days when dancing was a decorous affair and jazz unheard of. Kenny also had a cabin trunk full of sheet music and umpteen thick black gramophone records from which emerged the most amazing sounds that Jack Burnside had ever heard. When he sat in Kenny Cooper's kitchen and listened to scratchy recordings of King Oliver or the Dixielanders Jack's heart beat twice as fast as it had ever done over a test piece from 'Tannhauser' or the Overture from 'William Tell'. Released from the strictures of a conductor's stick and the brusque tone required to make the grade in brass band contests, Jack's spirit soared. Dance music, jazz, delighted him by its hot-blooded exuberance and he took to syncopation and *tempo rubato* like a duck to water.

On the raised platform under the rafters of the Cally's

Saturday night dance-hall, you were, so Jack fancied, about as close as you could get in Glasgow to the cathouses and speakeasys that Kenny had told him about or, by stretching the imagination, to some Wabash Street night-club where all the guys, not just the band, wore tuxedos and the women drank gin-slings. In fact, by half past nine or ten o'clock, when the floor was packed and the smell of cheap perfume and hair-oil and cigarette smoke hung in the air like steam, you could just about believe that the dancers were not shopgirls and apprentices but gangsters and their molls come slumming by the Clyde.

Bye, Bye, Blackbird.

Jack was on his feet, knees braced between the ram-shackle music-stands. Shoulders hunched, he angled the trumpet towards the roof. He had no notion of how the notes got from his head to the instrument's gleaming bell for what he seemed to hear, above the plinking banjo and the thud of the drum was someone other than himself playing music so sweet that he was entranced by it. Sweat ran down his cheeks. The heavy cotton shirt stuck to his spine and the ring of his half-starched collar was sodden and chafing, yet he felt no discomfort as the echo of his own talent came back at him, clear and dazzling, from walls and ceiling.

Blackbird, bye-bye, bye-bye, bye-bye.

Byyyeee . . . bye! He drew the trumpet away from his lips with a flourish and bowed. They applauded not like an audience but like dancers, applauded their own efforts not his, whistling and cheering, calling for more, because, Jack supposed, they felt as good as he did in this liberated atmosphere. He grinned and dabbed his lips with the back of his wrist and had just begun to edge towards his chair when a shrill voice rose out of the clamour. 'Jack, Jack. It's me. Down here.'

Jack was not oblivious to girls, not by a long chalk, but he did not share Kenny's keen appreciation of female charms or Sammy McGuire's predatory instincts.

'Me, me. Here.'

'Brenda?'

'Aye.'

At first he hardly recognised her. She had frizzed her sandy-blonde hair so that it stood out around her head like a halo, not much constrained by an embroidered bandana about her brow. She wore a party frock, a red object cut too low to be decent and hung with two big bows, one at the midriff, the other trailing from her left hip. From his vantage point above her Jack found himself treated to an unexpected view of his sister's chum's breasts as she leaned on the platform's edge and leered up at him. Two other specimens of 'flaming youth', girls of approximately the same age and dimensions as Brenda, stood behind her, simpering and smouldering.

'What're you doin' here?' Jack said.

'Enjoyin' myself.'

'I can see that. Our Alison isn't with you, is she?'

'Nah. This's Doris an' this's Vera. Say "hullo" to Jack, girls.'

''Lo, Jack.'

''Lo, Jack. Pleased ta meetcha.'

Jack managed a nod. He could not take his eyes off Brenda. The plump eager little face was unchanged and yet she seemed so different from the schoolgirl who hung about Wingfield Drive.

'Play somethin' special for us, eh?' said Doris.

'Aye, give's another good tootle,' said Vera.

Brenda leaned her bosom on her forearms, cocked her head and asked, 'Do you get, you know, time off?'

Kenny Cooper let out a mischievous chuckle but before

the bandleader could excuse him from the next set Jack snapped, 'Naw, Brenda, naw. I'm stuck here all night long. Sorry.'

'Hard cheese, eh?' said Brenda.

Vera audibly confided to Doris, 'Aw, he's nice too, i'n't he?'

'Aye, she's lucky havin' two o' them after her.'

Sammy, the drummer, beat out a roll on the rim of the snare drum and all five regular members of the Kenneth Cooper Moonlight Orchestra crooned '*Aaawwwwww!*' in unison.

'What would you like, ladies?' Jack said grimly. 'Foxtrot, modern waltz, tango, maybe?'

'Give'm "Black Bottom",' Sam McGuire suggested.

The girls giggled. '"Take me Home an' Tuck me Up,"' said Vera. 'Do ye know that one?'

'Oh, yeah, we all know that one,' Kenny said.

Brenda pushed herself back from the platform's edge and, flanked by her friends, gave a twirl that brought the drooping bows to life. Beads of perspiration glinted like seed pearls along the line of the bandana and her earrings – Ruby's best pair – swung each in an opposite direction to the other.

'Okay, fellers, let's play some more,' said Kenny.

Cringing with embarrassment Jack stepped back into the music stands as Mr Kenneth Cooper struck chords for 'Yes, Sir, That's My Baby', and in his droll, droning voice began to sing the verse.

Jack sighed, sank on to his chair. He placed the trumpet mouthpiece to his lips while Brenda, big bows bobbing, shimmied back into the crowd.

McGuire leaned towards him and muttered into his ear, 'By God, Jackie lad, you've got a right handful there, if you want it.'

'Don't want it,' Jack hissed, then, exactly on the beat, rode in behind Kenny's vocal just where the chorus began.

It was twenty minutes later before he spotted Brenda again.

The band were playing a quickstep and the floor was jammed with couples showing off their steps like mad. She came around below the bandstand and, in case Jack missed her, called out his name. She was locked in the arms of a young man in a baggy brown suit whose poise was perfect and whose technique put Brenda's to shame. Jack had a feeling that he had seen the chap before but he could not put a name to the face, distinctive though it was with a drooping eyelid and an expression of unsmiling seriousness.

'Jack, Jack!' Brenda winked at him over her partner's shoulder.

Jack waved his left hand half-heartedly, but long before the playing of 'Auld Lang Syne', he lost sight of her and assumed that she and her escort had left early to beat the curfew that old Ruby had imposed.

When, as usual, he reached for the bicycle Alison did not surrender it but clung to the handlebars possessively and engaged in a wordless little tug-of-war until he yielded and stepped back. Pushing the machine Alison started downhill away from the yew hedge at the mansion-house corner.

Walter hesitated then followed her. 'What's wrong with you?'

He spoke in a tone that indicated that he knew quite well what was wrong with her and that he had already decided there would be no contrition on his part, an explanation perhaps, but no apology.

'Tell me where you were on Saturday night?'

'So that's it?' Walter said. 'I suppose your brother clyped on me.'

'He didn't have to clype,' Alison said. 'I've seen the way Brenda's been clingin' to you all day long.'

'Gimme the bike, for God's sake, an' stop actin' like a child.'

'I don't need your assistance, Walter, thank you very much.'

He stuck his hands in his pockets and fanned out the jacket like bat's wings. 'She was there, I was there. What did you expect me to do, ignore her?'

'You've never invited me to the Cally dance.'

'I didn't invite her either. She turned up out of the blue along with a couple of females I've never seen before. Vera and Doris? Know them?'

'No – and I don't care to. I'll leave that pleasure to you, Walter.'

'I can't believe you're behavin' like this.'

'Like what?'

'Jealous.'

'I'm not in the least jealous.'

'You're doin' a damned good imitation, I can tell you,' Walter said.

The bicycle's wheels whirred and the pannier stuffed with Latin textbooks bounced as Alison, fists on saddle and crossbar, steered the machine around the corner out of the Kingsway.

'For your information my brother doesn't even know who you are,' she said, 'though he did mention he'd seen Brenda. Did you take her home?'

'What's she been tellin' you?' The languid gait had gone. He had to stride out to keep up with her and the brisk pace seemed to put him at a disadvantage.

164

'Has she been crowin' about it? All that happened—'

'No. I don't want to know.'

'Then why did you ask me?'

Alison swerved to a halt, the bicycle slewed across the pavement, and Walter had to skip nimbly to avoid collision.

'Did you kiss her?' Alison demanded.

''Course I didn't kiss her.'

'Didn't you take her behind a hedge or round the back of the shops?'

'Alison, for God's sake. I didn't—' The rising note in his voice died suddenly and when he spoke again his tone was laconic, almost smug. 'So what if I did?'

'Was she good at it? Was she better at it than me?'

'Jeez-us!'

'I'd prefer it if you didn't blaspheme.'

'Aw, cut it out,' he said.

'What else did you do?'

'For instance?'

'Did she let you take liberties?' Alison said.

'Define "liberties",' Walter said.

'Is that why you prefer her to me?'

'It's reachin' the stage,' Walter said, 'when I don't like either of you all that much.'

'Oh!'

Alison was completely taken aback. She did not resist now when he grasped the handlebars and hauled the bicycle towards him, bringing her with it. He leaned close, so close that she could smell the faint damp odour that seemed to cling to his clothing. The lazy eye glowered at her, his head tilted. If he had been hurt by her inquisition he gave no sign of it.

'But,' he said softly, 'just for your information, Brenda isn't in your class, not by a long, long shot.'

'I don't – I don't think that's a very nice thing to say,' Alison murmured.

'Think what you like,' Walter said and, with a tiny motion of his hands, pushed the bicycle back towards her and turned away.

'Walter?'

He paused. 'What?'

'Don't you want to—?'

'Huh!'

And with that he strolled off, heading for Dunsinane Street without her.

For some reason which he couldn't properly explain Alex no longer found himself quite comfortable in his daughter's company. She seemed to have grown up alarmingly in the past eight or ten weeks. He didn't even like going into her room now for the profusion of books and neatly folded clothing made him feel as if he were prying into a stranger's secrets. He was not entirely insensitive to Ally's moods, however, and prided himself that he could still tell when she was down-in-the-mouth. At such times he would offer her sympathy, if not always understanding.

She had come in from her class with Mr Abbott earlier than usual, had murmured goodnight and had gone straight upstairs to bed, leaving her brothers to forage for supper on their own account. Ten or fifteen minutes later Alex had taken her up a mug of hot cocoa and two biscuits smeared with butter. Pete, for some reason, had roused himself from a drowse by the fire and had pattered upstairs after him.

At first Alison seemed resentful of the intrusion and eager to get back to whatever she was doing at her desk. She wore an old dressing-gown over her nightie, a pair of Davy's thick woollen football stockings on her feet and

looked, Alex thought, both childish and mature at one and
the same time.

'Are you feelin' all right, sweetheart?'

'I'm fine, Dad.'

'What's that you're writin'? Is it in Latin?'

'No.'

'All these books—' He shook his head admiringly.

Alison watched him guardedly from the little dressing-
table desk, the paper she'd been writing on hidden by the
sleeve of her dressing-gown, the plump green fountain pen
which Jack had given her at Christmas poised in her fingers.
On the edge of the table the cocoa mug steamed.

'Pete, eh, Pete just wanted t' say goodnight,' said Alex
lamely.

Pete put his paws on the table's edge and declared his
interest in the buttered biscuits by sniffing the plate from a
distance of three inches. Alison snapped the Granolas in
half, held out the larger piece and smiled as the dog
delicately hoisted away the titbit.

'Goodnight then, Scrounger,' she said and looked up at
her father.

'I can see you're busy,' Alex said.

'A bit.'

'I'll go then.'

'If you don't mind.'

'No, no.' He caught Pete's collar and hauled the mongrel
towards the door. 'Sorry to disturb.'

'Dad?'

'Aye.'

'Thanks for the cocoa,' Alison said and, even before the
door closed, went back to work on her letter.

SIX

Paid Off

Henry arrived in the Cally dressed in the grubby jacket and muffler he'd worn to work. He was not in the best of moods for he had spent the weekend trying to sort out Trudi Coventry's financial affairs and had had precious little sleep. He had also got thoroughly behind with his copy for the *Banner* and hadn't a clue how to follow up his piece on Ransome's closure. God knows, he'd had plenty of time to think about it. The yard was unbelievably quiet. In the offices draughtsmen played cards and in the echoing reaches of the pattern shop and among the empty slipways impromptu games of football started up. Older men, disinclined to exercise, hung about the sheddings and discussed What Could Be Done as if they could conjure up orders where none existed or by gravity and concentration change the will of Whitton's board. Even the dimmest apprentice seemed to realise that there was no hope, that come Friday he'd be out of a job and that in hindsight the hard life of a shipwright would seem like luxury compared with life on the dole.

'Burnside, about time.'

It had been months since Henry had encountered Jock Ormskirk and he could not remember the last time he had seen all three members of the SPP's Steering Committee gathered together in one place. The tin-shaded lamp that overhung the printer had been tilted to light the area directly before Henry's office door. He looked past the human tableau and saw that somebody had been at the padlock and that only the weight of the chain had prevented his sanctum from being breached.

'What the hell is this?' he murmured.

He glanced around the loft in search of Eddie and found him hiding behind the printer's dented cowling. Eddie did not meet his eye, however, and before Henry could say a word vanished into the shadows.

Henry took off his cap, unwound his muffler, bowed and said, 'Good evenin', Mrs Chancellor. Glad to see you lookin' so well.'

'We can do wi'out the smarm, Burnside,' Jock Ormskirk told him. 'You're in trouble, you are.'

'Am I?' said Henry. 'You mean apart from being paid off.'

'Where do you work?' the woman enquired. 'Lobnitz?'

'Ransome's. Why am I in trouble?'

Hugh Niven was younger than the others, and shabbier. He wore an off-the-peg Co-op Drapery suit in a shade that reminded Henry of verdigris and had a high nervous voice which somehow matched his scrawny neck. He was standing beside Margaret Chancellor who had been given the loft's only upholstered chair, but he suddenly stepped forward and thrust a sheet of paper into Henry's face.

'This.'

'What is it?'

'Your head on the block.'

'Keep calm, Hughie, keep calm.' Margaret Chancellor tugged at the sleeve of the greeny-brown jacket as if she was afraid he might attack Henry physically.

She was ten or twelve years older than Henry and reminded him a little of Auntie Belle. Plump but not fat, she had a fair complexion and disconcerting hazel eyes. She opened her coat and spread her knees, the way a man might, so that Henry could see the shape of her thighs under the shin-length floral dress. She was the widow of a former Secretary of the Platelayers' Union and since the war had been a standard-bearer in the struggle against capitalist oppression but she had none of Ormskirk's pomposity or Niven's authoritarianism and was strong in a way that Henry respected.

'Let him see the letter, Hughie,' Margaret Chancellor said. 'He can hardly be expected to read it when you're waving it about like the Red Flag.'

'Thank you.' Henry plucked the letter from Niven's paw and, cap and muffler in hand, read it where he stood.

'Do you ken what it is?' said Jock Ormskirk.

'I ken fine weel.' Henry imitated Ormskirk's north-east accent, though he did not feel in the least humorous and clenched the letter tightly to stop his fingers shaking. 'It's an injunction against the *Banner*.'

'Like heck it is,' said Niven. 'It's an injunction against you, Burnside.'

'Let's not get carried away, gentlemen,' said Margaret Chancellor. 'It's not an injunction at all. Read it carefully, please, Mr Burnside.'

Henry nodded. 'You're right, Mrs Chancellor. It's an action for libel.'

'Not even that, Mr Burnside. It's the *threat* of an action for libel.'

'What the heck were you thinkin' of, attackin' the reputation of a fine upstandin' woman like Lady McCaine?'

'I was thinking of the hungry masses,' Henry said. 'I was thinking of the thousands of ordinary men and

171

women who'll face starvation because the owners of Whitton Engineering won't sacrifice a penny of their profits.'

'Rubbish!' said Margaret Chancellor. 'You were making copy, Mr Burnside, and very good copy at that, but for once you picked the wrong target.'

'How was I to know Elvira McCaine would read a rag like the *Banner?*' Henry said. 'What's it to her, anyway? She'll be back in her big house in Hampstead by this time and nobody any the wiser.'

'Oh, that's a sad mistake to make,' said Margaret Chancellor. 'It shows how little you know about rich women. The rich always have friends in low places and rich women – women like Elvira McCaine – are usually vain, Mr Burnside, vain beyond belief. It's not the fact you called her heartless that's spurred her to go to law, it's the fact you said she was ugly.'

'Did I?' said Henry.

'Check your copy,' Margaret Chancellor said. 'Your exact words were, I believe, "... her aged face was wrinkled in the sunlight." Nasty!'

'Well,' said Henry, 'it was. I saw it. A thousand others saw it too. I'm only tellin' the truth. Fair comment, it's called.'

'Not for a woman like Lady McCaine.'

'It seems you've managed to ruin us, Burnside,' said Jock Ormskirk. 'You an' your quest for the truth.'

'We can't afford to fight an action through the courts,' said Niven. 'What can we do, what can we do to save the situation?'

'Print a retraction,' Margaret Chancellor said.

And Henry heard himself say, 'No.'

'That's all she wants,' said Margaret Chancellor. 'She knows there's no money to be had from us and the last thing she wants is to fight a Scottish court case. Her solicitor will have advised her to that effect. I suggest you sit down now, Mr Burnside, and apply that fertile brain of yours to writing something nice about Elvira McCaine.'

'*Is* there anythin' nice about the bitch?' said Ormskirk.

'She's a good looker,' said Niven. 'Apart from the wrinkles.'

'Play up her involvement in charity work,' said Margaret Chancellor. 'Tell the world how caring and generous she is. How gracious, how concerned for the poor and needy. Apologise, Mr Burnside. Retract.'

'No,' said Henry again.

'Och, come on, Burnside, don't be so bloody stubborn,' Ormskirk said.

'I mean, it's no skin off your nose, is it?' said Niven.

'Huh!' said Henry, scornfully. 'And I thought you were men of principle to whom nothing mattered but the class war.'

'We can do without the clichés, Mr Burnside.' Margaret Chancellor got to her feet, carefully buttoned her coat and adjusted her hat. 'Are you aware that many people think I write those pieces for the *Banner*?'

'You should be flattered,' Henry said.

'Oh, but I am,' she said. 'Immensely flattered.'

'What Margaret – Mrs Chancellor – means,' Jock Ormskirk explained, 'is that we can do without your services.'

'You have talent, Mr Burnside,' the woman went on, 'a very great deal of talent. But you're too impractical. You don't have savvy.'

'Because I won't do what you want me to?'

'Because you're a nobody,' the woman told him.

'Who's kept your damned rag afloat for the past couple of years?'

'Without credit.'

'Pardon?' said Henry.

'She means,' said Ormskirk, 'nobody knows who you are.'

'No byline,' said Niven, 'no credit.'

'You don't speak for the People's Party in public. You've never attended conferences or turned out at rallies,' said Margaret Chancellor. 'You might have a strong voice, Henry, but you don't have a face to go with it.'

'Are you tellin' me I'm dispensable?'

'At the drop of a hat,' said Niven.

'The penalty of anonymity,' said Margaret Chancellor, 'is that you won't be missed. In fact, if you won't write a suitable retraction for Thursday's issue I'll do it myself.'

'An' you, Burnside, will never work for the SPP again,' said Ormskirk.

'Is that the democratic ultimatum?' said Henry. 'I lie my face off to pander to the vanity of some wealthy cow from London or I lose my job?'

'And your wee secret cubby-hole,' said Niven.

'I pay for that office.'

'You rent it from the SPP,' said Jock Ormskirk. 'An' we're verra fussy about who we have as a tenant, aren't we, Mr Niven?'

'That we are, Jock, that we are.'

Henry gave a little grunt. 'So you think I can be replaced, do you? Can you write as well as I do, Mrs Chancellor?'

'Not by a mile, Mr Burnside.'

'But the readers'll never notice,' said Jock Ormskirk.

'They're too stupid to tell the difference,' said Niven.

'Be that as it may,' the woman said, 'we don't want to be unreasonable, Henry, but no more will we allow you to be unreasonable with us. Our work's too important to jeopardise because of your pride.'

'Oh, bugger off,' said Henry. 'Some upper-crust bitch barks and you abandon your principles and crawl away like whipped curs. What sort of a revolution is that gonna bring you?' He glanced towards the door of Eddie's apartment and glimpsed his comrade's white face, all blank and shuttered. Poor Eddie, too scared even to show disapproval. 'Well, sod it!'

'What does that mean?' said Margaret Chancellor.

'It means,' said Henry, 'ta-ta.'

'You'll walk out before you'll compromise?'

'Yes.'

'Think of the money, Burnside.'

'You'll need every penny when Ransome's goes to the wall.'

'The office,' said Henry, 'is mine to the end of the month. I'll have my gear out of there by noon on the thirty-first.'

'You're a very foolish young man,' Margaret Chancellor said. 'But I do wish you'd reconsider, for your own sake as well as ours.'

'How long do I have to think it over?' Henry said.

The members of the committee exchanged glances and the woman said, 'Two days?'

'Not long enough,' said Henry as he wound the scarf about his neck and tugged on his cap. 'Try somethin' like a million years.'

'Is that your last word?'

'It is,' said Henry and, without speaking again, turned and quit the loft by the back staircase, leaving the Party, the Underwood and poor old Eddie behind.

The wire grid under the Bunsen glowed red hot and Boris

175

carefully removed the bubbling retort with a pair of tongs. Cigarette drooping from his lips, he carried the vessel to the long bench under the window and poured its contents into two none-too-clean glass beakers where it instantly turned a dark brown colour. The aroma of Camp Coffee mingled with the burnt-toast smell of coal gas and the antiseptic reek of chemicals from the open door of the science-room's storage cupboard.

Jim watched the science teacher carry the retort into the cupboard then he opened a tin marked *Poison: Do Not Touch* and helped himself to sugar followed by a Churchmans' from the box of fifty that stood quite openly on the desk. He lit the cigarette from the Bunsen flame and paused to warm his hand over the grid while he looked out at the cold spring rain which sprinkled the rooftops of Flannery Park.

Boris returned. He held up an unlabelled bottle.

'Milk, Jim? Mother's milk?'

'I'm teaching again in half an hour.'

'So what?'

'Righto. Just a drop, though.'

Boris poured whisky into each of the beakers and stirred them with a pencil. He lifted his glass, drank a mouthful of the scalding liquid, sighed and said, 'B' Goad, I needed that.'

Boris was a huge, stoop-shouldered man with enormous hands stained yellow with chemicals and nicotine. What little hair he had was cropped close to his skull and that, combined with his steel-rimmed glasses, gave him the brutal appearance of a Victorian convict. Even Jim was a little afraid of him. He had been a trench hero of sorts, though woe betide the person, pupil or peer, who dared ask after details for the very mention of war was enough to send Boris into a rage.

Jim hoisted a buttock on to one of the lab stools and rested an elbow on the bench. He had wrapped the beaker in a handkerchief and sipped the laced coffee cautiously while Boris, braced against the desk, drank deep again and peered out, scowling, at the rain.

The science rooms were separate from the main quadrangle and far from the headmaster's study. Mr Pallant knew perfectly well that Boris was a law unto himself, however, and, for fear of what he might find, made a point of never dropping in unannounced.

'So,' Boris said, 'what's bitin' your wee long-legged filly these days?'

'If you mean Alison Burnside,' Jim said, 'she isn't my filly, long-legged or otherwise.'

'Is she not now? She certainly thinks you're the cat's pyjamas.'

'What?'

'Haven't you noticed how she looks at you?'

'What?' said Jim again, flattered and intrigued.

Boris laughed. 'Just pullin' your leg, old son.'

'Oh, I see,' Jim said, disappointed and relieved.

'Fell for it too, didn't you?' Boris said. 'Occupational hazard, adoration. Suffer from it myself all the time.'

'I thought you had a daughter?'

'Two of 'um. What's that got to do with it? I can't help being irresistible.'

'Now you are pulling my leg.'

'Of course I am. Most of them think I'm Frankenstein's monster,' Boris said. 'And me such a sensitive soul.' He shook his head. 'Something is bitin' your Miss Burnside, though. Any ideas?'

'None,' Jim said. 'Unless it's the general Clydeside malaise.'

'The prospect of dole for Daddy?' Boris said. 'Aye, it

could be, I suppose. You wonder, though, how much they understand of what's going on in the wide, wide world.'

'They're bound to hear talk at home,' Jim said.

'Morgan's closing last month, Ransome's teetering on the brink,' said Boris. 'But do *les enfants* really comprehend what it means? They're such funny wee creatures. Close-mouthed when it comes to anything important. Did you hear about McLeod's dog?'

'No. What?'

'His old man put it down. Three days on the dole and McLeod senior takes the boy's best friend out to the canal bank, clouts it on the head with a claw hammer, tosses the body into the water, toddles home and tells the family that they've all got to make sacrifices now he's unemployed.'

'Good God!'

'There are worse things than not going on to university, Jim.'

'I wouldn't write off her chances just yet,' Jim said. 'Burnside seems very determined.'

'Maybe so, but you can't buy much meat with determination.' Boris poured more whisky into his glass, swirled it among the coffee dregs and drank. 'Couldn't you help her out?'

'No, no,' Jim said. 'It wouldn't look right.'

'Undemocratic?' Boris said. 'Or unethical?'

'Burnside would never accept financial assistance from an outsider. He has his pride.'

'Aye, that's one quality never in short supply, though you wonder what the hell they've got to be so proud about, most of them.'

'I wouldn't want to see her life wasted.'

'It wouldn't be the first, nor will it be the last,' Boris said. 'Pity you've squandered so much time tutoring her.'

'Oh, I don't grudge her that,' Jim said.

'And Giffard?'

'Giffard's another story.'

'Because he doesn't have big brown eyes?'

'Look, I'm not . . .'

'Just pullin' your leg, old son.'

'Well, don't,' Jim Abbott said and, rather to Boris's surprise, held out his glass for more.

'Alison?'

'Yes, Mr Abbott.'

'What's wrong with you tonight? You've hardly heard a word I've said.'

'I'm sorry.'

'All right. We'll try again. "*Quibus, Hector, ab oris exspectate venis?*"'

'I don't quite see what—'

'Case?'

'The nominative.'

'Look again. What's unusual about the construction?'

She lowered her head over the book. Her hair fell over her eyes and she brushed it back with her wrist. Her eyes were indeed big and brown but they also lacked comprehension.

Jim said, 'The participle, Alison, the participle.'

She remained dumb.

'Look at the blasted participle, will you?'

One tear fell on to the page, soaking into the paper instantly. She sniffed and dabbed at her eyes with her knuckle.

'Alison, Alison, what is it?'

'Nothing. I just feel stupid tonight.'

'Is there trouble at home?'

'No.'

'Has your father been paid off?'

She looked up suddenly. 'I don't want to do it any more. I'm tired of learnin'. I'm not sure it's worth it. What good's it going to do me, anyhow, learnin' how to translate the *Aeneid*? If I want to read Virgil I can buy him in English an' save myself a lot of time.'

'Alison—'

'Nobody cares whether it's nominative or vocative.'

Jim said softly, 'See, you did know.'

She sniffed and flung back her hair with her wrist and, still almost weeping, frowned down at the printed page. 'So it is – vocative, I mean.'

'Why?'

'A poetical construction.'

'Uh-huh.'

'I'm sorry.'

'*Are* you worried about your father's job?'

'Yes.'

'Money?'

'Yes.'

'You're not really sick of study, are you?'

'No, not really.'

He unfolded a spotless white handkerchief from the pocket of his cardigan and passed it across the textbooks to her. It was all he could do not to put an arm about her. If his sister had not been in the next room he would have touched Alison's wet cheek with his fingertip, would perhaps have kissed the tears away. The handkerchief was his servitor, his garland. He wondered if it was still warm from his body and, if so, if Alison was aware of it. When she glanced up he looked away quickly.

'Thanks, Mr Abbott.'

He cleared his throat. 'My pleasure.'

'I'm all right now.'

'Everyone's worried about losing their job right now.'

'Hmmm?'

'Your father – Ransome's.'

'Oh, that,' said Alison and with a quick little flick of her eyes looked to the clock on the sideboard which at that moment chimed nine.

'Who's in there?'

No answer came from behind the bathroom door. Davy rapped his knuckle on the pebble-glass and called out desperately, 'Is that you, Bertie?'

'It's me.'

'Ally? Are y' gonna be long?'

'Yes. I'm havin' a bath.'

'How long are you gonna be?' Davy shouted.

'As long as I like.'

'Alison, I need in.'

'Go away.'

The pale blue cotton curtain that covered the glass on the inside was damp with steam. He put his hand on the doorhandle then, because it was his sister, thought better of giving it a rattle and, closing his eyes, rested his head against the door. 'Are you not near finished, love?'

'*No.*'

'Awww, Alison!'

'What's all the racket?' Davy turned and looked down the staircase to the corner of the hall from out of which his father, one hand on the banister, glowered up at him. 'Do you not know what time it is?'

'It's only half ten.'

'Aye, well, there are people tryin' to sleep.'

'Ally's in the bath.'

181

'Leave her in peace then.'

'It's not her turn. An' she's usin' all the hot water.'

'Shut your face, Davy,' Bert yapped from behind the bedroom door.

'Do I have to come up there?' Alex shouted. 'If I do I'll take my belt to your backside, son, big an' all as y' are.'

'Dad, tell her I need in.'

'Tell her yourself. Quietly.'

'Aaalll-i-son, pleeease.'

'Go *away*.'

'Davy, stop tormentin' the girl.'

'Just go *away*,' Alison called, anger masking her tears. '*All* of you, just go *away*.'

'Aw – hell!' said Davy, and dove into Henry's room in search of the old floral chamberpot that lived on top of the wardrobe.

The bedroom, with its chintz and gilt, mirrors, jars and perfume bottles had rapidly assumed the claustrophobic atmosphere of a prison cell. Mrs Trudi Coventry seemed reluctant to leave her boudoir, not even to let him in each evening or to see him out again at night.

There were, however, indications that his ministrations, more out of bed than in, were having the desired effect and that if he persevered he might yet have her back on her feet and thinking straight before the weekend.

Being Trudi's warden was not without its compensations. In fairness, Henry could not put hand on heart and say that he had to drag himself up those gloomy baronial stairs of an evening or that it galled him to have her greet him propped up in the big bed, clad only in a silk nightdress or some frilly piece of lingerie. Certain signs indicated that Trudi was not quite so helpless as she pretended to be. The tray which held the remnants of last night's supper had, for instance, been removed, letters collected from the mat in the hall. Sheets had been changed, stockings and underwear washed, and Henry sensed that he was involved now in a contest less obviously perverse than their railway games but just as calculated.

Try as he would, though, he could wring no sense out of her. For a woman whom he had once considered shrewd she was behaving like a ninny.

When he attempted to pin her down about her financial situation she would squirm and wriggle and hide behind tears, the appealing Swiss-miss voice childish and whining. From the few crumbs of information that fell his way, though, Henry had gathered that Trudi had no income of her own, was entirely dependent upon 'allowances' from her ex-husband and that even the house would be taken from her as soon as the lease ran out.

Whenever Henry tried to quiz her about Coventry's legal obligations she would press a finger against his lips and say, 'You do not understand how it is with this man. But you are here now and you will look after me.'

'Sure I will,' said Henry, 'but we can't go on like this for very long. Any day now I'm goin' to be out of a job and . . .'

'You will leave me too?'

'No, no, for God's sake, that's not what I meant.' He put an arm about her and drew her to him. 'Trudi, you must have *something* of your own, stocks, a bank account, something you can fall back on.'

'He took it all.'

'What about your parents? Can't they—'

'I have no parents.'

'I thought your father was still alive?'

'He is a poor man. I do not know where he is.'

She was seated on the bed, knees tucked under her. Henry eased himself away from her. 'You don't know where your father is? I find that hard to swallow.'

'When I become married to Clive, my papa throws me out.'

'Why?'

'He does not like Clive.'

'Religion?' Henry asked.

She shook her head.

Henry had been reared with enough ingrained prejudice against the Roman Church not to want to have his suspicions confirmed. There was in the house, though, no trace of religious ornament and he had never seen Trudi with a crucifix about her neck.

'Are you sure Clive intends to throw you out?'

'I am certain of it.'

'What exactly *did* he say to you?'

'I have told you everything.'

'No you haven't. You haven't told me anythin'.'

'He cannot keep me. He does not wish to keep me. He has no longer need of me. He cannot afford to support me.'

'He'll never get away with it, not if there's been an agreement endorsed by the court.' Henry was not on firm ground when it came to the fine points of Scots law but he was willing to bluff in the hope of uncovering the truth. 'Anyway, why now? Why suddenly toss you out?'

'I think he is short of capital.'

'Gone bust, you mean?'

She could not, or would not, answer him. She rubbed her shoulder against his spine. Henry shivered and said, 'I reckon your lawyer had better talk to Coventry's lawyer at the first available opportunity.'

'Clive is not here.'

'Where is he then?'

She shrugged. 'New York. Berlin.'

'Berlin? What's he doin' in Berlin?'

'He looks for places to make money. Simple money.'

'Easy money,' Henry corrected. 'I'd have thought Germany was the last place to find easy money these days.'

She shrugged again and rubbed against him. What had begun as a sexual adventure with an older woman had become something else entirely. Precisely what, Henry could not yet decide. He turned and caught her by the shoulders, pressed her down upon the crumpled sheets. He did not kiss her, though. He pinned her like a butterfly against the silks and studied her face intently. If only he could figure out what he felt about her then he might still be able to make use of her.

'Tomorrow night,' he said, 'we'll go out for din-din, you an' me.'

'I have no money, Henry.'

'I have,' Henry said. 'No excuses, Trudi. You an' me, all dolled up an' out together on the town. Okay?'

'But tonight?' she said huskily. 'What will we do tonight?'

'We'll have to think about that, won't we?' said Henry and, still frowning slightly, began to unlace her gown.

When she was younger Alison had read H. G. Wells's novel *The Invisible Man*. It occurred to her now that there was something more than a nominal similarity between Griffin, the hero of that book, and Walter Giffard. In recent weeks, Wattie had seemingly acquired the ability to make himself transparent. He was still visible in class, on the verandahs and in the playground, but he had somehow developed the knack of not being where she was at any particular moment as if he could slide in and out of sight at will. Of course, she might have accosted him during lessons or called out to him as he disappeared across the playground but she refused to demean herself by grovelling in public and consoled herself with the knowledge that at least Wattie was evading Brenda too.

It comforted Alison to observe how hot and bothered her former friend became at Wattie's not-so-subtle rejections. No stoic, Brenda would pass crumpled notes to Walter during class and paid little or no attention to the substance of the lesson in her eagerness to wring a reply from him. She would shriek at him from the balcony and on more than one occasion had gone scampering after him – all to no avail. Walter, it appeared, was not inclined to talk to anyone and with a skill more scientific than supernatural, kept himself strictly to himself.

Alison's friendship with Brenda was over. They traded no more confidences and, indeed, exchanged hardly a civil word these days. If Ruby McColl guessed the source of the hostility between them she gave no sign of it and continued to treat Alison, and Davy too, almost as if they were her own. And as the Easter holiday approached Alison found that her anger at Walter's betrayal had diminished and she took to ignoring him and wondered only now and then if he'd noticed her new-found independence and, if so, if it troubled him.

Unemployment and yard closures ran like a threnody in the background of Alison's life during that blustery March. Anxiety pervaded the atmosphere and her brothers' heated arguments on the reasons for the dearth in world trade filled the house on many a night. She should have been worried too, she supposed, but she could not engage with those masculine issues, could not quite focus on how they might affect her. If Henry had been around, she might have asked him to explain it in simple terms. But Henry was hardly ever at home. He would come sneaking in long after midnight and be up and away to work without a word to anyone in the rushed and crabby half hour it took to shave, dress and eat breakfast.

'Gotta bit of fluff,' Bert declared.

'Has he said as much?' asked Alex.

'Not him.'

'How do you know then?'

'Look at him. He's walkin' around like a corpse.'

'Perhaps he's on the booze,' Davy suggested.

'Well, he might come in late,' Jack said, 'but he never comes in drunk.'

'Ask him what he's up to, Jack,' said Alex.

'Are you kiddin'? You ask him.'

'I'm only his father. He never tells me anythin'.'

'What if he knocks her up?' said Davy.

'Then he'll just have to marry her,' said Alex.

'Serve him bloody right,' said Bertie, finally.

In the tense atmosphere of domestic concern Alison floated like a soap-bubble, her head filled with Latin prose, class tests, grading examinations and, in spite of herself, with curiosity as to why Walter had rejected her when they had seemed such a perfect couple.

'Oh, it's you?'

He could not evade her in the narrow passageway that led to Snapes' meat counter and Alison, even if she had wished to, could not beat a ladylike retreat. Two women, big as buffalo, had entered the grocery store just behind her and the shop was, to say the least of it, congested.

'What are you doin' in this neck of the woods?' Walter asked.

'Our Co-op's run out of sausages.'

It was rare for Alison to shop in the stores at Summerston Street but she had planned on cooking a mixed grill for the boys' tea and no mixed grill, at least in the Burnside household, would be complete without spiced sausages. Walter studied her suspiciously as if he thought she had plotted to corner him against the wood and glass of the cold meat counter.

'What about you?' Alison enquired.

'Kippers,' he said, flatly.

It was hardly the time or place for a lovers' tiff or a passionate reconciliation. Alison could not imagine lovely Carole Lombard and suave William Powell mouthing words of love that appeared on the screen as *Kippers*, let alone *Sausages*.

'What are you grinnin' at?'

'I wasn't aware that I was grinning,' said Alison.

Before them two young housewives in chunky woollen hats and smart overcoats chattered with what passed for gaiety while Snapes's daughter, an almost exact replica of her father only with more hair, sliced gammon with surgical precision.

'Two ounces, Mrs Stover?'

'Aye, just the two'll do me fine the night.'

Mrs Stover, a seventy-year-old widow, was hardly bigger than a squirrel and had a squirrel's begging attitude, purse and shopping basket clutched in mittened paws. Even at the distance of a yard, though, she gave off a strong odour of grease and perspiration and the young wives had stopped chattering and were scowling at the widow in distaste. Gammon dropped in pink transparent leaves from the edge of the big steel blade and Alison, bullied from behind by the impatient buffalo, was pushed up against Walter who, obeying instinct, gripped her arm to steady her.

Alison said, 'You can't avoid me now, Wattie, can you?'

'Don't start.'

'You didn't answer my letter.'

'Nope.'

'Why not?'

'I'm not gettin' into that game.'

'It wasn't meant to be a game.'

'I know what it was meant to be,' he said from the side of his mouth. 'It was meant to make me feel guilty.'

'Oh, no it wasn't.'

'I've nothin' to feel guilty about.'

The hatted wives were breathing shallowly. One of them lit a Turkish cigarette and exhaled a protective cloud of smoke. Mrs Stover had been given a fragment of cooked meat to taste and nibbled it like a connoisseur while Miss Snapes waited for the widow's opinion with a professional smile fixed to her face like a grimace.

'Delicious,' the widow said. 'I'll take an ounce o' that too, hen.'

'A whole ounce?' said Miss Snapes.

'Aye, an' cut it thin.'

Alison said, 'I suppose Brenda's more accommodating than I am?'

'I'll say this for her – she sure can dance.'

'And what else?'

They spoke not to each other but into the sickly aura of foodstuffs and tobacco smoke, murmuring not whispering. It was furtive, not intimate, but the need for discretion lent a cool, quizzical quality to the exchange.

'You're jealous,' Walter Giffard said.

'Huh!' said Alison. 'I am not.'

'Anyway,' Walter said, 'I'm not interested in Brenda either.'

'Either?'

Mrs Stover, served at last, edged past them and, keeking up at Walter, gave him a nod of recognition. 'Lovely bit o' gammon, son, lovely.'

'I'm sure it is,' Walter said bleakly.

'Tell your mammy, son.'

'I will, Mrs Stover, I will.'

He blew out his cheeks in relief as the woman passed out of the shop as if she had threatened him not only with asphyxia but also with damaging revelations.

'A neighbour?' Alison asked.

'Unfortunately, yes,' said Walter.

Elbows on the counter, the young wives had fallen into a discussion of the cost of cosmetics. Here, even here, Alison realised, they were conscious of their looks. Behind her left shoulder the buffalo moved closer, grumbling ominously.

'What do you mean by "either"?' Alison said.

Wattie glanced at her sharply. 'That's what I can't stand about girls like you. Dig, dig, dig all the time. God, Alison, I used to think you were different.'

'You told me I was different.'

'Well, I take it back.'

'Am I to understand you think I'm tryin' to trap you into something?'

'Take it how you will.'

'Kippers, Walter?' Having disposed of the wives young Miss Snapes applied to handsome Mr Giffard a smile that was anything but professional. 'The usual two pair?'

'Please, Agnes.'

'They're fresh in today. Lovely an' plump. Look.'

'Yes, they look fine.'

'Smell that.'

'Great!'

When Agnes turned to the marble top to weigh and wrap the fish Alison inched closer and, chin almost touching his collar, whispered into his ear, 'Better watch it, Walter.'

'Uh?'

'The kippers are obviously a trap,' she said and, without waiting to be served, slipped lightly past the buffalo and out into the sweet fresh air.

Ruby was out of sorts. She was anxious, restless and perhaps a wee bit bored. Too much going on and, as it were, not enough *happening*. She longed for summer, wished fervently that Brenda might be settled in Singer's and the whole sorry business of slump and depression swept away. She was sufficiently in tune with the State of the Nation, however, to realise that Clydeside's economic woes would not be cured by a change in the weather and she did not accept the general opinion that a change of government would benefit the working man.

Poor old Mr Baldwin, for whose party Ruby had voted in the last election, was taking big stick from everyone but as barmaid, Ruby was obliged to remain, politically speaking, all things to all men. Politics was a mug's game anyway, and the best end to be served was that of the *status quo*, except, of course, where Brenda and she were concerned.

In the past three months her daughter had become not just morose but sly and secretive too. What caused this dark-blue mood Ruby did not know. She could wheedle nothing out of Brenda. She also tried to quiz Alison about it but Alison admitted that she and Brenda had fallen out and that she had no inkling as to what Brenda might be up to. She tried to discuss the matter rationally with Alex, to lean on him a little as if he was already the 'man in her life', but he was dismissive about Brenda's future, so airy in his attitude that Ruby became quite sharp with him and avoided 162 for three or four days. It wasn't Alex's fault, though; it was obvious, even to a less-than-doting mother, that Alison Burnside 'had it' and her wee Brenda did not.

Friday afternoon, half past three o'clock. Brenda still at school. Foxhill Crescent quiet as the grave. Weatherwise a day so grey and nondescript that Ruby looked forward to the coming of the dark and her trip into Glasgow where, amid the city's bright lights, she might find some relief from the general tedium of the times. She had whisked through her housework, fed Brenda and left soup and sandwiches at 162 for Davy and Alison. She had even bought a little piece of scrag-end from the butcher as a treat for the dog, for she was fond of the animal, and often kneeled in Mavis's kitchen and played with his ragged ears and petted him.

After Brenda had gone back to school, Ruby returned to her own house and, because the fire had been on all morning and the water was hot in the boiler, ran a bath and soaked in it for twenty minutes, bobbing and relaxed and nearly asleep. Fortunately she was out of the bath and dried before the doorbell rang.

She wrapped herself in her royal blue cotton dressing-gown and, all pink and warm, padded downstairs to the front door, unlatched it and peered around the jamb. She realised at once that something serious had happened and she did not have to wait long to find out what it was.

'Paid off,' Alex Burnside said. 'Oh, God. I've been paid off.'

'Where are the boys? Henry, Jack—'

'All of us, every last hand – paid off.'

He was still clad in the heavy, stained clothing that marked him as a shipyard worker. He had taken off his cap, though, and wrung it in his hands in shame and embarrassment.

'I never thought it would happen to us,' Alex gulped.

His face was ashen as if shock had drained him not just of dignity but of vital juices. On the doorstep lay an oily canvas bag, heavy with the tools of his trade, though what the bag contained or why he had taken to transporting it about with him Ruby could not fathom. Nevertheless, something had happened at last, something definite and, to Ruby's surprise, she experienced a sense of relief, almost of power, at his news.

She held the collar of her dressing-gown tight with one hand and looked down at him, her heart beating fast.

He hung his head, wrung his hands and mumbled, 'I'm – I'm sorry, Ruby, so sorry.'

'Sorry for what?'

'Botherin' you.'

'Och, Alex, Alex,' Ruby said warmly. 'Come away in.'

Until recently Brenda had been blissfully unaware of the existence of the old manufactory south of Dumbarton Road. Tucked into a clump of sixty-year-old tenements which stood like stumps at the bottom of the Kingsway, backed by the walls of the Highland & Western railway, the Bryce Walker Industrial Clothing Company occupied a peculiar wedge-shaped building topped by a hexagonal sandstone tower which seemed to stand guard not only over Greenthorn Street but over the freight yards and river reach beyond. Arched doorways and windows protected by heavy iron bars reminded Brenda of castles she'd seen in pictures and as she pushed in through the big wooden door at the main entrance she half expected to be greeted by men armed with axes and swords. Instead there was an empty hallway panelled in varnished oak and floored with wrinkled linoleum of a particularly nasty brown colour. There was one bench seat and a sort of shelf which supported a framed notice which said, *Ring for Attention*.

Brenda glanced this way and that, discovered a circular tumulus of wood with an ivory button in its centre protruding from the shelf and, sucking in a deep breath, dabbed at the button, *Breeeeeeeeee*. The din echoed across the hall and spiralled through the brown ceiling long after Brenda had released the button and, in panic, had stepped back six or eight paces from the counter. A panel in the wall grated open. A woman with a face like a cleaver snapped, 'Yass?'

Still backing away Brenda stammered, 'I – I – I've c-come a-about the job. I – I wrote in . . . about the job?'

'Nay-yim?'

'McColl. Brenda McColl.'

The woman was tall and skinny and wore a white shirt with starched collar like a minister's. Gimlet eyes fastened on Brenda over the edge of a brown card folder. 'Adder-ess?'

'Number twelve, Foxhill Crescent, Flan—'

'Naw-min, take 'er hup.'

Norman was clad in a uniform of sorts, green worsted with gilt epaulettes and gilt buttons. At first glance Brenda took him to be a boy of nine or ten but as he crabbed towards her she realised that he was forty if he was a day and belonged to that class of person which her mother, with unfashionable delicacy, referred to as 'very small'.

Resisting the temptation to run for it, Brenda simpered in response to the wee man's evil grin, meekly allowed him to take her hand and lead her through a doorway and into the cage of a clashing old elevator upon whose brass wheels and handles Norman performed with practised

194

ease. His eyes never left Brenda for an instant as the floor fell away and weights shaped like breadboards swooped past the sides of the cage.

Brenda got a grip of herself, managed to look down on Norman without flinching. 'Who's she?' she asked.

'Miss Brawn,' Norman answered.

'Brawn?'

'Brown then,' said Norman. 'We call her "Brawn", 'cause that's what she calls herself.'

'What's wrong with her?'

'Nothin'. She's gotta bee up her bum an' it makes her talk funny.'

He reached out and took her hand again. Brenda did not object.

'You're nice,' said Norman, squeezing her fingers.

'You're not so bad yourself,' said Brenda. 'I think my friend Doris, you know, warned me about you.'

'Doris, what Doris?'

'Doris an' Vera, my friends. They work here.'

'Oh aye. I know Doris an' Vera. An' they know me,' Norman said and nudged her shoulder with his epaulette.

Before he could expand on his relationship with Doris and Vera the elevator shuddered to a halt and Norman clashed open the gate. Brenda was confronted by a short corridor floored in the same shade of linoleum as the hallway below and a broad staircase of five or six steps at the top of which lay a door panelled in pebble-glass. Although the corridor was empty there was in the air itself a strange throbbing which felt, Brenda imagined, the way an earthquake must do, vibrating up through your feet and legs into your tummy.

She hesitated.

'Go on,' Norman said. 'He's waitin' for you.'

'Who?'

'Mr Walker, stupid.'

'Waitin' for me? What for?'

'T' take down your particulars,' Norman said and, sniggering, closed the elevator gates and dropped away, leaving Brenda all alone in the corridor of Bryce Walker's sandstone tower.

Bertie had laid claim to the armchair and Davy to the smoker so Jack pulled out a dining chair, planted it on the hearthrug and rocked back to rest his heels on the edge of the mantelpiece.

'Doesn't feel like a Friday,' he said.

Pete, who had narrowly missed being speared by a chair leg, shuffled on his belly and, to show there was no ill feeling, licked Jack's hand a couple of times before dropping off to sleep.

'Does to me,' Bertie said from behind the latest Lone Star Western.

'I don't know what I'm goin' to do,' Jack said.

'Go to band practice,' Davy advised. 'Worry about it tomorrow.'

'God knows, we'll have plenty time to worry about it tomorrow since there'll be precious little else to do,' Jack said.

'You knew it was comin',' Bert said.

'It's still a shock, though. Eight hundred men in the spar shed one minute an' the next the bloody yard's deserted.'

'Did you get paid?' said Davy.

'Aye, lyin' time too,' Jack said. 'Ransome did the best he could.'

'I'll bet Ransome's not worried about where his next meal's comin' from,' Bertie said. 'He'll have his bundle salted away.'

'Even so,' said Jack, 'he must be down in the mouth

about the closure. I mean, how would you feel if you saw a business that'd been in your family for a hundred years suddenly go to the wall?'

'No worse than I'd feel if I'd worked there for monkey nuts for forty or fifty years,' Bertie said. 'Where is the old man, anyhow? Alison, have you seen the old man?'

'Nope,' Alison answered from the kitchen.

'I expect he'll be in the pub, drownin' his sorrows,' said Davy. 'Ally, what's for tea?'

'Macaroni.'

'Macaroni! I thought it was to be a grill?'

'Have you seen the price of meat these days?' said Alison.

'Oh, we're at that stage already, are we?' said Bertie. 'It'll be bread 'n' drippin' next, I suppose.'

'An' tripe on Sunday – if you're lucky,' Alison said, as she brought in the big enamel ashet and placed it on a cork mat on the table.

'Aren't we waitin' for Dad?' Jack asked.

'Doesn't look like it,' Bertie said. 'What's the rush, anyhow? Are you out tonight, Alison?'

'Yes,' Alison answered.

'Gotta date, honey?' said Davy.

'Huh!' Bertie snorted. 'Fat chance.'

'Extra lessons?' Jack asked his sister.

'Yes, now wash your hands an' dig in before it gets cold.'

In the kitchen a moment later, while Alison arranged on a plate the six cream cookies she had bought as a treat, Jack turned from the sink, hands dripping, and said, 'You mustn't worry about this, Alison.'

'About what?'

'The yard closin'.'

'I'm not worried, not really.'

197

'We'll manage to keep our promise – somehow.'

'If it turns out you can't – well, I won't be too disappointed.'

'You haven't changed your mind, about university, I mean?'

'Certainly not.'

'I can get work, you know. Playin' the trumpet.'

'Where?' Bertie called from the living-room. 'In the street?'

'Don't listen to him.' Alison handed Jack a dry towel and, on impulse, kissed him behind the ear. 'Come an' get your tea.'

Jack nodded then, frowning, said, 'I wonder where Dad is, though?'

'I think I know where he is,' said Alison quietly.

'Where?'

'Across the road at Mrs McColl's.'

'You're kiddin'?'

'I'm not.'

'Where the hell have you been, miss?' Ruby said. 'I've been worried sick.'

'I met some friends,' said Brenda, 'and we got talkin'.'

'What friends, Alison?'

'I said "friends",' Brenda told her mother.

Buttoning her overcoat, Ruby said, 'Have you been with a boy?'

'Chance would be a fine thing,' said Brenda. 'Here, just look at the time. You'd better, you know, scram.'

'Tea's in the oven,' Ruby said. 'If it's dried to a crisp, don't blame me.'

Brenda slumped into the armchair by the fire. Though she wore her usual school clothes there was something different about her, a smartness not just of manner but of appearance. In full war-paint, ready for her night's work, Ruby stooped over to peck her daughter's cheek, then paused and sniffed. 'Is that my perfume you're wearin'?'

'Might be.'

'Where *have* you been?'

'I told you.'

The clock was ticking audibly and Ruby was already ten minutes late but there was something so horribly smug about Brenda's manner that she could not bring herself to leave without a straight answer. She perched on the arm of the chair and adopted a calm and rational tone of voice.

'I'm not leavin' until you tell me the truth.'

Brenda had intended to hug the secret to herself, at least over the weekend but, elated, she could keep it to herself no longer. She let her head drop back against the cushion, stretched out her feet towards the fire and announced as casually as possible, 'I've got a job.'

'What? Where?'

'Bryce Walker's. I start two weeks come Monday.'

'Bryce Walker's, that dump!'

'It isn't a dump. It's a nice place.'

'How would you know?'

'I've been there. Today, in fact.'

'And you didn't tell me?' Ruby strove to mask her disappointment, to hide the overwhelming fear that she had lost her daughter for ever. 'Oh, Brenda, why didn't you tell me?'

'Because you'd have tried to stop me.'

'Who put you up to this?'

'Nobody. I done it, you know, off my own bat.'

'Didn't they need a letter from your mother?'

'It was him himself, Mr Walker. Very nice he was too. Told me all about the place an' what they make. All sorts o' things. Rubber goods.'

'Rubber goods?'

'Aprons for nurses, gloves, special suits for firemen,' said Brenda with growing enthusiasm, 'an' those oilskins fishermen wear – we make those, as well as all the other stuff.'

'Don't you want to stay on at school?' said Ruby desperately. 'It might be a good idea if you stayed on at school.'

'Nup. I'm startin' in Bryce Walker's two weeks on Monday.'

'Doin' what?'

'Learnin' how to stitch heavy materials, for a start,' Brenda said. 'If I'm good at that, if I show, you know, aptitude, then Mr Walker says I could get moved on to the pressers where the big money's to be made.'

'Piecework!' said Ruby. 'Oh, Brenda, Brenda! Bryce Walker's is just a sweatshop, don't you see?'

'All I'm fit for really,' said Brenda with a shrug.

It had been a long, long time since Ruby had felt the urge to weep. Centuries ago, it seemed. But tears welled in her eyes now, big fat globules that clung to her lashes and which, if she'd allowed them to fall, would surely ruin her make-up. She sniffed and bravely turned her head away. What was she crying for, anyway? Brenda's innocence? Brenda's youth? For not having done better by her daughter? She flicked the tears away with a painted fingernail and got to her feet.

'I really *will* have to go now,' she heard herself say.

Brenda rolled her head on the cushion. 'Sure. Go.'

Ruby wetted her lips. 'What does this job pay?'

'Fourteen shillin's a week fixed rate for the first six months,' Brenda answered. 'Then I can get my hands on the big money.'

'What are the hours?'

'Half eight to six. One o'clock on Saturday. Not bad, eh?'

'No.' Ruby swallowed the lump in her throat. 'Not bad.'

'Vera says you can make four quid easy once you learn how.'

'Vera?'

'One o' my friends. Doris is the other one. They've worked in Walker's for years. They say it's great.'

'Where did you meet these girls?' Ruby asked.

'Met them at Ferraro's one night. We got on the chat, you know, an' they told me about Walker's. Said I'd fit right in.'

Bad company, Ruby thought, her daughter had already fallen into bad company. Whoever Vera and Doris were, however honest and decent, Ruby already had it in for them.

She recalled the hour she'd spent with Alex that afternoon, how he'd fretted about the rash promises he'd made to *his* daughter, promises he might not be able to keep. Was it worse, Ruby wondered, to break a promise to your child or to make no promises in the first place?

She leaned on the arm of the chair and suddenly found herself with an arm about Brenda's shoulders, patting her, kissing her brow and cheeks, clinging to her as if saying goodbye for ever.

'Hoi! What's this?' said Brenda, half smothered.

'I'm glad you've found work, that's all.'

'Are y' really?' said Brenda, surprised.

'Of course I am,' said Ruby, drawing back at last.

'I thought you'd be mad at me.'

'No, no.'

'About Singer's—'

'Forget Singer's,' said Ruby. 'It's their loss.'

'Really?'

'Really.'

A minute later Ruby bustled down the path into the March twilight with Brenda calling from the doorway behind her, 'Thanks, Mum, thanks. We can't all be lady doctors, you know,' a statement so true, so sad that Ruby, safe in the shadow of the hedges, stopped and burst into tears.

Alex pushed away his plate, wiped his lips with the back of his hand and said, 'Nothin' I like better than a dish o' macaroni cheese.' Without awaiting an invitation he plucked the last cream bun from the cake tray and bit greedily into it. His sons watched in sullen bewilderment while Alison, frowning, leaned across the table to pour Dad a second cup of tea.

Alex scoffed the titbit in two mouthfuls and only then seemed to become aware that he was the focus of family attention. 'What's wrong wi' everybody?'

'What's wrong wi' you?' said Davy.

'What makes you think there's somethin' wrong with me?'

'You're humming, Dad,' said Alison.

Alex dipped his head, sniffed at his armpit and said indignantly, 'No, I am not.'

'Hummin',' said Jack, 'as in *hmmmmmm*.'

'Aw, sorry. Just enjoyin' my tea, that's all.'

'Enjoyin' your tea?' said Bert. 'How can you be enjoyin' your tea?'

''Cause it's tasty.'

'Dad,' Alison reminded him, 'you were paid off today.'

'Aye, me an' another eight hundred honest workin' men. Make y' sick, wouldn't it? Ally, you wouldn't happen to have a chocolate biscuit lyin' about, would you?' Obediently Alison delivered him a Dainty wrapped in silver paper. He continued, 'I don't know what you're all goin' on about. We all knew Ransome's was on the skids.'

'We thought you'd be shattered,' said Davy.

'I'm not exactly over the moon,' Alex said, 'but I'm not goin' to let it get me down. It's not the end o' the world.' Just out of his father's line of vision Bertie tapped a forefinger to the side of his head. 'Yes,' Alex went on, 'we'll need to pull up our socks an' tighten our belts, but with a wee bit luck an' a wee bit help we'll pull through.'

'Help?' said Alison. 'Help from whom?'

'Friends,' said Alex. 'Neighbours.'

'So you *were* over the road at the McColls'?' said Jack.

Alex fiddled with the silver paper from the Dainty, folding it and refining it until it was hardly thicker than a human hair. 'Well, I wasn't goin' to say anythin' about this until we were all together but you may as well know now.' He leaned on his elbows and put the sliver of paper down gently on the side of his plate. 'I've sort of asked Ruby to marry me.'

Bertie was the first to find his voice. 'Oh, my God!'

Alex raised his hands placatingly and looked up and round at the shocked faces of his family. ''S all right, 's all right.'

'It's bloody well not all right,' Bertie shouted. 'I'm not havin' that woman come into my house. Mam's hardly cold in the ground an' here you've got another one lined up. Or were you on to that trollop before Mam died?'

'Steady on, Bertie,' Jack said.

Alison had never seen Bert so distraught. He flung his

203

book across the living-room, leapt to his feet and aimed a kick at Pete who, startled out of sleep, bolted for the kitchen. 'Can't keep your hands off her, can you? Been over there givin' her one, haven't you?'

'Bertie, for God's sake, ease up.'

'I'm leavin'. I'm packin' my bags an' leavin'. I will not stay in this house with that bloody woman an' her bloody daughter,' Bertie ranted. 'If you think I'm puttin' my wages into *her* hands every Friday—'

'Nobody's puttin' their wages anywhere,' Alex said.

'How *could* you do this to us?'

'I didn't do it to you,' Alex said. 'I did it *for* you, for all of us.'

'Come off it, Dad,' said Jack.

'Aye, Dad. You fancy her. Admit it,' said Davy.

'She's a very attractive woman, no doubt of that,' said Alex.

Bertie groaned as if in pain.

'But,' Alex said, 'she didn't say Yes.'

'Eh?'

Alex scratched his forehead ruefully. 'Apparently she's not ready to commit herself.'

'She turned you down?' Bertie whipped off his glasses and peered at his father through angry tears. '*She* had the cheek to turn *you* down?'

'Not exactly,' Alex explained. 'She didn't say Yes, but she didn't say No either. She said it was too soon.'

'Bloody right too,' Jack said.

Alex gave a sigh and a shrug of the shoulders. 'Pity, though.'

'Why, Dad?' Alison asked. 'Why Mrs McColl?'

'She's in work, isn't she?' Alex Burnside answered.

'Aw, naw!' said Davy.

'Aw, aye,' said Alex.

* * *

'Alison?' Jim Abbott said. 'What on earth are you doing here?'

'I'm sorry to bother you on a Friday, Mr Abbott, but if you could spare me a few minutes, I'd be grateful.'

She wore a green dress and a heavy dark green cardigan, stockings instead of socks and looked, he thought, a good two or three years older than she did in the uniform of a schoolgirl. Her height did that, he supposed, and the rearranged hair; a severe style, pulled back to show the shape of her face and the fine, poised line of her neck. She was bareheaded and there was no sign of the Raleigh, that cumbersome machine which, when she rode it, made her appear tomboyish. He glanced behind him then back to the girl on the doorstep and said, 'My sister isn't in.'

'If you're busy—'

'No, I'm not busy, not in the least,' he said. 'It's just that Winnie's not here and she probably won't be back for ages. Guild meeting. I think.'

Alison's solemn expression convinced him that she had no inkling that she was breaking the rules. She had caught him at his ease, waistcoat unbuttoned, collar off and sleeves rolled up. He was conscious first of how shabby and ordinary he must appear to her, and of an empty left sleeve too obvious to ignore. He imagined that she was staring at it and that her solemnity signified distaste.

'I'm sorry,' Alison said. 'I shouldn't have imposed.'

'You're not imposing.' He sensed her disappointment and, being fully aware of what had happened on Clydeside that afternoon, told himself that it would be cruel to send her away. He glanced past her. 'No bike?'

'I walked.'

'Come in, Alison.'

'Are you sure you don't mind?'

Mind? He felt his social inhibitions evaporate, common sense with them. He wanted to tell her that there was no other person in the world he'd rather have cross his threshold but instead he contented himself with ushering her into the living-room with a little wave of the hand.

Normally so neat, the room seemed to Jim to be suddenly cluttered. Exercise books scattered on the table, a coffee cup on the mantelshelf, the *Herald* with the crossword half done dropped on the rug, an ashtray perched precariously on the arm of his chair. He resisted the temptation to tidy up and, feigning ease, seated himself opposite the girl.

The parchment-shaded lamp on top of the bureau cast light along the side of her face and he could see the faint blonde-brown lashes and the darker arch of her brow. She looked almost Parisian. Stick her in a black beret and she would have been quite at home at a marble-topped table in a café on the boulevards, one of those mysterious intellectual companions with no past and no future. Calm yourself, Abbott, he told himself sternly, and said aloud, 'I heard about Ransome's closing its gates. Has your father changed his mind about keeping you on at school?'

'He hasn't said anything yet. I don't think it's quite sunk in.'

'Brothers paid off too?'

'Yes, two brothers.'

'Perhaps you'd better tell me what's troubling you, Alison?'

'They, the family, don't know I'm here tonight.' Jim nodded and Alison continued, 'So it isn't their decision. It's mine.'

'And what decision is this?'

'To leave school at the end of term.'

'No,' he said. 'You can't.'

'I don't think it's got anythin' to do with you, Mr Abbott.'

'Yes, it has.'

She frowned again, lips pursed. 'We won't have any money.'

'Yes, you will.'

'Mr Abbott, you don't understand.'

'I do, you know,' Jim said. 'Do you think I had it on a plate, Alison?'

She gave a little impatient sigh and he realised with gratitude that she was merely playing at martyrdom. He had seen this all before, had gone through the phase himself, damn it, before warfare introduced him to martyrdom of another sort. Once more, he had to remind himself that in spite of her intelligence she was still young and inexperienced.

'No,' he said, 'I'm not going to bore you with tales of hardship or with the history of *my* struggle against the odds. This I will say, however, you haven't even begun to feel the pinch, and already you're side-stepping responsibility.' He did not intend to sound pompous or patronising. He tried to relax. 'Education has nothing to do with money, Alison. It's there for the taking, like brambles on the hedges.'

'If I get a bursary.'

'Forget bursaries, forget grants and Carnegie trusts. You need a roof over your head, two squares a day, and a lot, a *lot* of determination. I've never deceived you about that, have I? I've never deceived any of my pupils about how much effort it takes to rise in the world. You have a special quality, Alison, and' – he hesitated then allowed himself to speak out – 'you mean a lot to me.'

'What about Walter?'

207

'I don't know about Walter,' Jim said. 'But I do know about you.'

'If I was a boy, I could see the point but—'

'Rubbish!' he said. 'Pure unadulterated tripe! Oldest excuse in the book. I'm the wrong sex, the wrong class, the wrong shape. Too much against me. Won't try. Won't make the effort. Save myself the bother and blame circumstances. I'll conform, do what's expected of me – which isn't very much – and that'll be enough to get by on.' He could tell by her wariness that he had forced an unwelcome understanding upon her. 'Who's against you, Alison? Give me a name.'

'My brother Bertie.'

'Why is he against you?'

'He thinks it's a waste of time for a girl.'

'Is he right?'

'No, well – no.'

'Who else?'

'My grandmother is – at least a bit.'

'Is she the marry-and-have-children type?'

'Yes.'

It was years since he had spoken with such passion. Once he had been full of zeal for the principles of education but he had lost it, somehow, along the way, had, God help him, shaken it off for comfort's sake.

'Is your grandmother right?' he demanded.

'No, I think she's wrong too.'

'And yet you're going to give in to her.'

'I don't see how it can be done.'

'Can't afford the tramcar fare? Walk. Can't afford the textbooks? Live in the library. Can't afford lunch? Go hungry.' He got up and knelt before her in a position not of supplication but of conviction. 'They'll scoff at you. They'll pretend they despise you. They'll hinder you if

208

they can, Alison. But in their trembling little hearts they'll be afraid of you because you'll have more than they'll ever have. I don't mean materially. I mean more fibre, more will.' He sat back on his heels. 'Do you trust me, Alison?'

'Yes.'

'You're not just saying it?'

'No.'

'Then trust *me* to tell you when it becomes impossible.' He got up, steadied himself with a hand on her knee, a brief, undeliberate touching. 'I'll be here whenever you need me. *I'm* not going anywhere, Alison, but *you* are.' He looked down at her, his passion modulated into tenderness. Perhaps for the first time she seemed aware of his feelings. Standing before her, he said, 'Aren't you?'

'Yes,' Alison said. 'Yes, Mr Abbott, I am.'

SEVEN

Deeds of Arrangement

Henry was conscious of the irony of taking out to dinner a woman who claimed to be broke but who appeared in an evening dress of ivory satin glittering with gold paillettes. He had told her to put on her best but he had not expected such a florid show. Where this expensive stuff had been hidden was something of a mystery for Henry had made a recce of the house late one evening when Trudi was asleep and he had found little of any value that wasn't nailed down in the inventory. He was not displeased by the lady's appearance, though, for she had regained her poise and would, he felt sure, turn every head in Pegler's, the swankiest restaurant in town.

He had broken the bank for the occasion. He had bought himself a three-piece navy blue suit, a pair of patent leather shoes and a new silk tie with a distinguished pattern upon it. He would have preferred to sally forth in a dinner suit but he could not bring himself to be quite so extravagant as all that, considering he would probably never wear it again and wouldn't dare turn up in the dole queue dressed like the Prince of Wales.

Henry could not remember who had told him that Pegler's was *the* place to dine in Glasgow. It certainly looked like the sort of establishment where the great and good would congregate to take a spot of supper, not all glow and glitter but discreet and, on the outside, even a trifle shabby. He had reserved a table, which was just as well. The place was packed, the narrow corridor which led from the doorway lined with furs and Chesterfields and black alpacas and guarded by a muscular flunkey in a uniform that made him look like Black Rod or the Moderator of the General Assembly.

Beyond the gloomy corridor were bright lights, snow-white tablecloths, gleaming crystal. As he waited for Trudi to emerge from the powder-room, Henry smoked a cigarette with all the style he could muster and felt his heart beat ten to the dozen with nervous excitement. Tonight was the acid test. Tonight he would discover if Mrs Trudi Coventry was nothing other than a hollow shell and if all the cleverness and influence with which he had invested her had been nothing but a product of his own imagination.

Trudi returned, gay and smiling. She took his arm.

Black Rod said, 'Surrr,' in a reassuring Glasgow accent, led them to the doorway and handed them on to a *maître d'* who, with all the shifty charm of a stage magician, whisked them to a table for two and performed a finger-snapping exercise which brought chair-puller-outers and deliverers of menus and wine lists leap-frogging to attend them.

'Okay wiff you, monsieurmadam?'

'Fine, thank you,' Henry replied to the already departing coat-tails. He heard Trudi laugh softly. He glanced at her quickly. 'Did I say the wrong thing?'

'Darling, how could you say the wrong thing when he is a servant of the establishment. It is you who foots the bill and you are his master.'

'By the way he goes on you'd never guess it.'

'It is how he likes to intimidate people. I believe he does not like to be a servant to the rich.'

'I'm not one of the rich.'

212

'Perhaps soon you will be.'

Henry opened the tall menu and flicked away the silky tassel which hung between the pages like a spider on a thread. The dishes were described in English and his eye went at once to the prices which he scanned with affected casualness.

He met Trudi's gaze over the rim of the menu and noted, with a little malicious satisfaction, that she was studying him very carefully indeed. She seemed to be quite her old confident, glamorous self, thoroughly at home in the glittering supper-room. He preferred her like this, sharp and shrewd, not clinging and dependent.

'Tell you one thing, Trude,' he said, 'I bet I'm the only shipwright on Clydeside who's celebrating bein' paid off by dinin' at Pegler's.'

'It is something to celebrate, no?'

'That depends,' said Henry.

'Upon what does it depend?'

He did not answer. He put the menu to one side and leaned away as a waiter, with tongs, put a bread roll on his plate and filled his water glass. Without effort Henry ignored the waiter and covertly scanned the room. He was not entirely sure who he hoped to find there, what faces he might recognise but he was keen now to see who recognised *her*, who knew Trudi Coventry.

Several men did, and at least three of the women. He watched the swift, furtive lift of a coiffeured head, the studied turn of a man's shoulders, a confirming nod; the language of gossip and speculation.

Trudi said, 'Do you wish me to tell you who they are?'

'That's what we're here for, Trude,' Henry told her. 'To find out who's still willin' to talk to you – now you're broke.'

'You wish to use me, Henry?'

'Absolutely.'

213

'Is that all I am to mean to you, a useful person?'

'Not at all.' He ordered for both of them, requested a bottle of Chablis to be served with the entrée and watched the man rise and come towards them, a small man, nimble as a weasel. 'Who's he?'

'My husband's lawyer.' She showed her small perfect teeth as the man approached, extended her hand towards him, and laughed. 'Gerald, I am delighted to see you.'

He was, Henry guessed, around forty. He was very dark and saturnine, with a neat little moustache that matched exactly the line of his pinched upper lip. He kissed Trudi's hand and bowed then turned to face Henry and said, 'I do not believe I have the pleasure of your acquaintance.'

The accent was educated Glaswegian with a purr of homespun sincerity carefully worked into it, ideal for pleading cases to others of similar ilk, old boys from the Academy or the Royal High, the *lingua franca* of the ruling class. Henry got to his feet, every movement as relaxed as he could possibly make it. He may not have been able to mimic the accent but he could drop his voice a full half octave when he wanted to and he introduced himself in a deep, masculine growl. 'Henry Burnside.'

The handshake, firm but not crushing, was held a second too long.

'Gerald Dante.'

'You are with someone, Gerald, or you would join us?' said Trudi.

'Alas, I've company.' His eyes were like blackberries and the backs of his hands and wrists were furred with dark hair. 'I couldn't pass by, though, without paying my respects. Have you recovered?'

'I am mending,' said Trudi. 'Have you lately encountered Clive?'

'Not for an age.'

'So it is true, he is out of the country?'

'Visiting New York, I expect.'

'I heard a rumour that it was, this time, Berlin,' Trudi said.

'Perhaps it is.' The little lawyer addressed himself to Henry. 'And you, Mr Burnside, what line of business are you in?'

'The business of buildin' ships,' said Henry. 'Or, at least, I was before I was paid off.'

To his credit Gerald Dante did not feign surprise. 'Ransome's?'

'That's the one,' said Henry. 'Come Monday, I'll be lookin' for work.'

Dante gave a little nod. 'Have you known Mrs Coventry for long?'

'My! You are full of questions,' said Henry.

'A bad habit one acquires in my profession,' Dante said.

'Henry has been taking care of me,' Trudi said.

'But,' said Henry, 'I might not be able to do so much longer unless I can find suitable employment. If you hear of anything, Mr Dante, you might be kind enough to let Trudi know.'

Behind the blackberry eyes there might have been a hint of amusement. 'It's unlikely I'll hear of anything that might suit a caulker or a plate-layer.'

'I'm prepared to do other things, different things.'

'I'm sure that you are, Mr Burnside.'

'Perhaps Mr Coventry might be able to find me something when he comes back from wherever he is right now,' Henry said casually.

'I'll mention it to him,' Gerald Dante said, 'if and when I see him next, which may not be for some time, of course.'

215

'No hurry,' said Henry.

A moment or two later the lawyer made his excuses and, with a parting kiss on the hand for Trudi, returned to his table.

'Who's he with?' said Henry.

'You must stop this, Henry.'

'Who's he with, Trudi?'

'I do not know them.'

'I think you do.'

'One of them, I believe, is Marcus Harrison.'

'That's handy,' said Henry. 'Very handy. And the other one?'

'I do not know him, truly,' Trudi said. 'Why do you bring me to this place, Henry? Only to make me ashamed?'

'Nope,' Henry said. 'I brought you here to fill you full of beef soup, Dover sole and a couple of helpings of toffee pudding. My other motives are strictly ulterior.'

'What does that mean?'

'Pure,' Henry answered as a waiter bore a soup tureen down upon them. 'Pure as the driven snow.'

Every sound, every little noise had meaning and Alison could follow them as easily as she might have tracked spoor on sand. She could identify her brothers and father by door-sounds, by creaks and coughs, the flushings of the lavatory. She heard the long, lazy, jaw-breaking yawn which signalled that Davy had turned on his side beneath the bedclothes, the pronounced click of Bertie's bedside lamp as he switched it off; her father's last-minute excursion into the kitchen to raid the biscuit barrel.

Only Pete was quiet, snoozing on a blanket beneath the big chair or, when the last noisy Burnside had finally gone to bed, spreading himself out on the hearthrug, fat as a seal. Sometimes, though not often, Alison would waken in dead of night and hear the click of Pete's claws from the hall, one wee muffled *wuff* of greeting as Henry arrived in from heaven knows where and, making hardly a ripple in the stillness, would feed the dog a few extra scraps and fill his water bowl before gliding upstairs to pass silent as a wraith into his bedroom across the landing. Alison knew better than to bother her eldest brother with her problems. Henry was so self-concerned, so intense these days that even Bertie did not dare rib him.

Seated at her study table, warmly clad in her nightdress, dressing-gown and woollen socks, she browsed over a geometry textbook, and waited for the rattle of the biscuit barrel which would tell her that her father was alone downstairs.

She caught him red-handed in the darkened living-room with two digestives glued together with butter, a cup of hot tea in his hand.

'God, you fair startled me, sweetheart.' He clutched his sagging trousers with his free hand and hoisted them into a state of comparative modesty. 'What's up then? Can y'not sleep?'

'No, I want a word with you, that's all.'

'Oh!'

'About Mrs McColl.'

'Uh-huh!'

He shuffled to the table and put down the cup and the biscuit upon the folded tablecloth. He found a clean cup, measured out half the tea from his own cup and gestured to Alison to join him.

'Ruby's a decent woman,' he said. 'In spite of what I told the boys I'd never take advantage of her.'

'But you would like to marry her?'

217

'I would, aye.'

'You're not just doing this for me, are you, Dad?'

'Don't you believe it.'

'Why did you choose today to propose?'

'Well, I didn't actually propose. I mean, she was there in her dressing-gown an' looked so nice. Naw, it wasn't even that.' He sipped tea, put the cup down. 'She's not like your Mam, Alison. I'm not lookin' for another Mavis.'

'What are you looking for – a breadwinner?'

'Naw, I just said that to get the boys off my back.'

'It sounded terrible.'

'I suppose it did.' He made a face, rueful but not repentant. 'I thought our Bertie was goin' to have a purple fit.'

'Davy likes her. He wouldn't mind.'

'What about you?'

'How hard are things going to be?'

'Now we're out o' work? Hard.'

'Can you not get another job?'

'I doubt it. Not in Glasgow, anyway.'

'What'll you do, Dad?'

'Sign on, fill in the forms, collect the dole.'

Alison nodded. 'I went to see Mr Abbott tonight.'

'Eh?' Alex's brows rose. 'What for?'

'To tell him I wasn't going to stay on at school.'

'Now, now, there's no need—'

'But I am,' Alison said. 'Mr Abbott says all I need is a roof over my head and two squares a day.'

'It doesn't seem like much when you put it that way.'

'I don't want you marrying Mrs McColl just to see me through,' Alison said. 'Besides, Brenda might have somethin' to say about it.'

'Brenda, aye!'

'We don't see eye to eye any longer,' Alison said.

'She's only jealous.'

'I know,' said Alison. 'She's made that all too plain.'

'Are you bothered?'

'I was,' said Alison, 'but I've got over it – I think.'

'You'll make other friends soon enough.'

'I won't have much time for gallivantin' with friends,' Alison said.

'Is that somethin' else the teacher told you?'

'He didn't have to,' Alison said. 'Anyway, I just thought I'd tell you where I stand, Dad. I'd still like to see what I can achieve, unless things get just too tough.'

'Ach, things are always tough,' said Alex. 'Always have been, always will be. We'll manage, though, never you fret.'

She got up and began to clear the cups from the table. It did not seem right that at sixteen, going on seventeen, she should feel pity for her father but she could not deny that she nursed an unfortunate sense of superiority towards him now.

'Will you miss Ransome's, Dad?'

'I don't know yet,' he said. 'If your Mam had been alive it would have been worse. She'd have been worried to death.'

'No, no. She'd have worked out a budget to make ends meet.'

'We'll do that tomorrow,' he said. 'All of us together, since we're all in the same boat. All right, sweetheart?'

'All right.'

She took the cups into the kitchen to rinse through and when she returned to the living-room she found, to her surprise, that he had gone into his room and closed the door. She hesitated, then, with an unconscious shrug, went back upstairs.

Below, alone, Alex Burnside thrust his face into the

feather pillow to muffle his tears and listened, distraught with anxiety, to the little sounds his daughter made as she climbed nimbly into bed.

Henry opened one eye and then the other, lids clicking like a china doll's. He stared up at the smear of tusk-coloured light that penetrated the curtains and transformed the cornices' rosebuds into gargoyles. For a moment he had no idea where he was. He felt as if he was floating in space with no more substance than a handful of dust; a peaceful sensation, until panic set in. He sat up and, still naked, swung his feet to the floor.

His head swam and his stomach churned. He felt as soggy as one of the dead dogs that Ransome's clean-up man would sometimes drag from the tide that lapped the slipways' edge and burn on a pyre behind the latrines.

The stench of burning seemed to waft into Henry's nostrils. He could taste beef soup and the acidic aftermath of too much wine and for three or four seconds he felt lost again, suspended between the glitter of Pegler's restaurant and the iron landscapes of Clydeside.

'What time is it?' he groaned.

'Are you unwell?' Trudi's fingers touched his back.

'What the hell time is it?'

He groped for his watch on the bedside table, found stockings instead, a garterbelt, something silken and slippery which he flung to the floor. He found the watch and pressed the glass against his nose but could see nothing of the numerals, though the watch, bought by mail order, had been advertised as 'luminous'.

'I'm late. God, I'm late. I've slept in.'

Trudi rolled away from him and switched on a lamp.

Henry blinked, screwed up his eyes and extended the watch to arm's length. Quarter past four. Relief. Then panic again. He shot to his feet and searched about the room for his clothing, muttering, 'I've gotta go home. Gotta go home.'

'Why, Henry? There is no work for you tomorrow.'

He found his shirt, his brand-new tie screwed up like a piece of tarry rope and automatically began to smooth it between his fingers while he struggled to get a grip on his senses. Too much food, too much wine, too much sex had brought him to this state. He glanced down at his body. Emaciated, almost bloodless, his tender parts shrivelled as if they had been scorched. He covered them with the hand that held the necktie and turned to the woman in the bed. Trudi did not seem wrecked by the night's excesses. On the contrary she appeared to have been invigorated and renewed.

Softly she said, 'It is too late to go home now, Henry. Come back to the bed.'

'No,' he shouted. He clutched his forehead. 'No, Trudi. I have to get back to Flannery Park.'

'You have hangover, my boy.' She chuckled. 'Come. I will soothe.'

He struggled to find the sleeves of his shirt. 'They'll be worried, my Dad especially. An' I've things to do tomorrow.'

'Tomorrow! Today is not over yet.' She sat back against the pillow, folded down the rumpled bedclothes and patted the sheet. 'Tomorrow is nothing if you do not sleep.'

Henry swayed slightly. He was afraid of what she might expect of him. He peered at the watch again. She was right, though, it would be daft to leave now. She was right about other things too. No work. No irksome Saturday shift. He felt stale and smelly, battered, out of control. 'Trudi—'

With her knees drawn up under her she reminded him of a drawing he'd seen of a mermaid luring sailors to their doom. She held out her hand.

He seated himself wearily on the bed and permitted Trudi Coventry to draw his head down to the pillow and fold the sheets over his bare legs.

'Oh, hell,' he said, 'why not!'

Satisfied, Trudi put out the light.

Mrs Marietta Giffard was having one of her 'turns' and had decided to remain in bed. It was not unusual for Mrs Giffard to remain in bed. Given the chance, Mrs Giffard would have permanently adopted the life of ease that 'her condition' demanded. What that condition was, what organs it affected and by how many years it would actually shorten her life were questions never asked, let alone answered, in the Giffard household.

Mrs Giffard certainly didn't look like an invalid. She was small and sturdy with a deep uncongested bosom, wide hips and a sallow, almost weatherbeaten complexion. She also had a good deal of hair, including a little moustache which she frequently tried to remove with a coating of white wax. Now and then in desperation, before the Manchester Crown General Life Assurance Company's annual dinner-dance, say, she would resort to peroxide treatment and would present to the world a gilded countenance, her upper lip alarmingly embroidered with bright blonde bristles. Waxing and peroxiding were exhausting procedures, of course, and invariably necessitated two or three days in bed, while the recovery period after a Marcel wave could be anything up to a week.

Mrs Giffard was, however, always wide awake when husband George or son Walter brought in the breakfast tray or served lunch from the three-tiered trolley, this last manoeuvre requiring all the skill of a Sapper since the trolley had four large wheels and the bedrooms in the Giffards' council house were both on the upper floor. George, dear George, did not object to waiting hand on foot on his wife. He had been born to be trampled underfoot and regarded Marietta's demands not as an unwelcome cross to bear but as signs of her gentility. Gentility was all to George and Marietta Giffard, that mannered, polished quality which marked the limits of aspiration and defined not only their relationship but the very centre of their being.

Now that elder brother Scott had fled the nest, Walter was the only fly in the Giffards' ointment. No matter how hard Marietta had tried she had never been able to bring her sons to heel. Even doses of the cane – administered by her husband while she wept in the lavatory – had not been able to bring the boys to the pitch of convention which Marietta expected of them. Nurture, it seemed, had lost out to some wild, rebellious gene which certainly hadn't come from *her* side of the family and for which poor George, innocent and servile male that he was, must shoulder *all* the blame.

Dancing lessons, violin lessons, Temperance lectures, Bible study, Choral Union concerts, even a brief season with the Pilgrim Way, had all failed to eliminate the scruffiness which Marietta so abhorred in her sons, a vice which, if only she'd known it, the boys had acquired to avoid being turned into duplicates of poor old hen-pecked Pop.

Scott, dark and handsome, had left home at seventeen to become a merchant seaman. He was currently serving as a steward on the P & O's Australian run. It was left to Walter, an imperfect version of his father, to carry all Marietta's hopes for the future.

223

She had never liked Walter much. The drooping eyelid and turned eye gave him such a shifty appearance that even when he was a baby Marietta had the impression that he was squinting at her as if he disapproved of and resented her motherly attentions. The 'lazy eye' might have been cured by surgical intervention but Marietta had begun to groom her elder son for 'big things' in life and consequently there wasn't a farthing left to squander on doctors' bills.

For most of their married life the Giffards had lived in a room and kitchen in what Marietta called Dowanhill but which, in fact, was only a tenement at the upper end of Gardner Street in Partick. The move to Flannery Park might have answered all Marietta's prayers, if only she'd had the gumption to drag herself out of bed and apply a little elbow grease to the semi's interior. As it was the council house in Dunsinane Street was just as grubby as the tenement flat had been, for which circumstance Marietta naturally blamed her husband and her left-over son.

'Walter?'

'What?'

'Has the postman been?'

'No.'

'I thought I heard the letterbox.'

'Nope.'

'What are you doing down there?'

'Doctorin' your porridge.'

'I'm sorry, I didn't catch that?'

'Hard cheese.'

'Have you looked on the mat?'

The voice of her son became clearly audible from the bottom of the stairs. 'Why, yes, Mother, there is indeed a spot of mail.'

'Anything for me, dear?'

'Bills, bills, an invitation to Buckingham Palace,' Walter intoned, 'bills, bills an' more bills.'

'Do stop teasing, Walter. If it isn't too much trouble would you be good enough to fetch the post up to Mama?'

'How do you want your egg?'

'Lightly boiled. Has your father gone?'

'Without givin' you a kiss? Nah, he's sittin' on the cludgie.'

'Please don't be vulgar, Walter.'

Walter in pyjama top and rumpled flannels, barefoot and tousle-haired, had slipped back into the kitchenette and was hastily sorting through the eight or ten pieces of mail that had whispered through the letterbox.

He did not expect Alison to write to him at home – he did not expect Alison to write to him at all – but he had a holy horror that some item from his private life would fall into his mother's hands. He was even more afraid of the weird little love-notes that Brenda had taken to sending him, the envelopes decorated with hearts and suggestive acronyms.

'Walter? Is there *nothing* for me?'

In the bathroom his father coughed politely and politely flushed the lavatory. Pop would shave and dress behind the closed blue-glass door of the bathroom. Recently his modesty had become almost obsessive, as if he feared that if Mrs G discovered a wrinkle here, a blemish there she would discard him like an old sock.

All of the letters, save one, were addressed to Mr Giffard, Insurance Agent. Walter put them carefully to one side of the oilcloth-covered dresser. The other envelope was addressed to his mother and carried a South African stamp. Without hesitation Walter slit the flap and shook out the card that the envelope contained. He turned it upright and looked at the picture with distaste.

He had no notion where his brother obtained such arcane postcards. Perhaps they were common truck in the Antipodes. But what was their purpose? Were they intended to stimulate the imagination of armchair travellers, to rouse enthusiasm in amateur anthropologists or just titillate a bunch of randy sailors whose concept of wit was, to say the least of it, unrefined? This particular offering depicted two male Aboriginals posed unself-consciously in the all-together by the carcase of a dead kangaroo. On the back Scott had written: '*How do you like these chaps, Ma? Aren't their boomerangs big? Happy Birthday. Home September.*'

The cards were intended not to amuse but to wound and Walter could not decide whether or not he was on Scott's side, whether or not his dislike of his mother had reached that peak of malice or if it ever would.

'Walter?'

'What?'

'Is my egg not done yet?'

'Comin', comin',' Walter shouted.

He studied the postcard again. If he rubbed out Scott's pencilled message he could ink in one of his own and send the card to Brenda. She, of course, would love it. He did not hesitate for long. He tore the card in half, tore it again, reduced it to tiny fragments which he hid in the bucket under the sink beneath a slurry of fish bones, bacon rind and potato peelings.

'Walter?'

'YES.'

He dolloped out porridge, filled the teapot, dropped an egg into boiling water, slid toast from beneath the grill and, minutes later, trudged upstairs with the breakfast tray.

226

She was propped up in bed, a knitted pink thing about her shoulders, an ancient cambric mobcap covering her thick dark hair. He put the tray across her knees. 'How d'you feel?'

'I'll be all right.'

'Good,' he said, half out of the door.

'Walter?'

'Yep.'

'Nothing for me in the post?'

'Nope.'

'No word from Scott?'

'Nope.'

She dabbled a spoon in milky porridge and then, without even looking up at him, said, 'Tell Dada I want a kiss.'

Ironically the new Labour Exchange was situated only three hundred yards from the gates of Ransome's shipyard. Registering was a slow business. The queue stretched around the corner and along the pavement as far as the Craigmore Bar which backed on to the patch of waste ground on which the Bureau of Employment building had been flung up. No sandstone pediments, no tiled halls or monumental notice boards here. The new 'buroo' was aggressively functional and reminded those who had served in the war of nothing so much as an artillery bunker.

Alex was embarrassed to be there at all. He did not see why a top-dollar riveter should be flung together with fitters, carters and storemen. Jack quietened him down though and together they shuffled into the unimposing building to answer the clerks' questions and be numbered and filed.

Monday was allotted as Alex's day for drawing dole. He

was awarded seventeen shillings, plus an extra two shillings for Alison who was currently his only dependent child. If Mavis had been alive he would have copped a further nine shillings but he did not even think of that as he came out into the spring sunshine with cap in hand. He sucked in a deep breath and lit his second last cigarette.

Jerry the apprentice, with a gang of his own kidney milling around him, shouted, 'Where's yer dog's breakfast noo, Mr Burnside?' and laughed when Alex shook a fist at him.

Sandy Simpson said, 'Aye, it's a sore day, this.'

'How much did they give you?'

'Basic. Twenty-six shillin's.'

'What about your wee daughter?' Alex said.

'She workin' now.'

'God, time flies,' Alex said. 'How's Peggie takin' it?'

'Bad,' said Sandy. 'Listen, I'd better away.'

'Aye, well – cheerio,' said Alex limply, then called out. 'I'll be seein' ye, Sandy.' But the big man, friend of thirty years, did not seem to hear him and did not even pause to wave goodbye.

Jack put a hand on his shoulder. 'All done, Dad?'

'Let's get outta here, son.'

Whistling softly and doing his best to appear nonchalant, Jack led his father past the queue and out on to Dumbarton Road. There was some trade at Ferraro's, not much, and a sullen little crowd had gathered outside the Warnock Bar to watch the almost empty tramcars rattle past.

'Twelve an' a tanner.' Jack patted his breast pocket. 'Eighteen bob down on the week. Could be worse, I suppose. What'd they give you for Ally?'

'Two bob,' said Alex, gruffly.

'Dear, dear! That's terrible,' Jack said and before his father could ask him to explain, picked up the tune again

228

and headed, whistling, across the Kingsway as if he hadn't a care in the world.

Bertie took off his raincoat and divested himself of the fancy little porkpie hat he had recently acquired for himself. 'Well, well, if it isn't my long-lost brother Henry! To what do we owe this honour, sir?'

'Don't be sarkie,' Alex said. 'Where have you been anyway? I thought you were on mid-shift.'

'Been to the pictures, if you must know.'

'Well, that's one luxury we can easy stroke off,' said Alex.

'Who says?'

'I says,' his father told him. 'Now sit there an' listen.'

'Listen to what?'

Bertie glowered at his brothers who were assembled at the dining table like a board of company directors. The cloth had been removed and on the rubberised under-mat were several beer glasses, two ashtrays, and a pile of papers made up of pay-lines, gas and electrical bills and, ominously, the rent book. Davy sat forward attentively, hands folded on the mat. Jack lounged. At the head of the table, back to the bow window, Henry tapped a pencil on a pad of yellow notepaper. Bertie dropped his coat and hat on to the arm of the smoker's chair and took his seat at the table. 'Listen to what?' he enquired again.

'Facts an' figures, Bertie,' Henry answered.

A half hour ago he had been in the stalls of the Astoria, absorbed in the adventures of Ronald Colman, one of his favourite film stars, who was playing the part of *Beau Geste*, a picture Bertie had seen three times before. The Astoria wasn't equipped to show talking pictures yet and the audience had been few in number, which was just how Bertie liked it. His head was still full of deserts and

courageous legionnaires and he could not quite bring into
focus the realities of a family pow-wow.

'Where's Alison?' he enquired.

'Gone to bed.'

'If this is another meetin' about her,' Bertie said, 'then
I'm off to bed too. I'm sick of discussin' her future night
after flamin' night.'

'Put a bloody sock in it,' Henry told him.

'Who put him in charge, anyway?'

Jack shrugged. 'He's got the pencil.'

Bertie snorted, folded his arms and scowled at the
patterns on the rubberised mat.

'Sulk if you like, son,' Alex said, 'just listen. Henry,
continue.'

'Davy, you're out of your apprenticeship in nine
weeks,' Henry said. 'Are you sure the builder will keep
you on?'

'Sure as I can be,' Davy replied. 'It's supposed to be
an eight-year scheme an' there's thousands of houses still
to be built. I should be on full wage from the first of
May.'

'Good,' Henry said. 'Very good. Jack, what have you got
to offer?'

'Band money,' Jack said. 'Kenny's promised me summer
work, if Stuart's not back by then.'

'What's wrong wi' Stuart?'

'Lungs,' Jack said.

'TB?'

'Might be.'

'Then you're in, son,' said Alex, with a happy little click
of the tongue.

'Dad!'

'Well, I don't know this Stuart chap, do I?'

'All right, all right,' said Henry. 'That leaves you, Dad?'

'Brown's are still buildin',' Davy said.

'Aye, but not employin',' said Jack.

'Maybe Davy could see if he can find me work with the Corporation,' Alex said. 'I'll even take road work if there's nothin' to be had in my trade.'

'Which there isn't,' said Henry.

'What about you, big man?' Bertie said suddenly. 'Are you movin' out?'

'No, I'm not moving out,' Henry said.

'What's your contribution then?'

'I've an iron or two in the fire.' Henry tapped the pencil on the pad. 'If things work out I could be startin' a new job in a month or so.'

'Just what're you up to, Henry?' Jack asked.

'Got a fancy piece, I'll bet,' said Bertie. 'He's hopin' to sponge off her.'

'Is that right, Henry?' Davy said. 'Have you got a girl?'

'Might have. Might not.'

'That means he has,' said Bertie.

Henry did not rise to the bait. He rubbed his eyes wearily, circled the notepad with his forearm, stared at the figures he had jotted upon it.

'What's the verdict, son?' said Alex.

'Oh, we can make it,' Henry said. 'If Davy gets kept on, if Jack gets a summer job, if things pan out right for me, we can make it.'

'On paper,' Jack said.

Henry nodded. 'You're right, Jack. On paper it looks fine but when it comes down to it – who knows?'

'And what about Ally?' said Davy. 'What about our plans for her?'

'Nothing's changed,' said Henry and left around the table an uncertain silence which not even Bertie had the gall to interrupt with the startling news that he himself had resigned from his job with the GPO that very day.

Soon after Easter the weather took a turn for the worse. Sleet brought winter back to the high hills north of the Clyde and the broad shoulders of Ben Lomond were white against a dark unsettled sky.

The Ben was both a barometer and a point of contemplation for the staff of Flannery Park Secondary School who, burdened by changes to the curriculum and an increase in 'teachers' estimates', were frequently to be found, teacups in hand, brooding on the view of the distant peak as if it was a symbol of escape from the grind of professional responsibility.

It was not to enjoy the view, however, that Mr Pallant stuck his head around the staffroom door and enquired if he might enter. Only Mr Borland and Mr Abbott were present. They had been left over from an informal meeting of the Scottish Teachers' Association which had been convened by Bob Morrison during the mid-morning interval. The meeting had been brief and lacklustre and Bob had been disappointed that his tentative proposals for improvement in pay and conditions had met with no support.

Boris was at the window, scowling at Ben Lomond, cigarette hanging from his lip, whisky flask tucked out of sight in his pocket.

'May I?' said Mr Pallant.

'Please do.'

Hastily Jim plucked his coffee cup from the table before Mr Pallant could sniff its piquant bouquet. Mr Pallant did not, however, sit down. He remained by the door, hands clasped at his chest in a manner that would have seemed obsequious in a man without power.

'What,' he enquired, 'is happening to us?'

Boris said, 'Pardon?'

'Where have they gone, the pupils? More to the point – why?'

Jim glanced at the science master who, blowing out smoke, had already twigged what the old buffer was on about. Since Easter the fifth year had been decimated by a sudden exodus of promising pupils and Mr Pallant's programme of academic advancement had taken a severe knock.

Jim said, 'It's the closures, Headmaster. I'm afraid that the parents no longer feel able to keep their children on at school.'

'But it costs them nothing,' said Mr Pallant.

'It costs them a wage,' said Boris.

'I cannot believe that the pittance a child earns is more important than educational opportunity.'

Boris said, 'Every penny counts these days. An extra shilling a week might just be enough to stave off the arrival of the Sheriff's officer.'

'But there are only fifteen pupils at most whose fathers are, or were, employed at Ransome's or Morgan's. Why have the others left?'

'Panic,' Jim told him.

'Or foresight,' Boris added.

'I'm not sure I grasp your meaning.'

'Ransome's today,' Jim said. 'Brown's tomorrow, Fairfield's next week.'

'Surely not?'

Again Boris and Jim exchanged a glance. They were puzzled at the head's naïvety, by what seemed like wilful ignorance of what was going on in the world. Mr Pallant, however, caught the glance and interpreted its meaning correctly. Without rancour he said, 'Is that really it?'

'I'm afraid so, sir,' said Boris. 'If a boy or girl finds a job now, then they might be able to hang on to it if and when unemployment increases.'

'But what *can* they do?'

'What we educated them for,' said Boris. 'Work as porters or counterhands, try to find apprenticeships.'

'The wage-packet mentality.' Mr Pallant shook his head. 'I had no idea that we were dealing with such narrow-minded people. I thought Flannery Park would be a beacon of opportunity for them.'

'Read, write, count – the rest isn't opportunity, it's waste,' Boris said.

'Do you really believe that, Mr Borland?'

'Oh, no, no, no. I don't believe it. But it's poisoning the air we breathe, Mr Pallant, and we've only just caught a whiff of it here in Flannery Park.'

The headmaster brushed his silver hair with the flat of his hand as if the wind from the hills to the north had found a way into the staffroom.

'Is this true, Mr Abbott?'

'I'm afraid it is, Mr Pallant,' Jim said.

The old boy looked so white and stooped all of a sudden that Jim had to resist an urge to put a hand on his arm to support him. After a moment, though, Ronald Pallant gathered himself together and offered a handshake to each of the teachers in turn.

'My thanks to you, gentlemen,' he said and abruptly left the staffroom.

'Well, well, well,' Boris said. 'What d'you make of that, old son?'

'I can't imagine he doesn't know what's going on,' Jim said.

'Of course he knows what's going on,' Boris said. 'He just can't bring himself to believe it.'

'Can you?'

'Definitely.' Boris sighed, slipped the bottle from his pocket, uncorked it deftly and sucked a mouthful of whisky neat from the neck. 'McNeillage, McLeod, Deans, the Phillips girl, Brenda McColl, him with the glasses—'

'Lawrence.'

'Yes.' Boris drank again. 'B' Goad, you begin to wonder who'll be left come June, who we'll have left to present for the Higher Leaving.'

'Giffard and Burnside?' Jim suggested.

'If we're lucky.' Boris corked the bottle and returned it to his pocket. 'Panic in the ranks. Are they right or are they wrong, old son?'

'They're right,' Jim said.

'Agreed,' said Boris and went off to do his duty by the handful of troops who still remained standing in the teachers' line of fire.

Eddie's domestic cubby-hole became more cluttered and filthy with each passing week. Henry made a point of never going beyond the door of the caretaker's flat if he could possibly avoid it. Beer bottles, old newspapers, pots crusted with gristle, unwashed cups, clothing, bedding, mouse dirt and cockroaches were all bundled together and all emitted the ineffable smell of Eddie, not an old man's smell yet but with the same sour odour of decay that some elderly bachelors trailed with them in lieu of glory.

Morning, about eleven. Eddie dead to the world in a swaddle of soiled sheets and blankets.

'Eddie,' Henry said from the half open door. 'Shake a leg.'

'Wha' – who—?'

Eddie sat up. He looked shocked. His eyes were weepy, his hair matted. He wore an ink-stained shirt, holed stockings and a pair of long combinations. Though the cubby was lit by gelid light from the slanting window of the loft, he groped about as if it was still pitch dark.

'Me,' said Henry. 'I've come for my stuff.'

Eddie massaged his face with both fists, coughed, spat into a rag, and laughed. 'Aye, I thought you wouldn't be able to stay away for long.'

Henry leaned against the doorpost and watched Eddie struggle into consciousness. 'Eddie, you know fine I'm not comin' back.'

'I thought maybe she'd changed her mind.'

'Who?'

'She was talkin' about it. She was askin' me.'

Eddie swung his feet to the floor. He did not seem to have found focus yet, however, and addressed himself to the door in the far corner of the room behind which lurked a sink and a leaky water closet.

'Henry, where are ye?'

'Over here,' Henry told him. 'Was it Margaret Chancellor who enquired about me?'

'Two nights ago when she come wi' her copy.'

'How was it – her copy, I mean?'

'Rotten.'

'How are the sales, Eddie?'

'Up.'

'What?'

'It's the lay-offs, she says.' He staggered to his feet. 'She says we're preachin' the right gospel for the unemployed. She wants you back, Henry.'

'Too late,' Henry said. 'I'm gone for good.'

'Come on back.'

'Can't, Eddie.'

'Is this the partin' o' the ways then?'

Henry hesitated. He watched his oldest friend, his last

link with his boyhood, grope towards the water closet until he could bear it no longer.

'Eddie, I'll be in the office.'

'Okay, okay.'

The big printing machine seemed to have deteriorated and the floor around it was strewn with ink-soaked sheets and screwed-up paper. Henry liked to think that the *Banner* would become equally rusty, its voice hoarse and unintelligible now that he had gone. But his affection for Eddie and the cheap weekly newspaper would not allow him to wish failure upon either one.

He let himself into the office for the last time. He opened the first locker, removed the padlock and put it in his pocket then carefully took down the photographs: Trudi, Mam, and a young boy he hardly recognised now. He slipped each photograph into a separate brown envelope which he laid on top of the typewriter.

It was definitely time to get out, to move on. Even so he could not bring himself to strike out nostalgia, to cancel all his debts. He could not, however, wait around for Eddie's Golden Age to arrive. He had himself to think about, and Trudi, and Alison.

In the silence of the loft he heard Eddie retching and hawking.

'Eddie,' he shouted. 'Get in here.'

'Wha' for?'

'To carry my bloody boxes, of course,' Henry yelled and listened, chastened, as poor little Eddie Ruff scrambled to do his bidding.

Alison was not surprised when Brenda announced that she was leaving school to go to work in Bryce Walker's clothing factory.

Alison had heard tales of what went on in Greenthorn

Street, of the 'wild women' that Walker employed and how, at dinnertime, the cul-de-sac was no place for a tenderfoot apprentice to walk alone.

Complaints against the factory girls were legion. Petty thieving was rife. Even the carriers, a hard-nosed breed, were careful to lock away their valuables, literally as well as metaphorically, before they drove their vans into the loading bay. Policemen went in twos into the building and presented themselves to the termagant behind the reception desk with an air of humility that ran counter to the constabulary's usual arrogant attitude towards women. As often as not, the innocent constables were sent away with a flea in their ear and the conviction that what Bryce Walker was running down there was not a legitimate business but a bloody madhouse.

Clannishness and security more than compensated for the fiendish noise in the sewing shops, the skin-shrivelling atmosphere of Adhesives and the all-pervading stench from Rubber Pressings, for filthy toilets, rats in the skirting and a piecework wage no man would work for eight, ten, twelve hours a day until the eyes blurred, the arms ached and your backside felt as if it had been kicked by mules. Brenda didn't mind. None of the girls seemed to mind. You were young in Bryce Walker's. You were paid to work hard and earn good money. You did what you were paid to do or your place was taken at bench or table by some other young flower who, for a day or two, was teased and tormented to see if she was tough enough to survive.

In this raucous female environment Brenda thrived.

Stitching interminable lengths of binding tape on a small, powerful sewing-machine was nobody's notion of heaven but camaraderie and exuberant vulgarity almost made up for the drudgery, and at the week's end she had money in her pocket and new friends to help her spend it.

Ruby had to admit that her daughter had changed for the better. No more sulks, no more blue moods. It was all Ruby could do to keep up with her daughter's chatter, accounts of scandals major and minor, of practical jokes involving lavatory seats and stories of young males who had been barraged with unmentionable objects from Walker's side windows or trapped on the stairs between floors and humiliated.

It was not Ruby's idea of fun but she convinced herself that she had lost touch with the younger generation and had better pretend to be tolerant. Meanwhile, Brenda smoked openly, laughed at nothing, ate like a horse, slept like a log, and rushed off each morning with an energy and enthusiasm that Ruby could only envy. What went on in the evenings, though, Ruby had no idea. She did not quite trust Brenda to give truthful answers to her questions.

'Where were you tonight, dear?'

'Pictures.'

'Who with?'

'Doris.'

'Just Doris?'

'Some o' the other girls too.'

'Just girls?'

'Aye.'

'Have you got a boyfriend, Brenda?'

'*Boy*friend! God, who needs a *boy*friend!' Brenda would declare with such conviction that Ruby was deluded into believing that, for the time being, her darling daughter had no interest in the male sex at all.

Gerald Dante did not seem dismayed to find Henry waiting in the outer office of his city centre chambers that fine spring morning.

As he followed the lawyer into the high-ceilinged room that overlooked the sober pediments of the National Bank and the busy junction of St Vincent and Buchanan Streets Henry wondered if Mr Dante had seen so many weird and wonderful things in and out of the law courts that one shipyard worker floundering like a fish out of water was nothing much to write home about. Whatever the reason Dante was brisk but affable and Henry's nervousness diminished as he was shown to a chair and given an opportunity to take stock of his surroundings.

The office was everything that Henry had expected it to be, grand and tasteful, with only the drone of city centre traffic and the rattle of the tramcars below to disturb its air of calm. The carpet was like a football field, the bookcases glazed, the books themselves, all bound in identical half-calf, seemed to add a certain ponderous wisdom to the chap behind the desk.

In flannels and sports jacket, Henry was determined not to be intimidated by the lawyer's hand-stitched black three-piece, the fine gold chain that draped the vest or by a manner which suggested if not impatience at least a certain hurrying along.

'Smoke if you wish, Mr Burnside,' Gerald Dante said.

Henry kept his hands on his knees. 'I see you remember me. That's good.'

'Why is it good?'

'It's goin' to save a lot of long-winded explanation.'

'In what connection?'

'In connection with Mrs Coventry.'

'I thought as much.'

'Did you now,' said Henry, trying not to wriggle on the frail little chair which had no doubt been occupied by more illustrious backsides than his own over the years. 'Did you now, indeed, Mr Dante.'

'Come to the point, please.'

'Clive Coventry, your client—'

'I'm not at liberty to discuss my client's affairs, Mr Burnside.'

'No, I don't suppose you are,' said Henry. 'But are you at liberty to put a proposition to him?'

'You want to borrow money, is that it?'

'Nope.' Henry paused. 'Not exactly.'

'Money is, however, involved?'

'Naturally.'

'Does Trudi – does Mrs Coventry know you're here?'

'She'd be mad if she did,' Henry said.

'Mad?'

'Angry,' Henry said.

Gerald Dante placed his elbows on the desk which was really too large for a man of such small stature.

Henry said, 'They aren't divorced at all, are they?'

'Did Mrs Coventry tell you that?'

'Mrs Coventry didn't tell me anything,' Henry said. 'But I'm not daft.'

'Oh, I know that much.'

'He wants rid of her, doesn't he?' Henry pressed on. 'I expect it's got something to do with finance, though I don't know for sure, of course.'

Gerald Dante did not confirm or deny Henry's speculations.

'Tell him I'll take her off his hands once and for all,' Henry said, 'if that's what he really wants.'

'How, may I enquire, will you manage this feat?'

'I'll marry her.'

The lawyer smiled. 'She put you up to this, didn't she?'

'No, she did not.'

'What do you know about Trudi Coventry, Mr Burnside?'

'She's thirty-nine years old an' needs somebody to look after her.'

'I won't insult you by asking if you're in love with her.'

'I won't insult you by pretendin' that I am.'

'What do you know of her family, her background?'

'Very little,' Henry said. 'But I don't much care about any of that.'

'Oh, you should, you should.'

'I'm not marryin' her for her money, you know.'

Gerald Dante leaned forward. 'Let's cut the cackle, Burnside. What's your proposition?'

'Two hundred an' forty pounds a year, for five years.'

'Paid how?'

'Monthly, in cash.'

'Twenty pounds a calendar month,' said Gerald Dante with a hint of scorn. 'You don't rate yourself very highly do you? Trudi can run through that much in a single day.'

'Not now she can't,' Henry said. 'If she marries me she'll have to live within our means.'

'All of this presupposes that the lady will take *you* on.'

'She will.'

'Cocky, aren't you?' Dante said. 'Trudi is not exactly ugly nor does she have one foot in the grave. She might still have her pick of men, you know.'

'True,' Henry said. 'But it's me she wants, apparently.'

'Why, I wonder?'

'She knows me better than you do. She trusts me.'

'Twenty pounds, paid monthly, in cash?'

'I reckon she must be costin' Clive Coventry ten times that much.'

'You must not jump to conclusions,' Dante interrupted. 'Nor, if you take my advice, will you pretend to understand

242

matters that you know absolutely nothing about. There's a point at which naïvety loses its charm, and we're close to that point now, sir.'

Henry felt deflated. He had been – probably rightly – taken down a peg. He cleared his throat. 'All right, Mr Dante. But do we or do we not have the basis for a negotiation?'

'The basis? Bare bones, more like.'

'Will you present my proposition to your client?'

'Yes.'

'That's all I need to know for now,' Henry said. 'There is, however, one more thing.'

'Which is?'

'I need a job.' He had the satisfaction of seeing surprise on the lawyer's brow at last. 'To be more specific, I'd like to try my hand in the newspaper business. I do have some experience in that line.'

'You wrote copy for the *Banner*, yes.'

Henry grinned and wagged a forefinger at the lawyer. 'Well, well! Don't tell me old Coventry's already had me vetted?'

Cocking his head, Gerald Dante studied Henry intently for several seconds before he answered, 'Surely you didn't expect him to take you at face value?'

'How did I fare then? Did I match up to his expectations?'

'You'll do,' said Gerald Dante, 'in the absence of somebody better.'

'Well thanks.'

'You're welcome,' Gerald Dante said.

Bertie had been only dimly aware that his application to become an assistant in the Flannery Park branch of the Scottish Co-operative Wholesale Society would incorporate him into an organisation of such breadth and depth that every aspect of his character would be called into question. Until that time he had been, politically speaking, neither one thing nor another but suddenly he was obliged to profess faith in the Labour Movement and the principles of Federalism and to explain why he had chosen to leave the Post Office and work for a lesser wage behind a Co-op grocery counter.

Some funny things had been said about Bert Burnside down at the Sorting Office. But there had been no real scandal and the Area Manager had no choice but to provide the departing employee with a letter of reference and recommendation which, it seemed, was all that the Co-op management had been waiting for. Dates of departure and re-employment having been negotiated to the satisfaction of all parties, Mr Robert Burnside left the Post Office on the third Friday in April and took up employment in the Co-op's Shackleton Drive shop at half past eight o'clock the following Monday morning.

Nobody had a clue that Bertie was embarked on a new career until he stepped into the kitchen at a quarter to eight and, with his brand-new white apron folded across his arm, announced to Alison, Davy and the dog, 'I've changed my job. I'm goin' to work in the Co-op.'

Alex, who had ostensibly been asleep next door, yelled, '*What did you say?*' and came galloping through to the kitchen, clutching his pyjamas at groin and chest. '*Who's goin' to work at the Co-op?*'

'I am. I start in half an hour.'

Alison snatched the teapot out of her father's path as he leapt at his son and, pyjamas flapping, grabbed him by the shoulders.

'What about the Post Office?'

'Left on Friday.'

'You idiot! You clown! What did you do that for?'

'Because I wanted to.'

Leaning against the sink out of harm's way, Davy munched a bacon and egg sandwich and watched with interest and even Pete, back to the door, cocked his lugs and growled reprovingly.

'Is it more money?' Alex roared.

'Less. Better prospects, though.'

'Less money. God Almighty, son! Don't you know the state we're in here? Don't you know every penny counts?'

'You'll get your housekeepin' same as before.'

'Bertie, Bertie! You bloody idiot!'

'Which branch?' said Davy casually.

'Round the corner in Shackleton Drive.'

'Regular hours?' said Alison.

'Eight thirty to six, half day Tuesday, one Saturday a month off.'

'He's proud of himself. Look at him,' Alex shouted. 'He's actually bloody proud of himself. What am I goin t' tell Ruby?'

'Ruby?' Bert, Alison and Davy chorused in unison.

'The neighbours, I mean. They're all gonna wonder what you're doin' in the Co-op when you were well set in the – Here, did you get your books?'

'I did not get my books,' said Bertie, haughtily. 'And as for the neighbours – stuff them.'

Alex would have stayed longer to argue with his son but nature drove him towards the stairs and the lavatory. He rushed away, still yelling, 'Clown! Idiot! The Co-op, the bloody Co-op! Is that the best you could do?'

Bertie's complexion had paled to the colour of egg white but there was in him a defiance which made him seem more manly. Alison adjusted his tie and gave his hair a pat with the flat of her hand.

Bertie said, 'I suppose you're goin' to tell me off too.'

'Nope,' said Alison. 'What do you want for breakfast?'

'An egg.'

'Boiled or fried?'

'Boiled.'

'Why did you do it, Bertie?' she asked him soberly.

'I fancied it, that's all,' Bertie answered. 'Fair enough?'

'Fair enough,' said Alison and, glancing at Davy, shrugged.

Light spring rain had cleansed the pavements outside the row of shops that bridged the corner of Wingfield and Shackleton Avenues. Butcher and baker had already been open for an hour and the bow-fronted newsagent's, owned by Mrs Powfoot, had done almost half a day's business in coping with the early morning rush.

It was quiet now along the avenues, the privet hedges rinsed by rain and trees budding into leaf. Shop fronts and windows had been washed and the suds, sluiced towards the gutters, lingered as freckles of foam about the drains and as a faint, soapy fragrance in the still, expectant air. Bertie dropped his cigarette and trod on it. He licked his fingers and brushed his hair, nervously adjusted his glasses. He pressed the new white apron against his ribs, took a deep breath, and advanced towards the Co-op's broad front door.

The gate had been taken down and the young man, no more than seventeen, who served the Society as a shop-boy, was just about to carry it all the way around the block to the back store where it would be kept until evening. The gate, Bert would learn, was never carried through the shop. Once, two or three years ago, it had been dropped and had wrecked a display of marmalades and Manager Lockie's predecessor had never quite recovered from the shame of having to write off stock and had requested a transfer to

Bradford where nobody knew who he was. Mr Lockie, a tight-lipped little martinet, wasn't going to let it happen again; so the boy was ordered to haul the heavy gate right around the block, once every morning and once again at night.

The current boy was blond, broad-cheeked, muscular. In the bright April sunshine the very sight of him made Bertie's pulses race.

'Hullo, Gavin,' Bertie said softly.

'Hullo, Mr Burnside,' Gavin answered shyly and, for some reason which neither boy nor man could explain, blushed scarlet as a rose.

EIGHT

Relative Perspectives

If Henry had supposed that Clive Coventry would leap to accept his offer then he was doomed to disappointment.

Days turned into weeks, spring slipped towards summer and still no word came from the lawyer or his client. Life on the margin of prosperity was not all that Henry had anticipated. He was stuck with Trudi in a limbo of uncertainty and the fact that he could not get her to accept that circumstances had radically altered galled him almost as much as idleness and the days' dithering pace. He had installed the Underwood on a table in the butler's pantry and had tried to hack out an article or two, strictly for cash. But he was too conscious of Trudi's presence upstairs for the creative juices to flow freely. He also found that he had nothing he wished to write about, nothing that would fit the declamatory style that years with the *Banner* had imposed upon him. Besides, he still nurtured a suspicion that Trudi had money tucked away and that earning a crust might no longer be a matter of necessity.

Meanwhile, every Monday, he continued to draw the dole.

Now and then, while Trudi slept, he would sit by the bed in the half-light like a doctor brooding over a patient and wonder what secrets she had kept from him, what lies she had told and how, without force, he might unravel the truth. He knew every inch of her body. He was privy to every whim and nuance that her imagination could devise, yet she remained a mystery, a woman outwith history, a woman without a past.

Soon, though, he would have to introduce her to present realities and he was not at all sure how she would take to them. Bearing this in mind, Henry assumed command. He insisted that all meals were cooked and served in the kitchen. He would not allow Trudi downstairs in her dressing-gown and slippers. He imposed a structure on the day. From the moment he arrived about half past ten o'clock to the moment he left about eleven at night, he found something, however trivial, for her to do but when she begged him to stay overnight Henry always refused.

Each night he returned to Flannery Park to sleep beside his brother Jack in the upstairs bedroom at the back, for the family was *his* link with reality, *his* handhold on a lifestyle that wasn't entirely bizarre.

In late April, without Trudi's permission, he sold off her sable coat for a price below its market value.

When he told her what he had done, and put the banknotes down upon the kitchen table to show her that he was not a thief, she simply shrugged. Four days later he sold a bracelet and a small diamond ring. When he told her of that, she laughed and, later that evening, brought down a ruby necklace and a string of fine old pearls, neither of which he had seen before.

'We have to do this, Trude,' he told her. 'We need a nest egg.'

'I know it, Henry.'

He waited for her to ask him what would happen when everything was gone, when the last expensive trinket had been sold, the last pair of kidskin shoes pawned. It was as if the question did not need to be asked, as if Trudi had already guessed the answer.

'You will look after me,' she said.

And Henry nodded.

Holding her dressing-gown to her breasts, Ruby leaned from the kitchen window and called out, 'What on earth are you doin' down there?'

Alex stuck the spade in the ground and looked up.

'Diggin' your garden.'

'At this hour?'

'Best time o' the day, this.'

She was conscious of her frowsy state, without a trace of lipstick, her hair fluffed everyway which. The sun was still so low in the sky that the shadow of chimneypots and gables slanted across the back garden's tangle of weeds and young, not-quite annealed grass.

'Is that my lawn you're demolishin'?'

'Aye. Not much of a lawn anyway,' Alex answered. 'I'm plantin' vegetables. Leeks, carrots, cabbages, onions.'

'What for?'

'To eat,' Alex said.

From the bathroom Brenda, newly risen, yelled, 'Who is that?'

'Mr Burnside.'

'What's he want?'

'He's doin' the garden.'

'Are you payin' him?'

'No, I am not.'

Alex had resumed digging. He had gone about it methodically, marking off a section of the lawn with stakes and string and cutting out the turf that the Council had been at such pains to lay three summers ago. Ruby noticed with something bordering on alarm that he had already cleared litter from the back of the green and had made a pile of it, ready, no doubt, for a bonfire.

'Don't you dare light that, Alex Burnside,' she shouted. 'I've a washin' to hang out.' He waved a hand over his shoulder and stooped into the spade. She had, perhaps, herself to blame. She had chinned him about his laziness only yesterday, had given him the edge of her tongue about his inability to find work. This, she suspected, was his revenge. She opened her mouth to give him a piece of her mind for taking such diabolical liberties with her nice patch of grass – then thought better of it.

He had such a contented look to him, kitted out in old boots and a rough tweed waistcoat, trousers tied below the knee with hairy twine like a tinker or a farmer. He stooped, edged the spade under a turf, lifted it cleanly on the blade and added it, neat as ninepence, to the long, brown row. Beneath the window, draped on the coal-bunker lid, were his jacket and cap and three or four parcels of plants ready to stick into the ground.

Ruby blinked. The sunlight had not yet melted the breath of icy white dew from the grass in the shadows and she could smell the sharp odours of the earth and the first whiffs of chimneysmoke from the houses round about. Close to her ear the drain gurgled like a mill-stream as Brenda flushed the lavatory.

She released her hand from her throat and let the gown part just a little, not to tempt the man below but to feel that clear, spring warmth upon her flesh. 'You'll want your breakfast, I suppose.'

'Aye,' Alex answered.

'Half an hour?' she said. 'After I've got shot of Brenda.'

'Ideal,' he said, and without pausing slit the moist grass with his spade's edge and, grunting just a little, turned over another sod.

* * *

Walking the dog last thing at night was usually Davy's job. But Davy had come down with a hamstring strain mid-way through the second half of a football match against Duntocher Juniors and, like a true athlete, had entered a state of complete absorption with his injury. Presently he was ensconced, moaning and groaning, on his bed with the limb supported by cushions. Bertie and Dad were at home but Bertie, surprisingly, had volunteered to crank the mangle while his father boiled shirts as if they were tripe and, in the big tub, steeped the week's sheets in something that smelled like Lysol. Alison did not have the heart to interrupt them and, calling quietly to Pete, slipped out of the front door with the dog at her heels.

It was mild out. Pete made his territorial marks along the hedgerows without urgency and seemed content to toddle, sniffing here and there, as far as the shops and back again. It was after eleven, late for Alison, late for the good folk of Flannery Park, those in work and out of it, and in the quiet avenue she felt strangely contented. Critical exams were coming up and she should have been worried about them but she had confidence in herself now, thanks to Mr Abbott's support and encouragement. He had assured her that if she kept calm and tackled the questions methodically she would pass easily in all five subjects.

As she approached the gate of 162 she glanced towards the McColls' house – and stopped dead in her tracks.

Pete glanced round at her enquiringly but did not bark at the man who had merged into the shadow of the hedges. A half minute earlier and he would have been gone, a half minute later and Alison would have been indoors again. But she had seen him and, in the glimpse she'd had before he hid himself, had recognised him. With the dog tagging at her heels, she crossed Wingfield Drive to the McColls' house.

'You're out late, Walter,' she said. 'Been visiting?'

Upstairs, the curtain which covered the window of Ruby McColl's bedroom lifted and Alison glimpsed Brenda's pale, startled face before the curtain dropped again.

'I think she's waitin' to blow you a kiss,' Alison said.

Walter slunk from behind the hedge like a tomcat. He looked more disreputable than ever in a collarless shirt and baggy grey flannels, jacket over his arm. Head tilted back he stared sullenly down at Alison. His eyelid fluttered nervously. For once he had nothing to say, no cynical remark or glib explanation to offer. Pete sniffed at the young man's ankles and then padded back to Alison's side where he flopped full length upon the pavement.

Alison smiled. There was no venom in her. It was more of a relief than anything to realise that the arrogant Walter Burnside was not so smart after all. In fact he appeared so discomfited that it was all she could do not to laugh in his face.

'For God's sake stop smirkin',' Walter blurted out.

'Sorry.'

'It's none of your business, Alison.'

'How long's it been going on?'

'This is the first time.'

'Really!' Alison said. 'So I don't have to iron my party frock just yet?'

'Party frock?'

'For the wedding.'

'Very bloody funny.'

'It won't be so funny, Walter, if her mother finds out.'

'You wouldn't—'

'No, I won't tell her. What do you take me for?' Alison said.

He jerked his head back again. 'I don't know,' he said. 'I've never known how to take you.'

'I gather that's not a problem you have with Brenda.'

'Ah, shut up!'

She saw, to her astonishment, that his eyes were filled with tears. She turned her head away and stared at the pavement in acute embarrassment while he slashed at his face with his wrist.

'Walter, I didn't mean—'

'It should have been you,' he said. 'Damn it to hell, Alison Burnside, it should have been you.'

And then he was gone, loping away up Foxhill Crescent until the hedges blotted him from sight.

The daffodils had been a little past their best but from a distance their yellow ranks had given the slopes of the Kelvingrove a gay and festive appearance and had set off the red sandstone towers and mirror-like windows of the Art Gallery and Museum, which, Trudi had told him, reminded her of Paris. Behind the gallery, on Gilmorehill, the spire of the university soared into a spring sky blue as an opal, and Henry had talked of his sister and the family's plans for her future. They had taken tea out of doors at a stall by the bandstand and had crossed and recrossed the little iron bridges, strolling and chatting in perfect harmony until five o'clock when, arm in arm, they wended their way back to Astor Gardens only to find Clive Coventry waiting for them in the drawing-room.

'Hah!' he said, turning from the window. 'What a fine couple you make, you do indeed. I'm rather surprised, however, that I didn't find you wallowing in bed. What's wrong with you, Trudi? Are you losing your touch as well as your looks?'

'I think,' said Henry, 'that's quite enough of that.'

'Do you really? Is that what you think? Gallant as well as gauche, I see. Stupid too by the looks of him.' Clive Coventry tripped forward, holding a whisky glass at arm's length, and, before she could retreat, kissed Trudi on the cheek. 'You're withering, my dear.' He sauntered on towards the Jacobean cabinet where the liquor was kept. 'I can feel it in the texture of your skin. Seems this young stallion does not possess the fountain of eternal youth after all. What a dreadful shame! He *does* want to marry you, however, so perhaps that's some compensation. Is a husband more rejuvenating than a lover? A profound question to ponder and discuss.'

He turned his back, lifted an almost empty bottle of Glen Grant from the cabinet and prepared to refill his glass.

Henry said, 'Hoi, you?'

'Hmmm?'

'Ladies first, Mr Coventry, if you don't mind.'

Clive Coventry bowed. 'Why of course. Do excuse me. What would you like, Trudi? No schnapps, I'm afraid. And not a drop of cognac in the house either that I can see. You'll just have to rough it on gin, my dear.'

'I want nothing,' Trudi said.

'Well, that makes a change.' He held up the bottle. 'What about you, Burnside? What do you want?'

'Only your wife,' Henry said.

'My God! Repartee! What *are* the working classes coming to?' He splashed whisky into a clean glass and handed it to Henry as he prowled towards the window, talking all the while. 'There, however, you err. Trudi is *not* my wife. Trudi hasn't been my wife these past eighteen months. Why didn't you tell him, darling? It would have saved a great deal of misunderstanding.'

'Dante led me to believe—,' Henry began.

'Dante's a lawyer, for heaven's sake. Don't ever believe

what lawyers tell you. Even our Trudi knows that much. Don't you, darling?'

Still Trudi said nothing. She seemed mesmerised by the man and without removing her coat or hat eased backward on to the arm of the couch. Henry took a sip of whisky then carried the glass to the woman and forced it into her hand.

Clive Coventry was younger than Henry had expected him to be, not much more than Trudi's age, though beefy cheeks, hanging jowls and high colouring added to his years. He seemed almost swollen, like an over-stuffed sausage about to burst out of its skin. His coarse-crinkled sandy hair was beginning to recede from brow and crown and, Henry guessed, he would be bald before he was fifty. The voice was incongruously light and fluid and flowed on without pause as if he did not know how to control it.

'Did you know that you had become an item of trade, darling? Oh, yes. Your charming young friend's been trying his hand at barter. At first I thought it might be your idea. But, no. You're much more subtle than that. Besides which, even you could not have forgotten that we're actually officially divorced. Why, oh why, didn't you tell him, Trudi my love?'

'I did not wish to discuss the matter.'

'In case you scared him off? Take more than that to scare away this young turk, I can tell you.'

Henry said, 'All right, it was my error. I admit it.'

'Now, I suppose, you'll make a run for it?' Clive Coventry said.

'What makes you think that?' said Henry.

'Well, you're not going to get any money out of me.'

Trudi said, 'I have money, Henry. It is not much but—'

257

'Surely, you don't believe her?' said Clive Coventry.

'I believe,' said Henry, 'now you've sucked her dry you want rid of her.'

'She didn't tell you *that*, did she?'

'It doesn't matter what she told me,' Henry said. 'Fact is, you wouldn't be here today unless you reckoned there was profit in it. So why don't we sit down and engage in conversation about compensation and maintenance?'

'Dear God! You make it sound like an industrial accident.' Clive Coventry laughed. 'Which perhaps it is – or might be – for you.'

'Clive, please do not,' said Trudi.

The man gave a snort followed by another bleat of laughter. 'She hasn't told you *anything*, has she? You're buying a little piggie in a poke just because you think she's rich. My friend, she isn't rich. Doesn't have a penny to her name. The fancy clothes, the motorcars, the jewels? I paid for most of them after her papa met his just deserts. Have you told Henry about your papa, Trudi? Have you told him where your papa lays his head?'

'Listen,' said Henry, 'I don't care about—'

'For a start, she isn't Swiss. She's German.'

'Stop it, Clive, stop, stop, stop it.' Trudi covered her ears with her hands as if her gesture might prevent Henry from hearing the truth.

'I had to marry her to save her being arrested.'

'For what?'

'For profiteering.'

'*Clive*,' Trudi screamed.

Clive Coventry ignored her and continued. 'Her papa, a model citizen, refused to let a little inconvenience like a war prevent him from coining profit. Do you know where Papa Keller is now? In prison. Near Dresden. Yes, serving time, a very great deal of time.'

'If you knew all this,' said Henry, 'why did *you* marry her?'

The question drew Coventry up short. He frowned and swirled the dregs of whisky in his glass, unable to find a ready answer.

Trudi said, 'Because Clive was also a part of the fraud.'

'Uh-huh!' said Henry. 'And now you're back doin' business in Berlin. Must be a wee bit risky that, Mr Coventry.'

'No risk at all. New policies rule in the new Germany.'

'What are you doin' exactly?' Henry said. 'Financin' loans to Germany through an American intermediary?'

He could tell by Coventry's astonishment that his guess had been reasonably accurate.

Coventry said, 'What do you know about American loan systems?'

Henry said, 'Do you think shipyard workers don't know how to read? It's been plastered all over the *Telegraph*. I often wondered what sort of odd fish would get up to tricks like that. Now I know.'

'Nothing illegal, nothing against the law.'

'It's why you need cash, though, isn't it?' Henry said. 'It's why you're scraping the barrel for every penny you can muster. I shudder to think what the capital investment charges must be like.'

'More than you can imagine,' Clive Coventry said.

'More than you can afford?' said Henry. 'Could that be the reason you want to welch on your financial obligations to your ex-wife?'

'He married me,' said Trudi out of the blue, 'because he could not bear to live without me.'

'Is that true, Mr Coventry?' said Henry.

'Do you know what a succubus is?' Coventry asked.

'Aye, I've a fair idea.'

'You should have,' said Clive Coventry, 'since you're sleeping with one. She'll have your heart and soul, laddie, if you give her half a chance.'

'I'm still goin' to marry her,' Henry said. 'The only problem is what we're goin' to live on.'

'Do you honestly expect me to pay to be shot of her?'

'I don't see why not,' said Henry, 'particularly as this'll be an end of it. One flat payment or, if you like, a modest sum per month.'

'Or a job?'

'I reckoned you hadn't come here empty handed,' Henry said.

'I'm not, as you've guessed, liquid in cash right now,' Clive Coventry said, 'but I can pull a few strings to help you find work.'

'With Blackstock Press?'

Coventry nodded. 'Don't imagine you're going to meet the great man face to face or that he's going to promote you to some exalted position in the editorial department. You'll have to prove yourself first.'

'I'm pretty good at proving myself,' said Henry.

'Make an appointment with Gerald. He'll arrange for you to be interviewed at the *Mercury* offices. Provided you're sober and have some sort of written material with which to satisfy the editor then you'll be offered a position on the reporting staff.'

'Guaranteed?'

'Guaranteed,' said Clive Coventry. 'Now, what about your side of it? What will you offer me in return?'

Henry turned to face the woman. She held the whisky glass in one hand, the other raised to hide her face so that he could not tell whether she was crying tears of happiness or of sorrow.

'Trudi,' Henry said, 'will you marry me?'

260

'If that is what you want.'

'It's you I want, nothing else,' Henry said.

'Is that the truth?'

'Yes, that's the truth.'

'Then, please, I will marry you,' Trudi said.

'God help you both,' Clive Coventry said and, shaking his head ruefully, rummaged in the cabinet in search of another Scotch.

'I've never done this before, you know,' Ruby said.

'Then it's time you learned,' Alex told her.

'Since when did you become such an expert?'

'Used to play when I was a boy. Went with my father round to the Crammond Bowling Club. Carried the baskets for a ha'penny until I was old enough to get on the greens for myself.'

'Then I suppose you became a champion?'

'Naw, naw,' said Alex. 'Good but never great.'

Ruby did not feel quite herself in the flat-soled rubberised galoshes that had been supplied to her from the little kiosk that jutted from the side of the pavilion. She also felt reduced in scale by the acres of green grass, trees and bushes that comprised the Flannery Park Tenants' Association recreational facility. She also wished she'd put on a loose skirt or summer frock and not the tight donkey-brown thing with the broad leather belt which Brenda said made her look like a 'groucho', which she gathered was some sort of cowboy. She hadn't known, of course, what Alex had had in mind. She'd supposed they were going for a stroll, not an afternoon of sporting activity.

Alex had replaced his cap with something that looked like a bandana knotted at the corners and carried the heavy wicker basket of bowls under one arm as if it weighed nothing at all. To Ruby's surprise there were other women on the greens. She squinted at them apprehensively as she stepped down from the pebble path to the close-mown lawn.

Alex crouched, knees splayed, and removed the wooden bowls from the cradle one by one. He held up a small white ball, so heavy it might have been made of marble, and showed it to her.

'This is called a jack.'

'I know that much,' said Ruby.

'We roll this up the rink an' then we see who can get nearest—'

'Yes, yes, get on with it.'

He clunked the bowls together with the side of his foot, slung a pimpled rubber mat upon the grass and, jack in hand, surveyed the green with eagle eye. Ruby stood back a little, watching him enjoy himself. She had to admit that it was a lovely day and that the park was a pleasant place to be, full of what she, a tenement girl, took to be the smells of the countryside. Above the hedges, though, she could see scaffolding and the raw brick of more council houses in course of construction.

'Right,' Alex said. 'Here we go,' and with a slow and careful motion dipped to deliver the small white ball on to the grass.

Behind him a voice said, 'Well, if it's not Alex Burnside, makin' a hash of things as usual.'

'Sandy! Sandy Simpson. Man, this is a surprise.' Ignoring Ruby, Alex clambered over the edge of the rink and pumped the big man's hand warmly. 'What are you doin' here?'

'Takin' the air, just takin' the air.'

'Gentleman o' leisure?' Alex said.

'More's the pity.'

'Somethin' to be said for it, though,' Alex said.

'Aye but, it's frugal, too frugal.' The man had a lantern jaw and enormous walrus moustache. Glancing at Ruby, he asked, 'Is this your daughter then?'

'Hah-hah-hah!' Ruby raised an eyebrow at Alex's laughter. 'Naw, naw. She's a neighbour, that's all. I just brought her out for the afternoon,' which explanation, Ruby thought, made her sound like an old lady in a Bath chair.

'Well, this is Peggie, my wife.'

The astonishment in Alex's voice was palpable. '*This* is Peggie?'

'Who d'you think I'd be walkin' out with?' Sandy said.

For a reason which Ruby could not fathom Alex had become embarrassed by this meeting.

As she hadn't been invited to join the group on the path she fished a cigarette from the packet in her skirt pocket, lit it and, sitting on the grass bank, pretended to observe the run of bowls on an adjacent rink. Out of the corner of her eye, though, she studied the big man's wife, big too and so burly that she might have been his sister rather than his spouse. She had heavy, sagging features and an expression so dull that Ruby wondered if she was in fact in possession of all her mental faculties. Conversation between the three was limping and tedious. Workmates for a quarter of a century, the men were like strangers now, the woman dim and uncomprehending. With a certain sense of triumph Ruby realised that Alex wasn't ashamed of *her*, he was ashamed of *them*, and could not wait to be rid of them.

'Eh, goodbye then, missus,' the big man said at length.

Ruby raised a hand in half-hearted farewell.

A moment later Alex, shaking his head, seated himself by her and she took the cigarette from her lips and gave it to him.

He glanced at her, accepted the smoke and inhaled

deeply. 'Well, well, well! Who'd have thought she'd be like that,' he said, wistfully. 'Makes great dumplin' and bakes great scones too.'

'So you thought she'd be a glamour puss, did you?'

'Well – you know—'

He turned his head towards her, kissed her on the cheek and patted her knee as if it was she, not he, who deserved sympathy.

'What's that for?' Ruby said, not at all sharply.

'For not bein' like her,' said Alex.

'What are you after, Alex Burnside?'

'You know what I'm after.'

'A meal ticket?' Ruby said.

'A partner for life,' Alex said.

'Is that another proposal?'

'Nope, same one as before.'

She took the cigarette from his fingers and put it between her lips again. She got up and stood before him, brown skirt draped neatly over her thighs, broad leather belt cinched neatly over her stomach.

He squinted up at her. 'Well, Ruby, what d'you say?'

'I'll think about it,' she told him and plucking up the jack sent it trundling down the green to vanish, thudding, into the ditch beyond.

Taxi-cabs were an uncommon sight in Wingfield Drive. When he came home late from town Henry would usually have the taxi halt at the shops and would walk the short distance to the gate of 162. On that Sunday afternoon, however, the cab stopped at the Burnsides' front gate in full view of all the neighbours, and Henry, like some old-world chevalier, stepped out on to the pavement and offered his hand to a very elegant lady clad in black.

In clear spring sunshine the woman was graceful and

Henry looked more handsome than ever in a new double-breasted lounge suit and matching snap-brim hat. He handed the woman down from the cab as carefully as if she was made of porcelain then stood by while the taxi-man hefted out four or five suitcases and one huge cabin trunk and piled them by the garden gate. Money, a banknote, changed hands. The taxi-man touched his cap obsequiously and drove away again and Henry unlatched the little iron gate and, leaving the luggage where it was, ushered the lady on to the path. The arrival of the prodigal in such grand style did not, of course, go unnoticed by members of the Burnside family who happened to be at home.

Seated on Mrs Rooney's front doorstep Davy and Alison had been entertaining one of the young Rooneys with a toy that Davy had made, a monkey-like figure which hopped on the end of a wire or, powered by an elastic band, spun dizzily in mid-air. Mrs Rooney was indoors, lying down. She was pregnant again and had been having a difficult time of it. Her husband was in the garden at the back of the house keeping the younger children in his sights while he engaged in conversation with Alex Burnside who, in shirt sleeves, leaned on the shaft of a lawnmower and, Sunday or not, talked about mowing the lawn. Slouched in a deckchair in the shade of the brick-built outhouse Bertie appeared to be reading but had in fact been drowsing over the open book, his head full of odd dreams.

Henry had been missing for three days and nights but nobody had thought much of it. Before he had the gate open, however, before the lady had set her dainty foot on Burnside property, the gang came rushing through the narrow close to see what all the commotion was about.

Alison got to her feet and eased the Rooney boy behind her as if the woman in black might represent a threat to small children. The monkey-toy dangling in his fingers,

Davy rose too and took an uncertain pace towards his brother.

'The stuff at the gate, will you bring it in, Dave?' Henry said. 'Perhaps Bert will give you a hand.'

'Uh?'

'The cases – into the house,' said Henry. 'We're stayin', you see.'

Alex careered out of the close with Bert, blinking, behind him. 'Who's stayin', who's stayin'? Nobody's stayin' until I say so.'

'Trudi,' said Henry. 'My father.'

'I – eh – pleased to meet you, miss.'

The woman glanced at Henry then offered her hand to Alex who shook it humbly. 'I don't think I – eh – caught your name.'

'It is Burnside,' the woman said, smiling. 'Mrs Henry Burnside.'

'*What?*'

'My wife, Dad,' Henry said. 'I'd like you to meet my wife.'

Brenda came home early. She clattered up the stairs from the front door and flung herself into the living-room, shouting excitedly, 'Mam, Mam, where are you?'

'Kitchen.' Ruby was leaning morosely on the dresser, nursing a cup of strong tea and a cigarette.

Brenda said, 'Is it true? Is Henry Burnside married?'

'Where did you hear that?'

'Met Mrs Oliphant. She told me. Is it, you know, true?'

Ruby, teacup in hand, went past her daughter into the living-room.

'Yes.'

'Henry married! I can't believe it? What's she like? Is she glamorous?'

'She's—'

'What, what?'

'Old.'

'What d'you mean, old?' said Brenda. 'Older'n you?'

'God, yes. Forty if she's a day.'

'Have you seen her? Have you been over?'

'I did drop in, yes,' said Ruby, 'before I was aware they had company.'

'I'll bet,' said Brenda. 'So, what? Tell me.'

'She's Swiss,' said Ruby.

'An old Swiss tart,' said Brenda.

'No, she's no tart,' Ruby admitted. 'She's pretty enough, I suppose. God, but she's got boxes of clothes piled all over the place.'

Hugging herself with delight, Brenda squatted on the hearthrug by her mother's side. 'You mean she's *rich?* You mean Henry's found himself a rich old widow? Good for him.'

'If she's so rich,' said Ruby, 'why are they staying here?'

'Visitin'?'

'Staying,' said Ruby. 'Moved in indefinitely as far as I gather.'

'Wait a minute,' Brenda bounced on her heels, 'where's she goin' to sleep? I mean, her an' Henry, man an' wife.'

'It's all organised. They'll have the big front room upstairs. Davy an' Bert will have the back room. Jack will share a bed with Alex.'

'What about Alison?'

Ruby shook her head. 'I wasn't there long. To tell you the truth, Brenda, I wasn't made welcome.'

'I thought you an' him were gettin' on like a house on fire?'

'Well, blood's thicker than water apparently.'

Brenda sat back against the armchair's cushion, purring

267

with pleasure at the scandal that had descended on the Burnside household and at the fact that her mother's pursuit of Alex Burnside had been thwarted.

Ruby exhaled smoke. 'Know what she said to me, this woman?'

'Tell me.'

'She asked me where they kept the omelette pan.'

'What's that?' said Brenda.

'An omelette pan, for makin' omelettes.'

'Never heard of such a thing,' said Brenda.

'What does she think we are?' said Ruby. 'Omelettes for a man's dinner! By the look of her she's never been inside a kitchen in her life. She's got a funny wee voice,' Ruby went on, warming to the account, 'this squeaky wee voice and she puts her hands out like this, as if she was afraid to touch anythin' for fear of gettin' her fingers dirty. By God, if the Burnside boys are dependin' on her for their chuck they'll starve to death inside a fortnight.'

Brenda giggled. 'Did nobody know about her?'

'Nope. Married by special licence in the registry office on Friday.'

'Where's he been since then?' said Brenda. 'As if I couldn't guess.'

'Honeymoon.'

'Ooo-la-la!' said Brenda. 'Gay Paree, I suppose?'

'Edinburgh.'

'Did she tell you that?'

'No, I overheard,' said Ruby. 'Henry had some sort of business in Edinburgh. Funny sort of honeymoon, if you ask me.'

'Maybe they'll make up for it, you know, tonight.'

'Brenda!'

'What?' said Brenda innocently.

'Where have you been anyway?'

'Down at Vera's,' Brenda answered glibly. 'Don't worry, I've been fed.'

Ruby seemed quite unconcerned about supplying her daughter with nourishment. Distracted by her own thoughts she sat on the edge of the sofa, cup in hand, gnawing at her lip anxiously.

She hadn't told Brenda everything. She hadn't, for instance, told her just how impressed Alex Burnside had been with his brand-new daughter-in-law or how much the woman's winsome manner had enthralled him once he'd got over his shock. She also kept to herself the hurt she'd felt at being unceremoniously bundled out of the Burnsides' house as if she was nothing but another nosy neighbour. Black lace at the throat, diamond earrings, dainty manners and a pitiful little bat-squeak voice and it seemed you could wrap any man round your fingers, even if you were forty years old and fading like an old net curtain. Well, damn it, she wasn't going to take this foreign woman's intrusion lying down.

Hoisting herself to her feet Ruby scowled at Brenda who, lolling against the cushion, chuckled gleefully to herself.

'What's so funny?' Ruby snapped.

'The big front room.' Brenda shook her head. 'Right next door to Ally-Pally. She'll learn a thing or two tonight, I'll bet.'

'Shut your dirty mouth,' Ruby shouted and, angrier than Brenda had ever seen her, stalked into the kitchenette and slammed the door.

Trudi had much to learn about the ways of the working class but she was a more eager student than anyone in Wingfield Drive, or Foxhill Crescent for that matter, imagined. Within a month of her arrival she had imposed upon the Burnsides a practical, down-to-earth regime. Money earned from the sale of her jewellery was invested in a savings account which paid low-rate interest on a weekly basis. The sum, counted in shillings not pounds, was sufficient to top up Henry's dole which, as a married man, had been increased to twenty-four shillings a week. By charm and tact she had wheedled out of her father-in-law an exact account of the family's financial status and had set herself to plug the leaks that careless spending caused. In this respect, she was a harder taskmaster than Henry had ever been. Her arithmetic was precise and her method of reckoning so sound and honest that no one, not even Bertie, could fault it.

Five labelled, lidded sweetmeat jars appeared one afternoon upon the sideboard in the living-room. Glass washed clean of stickiness, labels printed in Trudi's neat Continental script, they stood in a row on a polished wooden surface stripped of the clutter of ornaments and domestic bric-à-brac. *Rent – Food – Fuel – Insurance – Clothing.* Within each jar a little heap of copper and silver coins had already been sealed to breed like mustard seed or rise like yeast in dough. Into each jar, Trudi insisted, all income must in future go. There was, of course, a rammy about it. Alex approved but Bertie did not. Davy and Jack were unsure. A squabble took place at the tea table while Trudi, smiling, served ragout of beef, buttered cabbage, new season potatoes, and kept herself apart from the debate. She had made a pudding out of rice and cream, spiced with cinnamon and topped with granulated chocolate, however, and by the time the boys got through this the heat had gone out of the argument, common sense had prevailed over misogyny – and Trudi had control of the economy.

'Very clever,' Henry said in a whisper, as he lay with his

wife in his arms beneath the bedclothes late that night. 'You really are very, very clever.'

'They are just men,' said Trudi.

'So am I,' said Henry. 'Are you twisting me round your finger too?'

'I do not twist,' said Trudi. 'They can see where wages go now, how it is their money is spent.'

'Tell me, who actually pays the bills?'

'Papa.'

'Papa,' Henry said. 'I can't get used to you calling him that.'

'Why not?'

'Because he's my old man. And you have a papa of your own whom I've never met an' probably never will.'

Trudi snuggled closer, flank to flank. Come bedtime there was no desire in her, no desire left in Henry, for she made a point of satisfying her husband during the quiet hours of the afternoon. It was all part of her plan to make him forget that she was a cuckoo in his nest, an alien creature in the tawdry upstairs bedroom with its dusty, comfortable history written small in objects that meant much to him but nothing whatsoever to her.

It was not Henry's past she wished to share but his present and his future. Here in suburban Glasgow she felt safe from harm. She had often told Henry that she loved him but would never admit just how much she needed him. She had told him, truthfully, that he was the best lover she had ever had. She had even revealed a little about her chequered past and the illegal dealings on the post-war currency market which had led her father into a prison cell and caused her to flee with Clive Coventry to this little haven in North Britain. Now, lying in a big, squeaky bed in a cramped room in a council house in a raw estate on Glasgow's outskirts Trudi felt safer than she had done in a decade, Henry's arms about her and his family below and around her, yeomen and sentinels who would protect Papa – her Papa – and keep his enemies at bay.

'Oh,' she murmured. 'You will. Perhaps. Some day.'

Head resting on Henry's chest, she listened to the blissful silence of the Park in which, at this hour, not even a dog barked or a child cried in the darkness and everything was peaceful, safe and peaceful and secure.

It did not take Bertie long to learn the ropes. He mastered the intricacies of Credit Book, Dividend Slip and Outside Order list in no time at all and found serving in the Co-op much less demanding than mail sorting.

Bertie could not understand why Gavin Fairbairn thought he was a genius or why, to the consternation of other assistants, Mr Lockie treated him with favour. He had a trim, sanded look which reminded Mr Lockie of scrubbed counters and polished floors. He was polite to all the customers, without being over-friendly and, for some reason, women took to him. Perhaps they recognised that Bertie Burnside wasn't going to give them the glad eye or embarrass them with chirpy patter while he weighed potatoes, counted oranges or filled in their 'divvy' slips with quick, flicking strokes of his little red pencil. He was, in all respects, the perfect Co-op grocer, a fact that Mr Lockie realised long before it occurred to Bertie.

What Mr Lockie did not realise, however, was that Bertie Burnside's calm, sanitised appearance hid a swarm of contradictions, that the pale blue eyes behind the rimless glasses swam with nameless longings and that much of Bertie's day was spent striving not to mope after a sixteen-year-old gate-and-delivery boy named Gavin.

Teabreaks, mid-morning and mid-afternoon, were capsules of joy and torment for Bertie; ten-minute moments when he would squat on a tea-chest in the cluttered back shop, sip tea, smoke a Rocky Mount cigarette, dote on his muscular, fair-haired hero and discuss the one and only thing he seemed to have in common with the boy, namely a passion for the pictures.

Gavin's four sisters, Bertie's new and alarming sister-in-law, the state of the nation were subjects never raised. It was as if boy and man had tacitly settled rules which forbade the exchange of intimacies and opinions. Conversationally Bert and Gavin adhered to a narrow middle way, fenced in by stars of the cinema, faces so universally famous and familiar that they had become surrogates for family and a safe source of gossip.

'John Loder?'

'Oh, aye. He's got a dog, did you know that?'

'I did. I did. What's its name again?'

'Tangy.'

'Terrier, isn't it?'

'Don't know much about dogs. It's not very big, though.'

'Do you like his moustache?'

'Love it.'

'Six feet three—'

'Fought with the cavalry.'

'What's your favourite John Loder picture then?'

'*The Doctor's Secret.*'

'Saw it. Great, it was.'

'Where d'you see it, Bertie?'

'The Astoria.'

'I saw it in the Rialto.'

'What were you doin' there?'

'Somebody took me.'

An awkward pause. The question 'Who?' trembled upon Bertie's lips but he did not dare ask it. He watched the boy

273

lift the dark blue enamel teapot from the ring of the gas stove and, hot though it was, support the base lightly with the tips of his fingers.

It was cool and brown in the back shop at half past three o'clock in the afternoon. The dank smell of the sink in the corner suggested something vaguely Eastern, like the courtyard in *Morocco* or the harem in *Kismet*, which Bertie had seen when he was younger than Gavin was now. He held the tin mug steady and impassively received into it a golden stream of tea. Gavin offered the sugar jar, the long spoon.

Bertie helped himself while the boy, standing close, bent over him.

Bertie racked his brains then, with studied casualness, enquired, 'Ever see *The Eagle* then?'

'Five times.'

'Valentino?'

'Yeah!'

Gavin returned to his seat on the tea-chest.

And they were off again, safe again, all summer long.

'Oh, it's you, is it?'

'Aye, me an' my watering can.'

'What do you expect me to do with it?'

'Fill it up, please, Ruby.'

She didn't move but defended the doorstep with hands on hips, legs braced. 'Not content with diggin' up half my lawn,' she said, 'now you're goin' to flood the place, I suppose.'

'It's the leeks,' said Alex. 'They demand a lot o' water this time o' year.'

'What about your own garden? Is it dug up too?'

''Course it is,' Alex said. 'You've seen it.'

'Not lately I haven't,' Ruby said. 'Not since *she* arrived.'

'That's your fault, not hers,' Alex said.

'My fault? My fault?'

'She'll make you very welcome any time you care to drop in.'

'I never see Alison or Davy either, these days.'

'You've been very kind to them, to all of us, in our time of need,' Alex reached in desperation for platitudes. 'But—'

'Don't *dare* say it.'

'Say what?'

'Whatever you were goin' to say.'

'Do I get a canful o' water or do I not?'

'I'm thinkin' about it,' Ruby said.

He shrugged. 'It's your garden, not mine.'

'Huh! I'm not sure what's mine an' what's yours any more.'

Alex laid the watering can down by the doorstep and, head cocked, studied her for a moment. 'I'm comin' in.'

'No, you are not.'

'Aye, but I am.'

He reached out suddenly and, to Ruby's amazement, put both hands about her waist, lifted her backward into the hallway, stepped inside and, with his heel, closed the door.

She struggled, not violently.

It was the first time he had touched her body. She was shaken by his strength, affected in more ways than one by his unexpected assertiveness.

She put her palms flat against his shoulders as if to thrust him away but did not complete the gesture. She felt his fingers grip her waist between skirt and blouse. Thank God she'd discarded her apron before she'd answered the doorbell. He lifted her as if she weighed no more than a packet of leeks, placed her above him on the first step of the stairs.

Still holding her firmly, Alex said, 'She's Henry's wife, not mine.'

'She's old enough to be his – his mother.'

'Now, now, don't exaggerate. She's not much older than you are.'

'You don't need me any more,' Ruby stated.

'Wrong.'

'Alex, it's only half past nine in the mornin'. What are you doin'?'

'Courtin'.'

'Alex—'

He pushed her back until she lost balance and she was forced to rely on his arms to support her. She stuck out a hand to protect herself from bruising but Mr Burnside was not about to let her fall. He supported her for an instant then gently laid her down upon the staircase.

The thin strips of carpet felt gritty on her elbows, the old floral wallpaper faintly greasy against her forearm. She could smell burnt toast from the kitchenette, earth from Alex's jacket.

It was years – years and years – since she had been caught off guard by any man, rendered so pliant and vulnerable. Speechless, she stared up at him as he gallantly whipped off his cap and flung it away.

'What are you—?'

'This,' he growled.

Stooping on all fours over her, he planted a smacker full on her unpainted lips. She could feel his chest under the old striped shirt, the heaviness of his thigh pressing against her stomach. He kissed her twice and then pulled back and stood up. She could see that he too had been affected by the intimate contact and somehow that appeased her. He looked down at her for a moment. She couldn't tell whether he was smiling, or grimacing with the discomfort of desire.

Then he coughed, held out his hand and hoisted her to her feet. For a man so shy of women, Ruby thought, Alex Burnside was doing all right for himself.

'Now do I get my can filled?' he said.

And Ruby, still speechless, nodded.

For the first week after Trudi's arrival Alison had sulked.

It had not been a Brenda-type sulk though, not sour-faced and snarly, rather a meek, introverted moodiness which Henry and Henry's new wife had probably misinterpreted as bashfulness. In fact Alison had been filled with resentment at her brother's secret marriage and had fought one of her accustomed battles – common sense matched against emotion – with the usual indecisive result. It was not that she disliked Trudi but the woman's age and queer foreign accent, to say nothing of her sophisticated manner, were off-putting. At first Alison could not help but condemn her brother for betraying his ideals and, as it were, marrying against nature. Alison had to admit, though, that the woman was helpful and not at all haughty and that if she, Trudi, had found life with the Burnsides strange she had rapidly fashioned a compromise between their habits and her wishes.

It was left to Bertie to put the questions that his brothers and sister were too shy to ask. Thanks to Bertie's bluntness they eventually learned how Trudi and Henry had first met and what had come of it. The lady's peculiar history was so foreign to the Clydesiders that it seemed intriguing but somehow unreal, like the plot of an Arlen novel or a Garbo film.

In spite of herself Alison was drawn to Trudi, helped on by the fact that Trudi seemed willing to treat her as an equal.

The pair soon became conspirators in the kitchen and

allies at the dining table as Trudi replaced frying and boiling with grilling and braising and began to add herbs and uncommon spices to soups and stews. Not only was Trudi skilled as a cook, she was also good with a needle and could iron a pleated garment in the wink of an eye. Only the washing of men's clothes seemed to defeat her for she lacked the strength to crank the big, ugly iron mangle for long and laundry was a task in which Alison took the lead over her sister-in-law.

While they worked Trudi would tell Alison tales of life in Paris and Berlin, of the beauties of Alpine meadows and the excitements of New York. In turn Alison would talk of schoolwork and of her ambition to become a doctor, an objective which had recently taken on a more definite shape and become identified with knowledge of anatomy and the body's functions in health and in disease.

'You are not afraid?' Trudi would ask.

'No, why should I be?' Alison would answer.

'There is so much, so much to learn.'

'Mr Abbott says I've to regard the human body as a machine.'

'It is not a mechanical,' Trudi would declare. 'It is a mystery.'

'Not to doctors, it isn't.'

'You have a boy?'

'What do you mean?'

'A close friend who is a boy?'

'No, I haven't time for boyfriends.'

'A boy would teach you that your body is not a mechanical.'

If Henry had broached the topic – not that he ever would – then Alison would have retreated in embarrassment. With Trudi, however, the subject seemed as natural as breathing. Alison, therefore, was tempted to confide in her sister-in-law, to enquire about the strange and most unmechanical feelings which had disturbed her at the time of her friendship with Walter. But, now that she had turned seventeen, she felt herself too mature for all that sweetheart nonsense.

Strong feelings were dangerous and were best left to impulsive folk like Brenda. The most vivid and satisfying emotions that Alison experienced happened when she sat down before an examination paper – French, algebra or chemistry; it didn't matter – took out her sharpened pencils, her wooden ruler and read the questions carefully, as Mr Abbott had taught her to do. As knowledge poured from one side of her brain to the other Alison would squander thirty or forty seconds thinking not of Brenda or of Trudi, not even of Walter Giffard who was slouched at a desk only feet away, but of Mr Abbott's clean-shaven features and a smile that was both stern and warm at one and the same time.

Mr Abbott had already presented her with her first medical textbook, a huge quarto volume, thick as a kirk Bible. Sturgeon and McNeish's *Atlas of Anatomy* was filled with coloured plates and engravings which proved too grisly for Alison's brothers to contemplate. Davy, who professed a lordly intelligence about 'legs', had flicked through the book then, swallowing, had sauntered off as if he had better things to do. Bertie, who stumbled unwittingly on a diagram of a penis, went quite white and instantly took to shouting the odds about his sister going morally to the dogs. Only Henry could bear to look at the plates for long. He would utter little *huh* sounds of surprise and prod curiously at his hip joint or trace the long line of a vein with his fingertips, murmuring to himself, 'I see, I see, I see,' and no doubt salting the information away to amaze his acquaintances at some future date.

The *Atlas* lay open upon Alison's dressing-table and while she dressed in the morning or combed her hair before bed she would study it and do her best to relate the exotic Latin terms to the rivers, deltas and broad blue canals which the human body – her body – contained.

'Mechanicals?'. When Trudi smiled, the sinews which protected the roots of her bronchial tree stood out beneath her skin. 'Our bodies are mysteries, Alison, mysteries to us all.'

Unconvinced, Alison would politely nod agreement and think again of Mr James Abbott – while May, in a froth of blossom, rushed into June and the school year drew to a close.

The *Glasgow Mercury*, flagship of Lord Blackstock's publishing empire in Scotland, was the only serious challenger to the *Glasgow Herald* in the west. Ever since Blackstock had purchased the old Magdalen Building in Maldive Square back in 1919 and had equipped it with the latest printing presses the circulation war had raged. Not for the *Mercury* the traditional smugness of Outram publications. His lordship made little of history. He could not challenge the *Herald*'s predominance in this respect. Instead he set out to claim the no-man's-land of contentious feature journalism, backed by sound local and national reporting and an ultra-efficient city desk.

Editor-in-chief John Marcus Harrison was briefed to seek out budding talent and collar it for the *Mercury*, a task less easy than it seemed since literary talent was not so thick upon the ground as certain 'guid folk' imagined it to be. Harrison had not only heard of young Henry Burnside but had read many of his pieces for the *Banner*. Consequently the telephone call from Gerald Dante came as a pleasant surprise.

Harrison immediately telephoned Margaret Chancellor and arranged a lunch *à deux* at Pegler's during the course of which he extracted from the woman a lopsided recommendation of Henry Burnside's character and unstinting praise for his industry and ability. So, even before the letter granting an interview was signed, Marcus Harrison was inclined to appoint the ambitious and opinionated young man to serve as assistant to James Brewster whose column of news and views was as close as the *Mercury* dared get to heresy and treason.

Marcus Harrison, like Dante, was small but unlike the lawyer he exuded robustness. He sported a reddish-brown moustache and hair which hung about his head in loose auburn curls. About the Magdalen Building he wore expensive silk-weave jackets and, unusually, shirts with soft roll collars. No matter whether he was stationed in his office on the fourth floor or roamed the iron catwalks of the machine-room, Marcus Harrison, with a perpetual twinkle in his eye, seemed at ease with his status and power and had a cheery word for everyone.

He rose at once from behind the great streamer of proofs that poured across his desk and was round the desk and shaking Henry's hand almost before Henry had entered the room.

'Sit yourself down, Mr Burnside.' Marcus Harrison kicked out a chair and pushed it into position with the sole of his shoe. 'I say, do you mind if I call you Henry?'

'No, sir, not at all.'

'I feel as if I'd known you for years – from your stuff in the *Banner*.'

'How did you know it was me? No byline was ever published.'

'Friends in low places, Henry,' the editor told him.

'What did you—' Henry shrugged self-deprecatingly.

'What did I think of it? Well, you wouldn't be sitting here if I didn't think it was adequate.'

'Adequate?'

'Oh, you can handle the English language fine,' Marcus Harrison told him, 'and you're undoubtedly well read in literature and history but I'm less enamoured of your paste and scissors approach to hard facts and figures.'

'Cribbed,' Henry admitted. 'You know that.'

'Of course I do.'

'The only method open to me,' Henry said. 'I hadn't time to research.'

'Then you should have written less – or not written at all.'

Henry let this sink in then said, 'Are you sayin' there's no place for me on the *Mercury*?'

'Now, now, lad, no need to be so prickly. I'm just warning you, as politely as I can, that I'm a stickler for accuracy. The quality above all others which I demand from my staff isn't loyalty but integrity. Personal integrity. Do you have it or do you not?'

'Is that a rhetorical question, sir?' Henry said. 'Because if it isn't, I can't give you an answer.'

'You could lie to me.'

Henry laughed. 'That would hardly be a sign of integrity, would it?'

'Why did you quit the *Banner*?'

'I wished to advance myself in journalism.'

'Now you *are* telling me a white one.'

Again Henry paused. 'Who've you been speaking to, sir? Jock Ormskirk or Mrs Chancellor?'

Marcus Harrison smiled jovially but did not answer. Instead he put another question. 'Where are you living these days, Henry?'

'In Flannery Park.'

'I was led to believe you were married?'

'I am.'

'And your wife is quite happy to live with your family?'

'For the time being,' said Henry. 'Do you know my wife, Mr Harrison?'

'Yes, I made her acquaintance some years ago when she was married to Clive Coventry.'

'I don't suppose she's changed much,' said Henry cagily.

'No, I don't suppose she has.' Marcus Harrison got to his feet. 'Shorthand?'

'No.'

'Better learn a system. Pitman's is as good as any. Meanwhile I'll start you in the "Diary". You'll be working under James Brewster in Features. He'll show you the ropes.'

'I was hoping I might train to be a political reporter,' Henry said.

'One step at a time, lad, one step at a time.'

'Yes,' said Henry. 'When do I begin?'

'Monday, ten a.m.'

Heat from Pressings had gradually filled the whole building so that by mid-afternoon, when the slanting rays of June sunshine struck the fanlight windows, the machinists were sweat-saturated and near to swoon. It was then, out of necessity, that the gaffer sent for Norman to see what could be done about breaking the crusts of rust and lint that held the fanlights fast and to let in a little air. Norman arrived post haste, brandishing a window pole. Scorching summer weather was a hazard that nobody had foreseen and the opening of windows became an act not of common humanity but of commercial necessity. Not even the most dedicated pieceworker could be expected to keep up her tally while being slowly boiled alive. Matters were exacerbated by the fact that Bryce Walker's had won an urgent

order from the Royal Artillery for gunners' aprons and
hoods and the girls were working flat out to meet delivery.

The machinists' tables were littered with bottles of Cola
and Ginger Beer. Pole tucked under one arm like a lance,
Norman swigged his way down the side aisle. He still wore
the green uniform and his small, gnarled face was brick red
and he drank, without permission, from one bottle after
another, until he reached the gable wall where he stopped
and, burping, stared up at the fanlights far above his head.

The machines had fallen silent. Gasping like stranded
fish, the girls watched expectantly, Brenda among them.

Norman hoisted the pole and stretched. The hook
reached less than halfway up the wall. He jumped,
stretching again, and the sound the iron made as it
scratched across the bricks set everyone's teeth on edge.

'Awww God, Norman! Get a bleedin' ladder, eh.'

'Come on, Norman, come on. Don't clabber about.'

'Give's some air, for God's sake. We're dyin' down
here.'

Smirking, Norman looked round at his audience. He put
the pole carefully on the floor and stripped off the jacket of
his tunic. In spite of his diminished size he was well muscled
and Brenda, who had been sagging listlessly over her table,
raised herself up, curiously. She was close to the wee man
and the silence in the long oven-like room excited her
strangely.

'Puddy,' Norman said.

'What?' Brenda said.

'Gimme a puddy, girl. You're strong enough.'

She was so dazed by heat that she did not understand at
first and would not have moved from her table if Norman
had not dragged her by the arm and mimed his instruction
angrily. 'Puddy, puddy, puddy.'

'Aye!' Light dawned, 'I see what you mean.'

It was the old over-the-wall game. She did better than Norman had asked of her, offering not laced fingers but her back. She braced both arms against the wall and pressed her head forward. Norman grabbed a handful of overall and scrambled, chuckling, on to her back.

Behind them somebody – Vera, perhaps – yelled, 'Puddy, puddy,' and the chant was taken up. Brenda felt boots upon her shoulders and tensed, teeth clenched, to take his weight. Sweat dripped from her brow and her breasts hung, seal-slippery, in her sagging overall.

'G'an, Bren-*da*, g'an yersel', hen,' Doris shouted.

Slowly, very slowly, Brenda raised herself into a standing position and hoisted the janitor towards the steam-pipes which protruded from the brickwork eight or ten feet above her head.

Cheering filled her ears. She was amazed at her own strength. The fatigue which had plagued her all afternoon vanished into manic self-assurance. She jerked Norman higher. He was wriggling now. She could feel the weight of him all down her spine. None of it mattered except the cheers, the approbation, the admiration of her peers. Norman snatched at the pipes, gripped them with one hand and swung free of her.

Brenda staggered. Stepping back she watched Norman swing like a gibbon and swarm on to the top of the pipes. He rested for a moment only then danced along the metal crosstrees that bridged the corner and brought himself to rest on a narrow ledge that ran beneath the fanlights.

As she watched Brenda felt a terrible pang of envy and annoyance that Norman should be the one empowered to be the centre of attention. Taut and tense, she watched the janitor struggle with the window catches and, perched monkey-like between pipe and ledge, wrestle with the crusted mechanism.

285

Brenda heard herself shout out, 'I know what you need, Naw-min.'

'Not now, dearie.'

'You need a hand.'

'Brenda, for God's sake—'

'You'll never get up there.'

'She might, she might. Let her try.'

'Take him a hammer.'

'Aye, an' a screwdriver.'

'Here, Brenda, here.'

'Puddy, puddy. Puddy, puddy. You yins len' a hand.'

Hands fastened eagerly upon her legs, her arms. They raised her triumphally above their heads, while she, blood singing in her ears, straightened her back and saw her small, plump fingers grope for and close about the steampipe. At first the effort was quite free of strain. She girded her overall about her with one hand, tucked it between her thighs, then hauled herself up until she could stand on top of the pipe.

Suddenly, though, the girls below seemed very far away, the great stained ceiling and iron rafters too close for comfort. To her right, crouched on the crosstrees, Norman was screaming at her to get down. She hesitated, alarmed less by his temper than his poise. Altered perspectives of tables, machines, girls, slicing sunlight across the rough brick wall made her dizzy and she felt ugly and isolated so far above the ground.

Nobody cheered now, nobody egged her on.

She had chosen this route to recognition and did not dare fall. She had just enough sense to face the wall and, toe to heel, slip off her shoes. She heard them clatter to the floor far, far below.

'*Get back, y'stupid bitch,*' Norman was yelling.

He looked more stupid than she did, crouched on a

painted rafter. She gave him a sickly grin, curled her toes over the pipe and inched towards the crosstrees. She could no longer recall what she was doing there. Purpose, like her shoes, had fallen away. But the very idea of trying to climb down again numbed her with fear.

Vera called, 'Bren, be careful.'

Doris shouted, 'Stay where y'are.'

The fit of exuberance had passed and, with her limbs growing tired and rigid, she realised that she was stuck.

Humiliated, she watched from the corner of her eyes as Norman swung towards her. But she was mad at him for some reason and when he reached out for her she struck him with her forearm. Suspended from one hand he swooped away from her as if his sinews had turned to rubber, swung away then back again, boots scraping to find purchase on the big steam-pipe.

She smacked him again, heard a cheer rise up from below and with her prestige restored gave a stiff wave of the hand to her admirers.

The cheering ceased abruptly. She glanced over her shoulder.

Mr Bryce Walker stood, glowering, in the doorway.

Norman swung towards her again. His boots did not reach the curve of the pipe. She saw his face sag in alarm. The little trickle of blood at his nostril released a single red droplet – and then he fell, legs kicking, arms flailing, on to the floor below.

As a fifth-former Alison was permitted to take an occasional afternoon off school and on Thursday accompanied Trudi on the bus to Clydebank. Alison had never had much interest in clothes and was quite taken aback by the intensity with which Trudi approached their expedition to the Co-op's new emporium.

Money accumulated in the Dividend Book had been carefully tallied and a list of necessities drawn up by each of the boys in turn. Alison could not work up much enthusiasm for the purchase of gents' stockings or light-weight drawers, new braces for Bertie and a plain bow-tie for Jack who, at the end of the week, would be leaving for a stint with Kenny's band in Rothesay's Winter Garden. Trudi, however, had a shopping list of her own to fill, a suit for Henry being the prime item upon it. It would have been more sensible for Henry to accompany them for a fitting but he balked at that chore, meekly put up with the indignity of being measured inch by inch, and left choice of cloth, shade and cut to his wife.

'Something for you Alison?' Trudi had asked. 'A summer dress, perhaps?' Although she could think of plenty of things that she would like, Alison shook her head and assured her sister-in-law that she was well enough supplied.

To Alison's surprise no sooner had they emerged from the gate of 162 than Trudi, done up to the nines, took her arm and drew her into an unexpected intimacy.

It was a beautiful summer's afternoon, the streets of Flannery Park surprisingly busy for a weekday, the streets of Clydebank even more so.

Throughout the bus journey Trudi chatted about Henry, his new job with the *Mercury* and her ambitions for his future in journalism. Somehow it had come as no great surprise to Alison to learn that her oldest brother had been a reporter for the *Banner*. Her only regret was that she had missed the opportunity to read his articles as they appeared.

The Co-operative Wholesale Society's building in Clydebank had the grandeur of a cathedral. Beyond its doors glass display cases were arranged floor by floor beneath an open dome-like rotunda. Carpeted, gleaming and redolent of the odours of cloth and polish it seemed a most unlikely sort of store for the Co-op to open in this impoverished burgh but – unemployment notwithstanding – the aisles and staircases were thronged with women and small children and, here and there, a furtive husband condemned by idleness to wander in his family's wake.

Trudi's grip on Alison's elbow tightened. She sniffed the atmosphere and glanced at plaster-headed mannequins draped in the latest, not-quite-up-to-date tea-gowns, at slender amputated legs clad in sheer silk stockings and hands fanned out to exhibit gloves. All around were showcases and cabinets, trays of rings and brooches, mirrored panels, curtained alcoves and assistants quiet as moths; a far cry, Alison thought, from Gall's or Hoey's in Partick where garments were purchased out of necessity in a flurry of financial anxiety.

'Do they have them like this in Berlin?' Alison whispered.

'Oh, no, no,' Trudi whispered back. 'Not even in Paris do they have them *quite* like *this*,' and, giving Alison a little tug, started eagerly towards the staircase.

Millinery, on the gallery of the first floor, was all hats, heads and chromium stands.

Aunts Belle and Marion were positioned by the inner rail. A young slightly harassed female assistant was in attendance. A strew of chapeaux covered the oakwood counter and in one large triptych mirror Aunt Belle's moon face was reflected from several different angles. The hat which clung to her greying hair was hardly the pride of the Co-op's Summer Collection, a tall, stiff straw cloche over-decorated with stitched braid and a dyed feather ornament which not even an almond-eyed beauty could have got away with in broad daylight. Auntie Belle, however, was apparently entranced by it. She preened before the mirrors, cocking her head this way and that, swanning like a queen.

If Belle had been alone it might have been possible to slip away unseen, to hide in Modes or Mantles. But Marion, who had been acting as an arbiter of taste for an hour or more, spotted Alison at once.

'Well, well, well!' she said. 'Fancy!'

'Hello.' Alison stepped hastily away from Trudi as if she might yet fool her aunts into supposing that she was alone. 'How are you? I've come for stockings for the boys. Day off from school. How's Gran?'

'Who's she?' said Marion just as Belle tacked from the mirror and bore down, beaming, on her niece.

'Like it?' Belle said. 'Think it suits me?'

'Lovely,' said Alison, all too aware that Trudi had joined her.

'Honest?' said Belle.

'Really, really lovely.'

'Who's she?' said Marion again.

The gloved hand floated past Alison's shoulder. She was obliged to give a little start and, as if she had only just discovered the identity of her companion, say aloud, 'Trudi, these are my aunts. Marion, Belle, my mother's sisters. This is – this is—'

'Henry's wife,' said Trudi.

'*Eh?*'

'I am zo pleazed to make your acquaintinz,' said Trudi mischievously, Swiss-Missing it like mad. '*Enchantée*, I am zure.'

'What did she say she was?' Belle demanded, the hat forgotten.

'Enchanted,' said Alison. 'Delighted.'

'Henry's *what*?' said Marion.

'Wife,' said Trudi. '*Madame* Burnside.'

'Oh my Goad!' Belle reeled backwards. 'Madam! Did y'hear that, Marion? She's a madam – an' she's married to our Henry.'

'He's not our Henry,' Marion snapped. 'Thank God.'

'He is my Henry now, *n'est-ce pas?*' said Trudi, smiling gently. 'So you are *my* aunteez too, no?'

'Trudi,' Alison murmured, 'stop it. They don't understand.'

'Don't understand? I'll say we understand,' Marion told her. 'When did all this happen?'

'Aye, what was Henry doin' in foreign parts?' Belle leaned her backside on the counter while the assistant cautiously removed the expensive straw cloche from her head, soothed it and put it back in its bandbox to recover. 'I mean, what was he doin' over there now the war's over?'

'Pull yourself together, Belle,' Marion said. 'Alison, why were we not invited to the wedding?'

'No vedding,' Trudi answered before Alison could dream up an excuse.

'They're not married. They're livin' in—'

'Wingfield Drive,' said Alison, 'with us. And they are married. Of course they're married.'

'You vish to see my betrothal ring.' Trudi peeled off her glove and extended her hand. 'Tree diamonds. The vedding band – just gold.'

'Trudi, please,' said Alison.

'Tree – three diamonds?' Belle said. 'I thought Henry was on the dole?'

'He is,' said Alison. 'I mean, he was. He starts work on Monday.'

'Where? Brown's?'

'On the staff of the *Mercury*, actually.'

'The pub?'

291

'The newspaper. Vorking for Lord Blackstock.'

'Are you kiddin' us on, Alison?'

'No, Aunt Marion. It's all true.'

'Why weren't we informed?' said Belle. 'Henry should've told us.'

They were indignant because the grapevine had died. Ransome's closure had deprived them of a prime source of gossip.

'Why should he tell you?' said Alison. 'You never tell us what's happenin' with your lot. For your information, it was a quiet wedding.'

'I'll bet.' Marion eyed the stranger up and down and witheringly enquired, 'When's the baby due?'

'Tvinz,' said Trudi without hesitation, 'for Christmas.'

'Twins! How do you tell it's—?'

'She's lyin', Belle. Can't you see? She's makin' fools of us.'

Trudi's exaggerated accents were abruptly discarded. The twiddling little-girl voice deepened. Alison felt the knot of embarrassment in her stomach slacken as she realised that her aunts could not stand up to Henry's wife any more than they had ever been able to stand up to Henry. She, Trudi, was not constrained by the need to feign civility. Trudi was slender, elegant, sophisticated and perfectly, perfectly calm. She said, 'I cannot do what nature has done before me.' She paused then added, 'If you wish to visit my home I will welcome you but if you do not, I do not think that we will meet each other again. Goodbye to you.'

'Alison – Ally—?'

'Come, Alison, we will take tea in the tearoom,' Trudi said, 'which is, I believe, upon the third floor.'

'Yes, Trudi,' Alison heard herself say. 'What a jolly good idea.'

* * *

Ruby had been on early shift. She got home about a quarter to six and to her surprise found Brenda curled up in a chair in the living-room, crying her eyes out. Before Ruby even had time to take off her hat and coat Brenda hurled herself out of the chair and flung herself into her mother's arms, wailing, 'Aw, Mummy, I've been sacked.'

Ruby felt a wave of relief and was tempted to blurt out, 'Is that all?' but Brenda's distress was too great to treat lightly. She clasped the girl to her bosom, comforted her for half a minute or so then said, 'Now, darling, take a big deep breath an' try to calm down. Bryce Walker's isn't the first company to go to the wall.'

'Wall? What d'you mean – wall?'

'To close down.'

'Bryce Walker's hasn't closed down. It's me. I've been sacked.'

'What? What for?'

Brenda pulled back. She was flushed rosy red, cheeks so wet that they might have been daubed with glycerine. She sniffed, rubbed her nose with the back of her hand, suddenly less grief-stricken than furtive, a change that Ruby was quick to detect.

'Horseplay,' Brenda declared. 'Horseplay's all it was. I mean how was I to know he'd come into the bloody machine-room. If I'd seen him I'd have come down right away.'

Ruby's anxiety returned. She caught Brenda's arm a split second before the girl could beat a retreat to the kitchen. 'What is all this, Brenda? You didn't get the boot just for larkin' about.'

'I did. I did. I swear to God I never had anythin' to do with Norman gettin' his leg broke.'

'Leg broke?'

293

'It's not that bad, really, just fractured.'

'Norman's the janitor, isn't he?' Ruby said. 'What were you doin' to Norman that ended with him getting his leg broke – broken.'

'He was tryin' to open the window. His pole wouldn't reach so I was, you know, givin' him a helpin' hand.'

Under Ruby's astute questioning the whole sorry story emerged piece by piece. Ruby could make little sense of her daughter's behaviour, yet she felt that somehow it was her fault that Brenda had become so wild and unruly, so generally silly. She chose anger over guilt, however, indignation over reprimand.

Brenda said, 'An' then Mr Walker marched me into his office an' told me I was a silly wee bitch an'—'

'Did he actually say that?'

'Aye – said I was no use to him an' I could collect my wages for the week an' be on my way out the door.'

'What did you say?'

'I never said anythin'.'

Ruby wrapped an arm protectively about her daughter's shoulders. 'Did you cry, Brenda? Did Mr Walker make you cry?'

'Aye.'

'Do you still want to work there, darling?'

'Aye.'

'Then,' Ruby snapped, 'leave Mr Bryce bloody Walker to me.'

In the privacy of the upstairs bedroom Trudi knelt on the carpet before her husband.

'Stand still, please.' Three round-headed pins bobbed on her under lip as she spoke. 'I will be as rapid as it is possible to save you discomfort.'

'Take your time,' Henry said, not meaning it.

He pretended to be patient but he had been in a restless mood for several days now and could not remain motionless while she fussed with the suit. He swayed from foot to foot and now and then brushed her silky hair with the palm of his hand, speculatively. It wasn't that he disapproved of Trudi's choice of material but vanity had come to the fore during fitting and he had asked her to take in the jacket a little and peg the trousers to match his interpretation of current male fashion.

Trudi had informed him of her meeting with the Gilfillans and had confessed that the exchange had been less than friendly. Henry had seemed totally unconcerned. He had laughed dismissively and told her she'd done the right thing to give the patronising cows the brush-off.

Trudi unfastened the bottom button of the jacket and tugged at the sleeves to adjust them for length. She had marked the stitching lines with pins and was enjoying herself. In spite of the racket from the boys downstairs she felt intimate with her husband and took additional pleasure from the good smell of brand-new cloth. She placed a pin neatly into the trouser cuff and said, 'It will wear hard, this stuff. You will see, before I am finished you will be the Beau Bummell of the newspaper offices.'

'Brummell,' Henry said. 'Beau Brummell. How well do you know Marcus Harrison?'

The question caught Trudi off guard. She had just enough sense not to lift her head. 'I do not know him,' she mumbled through the pins, 'or hardly so.'

'He seems to know you pretty well.'

'I dined with him once with Clive, years gone by.'

'Why didn't you mention it?'

'I had forgotten it.'

'He hasn't forgotten it.'

'I am not one to be forgotten, no?' She tried to make light of it but her back had become stiff, the carpet's pressure on her knees increased. She planted a pin at random, sat back on her heels and looked up at Henry for the first time since he had mentioned Harrison's name. 'I did not think it was important.'

'He's my editor. Isn't that important to you?'

'What did he tell you, Henry, about me?'

'It wasn't what he said, it was the way he said it.'

Below, the dog barked, Jack Burnside laughed, Davy's voice was heavy and urgent in the warm evening air. One of the children from next door screamed as if he was being slaughtered. Trudi glanced towards the window.

'They're only playing,' Henry said. 'How many other men haven't you told me about, Trudi?'

'Marcus Harrison was a – what do you call it? – a passing acquaintance.'

'How many?'

Spitting the last pin into her hand, she shot to her feet.

'Ten, twenty,' she told him. 'A hundred, a thousand. What is the matter, Henry? I did not have Marcus Harrison to be my lover, if that is your meaning.'

'How many lovers *have* you had? I'm going to be meeting a lot of important people – men – from here on in,' Henry said, 'and I'd just like to know how many of them have been before me.'

'Damn you!' Trudi cried and then, forcing herself to be calm, said, 'I have loved two men, just two.'

'That wasn't the question.'

'I do not care about your question,' Trudi said. 'This is what I tell you, because it is the truth. Before you, Henry, I love only one man.'

'Clive?'

'*Phah!*'

'Who then?'

'My papa.'

'Baloney!'

'Now there is only you, no other. There will be no other ever again. I will die loving you.'

'Don't say that.'

'Why, when it is the truth?' Trudi told him. 'If I do not have you to love me, I will die.'

Suddenly contrite, Henry put his arms about her and drew her to him. She could feel the material of the suit slide against his shoulder blades. She clung to him defiantly, wallowing in a strange surge of joy.

'I'm sorry, Trudi. I shouldn't have said those things.'

'Are you jealous, Henry?'

'Yeah,' he admitted. 'Yes, I'm green with it.'

'You have no need to be so.'

'No, but I can't help it. I shouldn't go diggin' up the past, I suppose.'

In the garden the dog yapped, the child shrieked again. Trudi could almost sense the supple energy of the young men, Henry's brothers, who romped uninhibitedly on the lawn behind the council house.

'Henry?'

'What?'

'I think you are beginning to be in love with me.'

'Unfortunately, I think I am,' Henry said ruefully. 'How about that, Trude? Isn't that a turn-up for the book?'

'Take me.'

'What? Now?'

'Yes, now.'

'With or without my new suit on?'

'With,' said Trudi and, giggling softly, pulled him down on top of her across the width of the bed.

* * *

'I assume,' Bryce Walker said, 'that you've come about your daughter?'

'You assume correct,' said Ruby.

'I'd every right to disemploy her, Mrs McColl. Under the terms of her contract—'

'Don't give me that rubbish,' Ruby said. 'Contract! Huh! It's not worth the paper it's written on. No union in the country would—'

'This, madam, is a non-union establishment.'

'Slave labour establishment, more like,' Ruby said. 'What I want to find out is exactly *why* she was sacked.'

'She disrupted production and,' Bryce Walker held up a hand to prevent another interruption, 'she caused a member of my staff to break his ankle.'

'I thought he fractured his leg?'

'Ankle is bad enough,' Bryce Walker said, 'particularly when the poor chap's already partially malformed.'

'I suppose you paid him off an' all?'

'As a matter of fact I'm paying him a modest sum in compensation until he's fit to return to work. Money out of my own pocket, too.'

'Aye, so the Health and Safety Inspectors won't come down on you.'

Bryce Walker hesitated. 'None of us wants that kind of trouble, do we?'

'You may not,' said Ruby, 'but it's no skin off my nose what sort of trouble you get into, Mr Walker. My daughter's carrying the can for your negligence. Because she's young, I suppose, and can't answer back.'

'Can't answer back?' Bryce Walker said scathingly. 'Good God, she nearly chewed my ears off.' He cocked his head and studied Ruby suspiciously. 'You're not here to finish the job, I hope.'

'I'm here to ask you to take her back.'

'Why should I?'

'Because, for some queer reason, she enjoys workin' in this dump.'

'Very persuasive, Mrs McColl, very persuasive indeed,' Bryce Walker said. 'Oh, yes. I can see where Brenda gets her fighting spirit. God knows how your husband puts up with the pair of you.'

'That's none of your business,' Ruby said and then, changing her mind, added, 'As it so happens I don't have a husband. He was killed in the war.'

'You brought the girl up on your own?'

'You needn't sound so surprised.'

He cocked his head in the other direction. Brown-suited and smooth, he looked, Ruby thought, like an owl. He was of an age with her and, by God, he was handsome. She understood now why the factory girls, Brenda among them, spoke of the boss with such awe and admiration. He had fine, regular features and a deeply tanned complexion that made her think of the film star Warner Baxter, except that Warner Baxter had more hair.

Bryce Walker cleared his throat. 'On a widow's pension?'

'Pardon?'

'Do you work, Mrs McColl?'

'Of course I work.'

'May I ask where?'

'Why? Are you thinkin' of offerin' me a job?'

'I would too,' Bryce Walker said, 'if I thought you'd take it. But you wouldn't want to work in a dump like this, would you?'

'I might,' said Ruby, 'for the right sort of inducement.'

'Where *do* you work?'

'The Argyll Hotel in Glasgow.'

'Receptionist?'

'Barmaid, if you must know,' Ruby said. 'Why all these funny questions, Mr Walker? What does my occupation have to do with Brenda and whether or not she gets her job back?'

'I've already decided to give Brenda her job back.'

'Have you?' Ruby was unable to hide her surprise.

'In actual fact,' Bryce Walker went on, 'if you'd been just a wee bit more patient, Mrs McColl, you'd have received a letter to that effect by first post tomorrow.' He lifted a manilla envelope from his desk and held it out to her. 'I signed it half an hour ago.'

'Aye, because you knew I was comin' to read the riot act.'

'Not so. Brenda's too good a worker to lose.'

'Then why did you sack her in the first place?'

'Young girls do need a bit of discipline.'

He stepped closer, offering the letter. Ruby did not back away and as she took the envelope from him she felt his hand against hers at the instant of transfer.

It was Ruby's turn to clear her throat. 'What exactly did Brenda do?'

'Climbed the wall at the end of the machinists' room.'

'I thought she fell off a ladder?'

'Is that what she told you? No, Mrs McColl, when I appeared on the scene Brenda was dangling from the heating pipes and in a right old state.'

'Showing her legs, I suppose?'

'I hardly noticed. I was only concerned with fetching her down unscathed.'

'Are you really goin' to take her back?'

'Of course.'

'I must say I'm surprised,' said Ruby.

'Agreeably so, I trust?'

'Agreeably so, yes.'

'See, I'm not the ogre they make me out to be.'

'No, Mr Walker, that you're not.'

'To prove just how civil I can be, Mrs McColl, I'll even offer you afternoon tea, if you'd care to join me.'

Ruby paused for a second, the tip of her tongue against her upper lip. She tapped the manilla envelope against her chin while the man waited, amused by her hesitation and, she felt, confident of its outcome.

'Thank you, Mr Walker,' Ruby said. 'That would be very nice.'

NINE

The Turning Point

All summer Alison waited for the Gilfillans to arrive, singly
or in a pack. To her surprise none of the clan turned up at
162 and not a word was heard from Gran herself. One brief
encounter with Trudi Coventry Burnside seemed to have
put the wind up the in-laws good and proper; or perhaps
they did not wish to acknowledge that Henry had risen
above them by attaining a position of some public
prominence.

Henry did not yet have a byline in the *Mercury*, of
course, and had so far written nothing that could be
remotely considered a scoop. True to character, he was
most unforthcoming about the celebrities he encountered
in the course of acquiring titbits for 'Brewster's Diary'. In
fact he seemed to spend most of his time grumbling about
his mentor, James 'Brew' Brewster who, it seemed, did
most of his research in bars and public houses. The salary
made it worth while, however, and with Davy earning a
man's wage now and Jack sending home an occasional
Postal Order from Rothesay household finances were in a
pretty healthy state.

Alison had also found summer work. She served in Mrs
Powfoot's newsagent's shop from seven a.m. to one p.m.
each weekday, temporary replacement for Mrs Powfoot's
daughter who had gone off to have a baby. The wage was

hardly more than a pittance but Alison did not mind. Now that Trudi had removed the burden of housekeeping from her shoulders Alison found life comfortably compartmentalised. She saw nothing of Walter Giffard and very little of Brenda but there were 'drop-in' visits from Mr Abbott to look forward to. He would enter the shop and loiter by the magazine racks until Alison was free then order cigarettes or a newspaper in cod-Latin.

'What's this?' Mr Abbott would say, peering down at a bottle of turpentine or a block of Highland toffee.

'Is that not what you asked for, sir?'

'Certainly not. What's wrong with you, girl? Don't you understand the Latin tongue? In my young days all the shop girls spoke fluent Latin.'

'Was that when Agricola was buildin' his wall, sir?'

'Enough cheek out of you. Twenty Player's and a *Financial Times*.'

'We don't keep the *Financial Times*, I'm afraid. I can recommend the *Glasgow Mercury*, though. It's very intellectual.'

'That rag! Oh, all right. Twenty gaspers and a *Mercury*.'

'Will that be all, sir?'

'Well, I *could* do with a smile to cheer me up.'

Alison would show her teeth in a cheesy grin and say, 'Howzat, Mr Abbott,' and Jim would nod and say. 'Still needs some practice,' then, with a wink, be on his way, leaving Alison with a strange urge to laugh at nothing and a warm little glow just below her breastbone.

August was almost gone and the commencement of Alison's last year at school was only six days away when Uncle Jimmie McIntosh, Belle's husband, turned up in Powfoot's shop. At first Alison did not recognise him. She had been thinking dreamily of other things, of Mr Abbott, who had gone on holiday, among them. She had just served

two small boys with penny caramels and old Mrs Russell
with a tuppenny bundle of kindling and a copy of *My
Weekly* when a voice hissed at her from across the counter.
'Ally? Ally Burnside?'

She glanced up. 'Yes?'

'It's me, your Uncle Jimmie.'

Although the afternoon was warm he wore a greasy
boilersuit and a woollen cap. His moustache glistened with
perspiration and he clenched a blackened clay pipe
between his teeth like a bone. She hadn't seen him for
almost a year or more and he seemed to have aged
considerably in that time for he, like several of the Gilfillan
clan, had recently been paid off.

'What can I do for you, Uncle Jimmie?'

'She's no' weel.'

'Who's not well? Aunt Belle?'

'Hur. Yur granny.'

'Is she in the hospital?'

'Naw, at hame.'

'I'm sorry to hear it,' Alison said. 'I'll let my father know.
He'll probably want to call in just to—'

'She wants tae see you, hen, naebody else frum
your side o' the family. She sent me fur tae tell ye,
special.'

'How serious is it?'

'I think she's deein'.'

Alison felt an unexpected shock. 'Oh!'

'You've tae come for a visit tae hur hoose on Sunday at
half two. Jist you, naebody else.'

'Sunday? Will that – I mean, will that be soon enough?'

'Ye ken what's she's like, hen. If she says she'll be there
on Sunday then she'll be there on Sunday.' He removed the
pipe from his mouth and looked round as if in search of
somewhere to spit. Finding no suitable spot he swallowed

the brown juice that flooded his mouth and replaced the pipe between his teeth again. 'Okay?'

'Okay,' said Alison. 'Tell Gran I –,' But her uncle, message delivered, was already halfway out the door.

It was a fine hazy day, not unlike the one on which Mavis had passed out of the world nearly a year ago now. Sometimes Alex felt that she had been gone for much longer than that. At other times, though, he almost expected to see her in the kitchen, plump and aproned, as if she had never been away at all.

Seated on the doorstep he contemplated the lawnmower which, for the first time that year, he had dismantled and oiled. The parts lay scattered on an old teacloth, bearings and cutters steely white, the rest smeared with a blue-black grease that Bertie had scrounged from one of the Co-op's van drivers and had brought home in a cocoa tin.

Ten minutes would reassemble the machine. But once that was done he would be committed to cutting the grass front and back, and the Rooneys' bit of lawn as well. As if to remind him of his promise the Rooneys' brand-new infant wailed with surprising volume for a wee lass who had arrived prematurely. He had had his first sight of the morsel just half an hour ago when Mrs Devine, Mrs Rooney's mother, had risked bringing the baby out into the sunshine to show her off.

In spite of the fact that she was a Roman Catholic Alex found Mrs Devine to be a pleasant person and was not averse to wasting a quarter of an hour in chat with her. That morning he had been obliged to admire the wrinkled, red-faced ball whom the Rooneys had decided to call Juliette and of whom Mrs Devine was so proud. He had even offered little Juliette his oil-stained pinkie by way of greeting and had been slightly mortified when she had gaped at him out of vague petrol-coloured eyes and had promptly vomited milk all over his hand.

The arrival of Juliette Rooney had, however, caused Alex to regard his daughter-in-law with renewed interest for it had just recently occurred to him that Trudi might be young enough to bear children. He tried to imagine what it would be like to have a third-generation Burnside galloping round the garden and wondered if the inconveniences of sharing a house with a baby would outweigh the pleasures of being a grandfather. Trudi had not been slow to pick up Alex's hints. She had wagged her thin finger at him and had told him in no uncertain terms that she had no intention of embracing motherhood again just to please him.

'Mother Nature might have somethin' to say about it,' Alex had reminded her.

'I am too old for Mother Nature to take interest in me.'

'Nah, you're not. You're in the prime of life, Trudi, the prime of life.'

When he studied her carefully, though, he realised that Trudi was probably right. She was too pale, too brittle to bear children safely, let alone tackle the exhausting business of rearing them.

At the sound of her shoe heels on the kitchen floor, Alex turned and glanced over his shoulder. The rustle of her skirts reminded him, curiously, of nurses and hospitals.

'Tea?' she asked.

Obediently he held out both hands and took the cup and saucer.

Trudi squinted over his head and said, 'What is wrong? Can you not put your machine back together?'

''Course I bloody can.'

'Why do you not do it? Why do you just look at it?'

''Cause I'm havin' a rest.'

'You have rested all morning.'

'Nothin' of the kind.'

'If you do not work you will become fat and indolent.'

'Talk English, woman,' he told her, though he knew perfectly well what 'indolent' meant.

Standing behind him, she pressed her knees against his shoulder blades, placed one hand on the crown of his head, leaned over and plucked the teaspoon from the saucer and stirred his tea with it, all without spilling a drop. 'I have to do this for you too,' she said, shaking the spoon to one side as if it was a thermometer. 'Do you see how lazy you have become? It is wrong for you, a vigorous man, to sit and to do nothing.'

'I'm not doin' nothin'. I'm just about to cut the grass.'

'Before the snow falls?'

'Aw, go away,' Alex said, 'an' g'i'es peace.'

She crouched beside him, balanced on her toes. He sipped tea and tried not to stare at her slender neck, the wisps of fine blonde hair that escaped from the edge of the silk scarf which she wore when she did housework. God, but Henry had fair fallen on his feet with this one, Alex thought, and experienced a guilty little tug of envy for his son. He did not feel about Trudi as he felt about Ruby, however, and the absence of masculine authority left him vulnerable to other aspects of femininity, ones about which he knew nothing.

Soft and sharp at one and the same time, Trudi said, 'You have not been to search for work for many weeks.'

'There's no point.'

'Jobs are not to be found, no?'

'Not for the likes of me.'

'Are you too old?'

'Nah, nah.'

'So – it is that you are incompetent?'

He tried to pretend that he did not know what that word meant either but he could not hide from her. He fashioned a little *tsk* with his tongue and shook his head. Trudi moved even closer, her skirt crushed against his thigh. She always had a cool, almost icy look to her but up close she exuded a dry warmth, like the heat from a gas oven.

'They work to keep you,' Trudi told him. 'Even Alison. You are the only one who does not do work.'

'Here, hold on a minute. I put my share into your damned jam jars. I don't blow my money on drink or anythin'. I bring home all my dole.'

'It is not a thing to make a boast about – dole!' Trudi spoke in a voice hardly above a whisper as if she was ashamed of him. 'You will not be able to depend upon them for ever. Do you wish Henry to become master of this house? If I were a man I would not allow such a thing to happen to me.'

'You don't understand. Riveters are ten a . . .'

'How can Alison keep her head held up as a student when it is known that her father does not have employment?'

'Ally's not bothered about things like that.'

'No?'

She had pushed him too far. His initial impulse was to leap to his feet and sidle away to hide in the close. But he could not be angry with Trudi. She was too delicate, too – different to treat roughly. No matter how much it riled him he could not deny that there was more than a grain of truth in what she said.

'Has Alison been sayin' things about me behind my back?'

'Alison does not complain. She is loyal to you, though you do not deserve that she should be.'

'She's a good girl, I'll grant you that.'

'Yet you do nothing for her?'

'I'm doin' the best I can, damn it.' He rounded on her at last. 'Jesus, Trudi, what more do you expect me to do?'

'Find work.' Mouth against his ear, she whispered, 'So you can be a man again – like Henry.'

It had been two years since last Alison had visited her grandmother's tenement in Olympia Street, Clydebank. She had forgotten how mean and sunless the canyon-like street could seem on Sunday afternoons. Views from the windows of Gran's room and kitchen were of tenement walls and the blank brick walls of Morgan's Engineering Works, now closed, or, if you crouched by the sink in the kitchen cum living-room, of one gigantic crane that hoisted its beak high over the housetops like a huge metallic pelican.

The close, however, was spotlessly clean, steps lined in white pipeclay, gas brackets polished, the big iron gate to the backcourt swabbed free of grime. Water closets and landing windows gleamed. Even the coconut mats that fronted each threshold had been beaten free of dust and had a neatness that was obedient, almost smug.

Alison had cycled down from Flannery Park and left the Raleigh leaning against the gate at the rear of the close. She'd told nobody of Uncle Jimmie's call or of her grandmother's illness. She had no good reason to be secretive; nor could she think why she had fished out an old floral-patterned frock, ankle socks and brown sandals to wear for the visit. She was no longer afraid of Granny Gilfillan or of her web of maternal relatives but she did not want to hear her grandmother subjected to her brothers' hamfisted wit and her father's sarcasm, not least when the old woman was ailing and perhaps close to death.

310

Alison climbed the stairs quickly. Once, not so long ago, she'd had to be dragged up the steps by her mother. Now she felt that she was doing the leading and, pausing, glanced back into the lattice of sunlight and pale shadows that filled the half-landing as if she expected to find her mother lagging behind her, puffing and anxious.

The door to Gran's flat was ajar. Alison pushed it open and stepped tentatively into the cramped hallway that separated the kitchen from the 'good' front room. The house had no strong odour, no staleness; a faint soapiness in the air was almost fragrant, like flowers. From behind the closed door of the kitchen came voices, murmuring soft as prayer.

Alison tapped upon the door and waited.

She was suddenly very nervous, afraid of what she might find, afraid of being a witness to the sad state to which age and illness had reduced her grandmother.

The door was opened by an elderly gentleman whom Alison had never seen before.

'You must be Alison,' he said, jovially. 'Please do come in.'

For someone who was reputed to be at death's door Granny Gilfillan seemed remarkably chipper. True, she was in bed, propped up by pillows, but her nightgown and bed-bonnet were so prettily trimmed with lace that Alison was reminded of one of those Tudor portraits that graced the pages of her history book. Alison placed the pasteboard tray of fruit she'd had made up at the greengrocer's on the quilt and examined her grandmother more closely.

'What are you starin' at?' Granny snapped.

'You don't look all that ill to me,' said Alison. 'I thought you were breathing your last.'

'Who told you that?'

'Uncle Jimmie.'

'Och, he was always one for exaggerating.'

'What does the doctor say's wrong with you?' Alison turned and enquired of the stranger. 'Are you a doctor, by any chance?'

'Not me, love.' He had a crisp accent that marked him as a Londoner. 'If I was a doctor I'd a had 'er put down ages back.'

'I hope you don't think me rude,' said Alison, 'but who are you?'

'My name's Nelson.'

'As in "Admiral"?'

'Got it in one, love.'

Granny Gilfillan reached for the pasteboard tray. 'What's all this?'

'Fruit, a present.'

'What do you take me for – a monkey?'

'Very nutrit-ious, fruit,' said Mr Nelson. 'Shall I peel yer a 'nana?'

'No, you will not.' Granny sniffed suspiciously at the peel of an orange before she pushed the tray away. 'What you can do, since you're in a coddlin' mood, is make us all tea.'

'I'll do it,' Alison volunteered.

'He can manage fine. He knows where everythin' is.'

Alison tried to hide her surprise. It was obvious that Mr Nelson and her grandmother were close friends, and yet she had never heard mention of the man before. She was bursting with questions but would not give her gran the satisfaction of refusing to answer them. She noticed, though, that Mr Nelson did not scurry to do her grandmother's bidding but remained seated on a kitchen chair, his arms folded, grinning. He was smartly dressed in a hacking jacket and corduroy trousers and wore a cotton scarf in the collar of his shirt instead of a tie. His complexion was on the pink side of ruddy, his silver hair still thick and his blue eyes showed no sign of fading although, Alison guessed, he was no more than a year or two younger than her grandmother.

There was something disconcerting in the way Mr Nelson looked at her, however, and she slid on to the side of Gran's bed and said softly, 'I'm sorry to see you like this, Granny.'

'Like what?'

'So ill.'

'It's the legs,' put in Mr Nelson, 'that's all it is. 'Er legs went and she thought she were a goner.'

'You just leave my legs alone,' Granny Gilfillan said, snappishly. 'My legs have nothin' to do with you.'

Mr Nelson chuckled again then, with a heave and a grunt, hoisted himself from the chair and toddled to the sink to fill the kettle and busy himself with tea-making.

'What's wrong with your legs, Gran?'

'Age.'

'Age and 'igh-button boots,' said Mr Nelson from the sink.

'Get on with your work, Bill.'

'I will, I will.'

'How long have you known Mr Nelson, Gran?'

'Since Trafalgar,' Mr Nelson interrupted again.

'Hold your tongue or I'll send you packin'.'

'Not now, you won't,' said Mr Nelson. 'Got no excuse now, have yer?'

Granny Gilfillan shot him a glare but it did not, Alison thought, have its usual hostile edge to it. She sat upright against the pillows and beckoned Alison to come closer.

'Now,' she said, 'you tell me all about Henry an' this queer wife he's found for himself. Is she really goin' to have a bairn at Christmas?'

Alison laughed. 'Is that why you asked me here today, to gossip?'

'No, it is not – but tell me, anyway.'

For the next ten minutes, while the kettle boiled and Mr Nelson set out the rose-patterned china, Alison answered her grandmother's questions about Henry and Trudi and the rest of the Burnside boys. For once the old woman did not greet each item of information with scorn but nodded almost approvingly at Alison's account of the improvements that the summer had brought. Now and then she would dart a sly glance at Mr Nelson to see if he had heard, as if to say, 'I told you so.'

When at last Gran's curiosity was satisfied, Mr Nelson was packed off into the hall while the old woman got herself out of bed and with Alison's help put on a dressing-gown, stockings and slippers. Alison was dismayed at her grandmother's fragility but did not try to dissuade her from taking tea at the table. With a cushion at her back and her back to the fire she seemed strong enough to nibble on a scone and sip tea from a cup held in both tiny hands. Mr Nelson was summoned back from exile in the hall.

'Did I not tell you, Bill, what a clever girl she was?'

A little rivulet of tea trickled unnoticed down Gran's chin and Mr Nelson gently dabbed it away with a clean pocket handkerchief. 'So you did. And so she is,' he said. 'Going to be a doctor too. I say, won't that be a turn-up for the book, havin' a doctor in the fambly.'

Alison was embarrassed by the tone of the conversation. She was terribly aware that both the old man and the old woman were addressing her with something approaching fondness and she could not understand why. She wondered if age had softened not only her grandmother's attitude but also her brain, wondered too at the nature of the relationship with the Englishman, so easy and casual that they might have been sister and brother, if not man and wife.

'What do you think then, Bill? Is she worth it?'

'Oh, I'd say she's worth it.'

'Worth what?' said Alison. 'I wish you wouldn't talk about me as if I wasn't here.'

'May as well give it to her now,' Granny Gilfillan said.

'May as well,' Mr Bill Nelson said affably, digging into the side pocket of his jacket and extracting a little roll of banknotes neatly bound with a rubber band. He put the roll on Alison's teaplate and nodded at it eagerly, almost as if he was offering her a titbit.

'Take it, love.'

'But – what is it?'

'It's a hundred pounds, dear,' Gran told her.

'But – what's it for?'

'To see you through your education,' said Mr Nelson.

'But – I don't need it.'

'Yes, you do,' the man told her. 'If you don't need it now you'll surefire need it later.'

'An' that might be too late for us to help,' Granny said.

Alison felt her throat thicken. It was all she could do to hold back sentimental tears. She was touched by the magnanimity of the gesture but more puzzled than ever by its source. 'I can't accept your money. I don't even know who you are.'

'Well, that's easily remedied,' said Mr Nelson.

Granny Gilfillan scowled and shook her head at him before he could say more. She said, 'It's my money. All I've got to leave you, Alison. Take it an' don't ask questions.'

'Where on earth did *you* get a hundred pounds?'

'Saved it,' Granny said, promptly. 'A penny here an' there put past for my old age.'

'Then you'd better hang on to it, surely,' said Alison.

'I doubt if it'll be of much use to me now,' Gran said. 'If

the girls knew I had savings they'd be at each other's throats, so it's best if you take it away.'

'Gran, are you really ill?'

'Good for another ten years,' said Mr Nelson, patting the back of the old woman's hand. 'Make that twenty.'

Granny Gilfillan said nothing.

'It isn't your money at all, Gran, is it? What's going on here?' Alison spoke out. 'Just exactly who are you, Mr Nelson?'

Sighing, Mr Nelson sat back. The smile had dwindled and he too looked very old now, the blue eyes clouded. He said, ' It don't matter where the money come from, love. Take it as your due. As for who I am – plain Bill Nelson will do. London born and bred.' He paused then went on. 'I served under sail from the time I were a lad, then I skippered the *Zeelander* for the Glasgow Trading Company. Five forty-nine thousand tons gross, she were, steel hull, triple-expansion engines. Refrigerated hold. Carried ore from Port Pirie, frozen beef from New South Wales, live beef from La Plata.' He leaned an elbow on the table, hand to his mouth. 'This ain't really what you want to hear, love, is it?'

Alison said, 'How long have you known my Gran?'

'Fifty years,' Granny Gilfillan answered.

'Nearer sixty,' said Mr Nelson. 'I was mate to 'er first husband. Him an' me was the best of friends – until he died of a sudden fever at sea fifty mile off Port St Vincent.'

'Donald's heart was never strong,' Granny said. 'We hadn't been wedded for long, just a year.'

'We bringed him back,' said Mr Nelson. 'Against the company rules it were but we bringed him back any roads for 'er to bury in Scotland.'

'I'll never forget that act of kindness,' Granny Gilfillan said. 'An' Bill's part in it.'

'So, you see how it is, love? Been friends these many, many year, 'er an' me. Good friends.'

Alison hesitated. 'If you – if you liked each other so much why didn't you get married?'

'Well, I 'ad a wife at the time, down in the Smoke,' Mr Nelson answered. 'Wife an' three kiddies. Mouths to feed. Precious little time ashore.'

Granny Gilfillan said suddenly, 'Take the hundred pounds, Alison. It's all I can give you by way of blessin'.'

'Best do as she says, love,' Mr Nelson advised.

'What'll I tell Dad?'

'Tell him it came from me.'

'He won't believe me.'

'Tell him nothin' then. Aye, that's the best plan. Don't say a word about it to any of them, not even Henry.'

'Put it in a bank,' said Mr Nelson. 'Lord, you could be a-drawin' about four bob a week in interest without a-touchin' the capital. Four bob could make the difference between eatin' regular an' not eatin' at all, ain't that so?'

Picking up the roll of notes Alison held them uncertainly in the palm of her hand. She glanced from her grandmother to the stranger who gave her a grin and a wink of encouragement. 'Make 'er ladyship 'appy,' he said, 'there's a good girl.'

'Thank you,' Alison said, thickly.

'Ye're not a-goin' to cry, are you?'

'No.'

'Have you got a safe pocket in that skimpy dress?' Granny said.

'Yes.'

'Put it away then an' say no more about it, not to your father nor your brothers. Nothin' about the money – or Mr Nelson either.'

'Thank you, thank you both, Mr Nelson.'

317

'Me? What 'ave I done?'

'I don't know,' Alison admitted. 'But I'll try not to let you down.'

'I'm sure you won't, clever girl like you,' Mr Nelson said and patted her fondly on the shoulder as he passed on his way to the sink.

Brenda hated the countryside. She hated the wide open spaces that lay beyond the bus terminus, hated the exuberant hedgerows and lowering trees that flanked the lanes beyond the rim of posh bungalows that marked the city's outer limits. Cattle frightened her, crows too, and sheep, bleating unseen behind the thorn, sounded to Brenda like tigers in a jungle. On top of all that, she had no idea where Walter was leading her, though she had a pretty fair notion what they would do when they got there.

The country lanes were not exactly deserted. Ramblers in big boots tramped past, yelling a hearty 'Grand day,' to the couple before they hoofed out of sight, heading for the hills. Young boys spilled over fences, looking startled and guilty, like poachers caught in the act. An old buffer in a grey vest and green shorts pumped past on a bicycle, rump in the air, nose almost touching the mudguard, his weatherbeaten calves knotted hard as briar root. Deeper into the great unknown, on what Walter called 'the bridle paths', Brenda was treated to the sight of folk on horseback – and after that there was nothing much but fields and farms and a few couples like themselves, girl and boy, seeking what Walter called 'a bucolic idyll' by which Brenda reckoned he meant somewhere to lie down and smooch.

She was by no means averse to smooching, to the passionate kissing and fumbling that she had enjoyed throughout the winter and spring. She could not, however, understand why Wattie was so set on dragging her halfway across Scotland on a Sunday afternoon to do what they could do much more comfortably in her living-room back home.

Walter sucked in a deep breath and raised his arms to his chest like a strongman showing off his muscles. 'Taste that air,' he said. 'Marvellous!'

'I'm tired. My feet hurt.'

'I thought you fancied a picnic?'

'I thought we were goin' to the park.'

'Well, we're not.'

'Wattie, where *are* we goin'?'

'It's not much further,' he told her and then, addressing himself to the willow herb and thistles that shrouded the narrow path, intoned, ' "I know a bank whereon the wild thyme grows." '

'Wild what?' said Brenda.

'Shakespeare,' Walter told her.

'What does Shakespeare have t' do with it?'

'He used to do this too on Sunday afternoons.'

'I'll bet he bloody never.'

'He did, you know. Nothing the Bard liked better than roamin' in the woods with a pretty girl.'

'Well,' said Brenda, somewhat mollified, 'I don't feel very pretty. I'm all hot an' sticky.'

'Good.'

'Good?'

'Hot an' sticky, that's how I like you.'

'Waaal-ter!' Brenda feigned outrage.

But a moment later she wrapped her arm about Walter's waist and followed him eagerly into the tangle of bracken, alder and scrub-oak which choked the wagon track from an abandoned quarry where no one, not even other lovers, would be likely to discover them and, for an hour or two, their privacy would be complete.

'Ooooo, that's better,' Brenda said. 'Cooler.'

'Don't,' Walter said.

'Don't what?'

'Undo your buttons like that.'

'You weren't so fussy ten minutes ago.'

'Somebody might see you.'

'Well, what if they do? I don't care.' Sitting up from the jacket which Walter had spread on the grass, however, she buttoned her blouse carefully and patted her chest. 'Better?'

Walter did not reply. He had turned his back on her again, had drawn up his knees almost to his chin, as if he was nursing pain. He peered over the trickle of water that passed by the name of the Quarry Burn and studied the shale that showed through the vegetation on the far bank of the streamlet. He had been locked in that position for ten or fifteen minutes while Brenda had sprawled drowsily on his jacket, forearm shading her eyes.

Wide awake now she stole towards him on hands and knees like a cat and rubbed herself against his spine. When he failed to respond she snaked her elbow around his neck and, pressing her breasts against him, mewed in his ear, 'What's wrong wiff 'ou den?'

'I'm fine, Brenda.'

'You don't sound fine.' She sat back on her heels. 'Come on, Wattie,' she wheedled, 'a penny for them?' He remained motionless, staring across the burn as if she, Brenda, did not exist. 'Hell's bells!' Brenda exploded. 'You're not still mopin' about *her*, are you? Wishin' it was *her* instead of me?'

'If you must know, I was thinkin' about my brother.'

'Your brother?'

'My brother Scott – he's comin' home.'

'When?'

'In two or three weeks.'

'Is he nice, your brother?'

'A charmer,' Walter answered.

'Nicer than you?'

'That's a matter of opinion.'

'Will I, you know, get to meet him?'

'Sure thing.' Walter administered a smile which made Brenda go weak at the knees. 'We'll have a party round at our house. Bring your friends, Vera an' Doris.'

'A party? Is it his birthday then?'

'He'll think it is,' said Walter.

'Good to see you again, Alison.'

'Good to see you, Mr Abbott. You've certainly caught the sun.'

'Cullen sands. Hotter than Morocco. Went swimming every day and played a lot of golf.'

'Golf? How can you play – I'm sorry.'

'No, no. It's a perfectly reasonable question.' He came out from behind the desk into the empty classroom and, with a swish, demonstrated his swing. 'See, no problem.' Her question had challenged him, though, and he rattled on. 'Tennis is a bit trickier. I have to toss the ball up off the strings of the racquet and –' embarrassed by his own enthusiasm, he paused – 'and hit it.' He cleared his throat, adjusted his tie and retreated behind the desk again. 'Anyway, enough about my sporting endeavours. How was your holiday? Did you manage a few days down the coast?'

'No.'

'Powfoot's all the time?'

'I'm afraid so,' said Alison.

'Hasn't your father found work yet?'

'Not yet.'

Jim said, 'I hope you haven't come to tell me you're leaving?'

'On the contrary,' Alison said. 'I'd like to ask your advice – and a favour.'

Jim perched on the edge of the desk. 'Fire away.'

From the pocket of her cardigan she brought out a small roll of banknotes and, apologetically, held it to him. 'It's a hundred pounds.'

'Earnings from Powfoot's? Surely not!'

Alison laughed. 'Hardly.'

Jim's post-holiday yearning to be back on Cullen sands vanished. He said, 'Where on earth did you get so much money?'

Alison hesitated then plunged into an explanation which involved an ailing grandmother and an elderly gentleman.

When she'd finished, Jim asked, 'Have you counted it?'

'Yes, it's exactly one hundred pounds.'

'Scottish or English banknotes?'

'English.'

Jim inched towards the edge of the desk.

He said, 'What did your father have to say about it?'

Alison flushed. 'I haven't told him. I haven't told anyone except you, Mr Abbott. I'm not sure I should – tell my family, I mean.'

'Why ever not?'

'I don't want to start a row, not when things are settling down again.' She looked at the floor. 'I mean what if this Englishman's really a relative?'

'I think you're jumping to conclusions.'

'I mean, if he isn't a relative why would he give me money?'

'As a favour to your grandmother, perhaps.'

322

'She's known him for years, years before she married my grandfather, apparently.'

'Do you remember your grandfather?'

'No, he died soon after I was born.'

'What did he do?'

'Worked in Morgan's, I think.'

'I see.' Jim stroked his chin thoughtfully. 'Does it shock you that your grandmother might have had a close friend when she was young?'

'I can't imagine her young.'

'No, I don't suppose you can.'

'I didn't think it was like that in those days. I always thought things were very straitlaced and – well – moral.'

'Don't you believe it,' Jim Abbott said.

'Candidly,' said Alison, 'I'm more worried about what to do with the cash than about things that may have happened before I was born.'

'Is that the favour?'

'Yes, I'd like you to take care of it for me.'

'Why me? Why not your brother Henry? From what you've told me he's very trustworthy.'

'I'd rather you took it,' Alison said. 'Perhaps you could put it into an account in my name, let it accumulate interest.'

'I'm not sure this is a good idea, Alison. What if your grandmother mentions it to some member of the family?'

'She won't.'

'How can you be certain?'

'Because if she did then she'd have to explain who Mr Nelson is and why he gave me money,' Alison said. 'I think I prefer to leave that skeleton in the closet – if it is a skeleton. After all, I might be barkin' up the wrong tree.'

'You might,' Jim agreed. 'In fact, you probably are.'

She was almost as tall as he was now, balanced on those

long coltish legs. Her hair was shiny in the sunlight, her eyes solemn.

Jim said, 'Setting aside the matter of where the money came from, it was your grandmother who gave it to you. Why do you think she did that?'

'To help me through university.'

'I thought she was dead against education for girls.'

'Apparently not,' Alison said. 'Perhaps she just wants me to be less dependent on Dad and the boys. That would be typical of her, really.'

'Is that one of your objectives too, Alison – to be independent?'

'I just want to graduate with a medical degree.'

The babble of infants released into the playground rose from outside the window. At any moment the mid-morning bell would ring, Jim's single free period would be over and he would be obliged to organise himself for 3B's first lesson of the term.

'That sounds a bit glib to me,' Jim said.

'It wasn't meant to.' Alison glanced towards the door as the bell jangled. 'Thanks for listening to me, Mr Abbott.' She turned to leave.

'Wait.' He said, 'I'll do as you ask, Alison.'

'Are you sure? I don't want to put you on the spot.'

'I think I'm already on the spot,' Jim said. 'Come on, hand over the dough. I'll obtain a form for you to sign from the bank and a deposit book. Before you know it you'll be a woman of means.' He took the little wad of banknotes from her hand, put it directly into his watch pocket and buttoned it up safe and snug. 'We'll attend to the transaction when you come to my house on Wednesday evening.'

'What for?'

'Tuition, of course.'

'I thought we were finished with that.'

'Heck, no,' Jim said, 'we're only just starting.'

'On what?'

'Your education,' Jim informed her brusquely but he could tell by her expression that Miss Alison Burnside was no longer deceived.

September: it was growing dark early now and already the night sounds of the city had taken on a wintry tone. The last of the burgh fairs was over and commercial Glasgow had recovered its equilibrium and was battening down the hatches for a difficult year ahead. The Argyll Hotel had been quiet all summer. Bar takings were down, rooms remained empty. Agents and reps had lost their optimism and bottomless thirsts and would sit po-faced in dark corners nursing a half pint of bitter or a single dram of whisky all evening long.

Ruby was glad of the man's company between eight and nine. He was handsome, humorous and an extravagant tipper, even though he now regarded himself as more friend than customer. She rather missed him at weekends. He always went home at weekends. It seemed peculiar to Ruby that he didn't go home every night, for Helensburgh was only thirty miles down river from the factory in Greenthorn Street and his motorcar, so he'd told her, could do eighty miles an hour without putting the foot down.

'I really don't know why you hang around this place,' Ruby would say as she replenished his glass of Glen Grant. 'Do they not serve whisky in Helensburgh, or what?'

'My wife doesn't like me drinking,' Bryce Walker would answer. 'She's a wonderful housekeeper, a devoted mother, a pillar of the kirk but she just doesn't know what a man needs. Either that or she's forgotten.'

'I'm not surprised she's forgotten, since you seem to spend half your leisure time here and the rest of it sailin' in your boat.'

Ruby polished glasses, dabbed at spillage with a cloth and wondered what Brenda would say if she happened to walk in and find her boss perched on the bar stool, drinking, smoking and chatting up her mother.

'I'd love to take you sailing, Ruby,' Bryce Walker said. 'How would you like to sail away with me for the weekend sometime, hm?'

'I've told you before, I'm not that kind of girl.'

'What kind of girl?'

'Come off it!'

'Imagine, you and me alone on a desert island.'

'While your business went to pot, uh-huh, an' your wife sued you for divorce.'

'Margaret would never dream of divorcing me. She knows when she's well off – too bloody well off.'

'Anyway, why are you botherin' with me when you've a factory full of young things dyin' to give their all, no questions asked?'

'No questions asked? Don't you believe it,' Bryce Walker said. 'If I laid a finger on any of those sweet young things I'd be payin' through the nose for the rest of my natural. Discretion isn't a word they happen to understand.' He paused, sipped whisky. 'Besides, most of 'em look like the hind end of Slattery's donkey.'

'Dare I remind you that my daughter—'

'Of course I didn't mean Brenda.'

'No? What makes her different?'

'She's the fruit of your loins,' Bryce Walker said.

'Is that supposed to be a compliment?'

'Thus intended, Ruby, thus intended.'

'Know what? I think you're a snob, Mr Walker.'

'Defin-itely. I admit it – if being a snob means having taste and discernment when it comes to selecting a lady companion.'

In the shadows of the bar he looked more like Warner Baxter than ever. Square brown hands were clasped loosely upon the counter, a white cigarette, birling smoke, raked between his fingers.

Ruby could just imagine him in a yellow oilskin – own manufacture, of course – lashed to the wheel of a schooner, ploughing through a hurricane to rescue her from natives on a South Sea island. She wouldn't really mind being rescued by Bryce Walker, come to think of it, and surrendering, as they put it in *Lucky Star*, to his ardent embrace.

Patience seemed to be his middle name, though. He did not press for a meeting outside the Argyll and seemed content to drink whisky and drop risqué hints for an hour or two, two or three evenings a week. Naturally, Ruby said nothing to Brenda about her friendship with Bryce Walker. In any case the relationship had no future since Mr Walker was irrevocably, if not happily, married.

On Tuesday evening Bryce Walker dropped in early. He seemed less relaxed and cocksure than usual. He drank two quick whiskies and, hunched over the bar, spoke to Ruby of his wife. Margaret Walker, it seemed, was a member of a narrow religious sect and had inculcated his daughters, Jill and Sally, in the same beliefs and turned them against him. He was treated like a leper in his own house and was very lonely because of it. Ruby was not taken in. She had heard similar tales of woe from other men. He was only pleading for sympathy. She made appropriate noises, however, stood him a third whisky out of her own pocket and was relieved when, about eight o'clock, he left of his own accord.

She thought she had seen the last of him, at least for that evening, but she was mistaken.

Ruby left the Argyll at five minutes to eleven and, coat collar pulled up, heels clipping on the cold pavement, headed for the tram stop at the top end of Renfield Street. When the motorcar – shiny red, long bonnet, black hood – roared up alongside her and squealed to a halt Ruby almost died of fright. She would have taken to her heels and run if she hadn't recognised the driver's voice a moment before she saw his face.

'Ruby. Hop in.' Bryce Walker unlocked the passenger door from the inside. 'I'll drive you home.'

'No.' Ruby's heart pounded. 'I don't think I should.'

'I need to talk to someone, to you. Please, get in.'

She hesitated and then awkwardly clambered into the motorcar, swinging her legs over the high sill. She tucked her coat and skirt firmly about her and, following Bryce Walker's instruction, slammed the passenger door. The man said nothing until the car was in motion. Tram stops and familiar buildings whisked away behind them and, as he fisted the wheel, Ruby grabbed at the dashboard with both hands and, not without a certain ire, said, 'Well, what is it you want to say, Mr Walker?'

'Bryce. You really must call me Bryce.'

'I appreciate the ride – Bryce, but—'

'I'm thinking of asking my wife for a divorce.'

'What?'

'Been mulling it over for weeks. Ever since the day you stepped into my office, matter of fact.'

'Whoa, now, whoa,' said Ruby. 'I hope you're not blamin' me for your marriage going on the rocks.'

'No, not blaming you. But you're the cause, like it or not.' Bryce Walker took a hand from the steering wheel and placed it lightly on her knee. 'Only when I met you did it strike me what I'd been missing all these years. What a void, what an ache of emptiness there was in my life. I need you, Ruby. I really and truly do.'

'What is this?' Ruby said. 'I think you'd better let me out at the next corner, Mr Walker – Bryce.'

'Certainly not,' he said. 'Now I've got you I intend to keep you.'

She opened her lips to protest but could not think what to say. Her mind was clear and she understood perfectly what his intentions were. Talk of divorce was a smokescreen. She'd heard *that* one often enough before. She could not help but retain a tiny spark of hope that what he said might be true, though, that a handsome well-off gentleman *had* fallen madly in love with her and *did* intend to make her his wife.

'Don't be cross with me, Ruby,' he was saying. 'I didn't want this to happen. It caught me right off guard, I can tell you. I can't describe the effect you have on me.'

'This isn't the way to Flannery Park.'

'I want to show you something first.'

'And what might that be?'

She did not have the will to remove his hand from her knee. She fretted about the manner in which he steered the motorcar, though, shifting his hand from the steering wheel to the stick with an ease which added a touch of excitement to her alarm.

'Something nice,' he said.

She sat back. She watched the corners, sandstone buildings, tree-lined streets change and slide away. Tyres squealed on cobbles and the vehicle swayed as if Bryce Walker was a racer determined to reach the winning post before his rivals. Divorce? she thought. She knew only one person who had been divorced, the foreign cow who had moved into the Burnsides' house. Even so, Trudi Coventry had snared a handsome young chap and even if Bryce Walker wasn't quite so good-looking as Henry Burnside he was much better off. Could she possibly take Bryce's promises at face value or was she just being daft?

The motorcar came to an abrupt halt. Ruby jerked and shot forward and only Bryce Walker's arm saved her from being thrown against the dashboard.

He had his hands on her before she could open the door.

He kissed her, not tenderly.

'I adore you, Ruby. Honestly. I've never needed any woman the way I need you. It makes me ache just to think about it.'

She did not push him away but when he detached himself to breathe, asked, 'Bryce, where are we?'

He drew her forward with him, arm about her shoulder, so that she could look out and upward through the windscreen. She saw a handsome sandstone tenement, one of a long row, towering above her; broad steps, a glass-panelled door to the close, wrought iron railings, and a strip of garden, only a yard in width, in which the last of the summer roses bloomed. The terrace was lined with plane trees and the street lamps, large as lanterns, showed the trees' autumn tints and illuminated fallen leaves along the kerb.

'My house,' Bryce Walker said. 'Our house from now on.'

'Our house? I have a house.'

'I know, I know. But this is a place where we can be together,' Bryce Walker said. 'Until my divorce comes through. After that momentous event we'll never be apart again.'

'*If* your divorce comes through,' Ruby said.

'It will, it will. Might take a bit of time but—' He kissed her cheek this time, slipping his lips beneath her collar in

330

search of her neck. She felt his tongue upon her skin and, in spite of her apprehension, experienced a strange tingle of sexual excitement at his expertise. He pulled away once more. 'What's wrong? Don't you like it?'

'I haven't seen it yet,' Ruby said. 'The house, I mean.'

He laughed, leaned away from her, slid out of the motorcar and, a moment later, led her up the steps, through the big door and into a tiled close that smelled dank and, Ruby thought, almost ecclesiastical.

The apartment was on the first floor. The keys, Ruby noticed, were shiny new as if Bryce Walker had had them cut only that morning. She was tempted to enquire if he owned the flat or if he had just taken a lease on it but she resisted putting the question. Chances are, she thought, he'll only lie to me anyway.

The hallway was huge, with three or four doors opening off it. An expensive tassel-edged rug was centred on the floor and there was a table and a long hallstand and a selection of unhealthy-looking plants potted in big brass bowls.

'Coat,' Bryce Walker said, tugging off his own coat and gloves.

Obediently Ruby removed her hat and overcoat and handed them to the man. He draped them casually on the table and turned to her, saying, 'We'll leave the rest until later,' then with an arm about her he guided her to the door of one of the rooms, opened it and flicked an electrical light switch.

'Dining-room, for candlelit suppers.'

Ruby nodded.

He opened another door. 'Drawing-room.'

Very comfortable and elegant; a sofa, easy chairs, a cabinet with china ornaments in it, even a piano. Ruby nodded again.

He steered her across the hall. 'Bathroom. Kitchen.'

'Yes.'

'And here,' he said, still holding her, 'the bedroom.'

The bed was the size of a small cruiser, with a massive headboard of light, polished maple and a spread that looked like tapestry. The switch by the door did not trigger the overhead light but lit instead two lamps, one tubby Chinesey thing by the bedside and the other a standard with a painted shade that stood close to the windows which, Ruby noted, already had the curtains drawn across them.

He did not draw her away from this room; nor did he nudge her forward into it. He let her look her fill and Ruby obligingly leaned a shoulder on the doorpost and cocked her head.

'Like it?' Bryce Walker asked.

'Is it yours?'

'Ours.'

'I mean,' said Ruby, 'do you stay here when you're not at home?'

'Now and then,' he said. 'I haven't had it long.' He insinuated his arm about her and kissed her behind the ear. 'Do you like it, Ruby?' Before she could answer, he said hastily. 'Of course, if there's anything you don't care for I can have it changed. Anything you want, it's yours – within reason.'

'Reason,' Ruby said, almost under her breath.

'Look.' He held out the key ring, dangling it as if it was a diamond necklace. 'One set for you, all yours. Come when you like. Do what you like here. Liberty Hall, Ruby.'

'I have a house, Bryce.'

'Make this your second home.'

'Who does the cleaning?'

He laughed uncertainly. 'Let's worry about that later.'

'Where's the kitchen?'

'Never mind the kitchen.'

Ruby moved, angling her hips so that she was braced against the doorpost. She placed her arms on his shoulders, draped and loose, and let him nuzzle against her, his chest against her breasts, his stomach against her thighs. He was expert at it. His kisses, moist and lingering, were designed to demonstrate desire, a passion held on the very edge of control. He was certainly very handsome, very strong too.

She could not honestly say that she was repulsed by Bryce Walker or put off by his calculation. She had worked in the Argyll for far too long to be shocked by anything short of murder. What was strange, though, was that she did not respond to his embraces, to the stroking of his hands down her back, the tongue-tip tickling the side of her throat, not even to muffled evidence of his readiness to make love to her. She enjoyed his caresses but, it seemed, stood at one remove from what was actually happening, an observer as much as a participant; thinking, 'Not bad for an old girl, not bad at all.'

She said, 'Do you want me to take my clothes off?'

'God, yes.'

'An' get into bed.'

'Yes, yes.'

'Do you want me to come here two or three times a week, when you can be here too?'

'I want you every day, every night, Ruby.'

'Why? Why pick on me?'

He pulled back from her, an inch at most. But he closed his lips at last and frowned as if he sensed that it was not going to be all plain sailing.

Ruby said, 'Because I'm a widow, a barmaid, because I happen to live in Flannery Park, because you think I don't know any better?'

'Ruby, I assure you—'

To her surprise he yanked out a cigarette case and lit himself a smoke. He stepped to the bed and seated himself upon it. Ruby remained where she was, giving no sign of anger. She bent one leg, vampishly thrust out her chest. He smoked, a deep drag, and picked tobacco from his tongue.

'Look, I've been moving too fast,' he said. 'I apologise. It's just that I find you irresistible. I want you, Ruby. Desperately.' He waved the hand with the cigarette, scribbling smoke into the cold air of the bedroom. 'Perhaps this wasn't such a bright idea. I should have asked you first. Look, why don't you take your time and think about it?'

Ruby said, 'It's nice to know I'm allowed to have a choice.'

'Yes, sorry.' Bryce Walker patted the tapestry bedspread beside him and made a soft inviting gesture. 'Come on, come over here and we'll talk. No tricks, I promise. Come on.'

'No.'

'Ruby—'

'I'm not interested, Mr Walker. Not in your bed, your house or your offer. Even if you did get a divorce – which I doubt – I really wouldn't want to marry you, thanks very much.'

'You don't know what you're missing.' He was on his feet, furious at her rejection but cold, determined not to display his hurt. 'You could have had me and this place and other nice things, clothes, that you're never going to get otherwise.' He came towards her, prodding the cigarette. 'What you've got that's worth having isn't going to last much longer, sweetheart. When that kid of yours gets herself knocked up and leaves home you're going to be all on your own and it'll be too late by then, past it, way past it.'

'Is that what you think, Mr Walker?'

'I don't think – I know. I've seen it happen to your type before.'

'My type? What type's that?'

'Three or four good years left in you and desperate for a man.'

'Not desperate enough to take you on, Mr Walker,' Ruby said. 'Anyway, how do you know I don't have a man?'

'Oh! You mean somebody's set you up already?'

Ruby smiled. She wasn't daft enough to hand Bryce Walker more ammunition by mentioning Alex Burnside. But it was Alex she thought of, Alex who, if she just said the word, would fell the Helensburgh fancyman faster than you could hammer in a rivet.

Ruby said, 'I don't suppose you're going to offer to drive me home?'

'Out the door, turn right, keep walking. You'll find a taxi on the rank in Queen Margaret Drive. Here.' He pulled a ten shilling note from his pocket and tossed it at her. She caught it almost by accident as it fluttered towards the carpet. 'Have a ride on me.'

'Thanks, I will,' said Ruby and vanished into the hallway.

She reappeared in the doorway a second later wearing her hat and overcoat. 'By the by, Mr Walker, just in case you decide to do a bit of "disemploying" in the near future, I'd like to remind you that even an old biddy from Flannery Park can still look up the Helensburgh telephone directory.'

'What's that supposed to mean?'

'If my Brenda's sacked again, for any reason at all, Mrs Bryce Walker an' me are goin' to have a nice long chat.'

'Bitch! That's blackmail.'

'Too true,' said Ruby and, tossing him his key ring, walked out.

Sister Winnie had gone upstairs to lie down for a while. Jim had asked her if she was feeling unwell but she had just shaken her head and with a basket of mending and a copy of the *People's Friend* tucked under her arm had gone quietly upstairs only minutes after Alison had arrived.

Jim guessed that Win had guessed that something had changed, though he could not fathom for the life of him what clue he had given to his dear, sensitive sister to drive her to that conclusion. He could not say, however, that he wasn't glad to have her out of the way, for her presence just through the door in the kitchen was always just a wee bit distracting.

He had quite deliberately left off his jacket. The evening air was not cold yet and the fire in the living-room blazed brightly, so he had a viable excuse for informality. He wore his sleeveless tennis slipover and a white short-sleeved cotton shirt which left bare and exposed the shiny lump at the termination of his upper left arm.

Alison glanced at it then at him.

'Not pretty, is it?' Jim said.

'Not very, no.'

'There's a lot of ugly scarring here too,' he covered his ribcage with his right hand.

'Does it hurt?'

'No. At least, not much. Got a bit crackly and itchy because of the salt water and sunshine but usually I hardly notice it. They did a good job of patching me up.'

'I take it,' said Alison, sitting at the table and looking closely at the stump of his arm, 'that there was no possibility of saving the arm?'

'None at all. It was mostly – well, blown away.'

'You were lucky.'

'I suppose I was,' Jim said. 'I didn't used to think so.' He pulled out a chair and seated himself opposite her. 'But I do now.'

'Why now?'

'I feel better about everything now.'

'Did you think it was over?'

He didn't have to ask her to explain.

He said, 'I did. I must admit, I did.'

'But now things have changed for the better?'

'Oh, yes.'

'It's a long time since the war ended. Perhaps you've just reached some sort of turning point.'

'Perhaps I have,' Jim said. 'In any case, things are turning out well for you, Alison. Look here.' He handed her the neat, green cardboard bankbook, open at the first page. 'Money in the bank.'

'I don't feel I deserve it.'

'There's a difference been deserving something and justifying it.'

'That's too profound for me, Mr Abbott.'

'Rubbish! You know fine what I mean.'

'Yes, I do, actually.' She continued to study the single entry on the bankbook's page. 'It's nice to have something of my own, even if I haven't earned it yet.'

He opened a cardboard folder and slid it towards her. 'Tell me what you think of that?'

Alison scanned the document in the folder. Two foolscap pages, printed in an old-style type; it had the weight and substance of a legal edict sprinkled with Latin phrases which, to her relief, she found she could easily translate. 'What exactly is it, Mr Abbott?'

'What it says – an application to enter for the Tuxford Prize.'

'Tuxford, the printers?'

'That's them,' Jim told her.

'Why are you giving it to me?'

'Because I want you to enter.'

'It's a prize offered in history . . .'

'For the examination and essay of Scottish history, to be precise,' Jim said. 'Open to all Scottish schoolchildren, worth one hundred and fifty quid, no questions asked. There are two supplementary prizes of fifty pounds each for the essay alone.'

'Who sets the paper?'

'Some professor or other, in conjunction with the Education Department. The exam's held in St Cedric's College, first week in March. Two-hour question paper before lunch. Three-hour essay paper in the afternoon. It's a stinker too. Tuxford's don't exactly give their money away.'

'But I'm not doing history.'

'I thought you wanted to be independent?'

'Well – yes.'

'Even if you win it,' Jim said, 'it won't affect your chances of a Carnegie grant, which is more or less automatic for someone in your circumstances.'

'What's the competition like?'

'That's a much more sensible question to ask,' Jim told her, grinning. 'Stiff, very stiff. The cream of the crop. It's considered quite a coup to scoop the Tuxford. You'll get your name in the papers.'

'The *Mercury*?'

'Yes, that rag.'

Alison, for some reason, held the document up to the ceiling light and studied the watermark. 'Who's going to tutor me? Mr Brooks?'

'Me, of course.'

'Why?'

'I get pleasure out of teaching you.'

'What about Walter?'

'Walter?'

'Do you have a form for him too?'

'I can send for one. In fact, I think there's another one lurking in the headmaster's file.' He paused. 'Why are you so concerned about Walter?'

'He's cleverer than I am,' Alison said. 'If anyone can win the Tuxford for Flannery Park it's Walter Giffard.'

'Does that mean you won't enter?'

'Of course I'll enter,' Alison said promptly. 'A hundred and fifty pounds? I'm not passing up a chance to win that.' She put the document back into the folder, closed and leaned upon it as if to seal it away. 'Now, Mr Abbott, what else is tucked away in the headmaster's file?'

'Uh?'

'Competitive examinations? Prizes, bursaries, scholarships that pay cash money?'

'Alison, ease up.'

'You started it, Mr Abbott.'

'True.'

'After all,' said Alison, 'you never know your luck.'

'Even more true,' Jim Abbott said and, without really thinking what he was doing, brushed her nose affectionately with his knuckle and, early though it was, went off to make them tea.

As a rule Ruby enjoyed her afternoons in the park with Alex. She didn't even mind too much when he lured her on to the bowling green and at some point in the game contrived to lean his elbow on her backside and with palpable insincerity said, 'Oh, here, sorry. I was just havin' a rest,' and removed the offending joint before she could skelp him for his impudence. The only thing Ruby didn't like about afternoon excursions was that she would have to scurry home afterwards, throw together something for Brenda's tea and hasten away to a long shift at the Argyll while Alex would toddle into 162 relaxed in the knowledge that Trudi would be there to feed him chocolate biscuits and that he would be allowed, even encouraged, to have forty winks in his chair before the evening meal was served.

'When are you goin' to get work?'

'I'm lookin', I'm lookin.'

'You're not lookin' very hard.'

'Nobody wants riveters these days.'

'You weren't *born* a flamin' riveter, Alex. You *could* try something else.'

'It wouldn't be the same.'

On that particular September afternoon, though, Ruby was not in a sunny frame of mind. She had been upset by what had happened with Bryce Walker and had waited, with a certain amount of guilt, for Brenda to burst in and tell her that she'd been sacked. Several days had gone by, however, with no change in Brenda's attitude or status in the clothing factory. Needless to say, there had been no sign of Walker at the Argyll and Ruby knew that with that kind of man there would be no second thoughts, no second chances.

She had been offended by his proposal, his assumption that she would leap at the chance to become his mistress. Perversely, she was annoyed at herself for letting a good opportunity slip. And because she was not the sort of woman to blame herself she blamed Alex Burnside instead.

There was a moderate wind that afternoon. The young rhododendron bushes had dried out enough to clash like palms in the raw earth strips around the tennis courts. Leaf debris sullied the immaculate greens and the bowlers, pernickety devils at the best of times, were kept busy clearing their lines. The wind carried little wavelets of dark cloud out of the north and lapped them against the heather-clad moors that formed the horizon beyond Knightswood and Old Drumchapel. According to Alex there would be rain before nightfall.

He came, whistling cheerfully, out of the gents' toilet. Nursing a kind of ill-defined wrath, Ruby waited by the cradle of bowls at the side of the rink. The sight of him, cocky as a sparrow and dressed – as he usually was these days – in sporty flannels, Fair Isle pullover and open-necked shirt, was just too much for her.

She was on his top before he knew what hit him.

'I'm tired of waitin' for you.'

'Eh? I was only gone for two minutes.'

'I don't mean that. I mean waiting for you to make up your mind.'

'About what?' said Alex, mystified.

'About marryin' me.'

'Eh?'

'You heard.'

He looked around nervously but there was nobody within earshot and the bowlers were too concerned with games of another sort to pay any attention to a strident woman. Even so, he stepped closer to her and drew her away from the rink to a bench on the path by the side of the green.

'What's wrong wi' you these days?' he said. 'I thought we were havin' a good time together.'

'You are. You always are, you men. Come when you like, go when you like, kiss me when it comes up *your* back.'

'Steady on now, Ruby. I've never tried t' take advantage—'

'Why not?'

'Eh?'

'Stop sayin' that, for God's sake.'

He floated an arm towards her but could not quite bring himself to pat her shoulder. 'Are you no' well today, honey, is that it?'

'I'm perfectly bloody well,' Ruby snapped. 'Look at me. Sound in wind and limb. Fit as a bloody fiddle. And in my bloody prime.'

'Ruby, watch your language, eh.'

'Good,' Ruby exploded, 'God!'

Alex seated himself by her and sought for her hand which, of course, she would not yield up. She crossed one knee over the other and twisted her body away from him. A yard or two off on the verge the bowls waited, heavy and brown and patient in their wicker cradle.

Alex clasped his hands and hung them between his knees, hung his head too. He whistled soundlessly, not looking at her.

Seething, Ruby waited for him to say something, anything.

He cleared his throat.

She waited.

He cleared his throat again then said, 'It's difficult.'

'It's not difficult at all,' Ruby said. 'It's you, y' lazy bugger. You don't need me any more.'

'Eh? I mean – what?'

'Since *she* arrived, you don't need *me* any more.'

'Trudi?'

'Who bloody else?'

'She's got nothin' to do with us.'

'She treats you like a lord.'

'I wouldn't go that far.'

'Like a bloody lord. You don't know you're born, Alex

Burnside. What am I supposed to do, meantime? Hang about like an old coat on the peg just in case you ever need me again?' She gestured with her foot, kicking out in the direction of the verge. 'Play *bowls* with you.'

'I thought—'

'I don't *mind* all this,' Ruby said, heaving an enormous, angry sigh, 'but where's it leading? *That's* what you've got to tell me. Is it leadin' anywhere, Alex Burnside, or are you just leadin' me up the garden path too?'

'Too?'

'I've had another offer.' She hadn't intended to use the gambit but it was out before she could prevent it.

'What? Marriage?'

'More or less.'

'More or less what – marriage?'

'Are you daft? Are you thick? Yes – *marriage*.'

He raised himself up from his slumped position and was suddenly very erect and stiff. 'But who would – I mean, who do you know who'd – Who *is* this other joker?'

'It's no joke, Alex.'

'What did you tell him?'

'That I'd consider it.'

'Is he one o' the layabouts that hang round the Argyll?'

'No, he is not. He's better off and better lookin' than you.'

'Younger too, I suppose.'

'Younger too,' Ruby said, with an emphatic nod.

Still rigidly upright, Alex chewed this information over for a good half minute while Ruby, intrigued by the process of deliberation, glowered.

'Marry him then,' Alex said. 'What's stoppin' you?'

'You are, you idiot.'

He didn't cry 'Me?', didn't protest innocence or ignorance.

'Mavis . . .' He let the excuse trail off.

'Mavis has been dead for a whole year now,' Ruby told him.

'Come Sunday. Aye, I know.'

'So it's time to make up your mind.'

'If this other bloke's so wonderful why are you naggin' at me?'

'I wish,' said Ruby, 'I bloody well knew.'

Thirty seconds passed. He said, 'I never knew you swore so much.'

'Don't change the subject, Alex. Remember, you *nearly* got around to askin' me to marry you once or twice before. Now's the time. Now – or never.'

'It's – difficult.'

Ruby raised a hand to heaven and then in a tone that indicated total exasperation, said, 'What's so damned difficult about gettin' married?'

'You can't come to live in 162, not you an' Brenda, because there isn't any room,' Alex said. 'An' when Henry decides to buy a place of his own then I'll need to be there to look after Alison an' the boys. So, y'see, Ruby,' he shrugged, 'it's all sort of up in the air.'

'And always will be,' Ruby said thinly. 'You just don't want to work any more, do you, Alex? Come right out an' say it.'

''Course I want to work.'

'All right,' Ruby said, 'what if all these difficulties were swept away, what excuses would you find then for not wantin' to have me as your wife?'

'It's not that, not that at all. I'd have you in a minute – for a wife, I mean. You should know by this time how I feel about you. It's – other things.'

It was Ruby's turn to say nothing. He had assumed such a dour, hang-dog posture, stooped over on the bench, features sagging and hair wisped across his brow, that she was almost trapped into feeling sorry for him. But the little blaze of temper had done her a power of good, had revived her sense of perspective and her guile. She felt much less resentful now that she recognised his vacillation for what it really was, not antagonism towards her but simple bloody-minded male selfishness.

She got up, alarming Alex by the sudden movement. He shied away from her, not quite cowering, then got to his feet too.

'Well,' Ruby said, 'I thought we came here to bowl.'

'Eh?'

'There you go again,' Ruby said. 'Eh? Eh? Eh? – like a sheep with the croup. Are we here to bowl, or are we not?'

'We are, we are, of course we are,' Alex said and, thoroughly bewildered, stepped hastily back from her and down on to the smooth green turf. 'Ready?'

'And waiting,' said Ruby.

Henry had said, 'Yes, we have to go. All of us. Not you, though, Trudi. Cemetery opens at one o'clock. We'll go there early, do it, come home again for a late lunch. That way we probably won't have to encounter the Gilfillans.'

'If they're there,' Davy had said. 'If they haven't forgotten.'

'They won't have forgotten.' Jack had sailed home from Rothesay on Thursday and still wore the stunned look of someone who had returned from a distant land to find everything changed. 'Has anybody seen them lately?'

'Not a hair,' Davy had said. 'I think they've written us off.'

Alison had kept her mouth shut, tense with divided loyalty.

Henry had said, 'Right. Bertie – flowers. Two large bunches from the Co-op florists. Discount?'

'Yep.'

'The rest of you, best bibs and tuckers. I'll order the motorcar.'

'Motorcar?'

'I'm blowed if I'm wasting a half a day huddled at bus stops.'

'Visitin' your mam's grave is hardly a waste,' Alex had said.

'Does anyone object if we travel by hired car,' said Henry with exaggerated patience, 'to visit our mother's grave in a modicum of comfort?'

'Who will pay for it?' Trudi had enquired.

'I will,' Henry had said. 'My treat. Davy, Bertie – right?'

'Fine, fine.'

'Dad, Alison?'

'Aye, why not do it in style?'

'Jack?'

'Okay by me,' Jack had said and had gone back to staring out of the window as if he wasn't really there at all.

No sooner had the big black limousine – too much like a hearse for Ruby's liking – prowled away from the kerb outside 162 than Ruby was out of her house like a shot and across the road. She had been around the Burnsides long enough not to be surprised by the motorcar's appearance. She knew, of course, what day it was and where they were going and that they would not take the woman with them.

Trudi opened the door almost before Ruby took her finger from the bell. Ruby had put on her smartest clothes, a businesslike grey suit over a plum-coloured blouse but she had eschewed the wearing of jewellery on the grounds that she did not want to appear vulgar. Henry's wife wore a white shirt thing and a black skirt, had her hair pinned up and, Ruby thought, still managed to look like a million dollars.

The woman's efficiency was almost as galling as her ability to appear cool and good-looking at half past noon on a Sunday morning and the house, nest to five males and one teenage girl, was already trim and tidy. Over the road, Ruby's living-room looked as if it had been hit by a bomb, with bits and pieces of clothing strewn about and newspapers crumpled on every chair. It also smelled of cooking; not warm and welcoming, though, but stale, of lentils and hambones and mutton fat.

'They are out. They have gone to the gravestone.'

'It's you I want to talk to.'

Ruby seated herself on Alex's chair, the smoker, but did not relax. For a time she had felt more at home here than in her own house but that phase had ended when Henry had turned up with his new wife, the foreigner. Now Ruby felt uncomfortably like an intruder.

'They will be back by half past one, a quarter of two.'

'I'll not waste your time, then, Mrs Cov – Mrs Burnside,' Ruby said. She was dying for a cigarette but was not sure that the woman would approve of tobacco. 'I've a question I want to ask you.'

'Ask it, Mrs McColl.'

'I don't intend to sound impertinent but just what do you want here?'

'I want nothing more than I have. My husband, a family.'

'This isn't your sort o' place, though, is it?'

'What do you know of "my sort of place"?' Trudi said. 'How is it you can tell what place mine should be?'

'Flannery Park must be quite a comedown when you're used to a big house with servants.'

'Hah! Henry has been talking with you?'

347

'Henry and me don't have much in common. Never have,' Ruby said. 'It's just guesswork. I'm not wrong, though, am I?'

'What is your question, Mrs McColl?'

'How long will you be staying here, in this house?'

'For a long time. For ever, perhaps, if it is God's wish.'

Mention of God halted Ruby for a moment. She hadn't suspected that Henry's wife might be the religious type; then she realised that it was no more than a casual remark and meant nothing dark or sinister.

Ruby said, 'You're not looking for some place better then?'

Trudi shook her head. She seemed faintly, but not insultingly, amused.

Ruby said, 'I thought – I just assumed you an' Henry would be buyin' a place of your own.'

Trudi shook her head again. 'I am here to stay.'

'But what about Alex?'

'I will look after Alex.'

'I don't want you to look after Alex.'

'Is it that you wish him for yourself?'

'Yes,' said Ruby emphatically. 'Damn it, I do.'

'Take him then.'

'Take him? I can't just lift him up an' lug him off like he was a basket of clothes for the wash.'

Trudi smiled and raised a fine eyebrow. 'You do not need me to tell you how a man can be made to do things. You have made him attractive to you already, which is something in your favour.'

'It was joggin' along fine 'til you appeared on the scene.'

'I do not want him,' Trudi said. 'I have a papa of my own.'

'What *do* you want? I can't understand what you're doin' here.'

348

'I want the house.'

'This house? A council house?'

'I want it for my own.'

Ruby sat back. 'Well, that's a surprise. What does Henry have to say about that?'

'It is not discussed. Henry does not know.'

'I thought you were a lady. I thought—'

'You have been deceived.'

Ruby sat forward. 'You want the house. I want the tenant.'

'It is the mutual interest, is it not?'

'Very mutual,' Ruby said.

'We can together do something about it, no?' said Trudi.

'Oh, yes,' said Ruby, grinning. 'You bet your boots we can.'

The visit to Hallwood seemed somehow perfunctory. Because of the ease of riding there and back again in a hired car, which came complete with a driver in navy blue uniform and peaked cap, the whole episode lasted just a little more than an hour. Nobody, not even Bertie, managed to shed any tears and there was an aimlessness about the proceedings which Alison, though she tried to will it otherwise, shared.

She had one fleeting pang of emotion when she saw her mother's name engraved on the monumental stone but what that emotion signified – guilt, grief or impatience – Alison was not at all sure. It dissipated almost as quickly as it came and she was left with the bizarre impression that her mother had *become* the stone which bore her name, had been transformed, like a woman out of myth, into something cold and elemental.

They were back in Wingfield Drive by twenty minutes to

two o'clock. Henry paid the driver and the neighbours, ever vigilant, observed the less than stately procession up the path and into the house which, through its open door, released a rich aroma of baking and provided a glimpse of the new Mrs Burnside dressed in white and black, like a nun. Lunch, for some reason, was a little late; then it was time for dog walking and afternoon naps and an inexplicable avoidance of the subject of anniversaries, cemeteries and loved ones gone before, as if the future held too much promise to allow the past a breathing space.

Alison went next door to the Rooneys' house. Though she still found the Catholic icons a little disturbing, she was delighted to find Mrs Rooney restored to health and the new infant beginning to resemble a human being. Mrs Rooney's mother had gone home, taking the two youngest with her for 'a wee holiday'. Mrs Rooney's mother had left a very large, posh perambulator which had come into her possession at a church jumble sale. The pram occupied most of the Rooneys' living-room and little Juliette was quite buried in it, though she seemed to find the motion imparted by its gigantic steel springs decidedly soothing and would howl whenever she was removed from its cavernous interior for anything other than a feed.

It was Mr Rooney's turn to take the bairn for air but Mr Rooney, who seemed almost more exhausted than his wife these days, was not at all reluctant to relinquish the privilege to Alison who, in a new red winter coat, knitted cap and long scarf, bumped the pram gently down the steps and set off on a short tour of the neighbourhood before dusk came down. Before she had gone five yards from the gate, however, she was struck by a sudden sense of elation and a realisation that this was probably the most responsible thing she had ever been allowed to do in her whole life.

When she turned, smirking proudly, she saw that not only was Mr Rooney at the window but that Mrs Rooney and the two older boys were there too, watching anxiously, and that in the bay window of 162 her father, brothers and Trudi had gathered to wave and cheer.

She paused to fuss ostentatiously with Juliette's bonnet and then, chin up and chest out, headed for the high country at the top of the Kingsway on the off-chance that she might bump into Jim.

At first she could not be sure that it was him. He looked so ordinary there by the long hedge which fronted the garden in Macarthur Drive. He had on old flannels and a floppy, roll-necked cardigan and a cigarette was stuck in his mouth. He was sweeping leaves from the pavement: big tobacco-yellow palmate leaves that had dropped from the horse chestnut on the corner, the heart-shapes of a lime, moist and colourful, the long crinkled feathers from an elder and a rowan. He had fired a pile of them inside the confines of the gate and smoke hung downy soft against the late September sky. He worked well with a cut-down broom, the handle tucked under his armpit to give him leverage, and a coal-shovel which he held steady on the ground with his foot.

She saw him from a distance and would have gone on, pushing the pram quickly out of sight before he recognised her, if some intelligent impulse had not overcome her shyness. She turned the pram and, still proud, took the route along Jim Abbott's drive.

He looked up surprised, stopped sweeping and pointed the broom at her as she came towards him. 'What's all this?' he said. 'Something I don't know about, Alison?'

'Next door's.' She halted the pram and put on the brake. 'I was just out for a walk and happened to be passing when I saw you. I didn't think it would be very polite just to pass by.'

'I like babies.' Jim Abbott put down the broom, extracted the cigarette from his mouth and dropped it well away from the pram. 'What's this one called?'

Alison stood back a little but did not relinquish her hold upon the pram's bakelite-covered handle. 'Juliette.'

She watched him peep cautiously into the depths of the pram and then with a careful forefinger touch aside the coverlet so that he could look down on the sleeping child. In a whisper he asked, 'Is this the early bird?'

'That's her,' said Alison. 'Miss Juliette Rooney. Isn't she nice?'

'A knockout,' Jim Abbott said. 'Just think, in fifteen or sixteen years she'll be breaking some poor Romeo's heart. Amazing, isn't it?'

'It's a pity she's a Catholic,' said Alison.

'Why?'

'She won't have you for a teacher.'

'She'll do better than me at St Kentigern's.'

'I doubt that,' said Alison. 'She couldn't do better than you, Mr Abbott.'

He withdrew cautiously from the interior of the pram and lifted his head. For a moment he did not seem to know what to say.

'I mean it,' Alison said.

'Well – thank you, Alison.'

'No,' she said, 'I *really* mean it.'

'Babies,' – he cleared his throat – 'babies do funny things to women, Alison. Don't get carried away.'

'It isn't the baby,' Alison said.

The red coat, the tammy, the long scarf, her dark brown eyes more serious and solemn than he had ever seen them before; no matter what happened in future he would never forget how she looked that grey and hazy autumn afternoon with everything around him, and in him, still. He would never forget her compliment and how broken it made him feel.

He put his hand lightly upon the perambulator's canvas hood and gave it a tiny shake, a vibration that transmitted itself not only to the infant snuggled within but to Alison too. And then he tilted his head, sniffed smoke from the smouldering leaves and deliberately gazed past the girl, away over the spill of rooftops to the river and its silent cranes.

'Best not keep her out too late,' he said.

'No.'

'You can't be too careful.'

'No.'

'Alison?'

'Yes.'

'It was nice to see you.'

'Yes.'

'Tomorrow?'

'Tomorrow, Mr Abbott,' Alison said and, because she could find no words to express precisely what she felt at that moment, unlocked the brake and gently wheeled the Rooneys' child away.

TEN

Signs of the Times

The last thing that Mr George Giffard said to his sons, apart
from 'Goodnight', was to ask them if they had enough
money for their evening on the town. Offering pocket
money was George Giffard's standard method of express-
ing paternal affection. It was a mark of his sons' respect for
their father's generosity, or scorn for his naïvety, perhaps,
that neither Scott nor Walter had ever taken advantage of
it.

'Loaded, Pop, loaded,' Scott Giffard answered.

'Let him give you something,' Marietta shouted from
behind the bathroom door. 'I know you boys. You'll want
to buy a half pint of cider before you go dancing. I
remember when I was young, all the lads did that.'

'Christ!' said Scott under his breath, while Walter rolled
his eyes and shrugged. 'Isn't she ever gonna come out of
there?'

Father had wandered off into the kitchen, presumably to
look at his wristlet watch without giving offence. By now he
would probably be pacing the floor between sink and
cooker with a tread so measured that not one hint of his
seething impatience or resentment would show. In recent
years his gait had become as rigid as his facial expression.
He looked astonishingly controlled, though, and with that
control came an impression of masculine power which a full

355

dress suit – silk cummerbund, bow-tie and all – raised to a remarkable pitch of fulfilment. The boys, Scott in particular, were aware of this quality in dear old Dad. It irked them that while ladies swooned in his wake he was quite oblivious to his attraction for the opposite sex and remained in thrall to the woman who had mothered his sons and who, because of that harrowing ordeal, had felt entitled to treat him like a coconut doormat ever since.

'God,' Walter said in the side-of-the-mouth murmur which the Giffard boys had practised since both were in kneesocks, 'if I looked as good as he does in a dickie-bow I'm damned sure I wouldn't be scrapin' the bottom of the barrel for female companionship.'

'Yeh, he'll have them Manchester wives wettin' their knickers tonight,' Scott said. 'It's dickie that counts, though, not dickie-bows. Old Pop don't even know what it's for any more.'

It had been almost twenty months since last Scott had been in Glasgow and in that time he had been round the world and back again. He had changed physically, had become smaller and more whippet-like, at least in Wattie's eyes, and his soft, loose clothing and Anglified speech sprinkled with smart phrases had slackened the bond that had once existed between the brothers.

Only Marietta was blind and deaf to her elder's sarcasm, to his risqué remarks and smutty sailor's jokes. She was too adoring of the young man to harbour the faintest suspicion that he detested her and, even when she did pick up on one of his jibes, she would pretend that it was all just prankishness and boyish high spirits. Walter didn't mind all that. What he could not abide, though, were his mother's anthems of praise to her firstborn and the fact that Scott was held up as an idol worthy of worship, an untarnished hero possessed of virtues which he, by analogy, lacked.

'I wish she'd get a bleedin' move on,' Scott said. 'I'm as randy as a jack rabbit. When are they coming round?'

'Eight.'

'What's she *doing* in there?'

'Hair. She's worried about her hair.'

'I thought it was the earrings.'

'That too,' said Walter. 'What're we gonna tell her if Frankie turns up before they leave?'

'I'll tell her I told her and she must've forgot. Anyway, Frankie's an ace. He ain't gonna bite her hand. He's her type. He'll charm her pants off.'

From the hallway came a tentative sound, a discreet clearing of the throat. Pop said, 'Sorry to bother you, dear, but the taxi-man's waiting. I did, ah, indicate to Mr Walsh that we'd be there for the introductions.'

'Yes, yes. Do you want me to arrive looking like a trollop, George?'

Scott sniggered.

He was lolling on the couch pretending to read a copy of *Tit-Bits* but was in effect as intent as Walter on tracing his mother's progress to the door.

The cab had been parked outside, motor running and meter clicking, for the past fifteen minutes. It was now twenty-eight minutes past seven and Pop had little hope of arriving at the Global Hotel in Sauchiehall Street in time to be presented to his superiors from the 'home office' in Manchester, to have his hand shaken by no less a person than Sir Percy Blenkinsop and receive the accolades which were his due as Glasgow West's most industrious agent.

'If you don't feel like going, Marietta—'

'I'll go, I'll go. I wouldn't want to spoil *your* evening.'

'But if you're ill, dear—'

'I'll be all right, George. Never mind about me.'

In the living-room, listening to this exchange, Scott had

poked a finger into his open mouth, had mimed the act of being sick and had then silently parodied his father's obsequious responses, writhing and grovelling in a manner that made Walter want to look away; then, when Pop, in dress shirt and trousers had entered the room, Scott had looked up and brightly said, 'Hi, Dad. How're things?'

Tension made Walter's head ache and his eyelid flutter. He would have found it impossible to explain to his brother what it was that made him most nervous, the not-unfamiliar harangue of Mummy-on-the-move, sympathy with his father to whom the Manchester Crown's dinner-dance was an important event, or the arrangements – which he had contrived to make – for Scott's 'Welcome Home' party. In some ways he almost wished that his mother *would* fall suddenly ill and that the evening's entertainment at home would have to be cancelled.

He got up and crossed to the window, touched aside the curtain and looked out at the taxi-cab, black and somehow menacing beyond the front garden gate.

'Marietta, dear . . .'

'YES.'

She was out. She was ready.

Her timing was immaculate; instinctive, unintentional, but immaculate.

Thirty-five minutes into Glasgow, three or four to hustle up in the elevator to the hotel's top-floor ballroom; they would arrive, flustered and apologetic, just in time to catch everyone's attention, a split second before the reception line dispersed to the dinner tables.

'Tell me, darling, how do I look?'

She pranced before Scott, tilting her broad hips, flirting with the white coney jacket that came out of mothballs once a year. In the background Pop stood motionless, trying not to glance at his watch.

Scott leapt to his feet, beaming. When he smiled he showed small even teeth and his blue eyes lit up electrically. He had, Wattie thought, a charisma that he could never hope to match, a superficial charm that Mother fell for and was consumed by.

'Wonderful, Mum. Speck-tack-ular.'

'Do you really think so?'

'Oh, yes. Oh, you look so good I could eat you all up.'

'Scott! What a thing to say!'

She hugged him tight to her bosom and left a stain of moulting rabbit fur upon his jet black cardigan.

Pop took her arm and they went out. The door closed.

Walter, in a little voice too dry to be cynical, said, 'Bye, Mum,' and Scott scampered upstairs to dig out the booze he had bought and hidden away for the party.

It wasn't every day that Oswald Mosley, Chancellor of the Duchy of Lancaster and sitting member for Smethwick, deigned to show his haughty face in Scotland. He had no particular liking for the Scots, even less for Tory press barons who, in the heat of electoral debate, he had condemned as scurrilous and rapacious scandal-mongers.

Ramsay MacDonald's recently elected government was still hobbling, however, shackled with problems of rising unemployment and a heap of windy promises that could not possibly be kept. 'Comrade' Mosley, ambitious to a fault, felt that he had all the answers and needed only the support and understanding, tacit or otherwise, of the great and the good to push through his plans for Retirement Pensions and Public Works. For that reason he had reluctantly accepted Lord Blackstock's invitation to address a small and very select group of influential gentlemen at a private dinner in the Marlborough Club in Glasgow's Stockwell Street; a hit-and-run, whistlestop affair which, courtesy of the night train, would have him back in London in time for a late breakfast. Tom Johnston, Under Secretary of State for Scotland, had requested that the advent of Mosley be kept very quiet and Marcus Harrison had dished out no brief to his parliamentary reporters or diarists. Unless you took account of Charlie Blackstock, which Marcus tended not to do, he and he alone would represent the *Mercury* and use his editorial to bring Ozzie's not-so-daft notions to the readers' attention.

The five o'clock editorial meeting had gone smoothly and ended on time. Marcus had handed over without a qualm to Simpson Bond, night editor, and old Jimmie Dunn, chief sub-editor, who would see the morning editions safely to press. He had managed to chase everyone out of his office by half past six o'clock and, with a dry razor, had scraped off the day's stubble and begun the laborious process of getting himself into his dinner suit, a feat that seemed less a fashion problem than one of engineering.

He hated the damned monkey suit and paused frequently in his sartorial preparations to scan the massive file of Mosley's more recent declamations that had been sent up from the library and to fortify himself with snifters of Napoleon brandy. He was looking forward to the dinner, though, to meeting Mosley face to face and, abetted by his colleagues from the *Herald* and the *Scotsman*, to giving Labour's latest hot-shot quite a time of it in discussion and debate.

He had managed to adjust his garters and had one black shoe on and the other in his hand when the external telephone rang.

He hesitated and then, because he was congenitally incapable of letting a phone ring unanswered, snatched up the receiver.

'Harrison.'

'Marcus, is that you?'

'Who is this?'

'Trudi.'

'Who?'

'Trudi Coventry.'

'Look, Trudi, I—'

'One minute, it is all I ask.'

Marcus placed the shoe on the folder on his desk, sipped a little brandy and steadied himself. 'Yes, Mrs Burnside, what can I do for you?'

'Mrs Burnside?'

'Well, you're a married lady now.'

'I was a married lady when—' She did not complete the sentence.

She had, in fact, no need to complete the sentence for the casual reminder was more than enough to unsettle Marcus Harrison. He was very calm and relaxed about most things but he had committed two sexual indiscretions in his life, just two, one of which had been fleeting and unsatisfactory and had left him scarred with anxiety and regret; and the other . . . he had no wish to dwell on the other.

'Trudi,' he said, being hearty now, 'I'm dining out. Rather important. Got to pop in five minutes. Can you be quick, dear heart?'

'My father-in-law needs work. He is Henry's father. He must have a job of work as soon as possible.'

Marcus raised his eyes to the ceiling.

'What,' he said, 'does he do?'

'He rivets.'

'Pardon?'

'He is riveting, in a shipping yard.'

'Trudi, with the best will in the world I can't find work for a riveter.'

'You need caretakers, no?'

Two minutes ago he had been mulling over national statistics, comparing the number unemployed in shipbuilding and mining and engineering age group by age group. It had been a consoling exercise in the philosophy of government, a big issue writ suitably large. Now here was this woman, a German at that, nagging him about finding employment for some dole-queue nonentity. He felt more stifled by the pettiness of her request, by the woman's sheer brass neck, than by the weight of unwashed out-of-work millions.

'Trudi, I've already done you a favour by finding work for your husband.'

'That favour was not for me. It was for Clive.'

'You're hair-splitting, Trudi.' He sipped and swallowed then put the bottle firmly away from him. 'In any case it wouldn't be "caretaking". I suppose he might be useful in maintenance.'

'What is that?'

'Halfway between being a blacksmith and a mechanic. Of course we have press operators to run the – look, this is all irrelevant. I may be the editor of the *Mercury* but I've very little to do with the production side. I leave that to others, shop stewards, fathers of chapel, those sort of people. Trudi, I would like to help you but there are five men lined up for every job here.'

'How is your wife, Marcus?'

'That, Mrs Burnside, is clumsy.'

'Margaret Chancellor also is in good health?'

It occurred to Marcus Harrison at that moment that it might be simpler to employ Trudi Coventry Burnside instead of her father-in-law; elevate her to some position on the editorial board where her manipulative skills and outrageous cheek could be profitably channelled. He could just about imagine her in a smart little black suit and top hat, monocle too, blowing smoke over Oswald Mosley and tying him in knots with her literal interpretations of the English language.

He laughed. 'I don't know what to do about you, Trudi.'

'You do nothing with me now. I am a happily married woman. I do not want to see a good man brought to waste by idleness, that is all.'

'I wonder if the Burnsides knew what they were getting when they took you in off the street?'

'Henry knows.'

'I'll bet he does,' said Marcus Harrison. 'But I'll bet he doesn't know what you're up to.'

She had the decency to hesitate. 'No.'

'I'll see what I can do. No promises, though, Trudi. I can't conjure jobs out of thin air.' Marcus Harrison lifted the shoe from his desk, dropped it to the carpet and fished for it with his stockinged foot. 'This time you'll have to be patient, just wait for the right sort of vacancy.'

'But when it does?'

'I'll pass word down the line to Henry,' Marcus said, 'without mentioning our conversation or, for that matter, anything else Henry shouldn't know about.'

'Good, good,' Trudi said. 'Now, I will release you, Marcus, to go and eat your dinner with Mr Mosley.'

'How in the heck did you know about that?'

'Henry told me.'

'Henry? Dear Lord, it's supposed to be a state secret.'

'Is it not correct for a good journalist to know secrets?'

'Some of them, Trudi,' said Marcus Harrison. 'Some of them.'

He heard her laugh huskily and felt a strange little shiver

of apprehension lift the hairs on the nape of his neck, as if he was being mocked by a woman who may, or may not, be a witch.

And then, lightly, she hung up.

'What in God's name am I doing here?' Henry hissed as the party, so-called, moved from the public bar into the saloon in deference to the unexpected presence of ladies.

'Interviewing the greatest living Celtic bard,' James Brewster told him.

'But *you're* here,' Henry complained. '*You* know the old souse. You even speak the flamin' language.'

'Only when I'm sober.' Brew rolled bloodshot eyes in the boy's direction to indicate that he had just made a joke. 'It's you who'll be coverin' the presentation tomorrow night, so it is no bad idea to make the acquaintance of the main protagonist, particularly as he only shows himself in Glasgow once in a blue moon.'

On the tray in Brew's hands were four double whiskies and a half pint of lemonade, the latter being Henry's share of the refreshments. Brew carried the drinks as solemnly as if they were relics of state, the jewels of Scotland, say, which, Henry reckoned, might be a pretty fair analogy.

The 'party', one extremely elderly gentleman with features like a seal's and two husky handmaidens clad in Princes Street plaids, had settled in the corner by the fire.

This was the Sadducee's Head, a great sprawling public house near Buchanan Street railway station much favoured by journalists and the Glasgow literary crowd. In addition to its bars it boasted an upstairs room into which poetry groups were poured two or three evenings a week; also a long sandwich counter where impecunious novelists scrounged nourishment from journalists and liberated ladies, young and old, felt free to eye up the – literary –

talent and wonder how they could worm their way into somebody's good books and capture mention as a Muse in so-and-so's next slice of autobiographical nonsense.

Brew paused on his progress across the gilded room. He paused for several reasons; first because he had lost sensation in his left leg again and wasn't at all sure where his next step was coming from; second because he wanted to give roving reviewers from other journals time to admire *le roi*; and third because he did actually feel a certain professional obligation to break in 'the boy' to the cut-and-thrust world of feature journalism.

Henry, though, was still grousing. 'We shouldn't *be* here, Brew. We should be squatting on the steps of the Marlborough Club on the off-chance we could wring a word out of Mosley about this pension plan of his. It's fraught with problems and could backfire on Jimmie Thomas if the rail unions get wind of it.'

'See,' Brew said. 'See the danger. One injudicious word from you, son, could bring the government down. Safer to stick to Alasdair McWhirr. At least you know where you are with Celtic bards. You'll be writin' the puff for tomorrow's second edition, by the way, so you'd better pay attention. It's not every day the great man comes down from his Highland fastness. Nor is it every day the Ossian Society gives its special gold medallion to somebody who hasn't been dead for two hundred years. Anyway, you're booked for the ceremony at the Ossian Institute. Everybody who's anybody in Gaeldom will be there.' He progressed another three steps towards the trio in the booth who by this time were becoming restive and, like cormorants on a rock, had elongated their necks and started looking around for something to slip down their throats.

'Okay,' Henry conceded. 'Who are the girls? His daughters?'

'May be, may be,' said Brew and, having found his left leg just where it ought to be, tramped forward, offering out the tray like a society hostess.

James Brewster was also an islander. He came not from the remote Hebrides, though, but from Arran, which lay snug within the confines of the Clyde estuary and was as familiar in shape to Glaswegians as their own midden-heads. He had been a big city journalist for so many years, though, that his fluency in the language of the Gaels had deteriorated into a sort of hawk and spit arrangement, about as lyrical as a football chant. He was, however, a big man, broad as well as tall, and had a dignified head surmounted by a corona of wiry red hair. Though drink had aged him he still retained the proud dignity of his ancestors and had that long-snouted look which proclaimed him as a majestic force of nature, even when his balance left a lot to be desired.

McWhirr and the women plucked the glasses from the tray and uttered toasts by way of thanks. Brew plonked himself down on the padded bench and left Henry to perch on a quilted stool, notebook open on the table.

When he saw one of the women, Erica by name, looking at him Henry gave her his best smile and asked, 'Do you mind if I make notes?' to which she answered, with a majestic sweep of her blonde head, 'O-ooch, no-oo.'

The other one, Dierdre – Dier-*drah*, Dier-*drah*, with a sob instead of a hyphen between syllables, apparently – was dark not fair. Otherwise they were a matched pair. In fact they were a perfectly balanced trio if you took in the sallow little poet too; the Pict, the Viking and the Irish invader, all three sloshing it back good style in a Glasgow pub – a perfect paradigm, Henry thought, for contemporary Scottish culture.

He still hadn't figured out the relationship of the women

to McWhirr and was striving to frame a delicate question on the subject when, without any warning at all, McWhirr began to croon.

Henry's pencil stub poised over his notebook, Brew's right elbow froze in mid-air, the glass hovering close to his lips. The women, though, went into solemn raptures as the weird sing-song voice rose and fell. The Viking swept her head this way and that in restrained ecstasy, while the dark-haired Celt raised her eyes to heaven and clasped her hands not at but over her breasts, a gesture which Henry found just a wee bit disconcerting.

'Take this down, son,' Brew mouthed.

'What? It's in Gaelic, for God's sake.'

'No matter. Take it down.'

McWhirr had his eyes closed. He looked more like a seal than ever, silky lashes fluttering, mottled lips shaping each syllable while his nostrils flared with the falls in line and rhyme.

Dierdre took a big warm hand from her big warm breast and clamped it on Henry's forearm; he flinched. 'It is the story of the Merman of Loch Roag,' she informed him sonorously, 'and of the Foal-gathering Girl of Geshader. It is the story of their tragic love, each for the other, and of the child of their mating who is neither woman nor fish.'

'Yes,' said Henry, 'I've met girls like that.'

'Hush!'

'Sorry,' Henry whispered and, with the hand that wasn't pinned to the table, scribbled some gibberish down on his pad.

There was silence now in the saloon bar, silence in the public and, for all Henry knew, silence halfway down Buchanan Street. He couldn't be sure if the silence signified reverence or stunned incredulity but while the mourning voice rose and fell, collecting decibels verse by verse,

Henry was moved by a sudden impulse to make good his escape.

'Another wee dram, ladies?' he murmured hopefully.

'*Ssshhh!*'

'I think I'll just—'

'Hush, hush!'

'Sit still, son,' Brew told him. 'Listen an' learn.'

'Sorry, sorry.' Scrunched over the table Henry counted the bubbles in his lemonade in silence.

What stirred him was less the tragic incompatibility of Haddock-man and Donkey-girl than the even more tragic incompatibility of Reporter and Gaelic Bard, plus the dismal prospect of having to endure a whole evening dedicated to this pretentious nonsense.

He closed his eyes and tried to imagine the dinner table in the Marlborough Club, the wit of Oswald Mosley, the fire of political debate. He should have been there, not here listening to the last gasps of a culture dying on its feet, a culture to whom the Industrial Revolution was hardly more than an echo from the nether world, to whom Slump meant a sheep dead in the fank at Bernera and Depression was something you suffered from when the drink ran out.

It was Erica who first spotted the interloper, a second before Brew refocused his blank, bloodshot eyes and lifted his head from his chest.

'FIRE,' the man shouted from the doorway. 'FIRE.'

Henry whipped round and, the stool toppling, leapt to his feet.

The man was a five-eighter, common as muck in grubby scarf and greasy cap but to Henry he appeared radiant, a knightly saviour bathed in an aura of gold. Henry reached him a step ahead of the rabble and, grabbing the punter by the lapels, hoisted him clean off the floor.

'Where? Where, damn it?'

'Five bob,' the punter said, 'in advance.'

'Pay him, Henry, for God's sake.'

'The wee bugger's tellin' the truth. I can smell smoke off him.'

'Where, you wee runt, or I'll knock your block off?'

'Five—'

Brew flung two half crowns on to the floor and the pack of reporters and journalists which had massed out of nowhere bayed for an answer.

'Global Hotel,' the punter grunted and fell back, cowering, as the newsmen, Henry to the fore, streamed out into the ripe night air.

Even with her rudimentary knowledge of mathematics Brenda could multiply three by two, divide the number of beer dumpies in the crate and gin bottles on the table by six and realise that she had been lured into something that smacked more of a spree than a birthday party. Though she had no head for drink, she might have been all right with that if it hadn't been for the presence of the stranger. His name, she was told, was Frankie. He was a chum of Scott Giffard's, a Hull lad, a merchant seaman far from home. She didn't like the look of him at all. He was enormously tall, had a long neck, a prominent Adam's apple and almost no chin. He didn't seem to realise that he was such an ugly duck, though, and emanated an arrogance that gave Brenda the creeps.

Vera and Doris had no such reservations. They seemed not in the least surprised to find the so-called birthday party limited to three couples and no trace of cake, trifle or other party dainties laid out. Three bottles of Gordon's Dry Gin, glasses, four lemons on a saucer and a hexagonal cocktail shaker occupied the centre of the living-room table. The beer crate was propped on a chair. The room was lit only by a standard lamp over which had been draped a muslin scarf in peacock hues, which gave everything a funny russet tint. In the grate the coalfire crackled red and yellow and the atmosphere in the room was already hot.

Brenda was relieved of her coat and handed the gift she'd bought for Scott – playing cards in a box – to Walter to give to his brother later.

Walter slid the parcel casually on to the sideboard and, taking her arm, bare below the short sleeve of her party frock, led her away from the couch which faced the fireplace and steered her to an armchair instead. Brenda was already perspiring when Frankie, who was older than the Giffards by a good ten years, handed her a tall glass full of something pink. She drank two big mouthfuls before she felt the bite of gin in her throat. She coughed but managed not to splutter. Frankie laughed. Adam's apple bobbing like a cork, he towered above her, looking down speculatively.

'She's mine, Frankie.' Dumpy in hand, Walter seated himself on the arm of the chair and put an arm around Brenda's shoulders.

She felt better after that, much better. She'd heard Vera and Doris brag about 'gin parties' and how much fun they were but she'd been spared the more lurid details. She understood now why her pals had laughed when she'd turned up in her frilly old party frock, clutching a neatly wrapped birthday gift. She sipped cautiously from the glass, leaned in against Walter's chest and, tilting her head, looked up at him for reassurance.

His expression gave nothing away – it seldom did – but his eyelid twitched and he pretended that he did not notice her, turning his face towards the sofa where Frankie was serving drinks to Doris and Vera and, stooping over, getting an eyeful of what was on display. Brenda did not consider her pals 'forward' for wearing such revealing clothing. She envied them their suavity, the assurance that showed itself in knowing exactly what to put on – and what to leave off – for a gin party.

They had, all three, already met Scott Giffard at Ferraro's once or twice but Frankie was a novelty.

Once more Brenda drank. She could feel perspiration all over her now but with it came a comfortable warmth and an easing of tension.

Not looking at her, Walter said, 'Go easy, Brenda.'

'Go easy yourself,' she retorted, with a little more pith than she felt.

Walter nodded as if he'd expected her to say something of the sort and, lifting his left arm, sucked from the squat little beer bottle.

Brenda watched Frankie squeeze on to the couch beside Vera, and Scott ease himself down by Doris' side. The girls had adopted a strange, almost feline softness which Brenda had not detected in them before, not even at the Cally. Laughter broke out when Frankie, who seemed much prone to whispering, whispered in Vera's ear or, leaning, addressed Doris who was by now sitting on Scott Giffard's knee. It was a game with rules with which all the participants were familiar and only she, Brenda, remained a rank beginner. She stuck out her arm, empty glass in hand. 'More, please, somebody.'

Frankie rose, leggy, long-necked and took off his jacket and tie. He glanced at Vera, 'Can she hold it?'

'No – but I can.'

Doris gave her artificial laugh and rubbed her elbow against Scott Giffard's knee. He returned the compliment and, as Frankie moved to the table to mix Brenda another tall cocktail, leaned over and kissed Doris full on the lips as if he'd known her for months and not just a day or two.

'Uh-mmmmmm,' Doris murmured, nuzzling.

She pulled up one knee and twisted so that Scott could slip his arm about her waist and lift her towards him, very close.

'What are we gonna do?' Walter said in an unemphatic tone.

'Play games,' said Frankie.

'What sort of games?' Brenda heard herself ask.

'How about – Postman's Knock?' Vera suggested.

'Yeah, that'll do,' Frankie said. 'For starters, anyway. Scott?'

Scott had placed one hand on Doris' breast, quite motionless, almost unobtrusive. Brenda felt her mouth go dry at the suspicion that she might be looking at herself, plump legs in pinky-brown stockings, shoe dangling from one toe, dress crushed; in the midst of it Scott Giffard's black flannels and handsome head of hair. She watched him occupy himself with Doris and wave Frankie's question away.

With gin thawing her reserve and the example of the amorous couple to goad her on, Brenda heard herself cry out, 'Forfeits. I wanna play Forfeits.'

And beside her, Walter muttered, 'Oh, Christ, no.'

Whoever said that there could be no smoke without fire would have been proved wrong that Friday night at the Global Hotel.

Smoke was the signal that warned guests of danger and later entertained the crowd that gathered in Sauchiehall Street to watch firemen in frog-masks storm the foyer and their brethren on tall ladders smash windows in search of one wee lick of flame. Nothing livid or vivid belched from the building to give the crowds a thrill but, by golly, there was enough smoke to kipper half the herring in the North

Sea and a stench so acrid that you could smell it over on the Cathkin Braes.

Inspection was later to establish that the Global's newly installed gas ovens had suffered a blow back, the refrigeration system in cold-room and larder had been affected and had generated heat to an astonishing degree and, to cap it all, the sprinklers had shorted and failed. Tons of pork, beef and mutton in the cold-room were done to a turn in seconds and reduced to puddles of grease in minutes. Add varnish, flock, carpeting and lacquered plyboard to the smouldering mess from beneath and it was small wonder that the Global sizzled instead of igniting and a miracle that nobody, especially kitchen staff, suffocated on the fumes.

Having been the last to arrive at the Manchester Crown's reception, George and Marietta Giffard had not left the area of the door. Consequently when the shout went up – *Fire, Fire, Fire* – and gouts of savoury brown smoke issued simultaneously from several air ducts, the Giffards were first to the elevators. They might have been trapped there, trampled in the rush if Mr Giffard had not tapped into his expert knowledge of How Accidents Happen, dragged his wife bodily towards the stairs and given her an almighty shove.

Marietta was not best pleased.

She was screaming, '*My fur, my fur. George, go back an' get my fur,*' when Mr Giffard struck her in the small of the back. He swept her on to his shoulder, secured her flailing arms with one fist, flailing legs with another and sped down five flights of stairs with Marietta's head butting his backside and her shrieks – '*Mafur, mafur, mafur*' – ringing in his ears.

Somewhere en route Marietta lost one slipper and a wheen of hairpins so that she arrived in the street, still slung across her husband's shoulder, in a decidedly dishevelled state. The cheer that greeted these first survivors of the 'raging inferno' was accompanied by examples of pawky Glaswegian wit.

'She deid then, mister?'

'Pit hur doon, see if she can still dae a Heilan' fling.'

'Could ye no'uve found a better yin than that lyin' aboot, man?'

Finally, when George lowered his beloved to the pavement and Marietta hobbled dazedly about, some wag yelled, 'Hur spring's busted, mister. Awa' an' get yur money back.'

More fun might have been had at Marietta's expense if the simultaneous arrival of the constabulary, the fire brigade and a first flush of panic-stricken hotel guests, accompanied by a huge cauliflower of smoke from a third-floor window, had not distracted the onlookers' attention. The crowd, swelling by the moment, swayed forward then backward, sucking George and Marietta with it like flotsam on the tide.

A second or two later they were isolated in a shop doorway across the street from the Global. George smoothed his hair and brushed his lapels while Marietta, strung between wrath and relief, yelled at him to go back into the smoke-filled building, find her coney jacket and her shoe and not return without them or she would know the reason why.

George Giffard's back hurt, his thighs trembled and he had taken in a lungful of smoke which made his chest ache. He stared impassively over the heads of the crowd towards the red fire-engines, the mounted police and the smoke-wreathed façade of the Global Hotel while his wife beat her fists against his shoulder and clamoured for his attention.

'*George, do you hear me? Do you hear me, George?*'

He gave a little cough, said, 'Marietta, *eff off*!' and,

before she could recover from her shock, dragged her around the corner into Hope Street in search of a cruising cab.

The game had staggered on for the best part of an hour. The level of gin in the bottles had diminished considerably. The girls, the boys too, had shed their clothing down to that point where things were becoming both nerve-racking and very, very interesting. No imagination had been applied to calling the Forfeits. Five of the six persons in the Giffards' living-room had known from the beginning what the true objective of the party game was, though none could be quite sure if the ultimate goal would be achieved or if modesty and common sense would take over before all shreds of decency were thrown to the wind. That was part of the excitement.

Between the calling of each Forfeit, each Dare, there was ample time to drink and kiss, chest against forearm, hand against thigh. One by one trousers and underskirts were removed. The next obstacles to progress were garter belts and stockings, socks and vests and beyond that – beyond that Brenda did not dare contemplate.

Frankie poured gin into her. Frankie put his tongue in her mouth. Frankie was the first to expose his narrow, hairless chest and Frankie whispered in her ear, 'Your turn next, honey. Soon be your turn,' while she lay in Walter's passive arms. Walter was a stick-in-the-mud. Slow, sullen, sober, he tacitly resisted each cry for another Forfeit. He grumbled when Brenda, anxious not to be outdone, was summoned to perch upon a kitchen chair and remove one item of clothing after another, from hairband to shoes, stockings to underskirt. Initially Brenda was bashful but as Walter was left behind and Vera – mad Vera – claimed more of the boys' attention, Brenda hastened to catch up. She became, or seemed to become, brazen, duped into defiance by vanity aided and abetted by Walter's truculence.

'Take a gander at Mr Sour Puss there,' Vera jeered as she stepped down from the chair in garter belt, knickers and brassiere, one shrivelled stocking, just removed, coiled round her throat like a boa. She leaned over Walter who remained immobile in the armchair, Brenda on his lap. 'Don't ye like me then, Waaally, eh?' She arched her back and shook her upper body. 'Don't get many o' them in a punnet, do ye?'

Walter seemed to have to force himself not to look away. Brenda could feel his muscles harden under her thighs. She regarded Vera without embarrassment – comparing.

'Come on you, out o' it. Gi' me a shot. I know how t' make him smile.'

Grabbing Brenda by the arm Vera yanked her from Walter's lap and threw herself down upon the young man before he could escape. She covered him almost completely, her bushy red hair akimbo, breasts flattened against his unbuttoned shirt, her knees splayed on either side of his hips.

Walter's fists closed upon the arms of the chair and he let out a groan, half pleasure, half dismay, when Vera crushed her mouth to his.

Startled, Brenda stepped back. Frankie's arms snaked about her waist. His thin forearms each bore a misty blue tattoo, anchors and roses. Glancing over her shoulder she glimpsed Scott Giffard stretched on the couch with Doris on top of him. With a jolt of alarm Brenda realised that Doris wore nothing from the waist upward. Wattie groaned again, loudly. Then Frankie's hands were cupping her breasts. His tongue licked the back of her neck. He nuzzled against her, chaffing.

She was excited too now. Fear had been filtered out by resentment. She had expected Walter to protect her but at the first opportunity Walter had swapped her for Vera. When Frankie fumbled with the hooks at her back Brenda did not try to stop him. She let him loosen the garment, push it upward. She leaned her head against Frankie's shoulder, groaning too, as his hands stole to the elasticated waist of her underskirt.

Peeping out from behind the bush of Vera's hair Walter's eyes were upon her, cold eyes, calculating and uncaring. She stuck out her tongue and deliberately swung round to embrace Frankie. Numbly she lifted her face to accept his kisses, parted her lips to take his tongue. She heard nothing except an empty pounding in her ears and then there was an explosion of bodies in the living-room, a violent scramble that seemed to erupt out of nowhere. 'Hell's teeth!' Scott Giffard hissed and flung Doris from him on to the carpet. 'They're home.'

Walter struggled to disentangle himself from Vera but he was only half way up, back arched, the girl still clinging to his thighs, when the door burst open and Mrs Giffard stepped into the living-room.

'*Mama*,' Walter cried out abjectly. '*It wasn't me, it wasn't me*,' and, to Brenda's disgust, began there and then to weep.

'Far be it from me to preach,' Boris said, 'but I'd go easy on that stuff if I were you. One alkie on the staff's more than enough and the position, in case you hadn't realised, is already taken.'

'I can't stand this time of year,' Jim Abbott said. 'It makes me feel old.'

He leaned an elbow on the long bench and stared out of the window of the science lab at a bank of fallen leaves which, even as he spoke, rose on the wind and scurried away around the corner of the building as if his bleak stare had scared them. He sipped whisky from the beaker and glowered when Boris pointedly removed the bottle from his proximity.

'Drinking isn't going to solve your problems,' Boris told him. 'Besides, if you've decided to go to hell in a handcart I'd prefer it if you didn't do it on my territory.'

'Sorry.' Jim swung round. 'Would you like me to go?'

'No, stay if you like.' Boris pocketed the whisky bottle and returned to the pile of exercise notebooks which he was half-heartedly correcting. He cocked a leg over a stool and settled himself, beaker in hand, cigarette in mouth. He uncapped a fountain pen and scribbled a cruel comment in red ink in the margin of some poor third year pupil's homework. 'At least it's warm here and reasonably peaceful. Provided HMI doesn't barge in unannounced I can hole up here for the winter, snug as a bug.'

'I wish I could.'

Boris cocked his head and stared at his friend with that knitting of the brows which his pupils knew so well. 'Did you ask her?'

'Yes. She doesn't know.'

'Can't she find out?'

'It's all very much under the carpet, I gather,' Jim said. 'There are all sorts of wild rumours floating about, of course, but Alison's too sensible to set much store by them.'

'What sort of rumours?'

'Well, Alison didn't exactly say as much but—'

'Our roarin' boy's got somebody pregnant?'

'That's one theory, certainly.'

Boris grunted. 'Wouldn't be the first time.'

'It would for Flannery Park.'

'What can you expect if you keep the little beggars here until they're full grown. If I had my way ritual mating would be mandatory in sixth year. Get it over and done with, let them concentrate on more important things.'

Jim Abbott laughed in spite of himself. 'You'd never get away with that proposal, Norman. Just imagine having your name called by Nurse and being marched out to the clinic to – you know.'

'I can just see the parental letters. "Please excuse our Johnnie today's ritual mating. He has had a cold and still has a runny nose and I do not want him to have his trousers taken off." Aye, maybe you're right.'

'Damn it, why did it have to be Giffard? I had high hopes for that lad.'

'No higher than I had,' Boris said. 'He was always a bit on the fishy side, though, you'll have to admit.' He paused to grind his cigarette into a tobacco tin ashtray. 'I take it your wee filly's not involved?'

'No, Alison's far too intelligent to get into that sort of trouble.'

'So was Giffard. And he's gone west.'

'Did Pallant show you the parents' letter?' Jim enquired.

'I didn't ask to see it. You?'

'Yes. All it said was that Walter would not be returning to school, and a request for a Leaving Certificate up to the end of fifth year.'

'Signed by the mother?' Boris said.

'No, the father,' Jim said. 'Is that significant?'

'Search me,' Boris answered. 'I thought you might be able to deduce something from it. After all, you must have got to know Giffard quite well, all those evenings in his company.'

'Quite well!' said Jim. 'Are you serious? I knew even less about him by the time we'd finished than I did when we started. Our Wattie was not one for exchanging confidences. He came in, did his bit with the textbooks, drank a cup of tea and left. If I'd coached him from now to doomsday I doubt if I'd have found out much more about him.'

'Perhaps he was offered a job,' Boris said. 'His father's an insurance agent, isn't he? He might have gone to work with him.'

'Manchester Crown,' Jim said. 'Unlikely.'

'Joined the army, run off to sea.' Boris heaved a sigh. 'Anyway, Giffard's no longer our pigeon. Good luck to him, wherever he is.'

'I'll drink to that,' said Jim.

'No, you won't,' Boris told him, sternly.

Fear and trembling turned gradually to melancholy. Brenda passed three weeks in a state of abject terror sure that Mrs Giffard or, worse, Walter's father would eventually turn up on the doorstep to report the whole sordid and humiliating episode to her mother and demand that retribution be extracted from the guilty party, namely her.

Wattie's last pathetic utterance – 'It wasn't me' – rang in her head like a litany. She would hear it in the final few seconds before she fell asleep, would waken to it in the wee small hours, would have it along with breakfast and, worst of all, would catch its echo in the rhythm of Bryce Walker's sewing-machine, hour by hour, day after day.

There was no escape from the loneliness of guilt. She no longer had friends with whom to share her feelings. Doris and Vera had thrown her over. They blamed her, Brenda, for allowing them to be caught in a compromising situation, for being bundled half clad into the streets of Flannery Park in the middle of a Friday evening, for spoiling a great wee party. It was almost as if they thought the fire in the Global Hotel had been all her fault.

Doris and Vera were not ashamed of their behaviour or afraid of parental repercussions. There was nothing the Giffards could do to harm them. They sneered at Brenda's apologies, made jokes at her expense and spread slanders about her among their friends in the machine room. Brenda soon found herself cut off from sympathy and protection. It was bad enough that she had made a fool of herself once and caused poor Norman to break his leg; before the end of the workday every female in the factory had received some version of Brenda's latest escapade. She could hear them sniggering, see them smirking and, crouched low over her sewing-machine, she buried herself in stitching tapes to escape the opprobrium.

It did not take long for Brenda to begin to believe that she was to blame, that she would be condemned to bear the stigma throughout her life, that wherever she went, whatever she did, she would be chalked up as the girl who'd been caught with her pants down.

'What's wrong with you?' Ruby enquired anxiously. 'Are you not goin' out tonight?'

A shake of the head.

'What about your chums, aren't they comin' round?'

Another shake of the head.

'Oh, come on, Brenda. You can't just mooch about the house night after night. Here, eat your tea.'

'Not hungry.'

'Are you comin' down with somethin'?'

'I'm all right.'

'Has Mr Walker said somethin' to offend you?'

'No,' scathingly. 'Leave me alone, just leave me alone.'

Even after it became obvious that the Giffards intended

to make no more of the incident Brenda could not shake off her depression. She made no attempt to communicate with Walter. She'd hoped that he would contact her, would perhaps turn up at the house one night after her mother had gone to work. Then they would talk, kiss, make up and Wattie would tell her that he had explained everything to his parents and that they had forgiven her. But when Walter did not appear, when there was no sign of him in the streets, the cry in her head became louder – '*It wasn't me, wasn't me, wasn't me*' – until Brenda was so distracted by it that she wondered if she was going mad.

She took to skulking round Dunsinane Street and outside Ferraro's Café, to hanging about the school, even after darkness had fallen and the gates had been locked. But there was not a sniff of Walter or his brother or the man called Frankie, though she didn't care if she never saw *him* again. She pined for Walter, only for Walter. She longed for him to exonerate her and restore himself in her eyes. At length she could stand the silence no longer and, late one evening, waylaid Alison who was out walking the dog.

'Oh, it's you,' Ally said.

'Aye. Have you seen Walter?'

'No. I was about to ask you the same thing.'

'Has he not been, you know, at school?'

'He's left.'

'*What?*'

'I thought you'd be the first to know.'

'No, I—'

'Lovers' tiff?' said Alison, with a trace of sarcasm. 'Well, he's left school and, as far as I know, gone off to work somewhere.'

'When did this happen?'

'Three weeks ago. He was in class on Friday, gone on Monday. Is something wrong?'

382

Brenda pressed her wrist to her nose. 'Naw, naw, it's – it's okay.'

'Did something unpleasant happen between you?'

'Nothin' that concerns you.'

'Sorry I spoke,' said Alison. 'Brenda? Are you crying, Brenda?'

Alison could not recall the last time she'd seen Brenda run but the girl ran now, sprinting across the angle of Wingfield Drive to vanish into the unlit house on the corner, trailing behind her a faint little cry that sounded suspiciously like denial.

It had been years since Boris had extended his teaching beyond the elementary level and at first he was wary of the so-called 'new methods' which HMI, in their infinite wisdom, had advocated for the improvement of advanced students. Boris was not alone in feeling the strain. Wry comments in the staffroom indicated that the quick-mindedness of the sixth's young adults had other teachers backed into corners too and that all those involved in nurturing the careers of the academic whizz-kids had to give themselves a shake and, metaphorically at least, blow the dust off their mortarboards.

Even Mr Pallant had his problems – reorganisation of time-tables, the separation of subjects, the setting up of a prefects system and the selection of a representative Captain of School.

This last honour fell upon Charles Smailes known, without affection, as 'Snails', a small, gaunt, humourless item whose father, as it so happened, was a burgh councillor. Smailes was a safe bet. A mathematical genius bland to the point of invisibility and unlikely to abuse his position as leader of the 'student body', a definition of the rabble which most teachers found risible.

Alison was not disappointed in being passed over for the position of School Captain. She was the solitary female in the ranks of the sixth and had other, more important things on her mind.

Boris said, 'What do you know about Warrison and Nicholls?'

'Not much, Mr Borland.'

'How much?'

'They make scientific instruments and equipment. We have some of it here, don't we? The scales, the condenser—'

'We *could* do with a microscope, though, to keep you would-be medical types happy.'

'Well, I suppose we could, sir, yes.'

'There's one on offer, a prize from Warrison and Nicholls.'

'Ah!' said Alison.

'Test paper, short essay on a selected scientific subject. Saturday morning, November fourth, nine until twelve thirty. You and Wallace. Okay?'

'Okay, Mr Borland,' said Alison, unfazed.

Dave Wallace, though, was anything but unfazed. Tall, dark and acne-ridden, poor Dave had turned to jelly at the prospect of a competitive examination. On the morning of the test, it was all Alison could do to persuade him to leave the bus in Glasgow's Bath Street and accompany her to the long, cold basement room below Warrison and Nicholls's showrooms.

She was surprised at the poor turnout. Only twenty-six entrants were seated on uncomfortable chairs at the bench tables. Dave cringed at the sight of so many posh school uniforms, star pupils, confident and aloof, from the High School and the Academy but Alison, one of only seven girls present, suffered no sense of inferiority. She sat patiently through the preliminary speeches, listened with some scepticism as a representative of Warrison and Nicholls's board tried to convince the multitude that a career in scientific instrument-making was the way to fame and fortune. Then, at nine thirty on the dot, she gratefully received the first test paper from the hand of the appointed invigilator.

'Are you ready, children?'

The 'children' growled affirmatives and the invigilator clicked the button of his stopwatch and said, 'Begin.'

All the heads went down. Pens scratched. Little tinkling noises from uncapped inkwells and bottles filled the air. Somebody – not Dave – groaned and then there was a spate of throat-clearing, coughing and sighing followed by a peculiar gobbling noise which turned out to be a girl in glasses and a purple blazer having a nervous fit. She was instantly led away.

The room settled at last into a strangely dense near-silence, intensified by the grasshopper whisper of nibs on foolscap and the subtle murmur of young brains being cudgelled for forgotten facts.

Only Alison remained upright. She read the paper, selected the group of questions which seemed most suited to her knowledge and, as had become her habit, rested her mind quietly for half a minute before she tried to make it spin. She admired the prize microscope which was displayed on a table at the front of the room; a beautiful object, like something from a jeweller's catalogue, all steel and brass and mirrors, set on top of its walnut box. *The Alison Burnside Memorial Microscope, Presented to Flannery Park School by Doctor Alison Burnside, MD, FRCS, Regius Professor of Medicine, in recognition of the part played in her illustrious career by . . .*

Mr Jim Abbott – my teacher.

'Miss?' Alison blinked at the invigilator's question. 'Are you all right?'

'Fine, thank you,' Alison said and with a confident smile uncapped her fountain pen and began to write.

'Hey, Ally, how'd it go?' Dave Wallace asked as they scrambled up the steps into Bath Street at twenty minutes to one.

'All right, I suppose. Quite good, really. You?'

'Toffee,' Dave told her. 'Scooshed it.'

'Yes, me too,' said Alison. 'Fancy a coffee?'

'Sure do. Who's payin'?'

'I am,' said Alison.

'Are we celebratin'?'

'Of course we are.'

'Aye, one of us is bound to have won.'

'Me,' said Alison.

'Naw, me,' said Dave, grinning.

The microscope, needless to say, was not won by either of the pupils from Flannery Park.

ELEVEN

Looking Out for Number One

'It's not the night shift I really object to,' Alex roared, 'it's the noise of those damned machines.'

'You'll get used to it, Dad,' Henry said. 'Are you sorry I pushed you into applying for the job?'

'What?'

'ARE YOU SORRY I—'

'All right, all right. I'm not bloody deaf.'

'Lucky to get it,' Davy said. 'Must have been hundreds up for it.'

'Henry pulled the string, did you not, my darling?' said Trudi.

'Not me,' said Henry. 'No, really. I had nothing at all to do with it.'

'They would know it was your father,' Trudi said. 'It would be good for him to have a reliable son already upon the company's books.'

'Well,' Henry conceded, 'maybe.'

Trudi had one habit to which the boys could not adjust. She would sit with them at the end of a meal, smoke a cigarette, sip tea and join in their conversation. They had been used to having the living-room to themselves for a half hour while Mavis had scuttled off to wash up. Even Alison twitched a little restlessly and would have swept away the plates and cups if Trudi had not stopped her with a hand on the arm or a little shake of the head.

The family, in fact, seldom ate together these days. Through Kenny's good offices Jack had obtained a Musicians' Union card and had started rehearsals for the Alhambra's winter pantomime as a member of the pit orchestra. Henry's hours were, to say the least of it, erratic and Alex, three weeks into his new job at the *Mercury*, alternated week about between day shift and night shift.

Alex was still confused as to how he had got the job. He had no complaints about the nature of the work; general maintenance presented no problems in understanding or execution. Even so he remained bewildered by the ease with which he, one of shipbuilding's elite, had been snapped up for a job which any tuppence-ha'penny handyman could do. The wage was not what he had been used to in Ransome's but it was better by far than dole and he had to admit that he felt more of a man now that he was employed again.

There was something satisfying in being out in the streets before dawn, riding the tramcar along an empty Dumbarton Road, home to breakfast and bed. Something stimulating in the sight of feverish activity in Maldive Square when he arrived for nightwork – vans, vendors, paperboys and great thumping bundles of the morning editions, all flurry and bustle – and just along the cobbled lane from the despatch hatches a glimpse through basement windows of the presses, massive and brown and throbbing, and zigzag patterns of newsprint shooting through battens and rollers.

Alex would pause for a moment before he entered the building to sniff the hot, waxy steam from the air vents and feel the tremor of commerce in his feet, would look up at the Magdalen towering overhead and think of Henry somewhere up there. He felt remarkably secure in being part of an organisation so vast that neither boom nor bust could shake its stability and took pride in the fact that he helped tighten the nuts and oil the bearings that printed the words that Henry wrote.

Naturally, Alex told nobody of his feelings in case he opened himself to ridicule. He did, however, confess to Ruby that he had landed on his feet and guessed he had his eldest to thank for finding him permanent employment in the midst of a national slump.

Ruby nodded and held her tongue about Trudi's influence for she alone knew who was behind the sea-change in Burnside fortunes and that quite soon there might be a price to be paid for privileges received.

Bertie approved of recent domestic developments. He had never grown used to seeing his father lolling about the house, to confronting the old man's idleness. Bertie was priggish about work. He genuinely felt that work was the purpose for which man was put on earth. He loved routine and was never happier than when marking up Dividend Accounts at the day's end or counting piles of small change from the counter till, tedious tasks which Mr Lockie was heartily glad to relinquish to his eager assistant.

Mr Lockie was Bertie's role model. Now and then he might fancy himself tall in the saddle, fast with a gun but he was far too prim to entertain these daydreams for long. Instead he found a suitably grim and emulable reality in the manager. He even began to dress like Mr Lockie, to have his hair trimmed extra short and sport celluloid cuffs and an SCWS necktie.

Gavin did not like the changes in his friend, which was all the more reason for adopting them. At long last Hollywood had let the couple down. There was no more to say about films past and present, no more star gossip to exchange. Teabreaks had become unendurably dull. They would have been duller still if it hadn't been for the unacknowledged longing which grew in strength as Halloween nuts and dooking apples gave way to fireworks, fireworks to the first early boxes of tangerines wrapped in purple paper.

Bertie had grown disillusioned with Gavin, Gavin no less so with Bert. Spur-of-the-moment spats, nasty little arguments, back-biting and huffy accusations were followed by muted reconciliations in the course of which Bertie would do his best to apologise without actually saying he was sorry. He was often tempted to abuse his position of authority, to boss the lad about, even bully him a bit. Instead he strove to follow the excellent example set by Mr Lockie who was very firm and fair, never raised his voice above a shout and never let his favourites off with anything.

What galled Bertie most of all was that Gavin was not whole-heartedly committed to the Co-op. Gavin was for ever criticising the management committees, challenging the policies, questioning the bedrock principle of social equality upon which the movement was founded. And in the midst of one of their hair-trigger quarrels Gavin even admitted that he would be up and away the minute something better came on offer.

'But what about me?'

'What about you, Bertie?'

'Don't you want to stay?'

'An' be a delivery boy all my life?'

'What *do* you want to be, Gavin?'

'I want t' be rich. I want t' live in a big house in London—'

'London?'

'An' have fun.'

'Fun?'

'Fun, aye. You know what fun is, don't you, Bertie?'

'What sort of fun can you find in London that you can't find here?'

The tempo of the conversation slowed abruptly. With a pallet of self-raising flourbags lofted in his arms, Gavin squinted at Bertie and for a heart-stopping moment Bertie feared that he was about to learn something that would scar him for ever.

Gavin's blue eyes were blank, however, a little blemish of bewilderment dark between his fair brows. He shook his head.

'Dunno.'

'See,' Bertie said sharply. 'You're better off here. London – huh! Now get that lot to the shelves or we'll have Mr Lockie down on us, won't we?'

'Dunno,' said Gavin again, then, adjusting the heavy board across his chest, leaned on the storeroom door and swung through it into the shop.

It was one of the week's blank evenings, an evening on which Alison did not call. Jim was listening to a symphony concert on the wireless while marking third year compositions. He had seen nothing of Winnie since she'd cleared away the supper dishes. That was not of itself unusual. She had a sewing chair and lamp in her bedroom and, like Jim, was often content to seek her own company.

It was after nine o'clock before she reappeared in the living-room. Her specs hung on a silk ribbon about her neck, her cardigan was draped about her shoulders and she had replaced her comfortable broad-fitting house slippers with brown low-heeled shoes. This trivial detail immediately caught Jim's attention and indicated that Winnie had something weighty on her mind.

Concert music had been replaced by a broadcast talk and

Jim had no hesitation in switching the wireless off. The set was an Ormond five-valve portable model and he had already met half of the twelve monthly payments on the deferred terms agreement which Winnie had talked him into. He flipped the hinged lid to cover the dials but did not put on the dustcover. He closed the last of the essay jotters, gathered them into a bundle, snapped a rubber band about them and slid them into his briefcase.

Winnie said, 'Is that you finished?'

He looked round, not quite enquiringly. 'It is, thank goodness.'

She was standing by the fire. Her soft pink hands were folded about her elbows under the loose cardigan. She was younger than she appeared to be, not forty yet, but she had worn the faded air of middle age for so long that Jim had to remind himself that Winnie was still in her prime.

She said, 'I have something to tell you, Jim.'

'I guessed as much.'

'I had a letter from Mother this morning.'

Their mother, also a widow, was not a noted correspondent. She lived in Pitlochry not far from the Perthshire village where Jim and his sisters had been born and raised and where his father had earned a good living as a whisky blender. Jean and Constance, Jim's oldest sisters, were both married to hill farmers and lived within easy reach of the town. Mother, however much she might complain, was not lonely or neglected.

'What does she want?' Jim asked.

'She's unhappy.'

'No, she's not,' Jim said. 'She's just reminding us that we haven't been to visit lately. Do you want to go up this weekend?'

'I don't think she's well.'

'Have you been in touch with Connie?'

392

Win did not answer. She had stopped rocking on her heels, had stopped massaging her elbows with her fingertips. Jim had the sudden sinking feeling that this conversation might be important after all.

'She wants me to look after her,' Winnie announced.

'Well, she can hardly come here. We simply don't have room.'

'I'm thinking of going to stay with her,' Winnie said.

Jim hesitated. 'For how long?'

'For good.'

Another hesitation. 'If she needs medical attention—'

'It's not that.'

'Well, what is it?'

'Mother needs my company more than you do, Jim.'

'I don't think that's true,' Jim said. 'However, if you – if the time's come – what age is she? Sixty?'

'Sixty-two.'

'Not old.'

'To be frank about it,' Winnie said, 'I feel I'm in the way here.'

'Oh, for heaven's sake!' He slapped his hand upon the table and threw himself back in the chair. 'This sudden urge to dance attendance on Mother is because of Alison Burnside, isn't it? How ridiculous!'

'Is it?'

'Go,' Jim said. 'Go and stay with Mother if you must. She'll drive you batty in a fortnight, you know. Still, you can always come back.'

'You'll fare better without me. I know I'm holding you back from what you really want.'

'Holding me back? From what?'

'I'm not blind,' Winnie said. 'I can see what's going on between you and that young girl. I don't want to watch you make a fool of yourself.'

'Oh, come on,' Jim said, 'surely you don't suppose I'd take advantage of a—'

'You love her. Don't you love her?'

'That's immaterial. She's a young woman destined for a career. She's not interested in marrying some scarred old war veteran.'

'Don't you love her? She loves you.'

'Rubbish! Absolute rubbish!' he protested. 'At best – an infatuation.'

'No, it goes deeper than that.'

'Since when did you become such an expert? Alison doesn't know her own mind yet. Perhaps she does *like* me – I mean, we do get on well, but then we'd have to since I'm her tutor. What is it really, Win? Aren't you happy in Flannery Park?'

'Jim.'

'I thought you'd made friends in the Guild. You've never been exactly enamoured of Pitlochry, have you? You always said it was a stuffy wee town.'

'Jim.'

'What?'

'Don't let her go, Jim.'

He gave an uneasy laugh. 'Now there's inconsistency for you. First you accuse me of making a fool of myself and in the next breath you tell me not to let her go. I'm going to look an even bigger fool if you abandon me.'

'You can look after yourself well enough. You've done it before.'

'I don't mean that,' Jim said. 'I mean what will happen to Alison? I won't be able to tutor her, not a man alone in the house with a schoolgirl.'

'You'll just have to stop pretending.'

'Explain what you mean by that?'

'You can hardly keep your hands off her.'

'Hand,' Jim said. 'Just one, in case you'd forgotten.'

'Is that your excuse, Jim?'

'Pardon?'

'For not telling her, for not showing her how you feel? Will you make up her mind for her on that matter too? At least give her the chance to turn you down. Don't do the rejecting for her.'

'Winnie, what *are* you talking about?'

'I said I cannot stand to see you make a fool of yourself—'

'You did, you did. And—'

'—which is precisely the reason I intend to go and stay with Mother for a while. I don't want to watch you ruin your life through a stupid act of martyrdom. Stop being so *nice*, Jim Abbott. Start looking out for number one.'

'Winnie, I can't believe you're saying this.'

'Take a lesson from me. I lost everything I ever wanted because I was too indecisive and had too much regard for what people might think.'

'Winnie, Winnie, it was the war. Nobody could predict—'

'Who's to say there won't be another war?'

'That's just daft.'

'Who's to say we won't *all* be killed next time? If we are what will *you* have had out of life, James Abbott? Do you intend spending the rest of your days *waiting* for something good to happen to you? You love this girl. I know you do. At least allow her the opportunity of loving you in return.'

'I wish it was that simple,' Jim said.

'I mean within marriage, of course.'

'Of course, of course,' Jim said. 'But what purpose will be served by you leaving?'

'If I leave,' Winnie said, 'you'll no longer have to

consider my feelings or worry about what will become of me.'

'Winnie, I don't regard you as a burden.'

'I know you don't – but I am, none the less,' his sister said. 'You'll fare better on your own, Jim. With any luck, you won't be on your own for long.'

'Winnie – I don't know what to say.' Jim paused. 'When do you intend to leave?'

'Before Christmas.'

'Can't I persuade you to change your mind?'

'No.'

'Well,' Jim said, 'at least Mother will be pleased,' and, though the shaking in his legs had not quite gone, he got to his feet and went brusquely into the kitchen to put the kettle on.

It was raining, lashing in fact. Brenda put on her tomato-red oilskin, one of her mother's big hats and a pair of brown rubber galoshes. She realised that she looked a proper sight but she no longer cared.

At the back of eight o'clock she banged out of the house and ran into the rain-drenched streets as if pursued by demons. She hadn't a clue why, after weeks of lassitude, she had elected to do something positive on that particular night, in such appalling weather. Desperation, like a fever, had its own rhythm, she supposed.

Agitation had been mounting in her all day long. Latterly she could hardly bear to sit still and watch rain bring darkness to the big windows of the machinists' shop. It had been all she could do to get herself home without bursting into tears. She was mad at herself for yielding to such muddy surges of emotion. When the latest crying fit was over she had washed her hair, had wrapped her head in a towel and, in her mother's dressing-gown, had wolfed down the roll-mop herring and cold potatoes that had been left under the plate for her tea. Even then, even as she tinkered with her damp hair, put on a wool skirt and fished out the old brown galoshes from the cupboard, she was not quite sure if she could bring herself to do it. Eventually she dashed out of the house before fear got the better of her and condemned her to more days of miserable uncertainty.

She was soaked before she reached Dunsinane Street. Her stockings squelched within the rubber boots as she reached up to ring the doorbell.

'Yes, can I help you, young lady?'

She had been in Walter's house only once before, on that fateful night in September. She could hardly claim to have 'met' his parents in the usual sense of the word. She stared up at the man. He had a gloomy look to him, dark and glum. He wore the waistcoat and trousers of a heavy pin-stripe suit, collar and tie, shirt cuffs fastened by brass links.

'Is – is Walter . . . I'm lookin' for Walter.'

'Walter isn't here.'

'Where is – where can I find him?'

'Who is it, George?' a voice, female, enquired from within.

By the wan light from a shaded lamp in the hall Brenda could just make out the faint quirk at the corner of the man's lips.

'Are you one of those girls?' he asked. 'Walter's girls?'

'I – Yes, I think I am.'

'Come in,' the man said. 'Come on, don't be fright.'

He let her step past him into the hall.

'Who *is* it?'

'Nobody, Marietta. A client.' George Giffard frowned at the staircase that went up into the twilight. 'I'll take it in the living-room. Stay where you are. Stay in bed, please.'

He waited.

Brenda, dripping, waited too, both listening for sounds from the woman upstairs, for further interference, like static from a wireless set. After a moment Mr Giffard nodded, raised an eyebrow, put a finger to his lips and silently ushered Brenda into the living-room.

Brenda had expected the place to give her the creeps. She almost expected to discover bits and pieces of underwear scattered on chairs and carpet, an incriminating row of gin bottles still on the table, preserved like a tableau around which and through which the Giffards shuffled and shifted.

The room wasn't like that at all. It was trim, tidy and – different. Knobby green velvet covered the table. The long sofa on which Scott Giffard and Doris had grappled had been draped with a couple of tartan travelling rugs and the chair on which she'd cuddled Walter had been moved closer to the fire, a variation in angle which seemed to alter all other perspectives.

'Still pouring, I see,' said Mr Giffard.

Too nervous to speak yet, Brenda nodded.

He gestured to her to slip out of her coat. Very courteously he took her coat and hat, gave them a little shake over the fireplace then removed them from the room. On his return he motioned Brenda to the sofa, brought out a chair from the table and placed it almost against her knees. He seated himself and leaned forward, like a minister about to pray.

'Ah, yes,' he said. 'I recognise you now.'

Mr Giffard was handsome in a different way from Walter. He seemed stolid and firm, not arrogant. He was exactly the sort of man she'd have picked for a father if ever she'd been given a choice in the matter.

'I – I need to speak to Walter, Mr Giffard. It's, you know, urgent.'

'Can't be done, I'm afraid. Walter's no longer with us.'

'He's not, I mean, dead?'

'No, no. Departed but not dead. He's gone to sea with his brother.'

'Naw!'

'I gather he didn't have the gumption to tell you face to face.'

'Naw!' Brenda exclaimed again.

'Were you Walter's sweetheart?'

'I mean, I thought I was.'

'Yet when I saw you, you were embracing another young man.'

'He was embracin' me.'

'Who was the girl with Walter?'

'One o' my friends – leastways I thought she was a friend.'

There was nothing salacious in Mr Giffard's interrogation. His stare was inquisitive and sympathetic, not libidinous. He had large hands, Brenda noticed, and, unusual for a man, wore a gold wedding ring which he rubbed gently with his thumb as he spoke.

'You're a local girl, aren't you?'

'Foxhill Crescent.'

'I'm sorry I can't help you,' Mr Giffard said. 'I'd give you a forwarding address if I could but we have no idea at all where Walter is, or his brother for that matter. I'm not even sure what shipping line signed them on. Probably the P & O, Scott's company. You went to school with Walter, didn't you?'

'Aye, but I'm not at school now either.'

'He had a promising future, you know.'

'So everybody said,' Brenda responded.

Mr Giffard raised his shoulders. ' I can't honestly say I'm surprised Walter didn't persevere with his studies. Scott was always going to put a spoke in that wheel, of course. Scott wasn't going to let Walter gain too much favour. I miss him – miss them both, but Walter especially – but I think it's for the best in the long run that he's gone.' He paused. 'I hope you don't mind me taking you freely into my confidence, Alison?'

'I'm Brenda,' Brenda said. 'An' I'm goin' to have a baby.'

'Oh, you're not Alison? I thought you must be Alison.'

'Well, I'm not. I'm Brenda. Pregnant Brenda.'

'I don't think Walter ever mentioned you. Have you known him long?'

'Long, you know, enough.'

'Yes, I can see why you're anxious to get in touch with him.'

'Anxious?' Brenda said. 'I'm desperate.'

'I wonder, if you don't mind, if we might keep our voices down.' Mr Giffard did not seem particularly perturbed by her news. His facial muscles had slackened and he had that odd pursing about the mouth that Mr Abbott sometimes had, as if he was struggling not to smile.

'What age are you?' he asked.

'Seventeen,' Brenda whispered.

'Have you told anyone else of your condition?'

'No. I wanted to talk to Walter first.'

'So you haven't consulted a doctor – for confirmation?'

Brenda shook her head. It hadn't occurred to her that an insurance agent would be used to dealing with disasters.

Mr Giffard said, 'In that case how can you be sure you're expecting?'

Brenda felt her face flame with embarrassment. 'I just, you know, am.'

'When did the alleged act of conception take place?'

'The what?'

'Walter and you, together.'

'Lots of times.'

Mr Giffard asked her six or seven more delicate questions, not one of which seemed to relate to the fact that Walter had loved her and had left her in the lurch. He gave no indication that he intended to track down his errant son, to reach out the long parental arm and haul Wattie back to do the decent thing by her.

'Brenda – do you mind if I call you Brenda?' Mr Giffard said.

'Call me what you like. I want Walter. He should be made to marry me.'

'I realise,' said Mr Giffard, 'that you're feeling terribly let down. But you mustn't blame Walter. If anyone's to blame, it's me.'

'You?'

'I sent him away. I lost my temper and told him to clear out.'

'What's that got to do with my condition?'

'Unless a miracle has been visited upon us, Brenda,' Mr Giffard told her gently, 'you aren't expecting a baby. You can't be.'

'Can so,' Brenda said, petulantly. 'We done – done all those things.'

'But not the one thing that makes babies,' said Mr Giffard.

'How do you know?'

'Because you've just told me, as good as,' Mr Giffard said. 'In addition to which Walter confided in me before he left. He told me—'

'I don't care what he told you.'

'Brenda, it wasn't complete. It has to be complete.'

'Complete?'

'Inside you.'

'Oh!' Brenda's eyes widened. 'I thought – you know—'

She began to weep. Quiet tears, quite genuine. Relief mingled with disappointment. For days now she had prepared herself for dramatic change, for tempests of emotion, storms of recrimination, ultimate reconciliation. Now this man had taken it all away from her. She felt oddly let down.

'Walter may be a bit headstrong but he's not a complete fool. One thing he has always been is careful,' Mr Giffard said. 'If you feel there's something wrong with you then I suggest you visit your doctor and not leap to wrong conclusions.'

'I just thought we'd, you know, done it,' Brenda sobbed, 'an' Wattie would have to marry me.'

'A natural error.' Mr Giffard got to his feet, a trace of impatience in his manner now. 'Once, twenty-five years ago, I made exactly the same mistake. As it turned out, I was the fool. Some things never seem to change.'

Brenda struggled to her feet as a shrill female voice called from above, 'George, George, who *is* it?'

Mr Giffard directed Brenda towards the living-room door. 'You'd better go now, young lady, before my wife comes downstairs.'

'Is Mrs Giffard ill?' Brenda whispered.

'Yes.'

'Because of what happened?'

'So she would have us believe,' Mr Giffard said.

He accompanied Brenda out on to the path that flanked the house and, hands in pockets, watched her button her oilskin and adjust her mother's hat. He seemed quite impervious to the rain that wetted his shirt and plastered his hair to his scalp. Brenda could see Walter in him now, in the backward tilt of the head, the arrogance that was not arrogance at all but a kind of fatalism.

Rain hissed into the leafless trees and dowdy hedges, babbled along the eaves, splashed in the gutters.

Brenda stood below him, looking up. Relief, vast relief, far outweighed her disappointment and she realised what an idiot she had been. She really did wish she'd had a father like that, strong, stolid and sensible, to guide her properly through life and steer her direction. It was all she could do not to throw her arms around him, give him a hug, a hug to pass on to Walter.

'I'm sorry, Mr Giffard.'

'So you should be,' George Giffard said and, hands in pockets and head held back, solemnly watched her trot away down the path to freedom.

Now and then while Alex slept he would dream that he heard the voices of women murmuring around his bed; not loved ones gone before, though, not Mavis, not Olive, the sweet sister who had died when he was ten, or little Elsie Chalmers, the school friend whom he had worshipped in the cold, cruel world of Vine Street Infants, who had simply disappeared one day, plucked away into heaven by diphtheria. These were voices of the night, faint, ethereal and fairly uncommon. What Alex heard during his daylight slumbers were angels of a different order, too damned familiar to be veiled by anything more ectoplasmic than the back bedroom wall.

He would stir at their murmuring, at Ruby and Trudi giggling now and then, but when he opened his eyes there would be no sign of either one of them. He would lie in solitary state trying to adjust to the fact that it was still early afternoon and eighty per cent of the populace was fifty per cent of the way through the day and that it was he who was out of kilter, not them.

'Trudi?'

'What is it you want?'

'What time is it?'

'It is twenty minutes after two o'clock.'

'Is Ruby here?'

'No.'

'I thought I heard Ruby. I could've *sworn* I heard Ruby.'

'You are dreaming, Papa. It is the sausage which makes you dream.'

Breakfast – or was it supper? – did tend to lie heavy on his stomach. Sliced sausage, a fried heel-pad, had always been his downfall. Not even Trudi could talk him out of it. Dreams of fair women, it seemed, stemmed from nothing more exotic than a lump of ground beef bound with pork fat.

'Was she here earlier – Ruby, I mean?'

'In your bedroom? Now you do have a dream, Papa.' Trudi would pop her head around the door and smile, radiating brightness into the curtained room. 'Since she is not your wife our neighbour cannot visit your bedroom. It would not be respectable.'

'Oh, bugger off.'

Alex would wallow on to his side and cowl the quilt around his ears and listen to his daughter-in-law's tinkling laughter.

Although he would never admit it he liked being teased by Trudi, bossed by her, treated in some ways as if he were a boy again.

If he took Ruby to be his wife all that would have to change. As Ruby's husband he would have to stand up for himself, be too much the man of the house. He was reluctant to make the swap but had the feeling, the sneaky, sneaky feeling that others might be conspiring to make the swap for him while he worked and while he slept.

Aware of Alex's suspicions Trudi suggested that the morning 'kaffe klatch', as she called it, move on alternate weeks to Ruby's house. Pete went too. The dog no longer cared at whose fireside he snoozed and – just like any male – would waken only when titbits were offered him.

On that particular morning at the beginning of December, however, Alex was on day shift, Jack had risen early to go into town and the women had 162 all to themselves. On Trudi's orders they convened soon after nine o'clock to tackle the pleasant task of baking Christmas cakes. This was a new one on Ruby. Like most Scots folk she did not set much store by Christmas but confined her celebrations, such as they were, to New Year. Alex, Jack and Davy, Brenda too, would all be working on Christmas Day but Trudi would not be denied the pleasure of preparing for a grand Christmas feast and had coaxed Ruby into a session of baking which would eventually result in a rich five-pound plum cake, properly iced, for each of them.

Fresh butter, caster sugar, chopped cherries, sultanas and candied peel, walnuts and finely sliced dates all went into Trudi's mix. Eggs were languidly added to flour, plus allspice and several teaspoonsful of brandy from a half bottle bought specifically for culinary purposes. When the cakes were tinned and put in the oven the ladies, a little fatigued by creaming and whipping, refreshed themselves with hot coffee seasoned with what was left of the brandy which, as it happened, was rather a lot.

By eleven fifteen Mrs Burnside and Mrs McColl were, if not drunk, certainly tipsy.

'After which he says to me, "You vill not leef this boat as you boarded her. You vill first be mine or you vill be no manz's."'

'And what did he mean by that?' Ruby asked.

'He means,' Trudi gasped and whispered, 'a vigrin.'

'What's a vigrin?'

'Virgin, I mean a vir-*gin*.'

'Oh, my God! What did you say to that?'

'I said, "You are too late, m'sieur."'

'I thought he was a German?'

'He was. He was a German policeman. Big policeman. Important fellow. But I am pretending to be a French person. So I say to him, "M'sieur, you are too late. I am no longer what it is you take me for."'

'What did he do then?'

'He is not daunted. To be denied me. He says to me, "So, you vill proof to me you are not virgin or you vill not leef this boat."'

'What a predicament,' said Ruby, agog. 'Where was this?'

'On the Rhine, near – it does not matter where. He comes upon me, intent to take me. I am young and pretty. He does not know what I have learned already, so innocent I appear to him. He steps close to put out his big arms, the arms of a bear.'

'Dear God!'

'I have a parasol. It is sunny, so – a parasol. I hit him with the handle, which is of malacca, I think, if I remember.'

'On the head.'

'No, no, no, no. I hit him – *here*, down *here*.'

'You didn't!'

'He goes *ouuufff*. I see his eyes, they come out popping. I do not wait to watch him recover. I jump straight over the side of the boat in my nice summer dress. I swim to shore where Papa is and the big policeman's wife. I come drip-drip out of the river. And there I am safe.' Trudi drank from the coffee cup and added more brandy. 'I think I am safe.'

'He, I mean, he didn't get you, did he? The policeman?'

'No.' Trudi shook her head, more soberly. 'He get Papa, though. Later.'

'I never knew you'd led such an adventurous life,' Ruby said, sighing. 'Me, stuck here in Glasgow for all these years and all those things going on I never even dreamed about.'

'It is not always a dream. It is sometimes a nightmare.' Trudi leaned forward. 'I tell nobody of this. I tell you only because you will understand. We are not so different, I think, under the skins. We will have what we want to have, will we not?'

Flattered to be paired with such a sophisticated woman, to be treated if not as an equal at least as a friend, nevertheless Ruby could not help but wonder what Trudi would have done to, or with, Bryce Walker? With the taste of brandy in her mouth, the smell of plum cake in her nostrils, Ruby experienced a pang of apprehension at the realisation that she was perfectly content to settle for someone as ordinary as Alexander Burnside, a man whose only virtue seemed to be that, now he was in work, he would be able to take care of her in her old age.

'For you it will be a wedding in June,' Trudi said, patting Ruby's hand.

'Alex may have something to say about that.'

'He will not resist you. I can tell how it is with men.'

'Has he mentioned anything, you know, about me?'

'He dreams of you,' said Trudi.

'Get off!'

'It is true. He dreams of you. He hears your voice in sleep.'

'Sayin' what?'

'Saying, "Get out of bed you lazy bogger, get up and do your job." '

Ruby's face fell. For an instant she hated the blonde-haired woman with the brittle disparaging laugh. Trudi had made a joke, though, and expected her to laugh too which, obligingly, Ruby did. But only because of the plum cakes and brandy and because she'd suddenly realised that poor wee Alex Burnside deserved something better than this.

Poor wee Alex Burnside and similar souls who laboured in darkness had created certain rituals to see them through the night. The Magdalen Building was certainly one up on Ransome's when it came to creature comforts. No more gales blowing up your kilt, no frost to shrivel your tender parts, no reeking braziers and egg rolls tasting of tin. It might be noisy in the bowels of the newspaper office but by God it was warm and the chuck was infinitely superior to anything that came out of a shipwright's dinner-pail. Mind you, it didn't always look it. The blacksmith's stove in the low-beamed neuk below the gangway was ringed with pans full of glue and solder, flux and melted lead and it was sometimes difficult to tell which one contained the special dish, the *platter de jawer* as Tommy Bremner called it, which the smith had whipped up to sustain himself and his crew.

Minced steak and onions, brown and bubbling, was slabbered on to tin plates and served with piping hot rolls purchased directly from the bakers in Lorimer Street. Variety was provided by stew and beans, steak and kidney pudding or, as a rare treat, pork chops and apple sauce. Wiry little Tommy Bremner had a flair for cooking and an appetite to match and the men who worked in

Maintenance were the envy of all for their sophisticated dining arrangements.

A glass of red wine or a schooner of beer would have finished the three a.m. repast perfectly but Tom Bremner adhered rigidly to the No Booze rule. With welding torches and metal cutters, rip-saws, sledge hammers and bolting tools in constant use a man made muzzy by drink was a danger to all and if Tom caught you with a whiff of alcohol on your breath it was out on your ear and no appeal, an edict which Alex Burnside heartily endorsed.

They had been 'racking' that night, strengthening the huge metal pillars on which the paper platforms rested. Bolting and welding were the skills involved. Alex was happy to be working with metal again. He took to the torch – which as a riveter he had for so long despised – like a duck to water. No fear of trade union demarcation rows here. Maintenance men were expected to be jacks-of-all-trades. The internal noise still wearied him, though, and he was glad when the break was called and he could slump into one of the old broken armchairs with which the blacksmith's bothy was furnished. There was no door, only an arch of cement and tile beyond which the basement's long avenues stretched away under a web of pipes, beams and cables.

Tommy was already at the stove, stirring a pan of stew and beans. Kevin, the apprentice, and Jackie, the carpenter, were washing their hands at the deep stone sink which flanked the lavatory. Alex lighted a Woodbine and picked up a copy of the morning edition, literally hot off the press.

He hadn't much interest in headlines filled with depressing news about crashing stock markets in America and downward spirals in share prices. Henry had got all het up about the word from Wall Street and had chuntered on for days about bear markets, 'economic lifeboats' and the need for fiscal orthodoxy. Alex didn't know what the hell Henry was talking about or why his son was so indignant about toffs losing their cash. The Burnside boys were in steady employment and that, as far as Alex was concerned, was all that mattered. He glanced at the sports pages, scanned the 'Diary' to see what Henry had been up to – an interview with the driver of the *Flying Scotsman* locomotive and a 'date' with A. C. Astor, the ventriloquist – then out of habit turned to the pages which recorded births, marriages and deaths.

The aroma of stew wafted deliciously about the bothy as Kevin did his bit with ladle and spoon. Charlie, an oddjob boy, brought in a bag of bread rolls, received payment and departed again along the avenue, heading an imaginary football and practising body swerves as he went.

Alex yawned.

He swung his feet from the bench, made to toss the *Mercury* aside, then paused.

'Uh?' He grunted under his breath, grabbed the paper to him and, standing now, held it up to the light and reread the entry that had belatedly caught his attention.

'God Almighty!' he exclaimed in astonishment. 'She's dead. The old bitch is dead . . . an' she never even thought to let us know.'

Kevin slid two plates of stew on to the table. 'Who's that then?'

'Granny Gilfillan,' he said, more to himself than to the boy.

'Your granny, is it?'

'Naw, naw, my wife's – my mother-in-law.'

'Did you not know she was ailin'?' Tommy Bremner asked.

'Hadn't a clue.'

'Must've been took sudden. When's the funeral?'

410

'Good point.' Alex lifted the newspaper and studied the intimation. 'Day after tomorrow. Half past eleven at the Western Necropolis Crematorium. *Crematorium*! Jee-zus!'

'Aye, that's a rarity,' Tommy Bremner said. 'Never heard of a woman askin' to be cremated. She must've requested it special. Must've been stipulated in her will or somethin'.'

Kevin shook his head. 'Aye, well, she'll no' get into heaven now. Here, Mr Burnside, are you all right?'

'Fine, fine,' said Alex in a strange strangled tone.

'Up in smoke,' said the blacksmith wistfully. 'Somethin' to be said for goin' up in smoke. At least the worms canny get you.' He looked down at the plate of stew and beans, tapped his fork twice upon the table and then, with appetite, began to eat. 'Not fancy it, Kevin? Goin' out in a blaze o' glory?'

'Not me, Mr Bremner,' the boy answered. 'My mammy would have a fit if I tried that one on.' He held a spoonful of gravy poised short of his lips. 'She wasn't a Catholic then, Mr Burnside, your granny, I mean?'

'Hell, no,' said Alex. 'She's only doin' it so her damned daughters can be with her right up to the very last minute.'

'Like the Indians,' said Kevin.

'The what?' said Alex.

'Never mind the Indians, son,' said Tommy Bremner, anxiously studying the riveter out of the corner of his eye. 'Alex, are you upset?'

Alex hesitated then answered, 'Nah, not me.'

'Come an' eat your dinner then before it gets stone cold.'

'Aye, aye,' said Alex with a sigh and, casting the newspaper aside, seated himself at the table and obediently reached for his plate.

* * *

Naturally there was a scandal, so much chatter among friends and relatives of the deceased that at first it was all the minister could do to make himself heard over the buzz in the long, stone-built chapel crouched on the ridge on the outskirts of Maryhill. The minister too was quite a topic of conversation. Where was the Reverend Macdonald who had officiated at most of the births and all of the weddings in the Gilfillan family and who, though he was tottering towards the grave himself, had seen fit to visit Granny in her final illness to offer the promise of redemption and, if she kept her nose clean, eternal salvation?

Apparently Granny had said not a dicky-bird to Mr Macdonald about her plans for disposal of her remains and the old minister had had a purple fit when he was shown the document that his venerable parishioner had signed before a witness, a rather elegantly phrased form put out by the Scottish Burial Reform and Cremation Society. Mr Macdonald was vehemently opposed to cremation. He had ranted on about Mrs Gilfillan lying at the last with atheists and communists and in spite of all that Belle, Flora and Marion could do to persuade him had refused to lead the service.

The youthful Reverend Harry Steedman had been co-opted from the ranks of Reform sympathisers and, once he got them to shut up, he was certainly adept at making the mourners feel at home. He believed in the triumph of the spirit of corruptible flesh and seemed to be saying that cremation was clean, quick, inexpensive and definitely the modern way to go. His eulogy, just before the little coffin slipped out of sight, was moderate but sincere and suggested that he had known Granny Gilfillan most of his life instead of not knowing her at all.

Alison was impressed by her grandmother's courage in signing away her remains as far back as 1911, the original date on the document. She was even more impressed by the old woman's wiliness in masking one scandal with another. There was so much speculation on who was there and who wasn't, which of the neighbours had taken umbrage and which relatives had 'very nearly' put their foot down that nobody seemed to notice the elderly gentleman who slipped into a rear pew seconds before the service began.

The Burnsides had not been 'officially' notified of either Gran's death or the funeral arrangements. After a pow-wow it was, however, decided that Alex, Henry and Alison would show the flag and that Davy and Jack would be let off the hook. Bertie simply refused to have anything to do with it. He had a morbid fear of funerals and the very idea of being in the proximity of a *body* being committed to the *fire* was enough to bring him out in a cold sweat.

'Granny wouldn't mind,' he had said. 'She never liked me, anyway.'

'She never liked any of us much,' Davy had said.

Prudently Alison had kept her mouth shut.

She sat in the chapel in Sunday best coat and hat four rows back from the front and peeked at her pretty girl cousins and the glum and spotty young men whose names had been familiar since she was a babe in arms but whose adult features she barely recognised. The aunts were all down front, husbands by their sides. They were, of course, weeping. Alison felt no sorrow at her grandmother's passing. She was stimulated by the novelty of the proceedings and protected by the knowledge that Gran had shared with her a couple of months ago.

As she stood between Henry and her father or sat, head

bowed, while the minister intoned prayers she was in fact plotting how she could corner Mr William Nelson, one-time skipper of the *Zeelander* and her grandmother's oldest friend, before he slipped anchor and vanished over the horizon for ever.

'Is that it?' Alex hissed at the conclusion of the benediction.

'That's it, Dad,' said Henry.

And Alison said, 'Excuse me,' and hurried out of the chapel's rear door before anyone could stop her.

What she had taken to be a black overcoat was in fact a garment not dissimilar to a peajacket. It had broad lapels and patch pockets and, together with a black snap-brimmed trilby and black leather gloves, lent Mr Nelson the raffish air of an American gangster. He hesitated at the corner of the chapel's south buttress then disappeared. Alison darted a glance behind her, saw the main doors of the chapel start to open, and hastened after him.

He was waiting for her on the edge of a path that dipped down into the monuments. All around was sky, a panorama of still, grey cloud smudged with traces of last night's rain. On the horizon not ships but hills; the rhino-horn of Dumgoyne prominent at the rugged end of the Campsie Fells, Ben Lomond a pale grey silhouette to the west.

'Well,' Mr Nelson said, 'she had a good innings, the old gal did. Eighty-odd ain't bad by anybody's reck'nin'.' He blew his nose into a mushroom-coloured handkerchief and smiled at Alison. 'You'll be missed in a minute.'

'Were you with her when she died?'

'Nup. The daughters were there. Quite right too. She shuffled away fast at the last, though, 'ardly suffered at all.'

'She sent you away, didn't she?'

'Yup.' He put the handkerchief back in his pocket.

'I'm surprised you didn't just brazen it out.'

He laughed wheezily. 'I never could stand up to 'er, no more than nobody else. 'Sides, you keep a secret for sixty years why break the habit?'

'Where do you stay?'

'Lodgings.'

'I mean, normally?'

'Hm!' Mr Nelson said. 'They're all dead now. One wife, two sons – the war took them away – and now 'er ladyship. Hm!' He looked at Alison and said again. 'Lodgings.'

'I'm not going to see you again, am I?'

'I doubts it.'

'Then I have to ask you something important right now.'

They had stopped below the brow of the ridge, bungalows and dairy farms, ploughed fields and stubble pastures, string roads and suburban hamlets rolled out like a carpet before them.

'No, love, I'm not,' Mr Nelson said before Alison could put the question. 'You're not mine. She never carried none o' mine. I'm sorry for me own sake. And that's the honest truth. I could have done with one like you now, at the end of me days.'

Alison said, 'Did you sign the document, the cremation thing?'

'Nineteen hundred and eleven, I was the witness.'

'And Gran witnessed yours?'

'That she did.'

'And eventually,' Alison said, 'there'll be a brass tablet, a plaque on the wall of the chapel with her name on it?'

'Yup.'

'And yours?'

'Yup,' Mr Nelson said. 'You won't tell, will you?'

'No, I won't tell,' said Alison. 'But why did you let me into your secret?'

'She'd kill me for tellin' you, love, but she thought you was the only one she could trust not to make a fuss. Clever, she said you was, clever enough to understand. By gum, she were right. You're very like her, you know, not in looks but in character.'

'Oh!'

'She always said you were the one to keep the secret.'

'You didn't have to bribe me to do it,' Alison said.

'No, no, that were a gift, plain and simple.'

'From—?'

'From me, from her. It's all the same in the end.'

'*Why* didn't you marry her?'

He said nothing for a moment, looking first towards the fells and then over his shoulder to the two or three figures who had wandered to the edge of the gravel behind the chapel and were calling Alison's name.

'I missed my chance,' he said.

'Now you'll be two names on a brass plaque pinned to a chapel wall.'

'It'll do,' said Mr Nelson. 'It'll do, love. It'll have to.' He stirred himself. 'You'd better get back to your family.'

'What about you?'

'I'm a-going that way,' he said, nodding at the path.

She kissed him on the cheek, quickly.

'Goodbye, Mr Nelson.'

'Goodbye, love,' he said and set off through the gravestones down the path towards the bungalows and small sequestered farms without, to Alison's regret, once looking back.

* * *

'Who the heck was that?' said Alex.

'An old friend of Gran's,' said Alison then added, 'or to be more precise an old friend of Grandfather's.'

'Grandfather's? That old buzzard's been dead for years. God, I can hardly remember him. How come you're consortin' with his friends?'

'I met the man once,' Alison lied glibly, 'a few years ago when I was visitin' with Mam.'

'You never said.'

'Did too,' said Alison. 'You probably weren't listening. He just wanted to say how sorry he was – about Gran.'

'Funny way of expressin' his condolences,' said Alex.

Alison said, 'I don't think he wanted to impose.'

They walked a few yards in silence then Henry said, 'Is that Mr Nelson, by any chance?'

'Yes, that's the chap.'

'The sailor?' said Henry.

They were walking towards the main gate of the Necropolis, among the last to leave. The Gilfillans had gone off in two black motorcars and cousins and neighbours had dispersed towards the tram depot or downhill to the Maryhill Road in search of a bus.

Alison said, 'He used to be a sailor, yes.'

'Well, that takes you back a bit,' Alex said. 'Been a long time since there were seafarin' men in the Gilfillan family, a long time. What's his name again?'

'Nelson,' said Alison. 'Bill Nelson.'

Alex frowned, puffed on his cigarette, shrugged. 'Never heard of him.'

'Nice of him to turn up, though, after all these years,' said Henry.

Alison gave her brother a darting little glance but Henry, she felt sure, was only fishing. 'Wasn't it?' she said, and let it go at that.

* * *

The bar of the Argyll Hotel was quiet that weeknight and Ruby was perched on a padded stool behind the counter trying to decipher the *Mercury's* crossword.

One dour English shoe salesman and an Irish dealer in metal alloys were playing draughts in a corner and Mr Pickering, trade unknown, was brooding by the fire and nursing a whisky and soda to make it last. The wintry sounds from outside had not diminished but Ruby now reckoned that they had more to do with the lack of fizz in custom than some odd shift in climate.

The Argyll's oak corridors and halls had developed a strange hollowness over the past few months and three of the kitchen staff and two waitresses had recently been paid off. Ruby was not particularly prone to pessimism but there were times when she wondered if she too might be 'let go' or, if the fall in custom continued, the Argyll might be forced to close altogether and she would be left without an income. Brenda's contribution to the household purse was useful but, on its own, would hardly keep the wolf from the door. Perhaps, Ruby thought, with more rue than reason, she might finagle a job out of Bryce Walker, one that did not involve taking her clothes off. Meanwhile she went on as usual, with tips down and boredom rising, and wrestled nightly with the crossword puzzle as if solving it had become an important part of the job.

She heard the clack of shoe heels long before the customer reached the door of the bar, not light but rapid. When the door was flung open she twisted on the stool and looked into the mirror to her left. Just at first she did not recognise the new arrival. She thought, What a handsome chap, then, frowning, realised that the handsome chap was none other than her friend and neighbour, Mr Alexander Burnside.

She dropped the newspaper and tucking in her shirt waist and smoothing her skirt, rose hastily to her feet.

The draughts-players glanced up as Alex advanced around the corner of the bar in quick-march tempo, arms swinging and chest thrust out.

He still wore the dark blue suit and black necktie in which he had attended the cremation of old Mrs Gilfillan that morning. Ruby thought how odd the garb was since she knew that Alex had returned home at lunchtime and had spent the afternoon asleep in bed.

Soon after the family had left for the crematorium Trudi had arrived at Ruby's door. Ruby had been less than elated to see the woman but made coffee, served shortbread and chatted as if their friendship hadn't taken a knock in recent weeks. Trudi had been full of questions about the Gilfillans. Ruby saw no reason not to answer though, to be honest, she felt just a wee bit reluctant to tell the Swiss woman anything these days.

Alex reached the bar.

He planted his hands on the counter, looked Ruby straight in the eye and said, 'Marry me.'

Below the level of the counter Ruby's knees pressed themselves together in a girlish spasm of delight. Her facial expression, however, remained absolutely unchanged.

'Have you been drinkin'?' she said.

'Naw, of course I haven't been drinkin',' Alex retorted. 'Why would I be drinkin' at this hour when I've my work to go to?'

'Your work?'

'I'm on nightshift.'

'So you're just sort of passin' by, are you?'

'No, I am not. Hell's bells, Ruby, I don't go to work in my best suit.'

'Well, on a posh paper like the *Mercu* . . .'

'Stop it, for God's sake. I've told you why I'm here.'

'To ask me to marry you?'

'Right.'

'Done up like a dish of fish an' shoutin' the odds like an Ibrox referee?'

He leaned over the counter and, modulating his tone to a hoarse whisper, said, 'Ruby McColl, will you be my wife?' He pulled back, face flushed, and added, 'Don't tell me you'll *think* about it. I'm not *havin'* that. I'm askin' you proper an' I want a proper answer.'

'Okay.'

'Okay – what?'

'I'll marry you.'

'Good.'

'Do you want somethin' to drink?'

'Shandy, half pint, easy on the beer.'

'Oh, wild celebration!' said Ruby, smoothly drawing on the pump.

'It would hardly do if I got my books for boozin', would it?'

'No, hardly.' She put the half pint glass on a mat on the counter.

'Not now I've got responsibilities,' Alex said. 'Which reminds me, you'd better hand in your notice.'

'Hoi, not so fast, Sunny Jim,' Ruby said. 'First you'd better tell me why this sudden, unexpected rush to the altar.'

'Well, Trudi—'

'Trudi? Don't tell me it was her idea?'

'Not exactly. I was sittin' in the chapel today watchin' the old woman go down, an' I got to thinkin'—'

'My God!' Ruby interrupted. 'Don't tell me! You felt the wheels of time's winged chariot runnin' up your back?'

'Eh?'

'Never mind,' said Ruby with a sigh. 'Just tell me what Trudi had to say.'

'When I got home, she said – I was down in the mouth, see – and she said it was time I did somethin' about it. So I'm here to ask you to name the day. Okay?'

'June.'

'That's what Trudi said you'd say.'

'Look, are you marryin' her or me?'

'I'm marryin' you. I needed a wee push, that's all.'

'Do you think you'll peg out until June?' Ruby said.

Alex shook his head. 'This isn't what I expected from you, Ruby.'

'What did you expect – somersaults, cartwheels?'

'Naw, but Trudi said—' He bit his lip as a dark cloud crossed Ruby's brow. 'June's fine, June's great. You're right, you're right. We shouldn't be too hasty. Come June Mavis will have been dead near two years an' nobody can say you lured me into it.'

'Dear God, Alex!'

'I mean—'

Ruby tutted, then smiled. 'I know perfectly well what you mean. Drink your shandy.'

He did as bidden, wiped foam from his upper lip with his forefinger then said, 'I don't want you workin' here, not after we're married.'

'I agree,' said Ruby. 'I'll give the management three months' notice, which is more than they deserve.'

'We'll have a quiet church weddin' then a reception in the house.'

'I see you've got it all worked out.'

'I have been givin' it a lot o' thought,' Alex admitted. 'I've also been thinkin' it might be best if I flitted into your house. After we're married, I mean.'

421

Ruby hesitated then said, 'Is that another of Trudi's suggestions?'

'It's a good one, though,' said Alex. 'I'll transfer the rent book on 162 to Henry an' we can put your house into my name.'

'What's Brenda goin' to say to that?'

'Brenda?'

'I *thought* you'd forgotten about Brenda,' Ruby said.

'No, no. No, no. She can stay with us.'

'She doesn't have much option, does she? What about Alison?'

'She'll stay where she is. She'll need peace an' quiet for her studies.'

'Of course.'

'Is this not to your likin', Ruby?'

'What gives you that impression?'

'Well, you seem a bit sniffy, that's all.'

'It's emotion, Alex,' Ruby told him. 'Women are funny about proposals.'

'Oh, I see.' He drank a little more shandy and studied her over the rim of the glass. 'You're not goin' to cry, are you?'

'No, I don't think so.'

'I mean, I really do want to marry you, Ruby,' he said. 'I mean, I don't want to marry anyone else.'

'That's nice,' Ruby said then, hiding the gesture from the draughts-players as best she could, leaned over the counter and patted his hand reassuringly. 'Yes, that's really nice.'

'So we're definitely on for June, are we?'

'Yes, Alex, we are,' Ruby said and turned to the bottles behind the bar to pour herself a gin.

One thing Mr Lockie really cared about was tea. He made no bones about the fact that he considered tea-drinking one of life's great pleasures and, abandoning his usual modesty, bragged that whenever there was a tasting competition at an SCWS managerial convention he usually took first prize. The tea locker, therefore, was Mr Lockie's pride and joy. He had done much of the carpentry work on the big cupboard himself at no charge to the Society and had fitted a stout plywood-faced door to keep out dampness and contaminating odours. Nobody was allowed to enter the sanctum unless they were accompanied by Mr Lockie and nobody ever got to dip their paws into the packing chests, to turn the small tea and inhale the fragrant dusts released in the mixing.

Indian and Ceylon teas were favoured for general fixed-price quarter-pound packets, a mixture that gave the good thick, coloury liquor and the strong flavour favoured by the Scots. In addition to pre-packed quantity tea, however, Mr Lockie also stocked ten selected types of leaf which he would blend himself, going for clarity, delicacy and distinction. Mr Lockie's Special Blend was sold to certain discerning customers who considered the extra penny and a half per quarter well worth the price.

The key to the tea locker hung on a little silver clip attached to Mr Lockie's watch chain and to the best of anyone's recollection had never been handed out before.

What a shock then, what an honour, when, in the midst of a busy Wednesday afternoon just a couple of weeks before Christmas, Mr Lockie solemnly unclipped the key and laid it in Bertie's palm.

'What?' said Bertie.

'Go into the locker and measure out an exact pound of Pekoe Souchong. It's in the box on the second top shelf, second along, marked with a red stencil. Don't stir it. Don't dip the spoon too deep. And make sure the packet's white paper not brown.'

423

'Yes, Mr Lockie. Thanks, Mr Lockie.'

'Lock the door after you, bring me back the key and the one pound packet. It's for Miss Shirrif's special household order and you know how fussy she is.'

'Yes, Mr Lockie. Thanks, Mr Lockie.'

'Bertie.'

'Yes, Mr Lockie?'

'Wash your hands first. No soap, just water.'

'Right,' Bertie said.

Proudly holding the key before him Bertie stalked the length of the counters, letting everyone who wasn't too busy have an eyeful of the honour bestowed upon him. Then he entered the back shop and, nerves fluttering, unlocked the closet and stepped inside.

There was nothing to it, really. He spotted the Pekoe Souchong box at once, lifted it down and laid it on the broad oak board where the scales were then, remembering Mr Lockie's final instruction, went out of the closet to the stone sink by the half-open door to the lane. He rinsed his hands under the tap, dried them carefully on his own spotlessly clean handkerchief then headed back for the tea locker within which, to his consternation, young Gavin was already installed.

'What the bloody hell—'

'Cosy, isn't it?' Gavin said.

'Get out.'

'Keep your shirt on, Bertie. I'm only lookin'.'

'Out. Out.'

'Lockie's busy. Let me watch. I like tea, I do.'

'You can't stay here,' Bertie hissed. 'Look at the state of you. Where have you been?'

'Out on the bike, just back.'

'Look at the state – that apron. Is that ham fat? You're wet, your hair's wet, soaking wet. Look at the floor—'

424

'Don't be such an old wifie, Bertie. You never know, I might decide to become a tea blender one of these days. Go on, let me watch. Here, I'll even give you a hand.'

'No, don't touch. Please, Gavin, don't touch *anything*.'

To defend the precious chests from Gavin's inquisitiveness Bertie braced his buttocks against the board and spread out his arms. In the dry, confined space of the closet, wrapped in musky fragrances, a larger threat now swelled within him.

Fair hair darkened by rain, little droplets clung to the curls above the ears and at the nape of the neck. He could see nothing but Gavin, groping and chuckling, and beyond the boy's broad shoulder a tiny section of backshop, green and gloomy like a jungle. His anger was volcanic. Blind and irrational, it urged him to strike the boy down, to beat him to the ground, to kick him away.

'Go on, go on, go on,' Gavin taunted, nudging and butting against him. 'Don't be a spoilsport, Bertie, don't be such a mean old bitch.'

Then Bertie's arms were around him, nose crushed against the boy's cheek, glasses askew. And they wrestled, a step this way, a step that, swaying back. Then they were still, contained in a mutual cloud of breath, lips pressed together in a kiss.

'Stop it,' Mr Lockie said.

He stood in the doorway, arms by his sides, no expression at all on his face. Gavin fell back, cheeks flamered, ducked past him and was gone.

Bertie and the manager stared at each other.

'Give me the key, Bertie,' Mr Lockie said.

Bertie did. He shook his head, too numb to frame a question, too shocked to seek an answer.

'Go back to the counter, please,' said Mr Lockie.

'Wha . . .'

'Now, please,' Mr Lockie instructed and Bertie, broken, obeyed.

'What's this?'

'Toad-in-the-hole.'

'Good.' Brenda reached for the sauce bottle. 'Are you not out tonight?'

'Night off.'

'Celebratin' your engagement?' Brenda cut off a slice of the egg and sausage pudding and transferred it to her mouth.

'Is that sarcasm?' said Ruby.

'Nope.' Brenda chewed and swallowed. 'Do you want me to be, you know, sarcastic?'

'I just thought – I mean, you're taking it very well.'

Brenda puffed out her cheeks, raised her brows. 'Been on the cards long enough. Anyway it's no skin off my nose *what* you do.'

'I thought you liked Mr Burnside?'

'He's okay.'

'Brenda—'

'What do you want me to say? He's *o-kay*.'

'It's not going to make any difference to you, really,' Ruby said. 'It's not as if we'll be living somewhere else. Mr Burnside will move in with us.'

'With you.'

'Yes – but you've always rubbed along quite well with Alison an' the boys. It won't be so bad, Brenda, you'll see.'

'Up to you what you do. I might not be here much longer anyway,' said Brenda darkly.

'An' just what's that supposed to mean?'

'Nothin'.'

'You're not going to do anything daft, are you?'

'Like what?'

'Running off an' getting married.'

'Like you're doin'?' said Brenda.

'I mean married – just for the sake of it.'

'Now who would want to marry me?' said Brenda. 'A fat, ignorant wee lump like me?'

'Oh, Brenda!'

Ruby did not know what to say. Her throat constricted, anger mingled with pity. She would have put an arm about the girl's shoulders but Brenda, in her present mood, would have shaken it off or, more likely, would have given her that long, cold, withering stare.

She watched Brenda eat and when the plate was empty replaced it with a dish of tinned pears and custard. Brenda lifted a spoon and set to work at once on the dessert, saying nothing.

Ruby said, 'I need somebody to look after me.'

'Aye, maybe!'

'It hasn't been easy all these years. When you're older—'

'I'll understand?' Brenda looked up, spoon dripping pear syrup. 'There's nothin', you know, *to* understand. You're just lookin' out for yourself. Always have done, always will. But I don't care any more.'

'Brenda, that's not fair.'

'Nothin's fair in this world, is it?' She pushed away the dessert plate, dug a Woodbine from her mother's packet and lit it with a match.

'There's worse off than you, girl, let me tell you,' Ruby said.

'Aye, an' there's better too.' Brenda picked a fleck of tobacco from her tongue. 'Why did you have to pick him? Even at your age, surely you could have done better than Ally Burnside's old man.'

'Like who, for instance?'

'I dunno.' Brenda wrinkled her nose. 'Somebody better. Somebody like Bryce Walker maybe.'

'Bryce Walker!' Ruby exclaimed, taken aback by her daughter's suggestion. 'What – what's he been saying to you?'

'Who?'

'Bryce – Mr Walker.'

'Him? Nothin'.' Brenda frowned. 'He never says a word to the likes of me. Fact, I hardly ever even see him. Why should I? He's the boss an' I'm just a lousy machinist.'

'Why did you mention his name then?'

'God knows!' Brenda was suddenly on the defensive. She had lost the initiative but would not back down, would not dissolve in tears or petulant cries of frustration. 'Seems to me, though, if you wanted a man to take care of you, you might have picked one who was rich, not some bleedin' nobody who just happened to be handy.'

'Brenda, that's a terrible thing to say.'

'Just bein', you know, realistic.'

Ruby was dragged into a response in spite of herself.

'Did it not occur to you that Alex Burnside might be in love with me?'

'Love! Love's baloney,' Brenda said, 'a big fat load of baloney.'

'Oh, Brenda, Brenda, you'll learn different before you're much older.'

'I bloody hope not,' Brenda said and, with the Woodbine dangling from her lip, abandoned the kitchen for her favourite chair by the fire.

Bertie had slept not a wink the whole night long. In fact he had added to his term of torture by pleading a headache and by going to bed right after supper.

Only Trudi, noticing how ill he looked, had been

sympathetic. She had brought him up a hot toddy and two Aspro tablets and had laid her hand upon his brow and asked him if he wished her to call the doctor. He had lain back against the pillows, crushed against them as if by a great weight, and had stared at the blonde woman, fighting an urge to tell her what had happened. He didn't, though. He had said nothing, had swallowed the Aspros, had swallowed the toddy, had let her tuck him in and put out the lamp. Then he'd lain in darkness, listening to the woman go downstairs again, and had felt as he'd felt when he was a child, before Alison came, and he'd been left all alone in the front room, crying silently for his mam.

Hours later Davy had come to bed. Bertie had pretended to be asleep. He had listened to the sounds his brother made, the sighs and hearty little grunts as Davy had undressed, put on his pyjamas and had climbed into bed beside him. He'd felt the mattress sag with Davy's weight. He'd clung on to the edge with both fists as if he might be tipped inward and, like a child, clutch at Davy, weep into Davy's broad shoulder and confess to things that Davy could not be expected to understand.

Bertie was up long before it was light, long before the grey unspectacular frost had melted from the windowpane, before the kitchen had warmed with heat from the stove.

Davy and his father, on day shift, Alison and Trudi were all up and about before he could find an excuse to leave the house. He snapped at their enquiries, savagely dismissed their concern for his health, drank tea, ate nothing and left for the Co-op at twenty minutes to eight o'clock.

Mrs Powfoot's shop was busy, bright and warm in the frosty mid-winter gloom. Bertie did not go in. He walked around the block in search of Gavin. He did not find the boy, saw only the padlocked front gate, the Co-op's big blank plate-glass windows dark and empty. He looked at his watch and then, as if drawn by a magnet, wandered round the corner to the backyards.

He did not know what to expect. The Co-op Welfare Committee gathered in force to dismiss him? Two burly police sergeants come to arrest him for gross indecency? Gavin in hysterics?

Mr Lockie, in spotless white coat and starched apron, was waiting for him by the green painted door.

As if glued to a conveyor belt, Bertie shuffled past the manager into the rear stockroom. Mr Lockie followed him and closed the door.

There was one light on, a single bulb. In a tin ashtray a cigarette smoked. Mr Lockie lifted the cigarette, drew in a lungful of smoke then stubbed out the butt, very efficiently and carefully while Bertie, waxy with fatigue, waited.

Mr Lockie turned. 'You'll have to bring in the gate, Bertie.'

'Where's Gavin?'

'Gavin has gone.'

'Sacked?' Bertie cried.

'No. Resigned. Last night, after you'd left, we had words.' Mr Lockie exhaled the very last of the tobacco smoke. 'I offered to have him transferred to the warehouse in Clydebank but he would have none of it. He said certain things that were unacceptable. Gavin will not be coming back.'

'Oh, God! Oh, my God! What will you do to me? How can I live without him? What will happen to me now?'

'Nothing will happen to you,' Mr Lockie told him. 'As far as the staff are concerned Gavin left of his own free will. I'm not going to report you.'

'You don't – you don't understand,' Bertie wailed.

'Oh, but I do, son,' Mr Lockie said.

Bertie gaped at the manager, open-mouthed.

'It must never happen again, Bertie,' Mr Lockie went on. 'Not here, not anywhere. If you take my advice you'll never speak with Gavin again. He's not like you. He's weak. You're different. That's your burden, one you can't put down. I think you're strong enough to carry it. That's why I'm prepared to give you a second chance.'

'Mr Lockie, are you—'

'Promise me it won't happen again, Bertie,' Mr Lockie interrupted.

'No, Mr Lockie. No. Never.'

'Then bring in the gate, son,' Mr Lockie told him, gently.

'Aye, Mr Lockie.' Bertie struggled between tears and gratitude. 'An' thanks – thanks very much. I won't forget it.'

But the manager had already turned away and uttered no response but '*Huh*!'

Christmas fever may not have been general across Scotland but in a modern educational establishment like Flannery Park Secondary the winds of change were blowing fast and free and an unmistakable excitement, born of the festive spirit, thrummed in the air.

The piquant aroma of mince pies arose from domestic science room and stole down the verandahs to warm the dank December afternoons. Art classes were wreathed in homespun paper chains and bells, the floor littered with gougings from lino-blocks as the home-made greetings card industry went into full production. From the music room the cheerful sound of carols being murdered went on from dawn to dusk, accompanied by Mr Watson's despairing cries of '*A-A-Angels*, blast it! Not *Aaan-jee-ells*.'

Mr Abbott, in a special fruity voice, read passages from Dickens and old Boris, to demonstrate the dangerous properties of phosphorus, invented a species of sparkler bright enough to light up a football field. In playgrounds, fore and aft, the talk was all of Santa Claus and stockings, pantomimes, parties, pies and mistletoe. Even Alison, oldest girl in school and regal as a queen, was not immune. With Trudi's enthusiasm for the mid-winter festival running riot at home she soon gave up her lofty stance and threw herself into all the fun and games that came her way and, along with Smailes, even appeared for half an afternoon tricked out in a black-paper moustache and cardboard monocle until Mr Morrison, a diehard atheist, told them to remove them at once.

Burnsides en bloc, Bertie included, took themselves off to the Alhambra Theatre. There they craned over the front rail in the balcony and waved to Jack, a gentleman at last in black bow-tie and tails, down in the orchestra pit but when the girls came on, all legs and ankles, lace and tights, and comedians in skirts or kilts, the Burnsides whistled and cheered and congratulated themselves as heartily as if they, through Jack, had vested interests in the show.

Gradually, without willing it, Alison succumbed to the blandishments of the season. She knew she was an absolute goner when, late one night, she rested head on hand at her bedroom desk and realised that she had just decorated a margin in *Clinical Anatomy* with little Christmas trees and, with her fountain pen, had transformed a human kidney into a plum pudding, complete with custard and a sprig of holly.

'Oh, dear, Ally Pally,' she said to herself. 'Oh, dear, dear, dear,' and then she laughed as if she had no wits at all, leapt into bed and bounced up and down on the quilt like a bairn gone daft.

Christmas, it seemed, was an easy time to fall in love.

'Alison,' Jim Abbott said, frowning.

'Oh, didn't you expect me? You didn't tell me not to come.'

'Alison, I'm sorry. I forgot.'

He wore the big brown-bear cardigan, his school-suit trousers and had a frilly little apron tied about his waist.

'Did you forget that too, Mr Abbott?' Alison said, grinning.

'What?' He looked down. 'No, I was – my sister isn't here.'

'Oh, that doesn't matter any more, does it?'

'Well, it does rather,' Jim said. 'She's gone for good. Left yesterday.'

'Oh!'

'My mother's unwell – old age, I suppose – and Winnie's gone to look after her instead of me.'

'Does that mean I can't come any more?'

'You don't have to look so tragic about it, Alison.' Jim fumbled with the tie of the apron. 'I'll give you assignments and mark your—'

'That isn't what I meant exactly,' Alison said.

'You'd better come in,' Jim said, nervously. 'But only for a minute or two – while I explain.'

It was on the tip of Alison's tongue to assure him that explanations were not necessary, that she understood that decorum, decency and reputation were laws that had to be upheld even in progressive communities like Flannery Park; that he was a bachelor, she a spinster and that vindictive gossips lurked on every street corner and hid behind every bush.

'All right,' she said.

She took off her hat, scarf and overcoat and hung them quickly on the peg on the little stand in the hallway then followed him into the living-room. He was unusually agitated. The departure of his sister had probably upset

433

him. She stood by the door for a moment, deciding what to do then, as if out of habit, came forward to the table.

Hand stuck into his cardigan pocket, Jim had positioned himself by the hearth, as far away as it was possible to get without leaving the living-room entirely.

'Winnie—,' he began, then stopped. 'What's that you're wearing?'

'Oh, this? Do you like it?'

'Well, yes, but—'

'My party frock. My sister-in-law made it for me. *Très chic*, hm?'

'Very,' Jim said. 'Winnie—'

'I thought this might be the last time I'd see you alone before Christmas and I wanted to give you something, a gift, a thank you. It isn't much but it's all I could afford. All I could scrounge from my brother Henry to be truthful about it. Here.' She held out a small parcel, white shop paper neatly tied with crimson ribbon. 'Please take it, Mr Abbott.'

He wasn't looking at the parcel but at the shapes the green silk formed as it clung to her figure, at the curve of her arm, the swell of her breast, the fine line of her throat and the dusky hollows of bare skin half visible in the sag of the collar. As she leaned towards him her hair swung in a soft arc across her brow and cheek. She brushed the strand away with just a trace of impatience and then looked at him again, brown eyes eager and – yes, he thought, yes – tender. For a moment he could not speak. He was glad that he had had the foresight to keep the table between them.

She came around it with a confident little sway of the hips, sinuous but not consciously seductive and put her hand on his arm, holding the parcel by the ribbon, wrist arched.

'Please take it,' she said again, very softly this time.

He felt clumsy and wooden, maligned by age. He took the gift from her and stepped past her, brushing against her body, and put the parcel down upon the cloth and moved with elephantine slowness away from her again, lumbering to safety.

'I'll – I'll open it on Christmas morning,' he said.

'Aren't you going away for Christmas?' Alison said.

'No, not until Boxing Day. One of my other sisters – her husband has a car, an old banger. He's coming down to collect me and take all of Winnie's things back north with us in one trip. I'll stay there for the rest of the holiday.'

'So she isn't planning to come back here at all?'

'No.'

'I won't be able to come any more, will I?'

'It wouldn't be right, Alison. I'm sorry.'

'I'm sorry too,' Alison said. 'I'm really sorry. I'll miss—'

'Thank you for the gift,' Jim interrupted. 'It really wasn't necessary, you know.'

'Oh, but it was, it was,' said Alison. 'It isn't nearly enough. Nothing I could give you would be enough to repay you for what you've done for me.'

'Now don't be silly.'

'I'm not being silly. I'm being truthful.'

'I know you are,' he said. 'I didn't mean to hurt your feelings.'

'You couldn't do that if you tried,' Alison said. 'You're far too nice to hurt anyone.'

'I'm not – no saint.'

'Double negative,' said Alison. 'Tut-tut, very sloppy.'

'Just shows you, even teachers can be caught out now and then.'

'If they're not careful.'

'Yes,' Jim said, 'if they're not *very* careful.'

'Well,' she was suddenly brisk and efficient, 'I've shown you my new dress, given you your present and neither of us seems to be in the mood for learning anything tonight – so, if you'll fetch my coat and hat, please, I'll be on my way, rejoicing.'

'Madam,' Jim said, forcing himself to be jocular and teasing, 'your wish is my command.'

'I wish it was,' said Alison then, shaking her head, added, 'I don't mean that, Mr Abbott. That's cheek.'

'It certainly is,' Jim Abbott told her and a moment later, with a weird mixture of relief and regret, saw her out into Macarthur Drive.

Alison popped her head around the door.

'Hullo,' said Davy, 'you're back early.'

'Things to do,' said Alison. 'Is Henry in yet?'

'In, fed an' watered,' said Bertie from behind a book.

'Where is he?'

'Henry is in our room, typewriting,' Trudi called from the kitchen.

'Good,' said Alison. 'I want a word with him.'

'What sort of word?' said Davy.

'Advice,' said Alison and promptly disappeared upstairs.

'Well, it's not what you're used to, I know, Mr Abbott,' Alex Burnside said, 'just plain farin' in this household, but I hope you've enjoyed it.'

'Every single mouthful.' Jim dabbed his lips with his napkin and politely stifled a burp. 'I am, if you'll excuse the expression, stuffed.'

Pudding plates and the remnants of paper crackers lay all about the Burnsides' dining table and the living-room seemed to glow with the heat that the dinner had generated. There was an atmosphere of repleteness, almost of luxury in the room as the men, tight-tummied and unbuttoned, reached for the cigarettes that Trudi had put out for them in a wine glass. There were also a brand new box of matches, large size, a bowl of nuts and raisins, a bottle of whisky, another of brandy and the special thistle-shaped glasses that Alex had won in a raffle years ago and that only usually appeared on Hogmanay.

It would have been a pleasant and unusually rich celebration of Christmas for the Burnsides even without the presence of a distinguished guest like Mr Abbott to add an extra fillip to the proceedings. They were all there, all except Jack. And they were all curious as to how someone as educated as a schoolteacher would behave in their company. At first there had been a decided awkwardness, a minding of manners, that had made the boys seem sulky. But Henry and Trudi apparently knew how to treat a guest, what to say to him and how to make him feel at home. And before the soup had been served and bread rolls broken, the stiffness had all gone and Mr James Abbott was telling jokes and arguing his corner with uninhibited fervour. He did not even bat an eyelid when Bertie asked him outright if he wanted his slice of goose cut up for him.

'Kind of you to ask, Bertie,' Jim Abbott said, 'but no. I have perfected the technique by practice. Watch this.'

He put his fork in his mouth, bit on it hard with his front teeth, leaned forward and accurately speared the slippery slice of goose-breast that rested in a little lake of sauce on his dinner plate. Pressing down, he took his knife in his right hand, gave it a showy twirl and with four or five neat strokes cut the meat into manageable pieces. He put the knife on the edge of the plate, removed the fork from his mouth and, with a modest grin, said, '*Voilà!*'

'By gum, Mr Abbott, that's a trick I've never seen before,' Alex said, drumming his fingers on the tablecloth. 'Never thought you'd see that, did you, Bertie?'

'It's a fine trick right enough,' Bertie said. 'What d'you do about shoelaces?'

'Ah, that's harder. I've a machine, a device, to assist with those.' Jim Abbott helped himself to a baked potato from a floral dish. 'It's a sort of hook and eye arrangement. Takes a bit of manual dexterity but works well enough.'

'Buttons?' said Bertie.

'Bertie, that's enough,' said Henry.

'I'm not embarrassed about having lost an arm,' Jim said. 'It's not very pretty but it's more of a problem for other people than it is for me, really.'

'You lost it bravely defendin' the country,' said Alex, 'why should you be ashamed about it?'

'Hey, did you kill any Jerries?' Davy asked. 'Did you bayonet them or shoot them? Tell us about it, Mr Abbott.'

Bustling in from the kitchen with dishes of peas and buttered carrots, Trudi intervened. 'War is not a subject for the Christmas festival, Davy. Pour Mr Abbott a glass of wine and the topic change. Henry,' Henry looked up, 'you may tell Mr Abbott about your encounter with the Crocodile Lady.'

'Now that sounds much more interesting than my departed fin,' Jim Abbott said and, with a quick, amused glance at Alison, skilfully divided his attention between hearty eating and listening to Henry's circus anecdote.

Dinner spun itself out until after ten o'clock.

Trudi did not conform to the Scottish habit of whisking through courses and between each serving would sit at table, would sip wine and slide her eyes, merry with speculation, from the guest to Alison.

Alex and Davy were oblivious to the little pink ribbons of

tension which stretched between the schoolmaster and his pupil but Henry and Trudi were not and even Bertie eventually seemed to twig that there was something more than seasonal charity involved in having the teacher to dinner.

It was Henry – prompted by Alison, of course – who had delivered the invitation to Jim Abbott's doorstep, who had undertaken the not-very-difficult task of persuading the teacher that he would be welcomed by all, not just Alison, at the Burnsides' Christmas Day dinner. Jim had been delighted, Alison elated, Trudi quietly pleased and only Henry, who was not so much under his wife's spell as all that, had felt a twinge of doubt that anything beneficial could stem from this unusual relationship.

He had cautiously raised the subject with Trudi.

'She is fond of him,' Trudi had said. 'Is it not a natural thing for a young girl to be fond of a man who gives her so much of his attention?'

'It's more than that,' Henry had said.

'Do you think she is in love with him?'

'Stranger things have happened.'

'What would be wrong for her to have him as a lover?'

'Trudi, for God's sake. She's only a girl.'

'Like the heck she is,' Trudi had said. 'She is a grown-up woman. When I was her age I had had—'

'I don't think I want to hear any more about your reckless youth, thank you,' Henry had said stiffly. 'I don't mind him coming to dinner. He seems like a nice enough bloke even if he is almost twice her age.'

'How can *you* say such a prejudice?'

'True,' Henry had admitted sheepishly. 'It's just that Ally's not ready for a husband at this particular time.'

'Love does not choose to be convenient.'

'I don't think you've got the picture, Trude.'

'She cannot marry him? Why can she not? She can marry him and live with him as his wife if that is what she wishes. He works, he can afford to become a husband. It is a good occupation this teaching, no?'

'Yes, but *he's* the one who pushed Dad into promising to send Alison to university. He – Abbott – he's the very chap who believes my sister should be given every opportunity to make a career in medicine.'

'She will become a *married* lady doctor,' Trudi had stated.

'Not so damned easy,' Henry had said. 'Suppose she has a child half-way through her studies?'

'It can be nursed. I will nurse it.'

'No, that's impossible,' Henry had said. 'It's going to be difficult enough for Alison to put up with five or six years of hard graft without having to cope with a husband and children as well. Anyway, I'm not entirely sure the University Court would wear it.'

'Court? What is this Court? Is it a judgement of men?'

'It just wouldn't be practical,' Henry had said. 'What's more, it wouldn't be – well – right.'

'Bigot.'

'Oh, cut it out, Trudi,' Henry had said. 'I'm tryin' to look at it from Abbott's point of view. From what I gather he's even more ambitious for Alison to succeed than we are. It's like she was some sort of cause for him, a guinea-pig.'

'*Phah!*'

'He might not be in love with her in the way she's in love with him,' Henry had said. 'In fact, I'll stick my neck out and say I think you've got it wrong, Trudi. Abbott's just coddling her because she's clever. I doubt if he's even thought of her as a woman, let alone imagined her as wife material.'

'*Phah and phooey!*'

'If he has – fallen for Ally, I mean – then he's got a big, big problem.'

'No problem,' Trudi had said. 'Marriage.'

'Sell out his idea of opportunity, of independence, and scuttle Ally's chances of ever making anything of herself in the process?' Henry had said. '*He* can't have it both ways. And he knows damned well *she* can't either. I suppose if he's really, truly stuck on her he might wait six years, though.'

'No, not wait.'

'Why, all of a sudden, are you so keen to push Alison into marriage? I thought you were the one who'd advocate caution, who'd back her to the hilt if she went for a career. Now, suddenly, it's grab a husband while you can. Why the change of course, Trudi, eh?'

'He will look after her if he loves her.'

'Good God, do you want rid of her too?'

'No. No. Not so, it is not so.'

'What, then?'

Trudi had hesitated and had shaken her head as if she had no ready answer to his question. 'It is for him, for her Mr Abbott, to puzzle his head over. As you say, it is a dilemma – but for him, not for us.'

'If, Trude, he's in love with her at all.'

'You see,' Trudi had told him. 'You see on Christmas Day.'

'How will we be able to tell?'

'No problem,' Trudi had answered and, not for the first time, Trudi had been absolutely right.

Henry could see it as plain as a pikestaff in the language of gesture, in the soft looks that Alison exchanged with Abbott and the way they managed to sit together, apparently casually, almost, *almost* touching. His sister's gaze hardly left the man for an instant throughout the course of the evening and if he, the teacher, was a model of propriety on the outside Henry, of all people, could certainly read the tiny signs of ardour and desire that Abbott emitted like radio waves.

Now and then Trudi would meet Henry's eye and give that fine, smug little smile as if to say, 'I told you so.'

Since the Burnsides were not inclined to indulge in community singing or the playing of charades and Bertie's suggestion that they bring out the cards for a hand or two of Newmarket met with a universal groan, there was nothing left to do but drink, smoke and argue, pastimes beloved by most Scots including, it appeared, Mr James Abbott.

Everyone had an opinion about something and was not afraid to express it. Politics, social theory, religion were all grist to the mill and soon voices were raised – Jim's too – and goose and pudding were digested and transformed into energy and adrenalin. It was left to Alison to act as mediator, as umpire and, when debate got heated, to cool it down and change the tack as best she could. By half past eleven, though, jackets were off and battle lines drawn, Jim, Henry and Trudi on one side, Alex, Bertie and Davy on the other, and the discussion had somehow gravitated from the Rights of Man to Free Love, Pro and Con.

On this subject Bertie was irrationally opposed to the motion. He had just about reached the stage of spitting and ranting in the face of Jim's calm assertions that freedom of choice and moral degeneracy did not necessarily go hand in hand when the doorbell rang.

Alex scuttled off to answer it and returned a moment later with Ruby, back home from her Christmas stint at the Argyll.

'A case in point,' Alex shouted, dragging Ruby into the living-room by the arm. 'A perfect bloody case in point.'

'What are you talkin' about?' Ruby asked, bewildered but amused. 'I could hear the shoutin' half way to Partick. What's got you all so heated?'

'Free love, dear,' Alex told her.

'No such thing,' said Ruby instantly and, shoving a bottle of Gordon's gin at her best beloved, plunged willy-nilly into the fray.

'I'm sorry,' Alison said. 'I don't know what came over them.'

'Aren't they usually like that?'

'Well, yes, actually they are.'

'I loved it,' Jim said.

'Even when Bertie threatened to punch your nose?'

'Especially when Bertie threatened to punch my nose.'

'He didn't mean it,' Alison said.

'Of course he did,' Jim said. 'It wouldn't have been half so much fun if he hadn't meant it.' He chuckled. 'I felt very flattered when Brenda's mother leapt to my defence.'

'By planting herself right in front of you,' Alison giggled. 'Poor Bertie didn't stand a chance after that.'

The evening had ended well after midnight with hot tea, buttered toast, great wedges of Christmas cake, handshakes and back-slapping all round. It was as if the clan was dispersing to distant villages across the mountains instead of being herded into the kitchen to do the washing up. Only Alison was excused. Her chore, Trudi had told her, was to walk the dog and, at the same time, escort her guest safely home to Macarthur Drive.

'Do you think they liked me?' Jim asked.

'Absolutely.'

'I mean, I didn't offend them?'

'No, no. There's nothing like a really good argument to bind folk together,' Alison said. 'It would have been a lot worse if you'd just sat there with your thumb in your mouth and said nothing.'

'I liked them,' Jim said. 'And I'm grateful to you for inviting me.'

'Better than sitting alone, moping.'

It was cold and quiet in the streets, cloud covering the stars and smothering the wind that had had such an edge to it that afternoon. Though it was very late there were still lights in windows, upstairs and down, and at the foot of the Kingsway a party of young people, flushed and excited, were breaking up into couples, arm in arm, and calling out cheery farewells.

'When do you leave for Pitlochry?' Alison asked.

'I expect my brother-in-law to arrive about ten.'

'You won't get much sleep, then,' said Alison.

'No, but I seldom do.'

'Because of your arm?'

'Too many thoughts racing and chasing about.'

'Oh, I know that feeling,' Alison said. 'Tomorrow, tomorrow, tomorrow. I want it to be tomorrow.' She glanced behind her at Pete who was padding along in the lee of the hedges, sniffing at roots. 'But not tonight. Tonight—' She paused, embarrassed.

'What?'

'I think I want tonight – right now – not to end at all.'

Jim said, 'I'll probably sit up and read *Prufrock* again.'

'I didn't know what book to buy you. I wasn't sure you'd like T. S. Eliot.'

'Why not?'

'Well, he's not very romantic.'

'Is that how you see me, Alison, as a romantic?'

She slipped her arm through his, leaned against him a little and did not answer his question. They walked on, saying nothing, into Macarthur Drive.

Council houses closed comfortingly about them and the hill between the hedges did not seem steep. The bell clock in the steeple of old St Silas's chimed a single note which quivered, muffled, in the river fog below. Alison could hear their isolated footsteps on the pavement, see their shadows swell and faint away in the passing rings of streetlamp light and wondered, very vaguely, where Walter was this Christmas night and why Brenda had stayed, sulking, at home. She felt a peculiar warmth spread out from her now, an all-inclusive warmth, absorbing past as well as present and she knew that this was a moment she would remember, clear and sharp, no matter how long she lived or what other happiness awaited her.

'Well,' Jim said, 'we're here.'

The house was dark, all dark, the curtains drawn. Only the big leafless tree to the left of the lawn had shape and definition, sheened by the streetlight for half its height.

Pete, behind them, stopped and lay on the ground.

It did not occur to Alison that this was a man's house, *his* house and that he might take her in.

Already she had begun to obey the rules of the system by which she and Mr Abbott might survive. Christmas night, New Year, the uncertain years beyond? There would be time enough tomorrow to think of gates and keys, of doors opened in welcome, of love unlocked.

'Thank you again, Alison,' Jim Abbott said.

She reached forward. She did not have to reach up. She did it without evidence of impulse. She sought out his mouth and kissed him. It was awkward, more awkward than it had ever been with Walter, but it filled her with a happiness that swept away her doubts, a feeling of release and certainty that came close, she supposed, to joy.

'Merry Christmas, Mr Abbott.' She kissed him again,

deliberately this time. 'Merry Christmas, Jim,' she whispered, then, with poor old Pete loping to keep up, she ran like the wind for home.

TWELVE

The Penny Wedding

Easter fell late that year which was perhaps just as well for March was cold and blustery and bothered by big winds which grew more bold and boisterous as the month progressed and eventually swept away in a night of violent storms. Tenement slates came clattering down, chimneypots crashed into backyards, rhone-pipes were ripped off and buried themselves like spears in all sorts of odd places which photographers from the *Mercury* duly photographed to amaze the paper's readers. Henry quickly put together a piece on steeplejacks which was hooked from the 'Diary' by Marcus Harrison and appeared, with by-line, as a feature in all the Saturday editions.

Construction work in Flannery Park, delayed by January's frosts, was held up now by dangerously high winds and Davy spent a great many hours huddled in an on-site hut waiting for the rough weather to abate. In March too Jack's stint at the Alhambra came to an end. He scrounged weekend engagements here and there and hoped for regular employment on the coast when the summer season started. Bertie, though, had never been busier. At Mr Lockie's instigation he had joined the SCWS Welfare Club and had promptly been elected to one of the sub-committees, a job which seemed to involve a mass of paperwork and umpteen 'important meetings' in Clydebank.

Alex too was a busy wee bee in the spring month. To Brenda's disgust her future stepfather had found his true métier and, temporarily abandoning the garden, had taken to papering and painting with demonic passion. Consequently the McColls' semi in Foxhill Crescent became a hellhole of wet paint and soggy wallpaper, so thick with the stench of turpentine that Brenda was scared to light a cigarette indoors. In the evenings after work she took to wandering the windy streets of Partick or Clydebank just to get away from the whistling paperhanger and his erstwhile female assistant. She still hadn't made up with Doris or Vera and her one and only ally in Bryce Walker's was Norman who, in spite of his limp, seemed to bear no animosity.

From Walter – nothing. Not a letter, not a card. It was as if the sea had swallowed him up. Brenda's one consolation was that Alison was equally in the dark about Walter's whereabouts and even Mr Giffard, whom she met by chance in Dumbarton Road late one Friday night, knew only that his sons were serving together on a P & O vessel bound for New Zealand.

Alison was blissfully unaware of Brenda's blustery moods. In the lingering weeks of winter Alison was blissfully unaware of most things. She was completely wrapped up in schoolwork and school affairs and in expanding her horizons by stretching her mental capacity to its limits. She was careful to obey the rules of the game *apropos* Mr James Abbott but in general she was far too busy to mope about things which had slipped away or even to remark the current of change upon whose breast she floated.

She longed for her schooldays to end, longed for her student ticket, longed for Jim to become her lover, her man-friend. She told herself that it would be a very intelligent sort of affair, disciplined, not sloppy. Meanwhile she was meticulously correct in her behaviour towards him, careful to give no sign of how she really felt unless, that is, they were alone. Then she would relax, smile, call him 'Jim', would even touch him in a manner that was tender and affectionate not – so Alison believed – tantalising and teasing. She no longer went to his house for tutoring. Jim had been adamant on that point. Instead he toddled down to 162 from time to time, sat in the living-room and gassed with Henry or Trudi or Alex. Alison would fuss over him, make tea, butter scones, find him an ashtray and talk, talk, talk about school, about university as if her breathless concerns, her youthful perspectives must be his too and a source of mutual involvement.

She had no Dave Wallace to keep her company when she went to sit the Tuxford Prize Examination. She was all tuned up for it, had Scottish history running out of her ears, significant dates printed on the back of her eyeballs. Her hands were steady, her nerves steely. The vast eighteenth century hall of St Cedric's College, where the examination was held, did not daunt her, nor the array of precocious talent that had been assembled to do battle for the prize. Two hundred young adults, licked and polished to perfection by masters all across the country, handsome calm young men and well-groomed young women all coldly eyed each other with an arrogance that seemed to declare, '*Forget it, chaps, I'm the one.*'

As she sat there with the first of the sealed papers before her, waiting for the invigilator's signal to begin, Alison too thought, '*No, I'm it. I'm definitely the one,*' and looking up at the rail of the carved gallery imagined that she saw Jim there, solid not shadowy, nodding approval at her presumption.

Alison stepped out of the college into an inimitable spring evening. Salmon pink and lavender clouds, scattered among scourings of grey weather, whisked across the cold evening sky and even on the train she could hear the wail of the wind and feel how it shook the carriages. She was dog-tired. She felt as if her brain had collapsed so that there were no thoughts left within her head. She dozed on the homeward journey, school hat awry, eyelids gritty with strain. It was all she could do to stumble out at Flannery Park station and look about her, dazed.

The wind roared under the road bridge like an invisible express and badgered the cluster of rooks that clawed at the elms that soared above the booking office. Fresh air revived her. She took in a deep breath of brisk evening air and let it out again with a whoosh.

Jim said, 'Tough, was it?'

He had been sheltering behind the battered hoardings by the ticket gate while a gaggle of schoolchildren had gone billowing past. There was nobody in sight now except the ticket collector and one elderly gentleman waiting on the platform on the up-line.

Alison sucked in another breath. She was on the point of putting on a swagger and telling him that the Tuxford exam had been incredibly simple but she was so relieved to see him that she simply shook her head and leaned against his shoulder for a moment as if the wind had pushed her.

'Tough?' she said in a croaky voice. 'Are you kidding?'

'Have you won, do you think?'

'I doubt it,' Alison said. 'Believe me, Jim, the first paper was a killer.'

Jim grinned and raised an eyebrow. He put his arm about her for a fleeting moment and then, separating, said, 'Come on, I'll walk you home.'

'Will it be all right?'

'It'll be fine,' he said, then, as if that had been his purpose in showing up at all, questioned her at length about the test papers.

By the time she reached the gate of 162 Alison was quite her old self again. Jim gave her a little pat on the shoulder by way of farewell and, walking briskly now, headed off up Wingfield Drive.

Alison let herself into the house by the front door and called out, 'It's me, Trudi. I'm back.' At first there was no answer, except a drowsy bark from Pete in the living-room, and there was no sign of anyone being home.

'Trudi?'

'Up here. I am up the staircase. Come up to see me.'

Intrigued, Alison climbed the stairs, gave the bedroom door a little push and peeped round it.

The usually neat room looked as if it had been struck by a bomb. The wardrobe lay open and clothing was strewn across the bed. A dark brown leather valise yawned on a chair and Trudi, in underwear, was holding a tweed suit against her body to test it for size.

'I am packing, you will see,' Trudi told her.

'Packing? But why?'

'To leave.'

'Leave? Surely you're not leaving us, leaving Henry, I mean?'

Trudi managed a small, tight smile and shook her head. 'No, I will come back to you in five or six days.'

'Where are you going?'

'To Germany.' Trudi slipped the tweed jacket and skirt on to a hanger and draped it from the wardrobe door. 'It is my Papa. He is very sick. I am to go to see him. I must leave by the sleeping car tonight.'

'Does Henry know about it?'

'Yes, I tell him last night.'

451

'Well,' Alison said, 'well, this is a bit of a shock.'

'You will feed them, will you not?'

'Oh, yes, don't worry about that,' said Alison. 'I just hope your father – I didn't actually know you had one – I just hope he's all right.'

'He is old and he is not close to me.' Trudi plucked black silk stockings from a drawer. 'Nevertheless, I must go to see him at once. In case he dies.'

'Of course, of course,' said Alison. 'Where is he exactly?'

And Trudi, without thinking, answered, 'Berlin.'

She had shown Henry the letter late the previous evening, slipping it from the long grey-green envelope emblazoned with official markings. The letter, of course, was written in German. Her father's fine, neat script had grown even smaller over the years so that the single-sheet page appeared packed with information.

She had masked her elation with a show of anxiety so convincing that Henry, who had learned to see through many of her minor deceptions, had been taken in by it. 'Will they let him out of prison?' he'd asked.

'I do not know. I will have to see to it.'

'How sick is he?'

'It may be that he is dying.'

'Do you want me to come with you?'

'No, Henry, darling.' She'd clung to him for a moment, head against his collar. 'But I will need to take some money from the banking account. What is left over from the sales of my fur.'

'I'll draw it first thing tomorrow.'

'I will go to London tomorrow night on the sleeping car.'

'And then?'

'I will take an aeroplane, to save much time.'

'An aeroplane?'

'From London to Germany.'

'Is your father still in Dresden prison?'

'Yes,' Trudi had lied.

Henry had seated himself on the side of the bed. 'Have you visited him there before?'

'Once only, many years ago.'

'I don't like you making such a long journey on your own,' Henry had said. 'I think I should ask for time off and come with you.'

'No.' She had sounded sharp and had modified her tone. 'No, my darling. It is too much money for two fares. He will be in the prisoners' infirmary and I will talk to him. I will talk to the Superintendent to see if he can be released soon.'

'What if he is released?'

'I will stay with him for six days or a week.'

'Trudi, do you want to bring him back here?'

'No, I will take him to my aunt in Berlin.'

'I didn't know you had an aunt in Berlin.'

'She too is old.'

'You can't just abandon him. I mean, whatever he's done, however much you dislike him, Trude, you're his one and only.' Henry had hesitated, hands on his knees, mouth twisted with indecision. 'Look, if he is released and if he's well enough, bring him back with you, back here to our house.'

'He is an old man. He speaks few words of English. What can I do with him in our house? Where will he be put to sleep?'

'If the worst comes to the worst we'll find a convalescent home to put him in. Somewhere decent and not too far away.'

'How will we pay?'

'I take it he has no money?'

'It all went back,' Trudi had lied again. 'He owed much to so many men, so he is penniless now.'

'What do you want me to tell them, downstairs?'

'Not of the prison,' Trudi had answered. 'Tell them how my Papa is sick. They will believe that, no?'

'It's the truth, isn't it?'

'Yes, it is the truth.'

Henry had taken her into his arms and she had wept little tears to disguise her satisfaction in the knowledge that her plan was working out perfectly and that Henry, even darling Henry, had been thoroughly taken in.

'Brew,' Henry shouted at the top of his voice, 'do you want another?'

'Certainly, my boy, certainly.'

Lunchtime in the Sadducee's Head.

Ham sandwiches, mutton pies, sausage rolls, tureens of greasy Scotch broth, plates of boiled cod and mashed potato. Beer by the quart. Whisky by the gill. Crowds swarming around bar and luncheon counters, mobbing the coffee urns. Broad-hipped waitresses in grubby black dresses struggling to serve steamed pudding to impatient regulars. Stout men in bowler hats. Boys in natty trilbys. Noise like a parrot house, smell like a chimps' teaparty, and pandemonium everywhere.

Henry clawed his way to the bar, elbowed through a bunch of *Citizen* reporters, trampled over an elderly solicitor, knocked the cap off a notorious bookie's runner – apologies, apologies – and finally secured a foaming pint of 90/- Alloa beer and juggled it back to the window table.

Brew grabbed it, hoisted it to his mouth. 'Your health, son,' he said and sank half the glass in one long heroic swallow. He was due to interview the prima ballerina from a Parisian touring company at half past two o'clock and obviously required fortification before the ordeal. Henry shoved away plates, got an elbow on the table, close enough to make himself heard.

'Brew, what do you know about Berlin?'

'It's in Germany – I think,' James Brewster answered.

'Hah-hah,' said Henry. 'Seriously?'

'Never been there. I never fought in the war, thank God. I avoid the Germans at all costs, though. Why?'

'My wife's gone there,' Henry said. 'She's flying—'

'A feeling I know well,' James Brewster said, '*sans* acroplane, of course. She's German, your wife?'

'Swiss,' said Henry. 'She should be landing about now.'

'Safe as houses, aeroplanes.' Brew drank. 'London to Paris? Hardly time for a cocktail. Lufthansa has an impeccable record. Don't worry, the Jerries won't let her fall.'

'I'm not worried. I just wondered if you knew if anything special might be happening in Berlin this week. Something out of the ordinary.'

'Me, why ask me?'

'Well, you seem to know a helluva lot about everything.'

'True, very true,' James Brewster said. 'But in this instance I confess my ignorance. What do you think's going on in Berlin?'

'I dunno. I'm just sort of fishing.'

'If you're really eager for information on what the Hun might be up to then give old Marcus a ring. I'm sure he won't mind.'

'Marcus Harrison?'

'Aye, aye. How many other Marcuses do you know?'

'What does he know about Germany?'

'Lots.' Brew polished off his ale and glanced at his pocket

watch. 'He's by way of being our Teutonic expert. He trots around the Fatherland a fair old bit, does our lord and master.'

'What for?'

'Ask him, not me,' said Brew.

But Henry was not so bold as all that and, for the time being, preferred to let the matter ride.

Trudi could not believe how much Berlin had altered in the time she had been away. Eight years ago the land on which Tempelhof airport now stood had been nothing but a dusty plain. Now it was one of the busiest airports in the world with planes arriving every few minutes from Stockholm, Moscow, London, Paris or Milan. The field itself had become a Mecca for aviation enthusiasts and was set about with restaurants and beer gardens to which the public flocked as if to a military display.

As the flight from London had approached the city Trudi, eyes widening, had been awed by the transformations that had been wrought by systematic government in just a few brief years. On landing she had been treated like an honoured guest, whisked off in a comfortable motorbus along a newly constructed autobahn and deposited at a terminus not far from her hotel, the Berlin-Palace, near the western end of the Kurfürstendamm.

She had stayed at the Palace before. Under the imperial windows of the wedding suite Clive and she had made love to the sound of jazz saxophones, a babble of traffic and café small talk from the promenade half a block away. On that trip they had tasted the dust of desperation and defeat in the city but also an underlying whiff of greed which had made Clive feel potent and alive. The Palace, however, had changed too. It had shed rococo gilt in favour of brushed steel, exchanged its famous potted palms for kiosks selling perfumes, cigars, expensive leather goods and even, to Trudi's surprise, exotic lingerie.

Within hours of her arrival she was thoroughly unsettled. Berlin was too bold for her now, too muscular, too big. She wanted it to be the way it had been when she was young, elegant and poised, opportunistic but not so calculating, so cold-bloodedly republican. Perhaps what she really missed was the sense of pageantry that the warriors of the old imperial Germany had imparted, the sedate civilising presence of horses and beautiful well-mannered women. Perhaps what she really missed was the girl that she had been, with Otto and Papa, long ago before the war, before Mama had died and everything had fallen apart.

She ate dinner alone, modestly avoiding the inviting glances of men from other tables. She was no longer flattered by their interest. She resented the fact that they recognised her as one of their own kind, as a woman who might be wooed into bed by casual flirtation.

Meanwhile, she ate veal of such delicacy that it melted in the mouth and a sorbet pink as a carnation and thought all the while of what might be happening back in Flannery Park, fretting in case Henry missed his supper or Alison scorched the collar of Bertie's new white shirt. Provincial trivia bound her to Glasgow and she felt peculiarly alien in the Berlin-Palace, threatened by a culture whose values she had once fondly embraced.

How long they had been staring at her Trudi had no idea.

She had not anticipated that Papa would turn up at her hotel. She had expected him to be furtive, to leave a mysterious message arranging a rendezvous in some sleazy café near the Nollendorfplatz or the public gardens east of the Zoo. At one time the Kroll had been a favourite place for Papa's assignations. There he could lose himself in the huge open-air café that sprawled beneath the bandstand, merge with the crowds that gathered to drink lager and listen to the music of Strauss and Waldteufel and Meyerbeer. He had met Clive in the Kroll, Clive and other men – civil officials, loan sharks, shady bankers – to hatch the deals that had landed him in prison.

Suddenly there they were – together – by the pillar at the door of the dining-room. She felt her breath catch in her throat and a hard lump form in her chest. The silver spoon balanced in her fingers dripped a sliver of water-ice into the silver dish.

It was not the sight of her papa that affected her so much as the shock of seeing her son. She did not doubt the identity of the handsome young man who stood by her father's side.

The last time she had seen Otto he had been four years old, a romping little toddler playing the devil with his nanny on the terrace overlooking the lake behind the Dahrendorfs' summer residence in Bad Wiessee. On that simmering August afternoon she had given him over to the Dahrendorfs, signed him away for the child's own good and in exchange for her freedom. When she stared at him across the Palace's tablecloths and glassware she saw not his father Otto nor his grandfather Keller but herself in him; blue eyes so pale as to be almost luminous and white-blond hair fine as gossamer and already beginning to recede from his youthful brow.

Trudi had no inclination, no strength, to start up in welcome.

She put down the dripping spoon carefully as her father and her son advanced stiffly towards her through the dining tables.

She could hardly take her eyes off the boy.

His style, his arrogance were terrifying. Pale eyes and hair were set off by a deeply tanned complexion, further enhanced by his uniform of black and brown. He had taken off his cap and held it across his chest as if swearing an oath. His boots clicked in an echo of imperial gentility and Trudi noticed how all the women in the dining-room ogled him and, in spite of her fear, felt a soft suffusion of sentiment and pride.

Papa was not ailing and skinny as she'd imagined he would be. He had put on weight, had the girth of a burgomeister, a great round belly that bulged against his coat and mottled silk waistcoat. His hair was as black as it had been in his youth, his faintly ridiculous quiff was still prominently in place.

Trudi waited, ladylike and cool.

Otto clicked his heels and bowed. Papa, still without the vestige of a smile, took her hand and kissed it.

'I did not think that you would come,' he said.

'I told you I would come,' Trudi said. 'If I had not told you how would you have known where to find me and when I would be here?'

'Do you know who it is I have brought with me?'

'It is, I believe, your grandson,' Trudi said.

The other diners were still watching Otto out of the corner of their eyes as if they had never seen a uniform in the Berlin-Palace before. In the old days the room would have been full of officers and unbearded cadets, in blue and scarlet, though, not black and brown and without the armband of the *Schutzstaffel* to declare their allegiances.

'Has he not grown well?' Papa said.

'He has grown handsome,' said Trudi, trying to control herself.

Otto inclined his head. His manner was icy, bullyingly courteous.

He did not approve of her. He had no feeling for her. Trudi felt her lip tremble. Whatever bond was alleged to exist between mother and son was absent. For all that, he did not seem like a stranger for she still recognised in him the shape of the toddling child who had made her weep and weep as if her heart would break in the weeks after she had said goodbye.

'Are you an officer, Otto?'

'I am a *Führer*,' Otto told her.

'He is honoured because of his family,' Papa said. 'He has carried the "Blood Flag". Do you know what that is?'

'No,' Trudi said.

'He is a guardian to the party, to the person of the leader,' Papa said.

'I did not know that you and he were acquainted?' Trudi said.

With pride, with love, the old man looked at his grandson. 'He has been to visit me in Dresden many times. It is he who has secured my release and who will have the charges against me eradicated. It is more than you, or your husband, ever did for me.'

'My husband is not in a position to do anything for you.'

'It is Coventry I refer to.'

'Papa, Clive left me, divorced me. I am married again. To a nice man.'

'A Scotlander,' Papa said with just the trace of a sneer. 'He does nothing, you say, this new man of yours.'

'He is a journalist.'

'In Scotland?'

'Yes, of course.'

'What do they read there? Have they learned to read at all?'

Otto laughed.

It was the first sound her son had uttered and it caught Trudi by surprise. She smiled automatically just before she realised how disloyal it was to Henry to do so.

She said, 'Will you dine with me?'

'No,' Otto said.

'We have much to talk about,' Trudi said.

'We have nothing to talk about,' Papa said.

She might have accepted the statement from Otto but coming from her father's mouth the words were heartless.

She said, 'I have come to take you back to Scotland, Papa.'

'I do not wish to go to Scotland.'

'I have made a home there for you,' Trudi said. 'There is no place more safe than Scotland, I think. Your enemies will not find you there.'

'My enemies? What enemies?'

'The men who had you put in prison.'

'Those fools. I have no fear of them. It is they who should fear me.'

'What is it you mean?'

Otto leaned towards his grandfather. 'I thought you told me she was clever. She is not clever at all. She understands nothing.' He addressed his grandfather as if she, his mother, did not exist. 'She does not know how things are changing here in Germany and what use can be made of men like you, men who are not afraid of the future.'

'What is he saying?' Trudi asked, as if deafness had come with age.

'You see.' Otto draped an arm over the chair back and laughed again.

The mirthless laugh reminded her of her first husband. It had been a brief marriage, forged out of necessity. In retrospect it seemed that everyone had benefited from it. The Dahrendorfs had collected a legitimate heir. Her papa had obtained money and 'connections' and her son had been brought up in an atmosphere of privilege and wealth. Only she had suffered. Seven winter months hidden away

461

in Bad Wiessee had been a torment and when the child had been born she had not loved him. Soon after the birth her father had persuaded her to agree to separate, to sign the child away so that she might get on with the business of being young again in Berlin and in Paris.

How much, she wondered, did Otto know of this?

His anger was more than skin deep. That taut, cold rage had been in his father too, however, an imperiousness which had made Otto Dahrendorf seem, for a time, irresistible. She studied her son without fear now, without guilt. Somehow she could not imagine that fish-hook-shaped mouth ever uttering the word 'Mama' without derision. Was that her fault or was it bred into the bone, an irremediable flaw in character? She would never unravel the answer to that question.

To her father she said, 'Have I have wasted my time and my husband's money by coming here? Are you not ill after all? Do you not need me?'

'No,' Papa said. 'I do not need you.'

'I am here for him,' Otto said.

'He will take care of me now,' Papa said.

'In that case,' Trudi said, 'I will take the morning aeroplane back to my own country.'

'Germany is your country,' Otto said.

'To my home then,' Trudi said, 'if you wish to be exact.'

For a split second she detected alarm in her father's eyes as if he suspected that he had pushed her too hard. He had deliberately engineered the confrontation to cause her distress, of course, but somehow she had managed to turn it against him, to regain control. Regret flickered in his expression and the fat face aged before her eyes. In the past she would have given in to whatever plan he had in mind but she was no longer a trusting, doting child dependent upon him for love.

'What is the nature of this "home" you talk about?' Papa said. 'Tell me, are you happy with your new man, your journalist? Is he more satisfying to you than Coventry?'

'Infinitely more satisfying,' Trudi said.

'Is he powerful in his country?'

'Powerful? No.'

'Does he have money?'

'Not that either.'

'So what does he offer that you find attractive?'

Trudi gave a little smile, thinking not of the past but of the present, of the unremarkable Henry Burnside and his undistinguished family, of how she had tried to manipulate them and how instead they had taken her in without her even being aware of it.

'Is he so good a lover?' said Otto, trying to embarrass her.

'He is that, among other things,' said Trudi, without a blush.

'Other things?' Papa said.

'He is an honest man,' Trudi said. 'He supports his family.'

'And the house?'

'Small and crowded.'

'*Phah*! It is to this – this *cottage* in Scotland that you would take me?' Papa said. 'God in heaven, Trudi, it would have been worse for me than jail in Dresden.'

'Yes,' Trudi said. 'I did not understand before. But now I do. It is clear that you are better off with your grandson Dahrendorf. My only regret, Papa, is that you kept so much from me.'

'So much of what, Trudi?'

'Of everything, of what you felt, what you wanted.'

'It was better that the options be kept, as it were, wide open.'

'Better for who?'

'For me, of course,' her papa said. 'For me.'

Suddenly she wanted Henry so badly, wanted him to walk into the dining room in his Co-op suit, hair untidy, shoes just that little bit down at heel, to see him size up the situation and to watch the dark, disapproving look on his face turn to anger. What would he say to Papa, to Otto, to the ugly death's head brooch and proletarian tie? '*Trudi,*' he would say, '*are you okay?*' and in the doorway, like a gang of affable villains, perhaps she would see the rest of the Burnside boys come to collect her and take her safely home.

'What is good for you, Papa,' Trudi said, 'is it also good for the Fatherland? Will you prey on each other, perhaps?'

Her waggishness was intended to rile. Instinct had already told her that there could be no civilised exchange between them. Her son's life as a Dahrendorf and her life with the Burnsides must remain mysterious each to the other. At least she knew where she stood now and that her papa was best left to take care of himself.

Otto shot to his feet. Chairs grated, knives rattled. Diners and waiters darted apprehensive glances towards the corner table.

Otto's anger was quite awe-inspiring, Trudi thought, but the mouth remained weak and that weakness extracted from her a last little gush of sorrow for the child she had sacrificed so long ago.

'I have had enough of this woman,' Otto shouted. 'It was a mistake to bring her back to Berlin, for you to fetch me to meet her. I told you originally that I saw no beneficial purpose in it and she has proved me correct. It is a masquerade, a sentimental farce. She is of no use to us, no use at all. Please.' He clicked his heels and with a deference that revealed the boy in him bowed to his grandfather, 'Please, I wish to go home.'

'Trudi, I . . .' Papa began.

The young man's hand tightened on his shoulder.

'Go with him,' Trudi said. 'He is more yours than mine. He will take better care of you than I can. Go.'

'*Now*. I wish to go *now*,' Otto cried.

'Yes, Otto. Yes, I hear you,' Papa said and, easing his bulk from the chair, kissed Trudi lingeringly upon the brow then, with a shrug, let his grandson lead him out into the rain-wet streets of Berlin.

It was after midnight. Henry had been in bed for twenty minutes and was just drifting off to sleep when the bedroom door creaked open. He opened his eyes, rolled on to his right side and drowsily enquired, 'Dad, is that you?' Stealthy sounds, the covers drawn back, arms about him, breasts brushing his cheek, his chest. 'Trudi!'

'Oh, so you guessed that it was me, your wife.'

'For God's sake! How did you get back?'

'Aeroplanes.'

She was naked, her skin cool but not cold. He drew her under the covers and hugged her with both arms.

'I didn't expect you back so soon,' he said. 'What happened?'

'Papa is not sick. He has been released from prison and he has found a place for himself in Berlin.'

'Place? What d'you mean?'

'To stay, to work. With a relative,' Trudi whispered impatiently.

'And he didn't think to let you know? Huh!'

'That is Papa. He has not changed,' she said. 'Henry, no more talk tonight. Hold me close.'

'Sure.' Henry opened his knees, snared her legs and

brought her on top of him. He kissed her. Her lips tasted of cachous and cognac. 'Have you been at the bottle?'

'Brandy, on the train. *Ssshhh*, my love. *Ssshhh*!'

'Is anybody else still up?'

'Only Jack. He is downstairs.'

'In that case—'

'Yes,' she said. 'Yes.'

Henry chuckled and for the time being put all his questions about Papa Keller, and Marcus Harrison, far to the back of his mind.

For the best part of eight months Jack Burnside had been mooning over a tousled-haired lassie he'd met in Rothesay last summer. She was a native of the town, worked as a waitress in the Winter Garden Tearooms and her name was Dorothy Smith. He had written her a couple of letters, sent birthday greetings, a Christmas gift and a grisly St Valentine's Day card, and in response to this long-distance wooing had received not a cheep in reply. He had kept the flame of love alive only by remembering the velvet nights – well, two velvet nights – last August when he had walked under Rothesay's stunted palm trees hand in hand with the love object and had managed to extract a kiss from her coy lips round the back of the fish and chip shop in Wedmore Street.

By February even Jack's romantic inclinations had begun to wilt under the deluge of silence from pretty Miss Smith and he was down to worshipping a dim memory, an image of love far removed from reality. In fact he could hardly remember what Dorothy looked like and only kept himself going by playing 'I Can't Give You Anything But Love, Baby,' in muted *legato* now and then and telling himself how great it was going to be when he got back to the Winter Garden next summer.

When Kenny informed him that Rothesay was 'Off' and the new Barrfields Pavilion at Largs was 'On' poor old Jack didn't know whether to laugh or cry. Still, he had a fine time crooning all the broken-hearted ballads he could think of in that long showery spring, secure in the knowledge that only cruel fate was keeping him apart from the love of his life, even if the bitch was too mean to buy a bloody postage stamp.

Meanwhile Kenny's boys were playing the Cally regularly every other Saturday night in a sort of bandstand war with Ronald Mitchell's Moonlight Orchestra and seemed to be gradually winning the favour of the crowd with a weird mixture of novelty numbers and treacly foxtrots.

It was during the playing of one of the latter – 'Always' – on a shivery evening in mid-May that Jack became aware that he was once again the focus of female attention. Nothing unusual, really. Jack's fans were legion. The only odd thing about it was that Jack did not exploit his sway over the ladies with a mite more *savoir faire*. In band circles Jackie's shyness was a standing joke for, in spite of having wives and children at home, Kenny and his cohorts all fancied themselves as terrific Don Juans.

The female in question wasn't lolling against the edge of the platform in the hope of catching the handsome young trumpeter's eye, however. She was dancing with, of all people, Eddie Ruff who, as usual, was somewhat less than sober and kept bumping into folk.

In the past year Eddie had become 'a character' in Partick lore and, like all colourless eccentrics, was treated with a mixture of affection and irritation. Drunk most of the time, none too clean in appearance, he had recently taken to shouting crude political slogans at street corners while delivering bundles of the *Banner* to shopkeepers who wanted nothing whatsoever to do with the newspaper or Eddie's radical politics.

It was mercifully rare for Eddie to roll out of the pub in time to attend the Cally dances. In any case he was, as a rule, too far gone in drink to make it past the bouncer. Tonight, though, he had a girl in his arms. She, it seemed, was willing to put up with his beery breath and body odour and guided him patiently through the steps of the foxtrot, steering him in a shallow circle just below the bandstand and creating just enough kerfuffle to attract the attention of the bandsmen, Jack included.

'It's her again.' Sammy McGuire put in an extra little *ta-ra-diddle* to emphasise his point.

'Ain't seen her in months,' Kenny remarked to the lid of the piano.

Seated now, Jack took the mouthpiece from his lips and, at the end of a phrase, told them, 'It's Brenda McColl.'

'Oooo-eee! He knows her name already. Fast worker, our Jack.'

'His type, d'ye think?'

'Shy an' retirin'? Yeah.'

'Whaddya say, Jackie boy?'

Playing again, Jack extended his left hand behind him and made a rude gesture by way of reply.

'See. He fancies her.'

'Look at him slaver.'

At this point Eddie, dizzy with dancing, dunted the platform's edge and in desperately trying to stay upright fell to the floor, taking not only Brenda but another two couples with him.

Brenda let out a shriek and looked straight at Jack as one of the fallen couples divided itself into two separate parts, one part of which was an Irish navvy, six feet tall and built like a brick washhouse.

'Oi, you,' the brick washhouse rumbled.

'Uh-oh!' Kenny muttered.

They were not friends, they had never been friends. Though he knew of his brother's connection with Red Eddie, the depth and duration of that friendship meant nothing at all to Jack Burnside.

He didn't know why he did what he did.

Whenever there was trouble on a dance floor Jack, like all musicians, protected his instrument and his person and did not interfere.

Tonight, though, was different.

Still playing, without a wobble, Jack leaned forward and peered at the lop-sided struggle as it evolved below the bell of his trumpet.

He saw Brenda flattened by a shove. He watched the brick washhouse kick Eddie in the ribs then, laying his trumpet carefully aside, Jack got slowly to his feet. Somebody said, 'Ach, it's only daft Eddie,' and there was laughter. Jack leapt off the front edge of the bandstand, landed on the brick washhouse's back and carried the bloke to the floor.

Brenda screamed, '*Jack, Jack. Kill the bastard, Jack!*'

The bouncer came bustling from the doorway and now that the music had stopped the dancers had formed a circle round the disturbance and were egging the pair on to murder each other. Jack was oblivious to the crowd. He'd had a glimpse of Eddie Ruff crouched on all fours like a dog, mouth open and bloody, and he'd heard Brenda screaming in his ear; then the brute beneath him rose, growling, and Jack slid off and stood his ground.

The navvy swung round. The meaty young face, flushed with rage, was thrust towards him. Without pausing to think about it, Jack popped two short jabs to the bloke's jaw before a roundhouse Irish right connected with the side of his head and a thin high strident note, like the last bar of a Suppé overture gone wrong, filled his ears.

He shook his head. He ducked. He flicked out his right hand then, without heat, drove his knee into the navvy's groin and, rather to his surprise, saw the bloke double up and sink slowly, very slowly, to the floor.

Sammy let out a whoop and a drumroll.

Kenny strummed his nails across the keyboard and shook out the notes of '*Good Evening Fri-eeeeends*,' while the bouncer hauled the troublemaker away by the heels.

Still dazed, Jack leaned back against the bandstand while everyone cheered and whistled and Brenda hugged him frantically.

And on the floor, neglected, Red Eddie vomited blood.

Above the clatter of the tramcar, Brenda cried, 'Nobody's ever done nothin' like that for me before. I don't know what to say.'

'What were you doin' with Eddie in the first place?' Jack said.

'I never started out to go to the jiggin', y'know.' She was pressed against Jack's flank on the long bench towards the nose of the car but still had to shout to make herself heard. 'I was down in Partick for no special reason when I met, you know, wee Eddie. He was comin' out the pub right enough but I never realised he was drunk or I wouldn't have asked him to get me into the Cally.'

'Is that how it happened?'

'Aye, that's just how it happened.'

The trumpet case was securely wedged between Jack's feet and he held a cigarette in his left hand. His right hand rested loosely on his knee, knuckles swollen and throbbing. He hoped to heaven nothing was damaged for a broken bone in the hand would wreak havoc with his earning power. Never having punched anyone before he hadn't appreciated how painful the experience would be.

He did not object to Brenda leaning against him, rocking in unison to the sway of the tramcar. He glanced down the car at the other passengers, a solitary drunk, a young couple with a baby wrapped in a shawl, an off-duty constable, big and solid and passive, probably going home to bed.

'Do you always wear your party frock when you go to Partick?'

'This isn't my party frock,' Brenda said. 'Nice one, though, isn't it?'

'I like the colour.'

'Green always suits me,' Brenda said.

Jack didn't have the heart to disillusion her, to inform her that it wasn't her cry for help that had prompted him to leap into the fray. If Eddie had been sober and the brick washhouse smaller in size then he wouldn't have intervened at all.

'What were you doin' in Partick on your own on a Saturday night, anyway?' he said casually.

'Takin' a stroll, lookin' at the shops.'

'Does your mother know where you are?'

'She doesn't care.'

'I thought you had friends, chums you went dancin' with?'

'Can't go dancin' on your own, not if you're a girl,' Brenda replied, neatly evading the point of the question.

'You should've come over to our house,' Jack said. 'Davy would've took you dancin'.'

'I don't like to, you know, impose.'

'It'll not be an imposition much longer,' Jack said, 'not when we're all just one big happy family, eh?'

'Huh!' said Brenda.

'You don't like the idea of us bein' related?'

'It's got nothin' to do with me. She does what she likes.'

'Your mother?'

'Aye, my mother.'

Jack said, 'My old man's all right, you know. He'll treat you fair an' square. His bark's far worse than his bite.'

'Do *you* like the idea of them gettin' married?'

Jack paused. 'Not much.'

'See!'

Constable and conductor, linked by the bond of public service, were chatting. The drunk was slumped full-length across the seat, dribble at his lips, eyes screwed shut. He would ride on past his stop, be deposited at the terminus miles away, bewildered and helpless. Brenda was looking at the drunk too.

She said, 'What'll happen to Eddie?'

'He'll be all right,' Jack said. 'He'll feel rotten in the mornin' but I expect he's used to that.'

'He looked awful sick to me.'

'Nah, his kind never get sick, really sick.'

'It was some kickin' he got.'

'He'll be all right,' said Jack again, flexing his knuckles cautiously against his knee, listening for the telltale crackle of bone.

Brenda said, 'Mind you, I can see there'll be advantages.'

'What?'

'To my mum bein' married to your dad.'

'Advantages?' said Jack.

She leaned closer, insinuated an arm about his waist and laid her head on his shoulder. Jack had a sudden flash of memory: Rothesay's palm trees, the Firth, silvered by moonlight, still as a millpond. As if by accident he let his brow rest against Brenda's hair.

'I'll always have somebody to look after me then,' she said, 'won't I?'

'Like who?'

'Like you.'

And Jack, rather innocently, said, 'That's true.'

'Well, well, fancy meeting you here,' Henry said. 'You're the last person I expected to see in this place.'

'I might say the same about you.' With neither surprise nor animosity in her brown eyes, Margaret Chancellor glanced up from the long bench which was backed against the corridor's tiled wall. 'You're looking well, though. Working for Marcus Harrison obviously agrees with you.'

'Oh, yeah,' said Henry. 'I'm doing fine, Mrs Chancellor. At least I'm being paid a living wage for all my hard labour.'

'For selling out your principles, you mean.'

'Don't start!' said Henry. 'This is neither the time nor the place for political argument.'

'You're right,' Margaret Chancellor agreed, nodding.

Henry glanced along the corridor towards the ward's swing doors. They were firmly closed, and defended by a prim starched woman in the dark blue garb of a Ward Sister. He hated the Western Infirmary. It had cost him an effort of will to attend afternoon visiting, to climb the hill and enter the great, rambling grey fortress, smelling not of sickness but of disinfectant, so clean, so sanitised, so orderly that even the patients seemed like mere adjuncts to a system organised for its own glory and advancement.

'How is Eddie? Have you heard?'

'He'll live to fight another day,' Margaret Chancellor said.

'You've been before?'

473

'Of course.'

'So what's the diagnosis?'

'Ruptured spleen.'

'Will they operate?' Henry asked.

'Apparently Eddie's not well enough to undergo surgery.'

'But he will get better?'

'Oh, yes.'

'And then what?'

Henry had remained standing, one hand braced against the wall above the woman, the cake box tucked under his left arm. He preferred a position of dominance and the advantage of height when he talked to Mrs Chancellor.

She was well dressed, well groomed and looked plump and sleek. Left-wing radical politics were obviously paying well. She said, 'He'll return to work on the *Banner*, of course.'

'And drink himself to death?'

'That's hardly our fault, Henry. You can't hold the SPP responsible for a man's endemic weaknesses.'

'Endemic,' said Henry. 'I like that. That's a good word.'

'Won't you sit down?' the woman said. 'They won't let us in until the stroke of two thirty, you know.'

'I'm happy where I am,' said Henry. 'Tell me, what will you do for a printer while Eddie's in dry dock?'

'Niven has a cousin who'll stand in.'

'Trained and unionised?'

'I haven't enquired.'

'What will happen to Niven's cousin when Eddie comes back?'

'You are full of questions, aren't you?'

'It's what I'm paid for,' Henry said. 'You never know, I might get an article out of it.'

'Injustice in Labour circles?'

'Victimisation among the victims,' said Henry. 'Yes, something along those lines.'

'May I ask *you* a question?'

'By all means.'

'Were you always a damned hypocrite?'

'Don't know what you mean.'

'Out for fame and fortune at any price? I mean,' the woman said, 'did you always despise what the SPP stands for even while you were writing such eloquent propaganda?'

'It's a wee bit like religion, I suppose,' Henry said. 'I'd like to believe but I can't.'

'Ah, but do you respect those of us who do – believe, I mean?'

Henry was taken by her sharpness. He had always respected her intelligence and wit. Not that he would ever tell her so, of course.

He said, 'Some of you, I suppose, a very few.'

'Why do you write such trash for Marcus?'

'He pays my salary.'

'It's a crying shame, Henry, to watch you squander your talent hacking out trivia for Brewster's Diary.'

'I won't be Brew's dogsbody for ever.'

'Don't be too sure,' Margaret Chancellor said. 'Even the most ambitious among us can easily tumble and fall into the pitfall of compromise.'

'That won't happen to me,' said Henry, uncomfortably.

'If it does, you can always come—'

Her promise was drowned out by a clanging handbell as a young nurse marched through the corridors to announce the commencement of the visiting hour. Ward doors swung open and Henry, staring into the long perspective of the ward, saw iron bedsteads, lockers, flowers, and patients squaring themselves up as if for military inspection.

He could not see Eddie, though, and quite suddenly did not want to see Eddie. He could not face the sight of his old pal lying wrecked in this starched and sterile environment.

'Wait,' he said.

Margaret Chancellor was on her feet, preparing to join the troop of visitors which headed through the doors.

She glanced at Henry enquiringly.

Henry said, 'How did you manage to keep the police out of it?'

'Pardon?'

'Eddie was the victim of a serious assault, before witnesses too. How did you square it with the law?'

'Oh, Henry, you're not going to make trouble for us, are you?'

'You don't want to lose the licence, do you? For the Cally?'

'That's right.'

'So you covered up the fight?'

'It was hardly a fight. And Eddie was drunk. We don't even know if his injuries were sustained on the premises or acquired beforehand.'

'What if Eddie dies?'

'I'm assured that will not happen.'

'Will the SPP bury him?'

'What?'

'You heard me, Mrs Chancellor.'

'Yes, we'll pay for the funeral.'

'I mean,' said Henry, 'bury him?'

She stared at him for a long moment while the good citizens of Glasgow, cowed by their surroundings, trudged past to offer succour to ailing relatives and friends.

She wetted her lips before answering. 'If we bury him, Henry, will you dig him up again?'

'Oh, yes,' said Henry. 'Damned sure I will.'

She continued to stare at him, brown Aunt Belle-like eyes softened by something akin to admiration. She smiled.

'There's hope for you yet, Henry Burnside,' she said. 'Hope for you yet. Are you coming?'

Henry shook his head. He pushed the cake-box towards her.

'I'm not going in. Give him this. From me.'

'What is it?'

'Doughnuts,' said Henry. 'Jammy variety.'

She took the box by the string. 'Any message?'

'Yes. Tell the little bugger he'd better not snuff it or I'll want to know the reason why.'

'Is that it? Is that your tender greeting?'

'Eddie'll understand,' said Henry, and left.

Ruby felt like a fool in Trudi's floppy old straw hat and the wash-leather gauntlets Alex had purchased in the Co-op hardware store. She hoped the neighbours weren't watching, that Mrs Harris wouldn't come out to take in clothes from the line or Mrs Wilkie stick her neb over the raspberry canes and make stupid remarks about Adam, Eve and the Garden of bloody Eden.

'*Now* what do you want me to do?' Ruby demanded irascibly.

'Take the watering can,' Alex told her, 'an' gently pour a wee dollop on each of the sets. The liquid's quite thick but I've a coarse spray on the nozzle so if you hold it up high – about here – it'll spread itself fine. See.'

'God, it smells awful. What is it?'

'Liquid fertiliser. Blood, bone, fishmeal, stuff like that.'

'These flamin' onions are better fed than I am,' Ruby said, holding the can out in both hands at arm's length.

'We'll need them when the winter comes.'

'Why?' Ruby said. 'Are the greengrocers goin' on strike or are we declarin' war on Spain?'

'Nothin' like a big fat onion you've grown yourself,' Alex informed her, 'nothin' like it for flavour an' texture, sidlin' up white through the mince. An' there's onion soup. I reckon you should learn how to make French onion soup.' Alex leaned on the rake and smacked his lips enthusiastically.

'Listen, m' lad,' Ruby said, 'I'm not Marie-Antoinette an' you're not Louis-the-Whatsit. You'll get pea an' ham and barley broth just like you've always done an' eat it with your lip tremblin'.' She dribbled a quantity of the disgusting liquid from the spray of the watering can on to the dry earth and wrinkled her nose at the stench. 'Anyway, much more of this gardenin' lark an' you'll be makin' your own dinners for I'll never be able to look an onion in the face again.'

'If you don't know how to do it, Trudi can teach you.'

'Trudi can teach me nothin',' Ruby said. 'I've forgotten more about pleasin' a man than Trudi ever knew.'

'Oh! Oooh?'

'At the table, at the table, I mean.'

Alex laughed and, glancing round, Ruby realised that he'd been teasing her all along. She wondered if he'd ribbed Mavis too, had made fun of her. Ruby did not resent it. She saw it as a healthy sign, indicating an easiness in their relationship. She had become far too wrought-up about everything to realise that what she missed most about not having a man were really these nonsensical conversations, the foam and froth of communication. She expected another quip, something mildly ribald, and had an answer ready on the tip of her tongue. But Alex said nothing.

He'd tilted his chin and was peering up at the sky. He seemed to be studying the squashy cauliflowers of summer cloud that floated above the rooftops and the faint kipper-coloured haze of chimney smoke. He sniffed and rubbed his forefinger against his upper lip.

'What's wrong with you?' Ruby asked.

'I'm so happy,' Alex said thickly.

'Eh?'

'It was never like this before,' Alex went on. 'I never did any of this with Mavis. Maybe it was because there were always weans runnin' about your feet or we were perpetually worried about money. Whatever the reason it wasn't like it is with you an' me, Ruby.'

She put down the can, stripped off the gardening gloves and tossed them on to the grass.

She didn't care if Mrs Harris thought she was a shameless hussy or what Mrs Wilkie said about her morals. She put an arm round Alex and drew him to her just firmly enough to show understanding without bruising his pride. 'Surely you're not feelin' guilty about bein' happy?'

'Somethin' like that, I suppose.'

'Because of Mavis?'

'Nah. She wouldn't have minded. She always liked you.'

'What is it then? Can't you tell me?'

'I'd tell you if I could.' Alex sniffed and buffed her chin with his knuckles. 'I'm all right. I'm absolutely dandy, in fact. I just wish – I just wish it had been like this before, this good.'

'No use lookin' back, Alex.'

'Aye, you're right there.'

'What we've got to do,' Ruby told him, 'is make the most of the time we've got left.'

'How long's that, though? Ten years, twenty at most?'

'Forty,' Ruby told him firmly. 'In my case, fifty.'

'Aye, but we'll not be plantin' onions together when I'm ninety-seven.'

'You never know, Alex Burnside, you never know what we'll be doin' forty years from now.'

'Be nice,' he said, 'if it lasted for ever.'

'You an' me, do you mean?'

'That's just what I mean,' he said. 'Funny, an ordinary night like this in an ordinary place like Flannery Park, me so happy to be here an' so sad because I won't be here for ever. Daft, eh?'

'For goodness sake, enough,' said Ruby. 'You'll have me blubbin' in a minute. Know what?'

'What?'

'It's high time we were married.'

'Yes,' Alex said, giving himself a shake. 'It'll not be long now.'

'Three weeks. And then,' Ruby said, 'I'll show you what happiness is really all about.'

'Onion soup?'

'Think again, Sunny Jim,' said Ruby.

One of the most difficult things to do in any school is keep a secret. Sooner or later a beady-eyed coterie of bright sparks will notice 'something going on' and, before you know it, will put two and two together and come up with a rumour which, like a hare coursing a field, will dart desperately about corridors and playgrounds until one spark, even brighter than the rest, leaps on the truth and pins it down.

Mr Pallant did not intend to have his fun spoiled by a sudden outbreak of deductive intelligence, however, and went about the business of keeping things dark with unexpected deviousness. He enlisted the assistance of trusted colleagues and briefed them behind locked doors. He wrote letters, made telephone calls, paid a personal visit to the sign-writer in the huts behind the railway line and had poor Jim Abbott running hither and thither during the lunch hour. Old Ronald's efficiency had never been so well demonstrated and come Thursday, exactly a week before end of term, every detail was in place and everything was ready to roll.

'Nervous?' Boris asked.

'Heck, no. What have I got to be nervous about?' said Jim.

'Try these.' Boris offered a hip flask in one hand and a tiny sweet reeking of peppermint on the other. 'Nerve tonics, tried and true.'

Without hesitation Jim took the flask, uncapped it, wiped the rim and slurped down a mouthful of brandy, followed by the peppermint. He gasped and fanned his mouth with his palm. 'Dear God!'

'Potent, eh? Put hair on your chest that will.'

Jim blew out his cheeks as the fiery liquid burned the back of his throat and coasted down his gullet into his chest. He let the fierce little peppermint tablet dissolve slowly on his tongue.

The teachers were stationed on the upper verandah and had a bird's eye view of the front playground and the steps that led down from the gate. Smailes and Dave Wallace, Mr Pallant's trusties, had greeted the guests from the District Education Office and had led them to the Head's study where light refreshment was on offer. A second lot of specially invited guests had also arrived and had been taken directly to the gymnasium which served the school as an assembly hall. Teachers had vacated classrooms on a rota and for the past ten minutes crocodiles of children had been crossing the playground and vanishing into the gym through the fire doors.

The rabble's fear of the unexpected had been partly allayed by a wee white lie – 'Mr Lapsley will lead us all in

481

prayers' – but the miasmic feeling of holiday was already in the air and the mutter of conversation from the gym soon rose to a roar. Prayers? Teachers in clean shirts and blue suits? Flowers in a vase on the table on the platform and Mr Watson shuffling sheet music across the top of the piano? Nothing much to get excited about. And the fact that the quarterly religious service was taking place on Thursday afternoon instead of Friday morning was dismissed as adult idiosyncrasy.

The structures of school life in Flannery Park had not had time to form properly and, like young bones, were still light and flexible. That, thanks to Mr Pallant's opportunism, was about to change. Though the pupils were unaware of it, the first chapter in their school's history was about to be inscribed for posterity, to challenge and to plague their sons, daughters and grandchildren with memories that time would fade but not obliterate.

'Whozzat?'

'Where?'

'There. Front row.'

'Who? The big bloke?'

'Aye, an' the wifie in the funny hat?'

'Search me.' Turning, 'Hey, Andy, who's that down yonder?'

Ripples of curiosity, tinged with anxiety, spread like flames through bracken as the adults in the front row were finally identified.

There was hardly time for speculation on what the intrusion of strangers might portend – Walter would have known but Walter was gone and long forgotten – before the small door at the back of the platform opened and the minister, Mr Lapsley, and Miss Stewart, domestic science teacher and assistant deputy head, emerged through the dust-motes and took their seats on the platform. Next came the Education Office's official representatives accompanied by Mr Pallant. They all appeared to be quite jolly, simpering and handshaking and changing chairs until they were finally seated, like stuffed dummies, facing out towards the multitude.

Miss Stewart looked along at Mr Pallant. Mr Pallant nodded.

Miss Stewart got to her feet, patted her bosom, then raised her right hand as if for a swearing in.

Comparative silence in the ranks.

All was about to be revealed.

'Let us begin by giving praise,' said Miss Stewart in a deep, syrupy voice. 'Hymn six hundred and seventy: "O, What Can Little Hands Do?"'

With a terrific flourish Mr Watson struck the opening chords and the multitude rose amid a thunder of coughs and scraping chairs.

'Prayers?' muttered Andy suspiciously.

'Looks like it, pal. Looks like it.'

"*Oooh Whaaat Can Liii-tle Haaa-nds Do t' Please the Kiii-ng of H'vin.*"'

On the battlements Boris dropped his cigarette and ground it out with his shoe heel.

'That's it, Jim,' he said. 'Go fetch your lamb to the slaughter.'

'Now, Alison,' Jim said, 'just try to keep calm.'

'I'm perfectly calm, thank you.'

'Nothing to it. Go forward when your name's called and deliver your speech. Have you got it in your pocket?'

'I've memorised it,' Alison said. 'I still don't see what all the fuss is about.' They reached the bottom of the stairs, hurried out into bright June sunshine and crossed the playground towards the gymnasium.

'I told you,' Jim said, 'Mr Pallant's very keen to show off the new sixth form and because members of the Education Authority are here he wants to involve the pupils.'

'Yes,' said Alison, 'but why do I have to stand up and tell everyone I'm going on to study medicine at Glasgow University. It just sounds like boasting to me.'

'It is,' Jim said. 'Boasting on behalf of the school.'

'Why can't Smailes do it?'

'Smailes and Wallace will also have their say.' He stopped, put his hand on her shoulder and spoke with unusual gravity. 'Mr Pallant has every right to be proud of you. It's no mean achievement for a council school to have three pupils entered for university.'

'Jim,' she whispered, 'I do understand, honest I do. I don't fancy being the focus of attention but I am prepared to go through with it.'

He managed a smile. 'Good.'

A moment or two later they were lying in wait behind the small door that led to the platform.

Alison could see the three members of the Education Authority, very attentive, and Mr Lapsley. Miss Stewart, on her feet. Mr Watson swung round on the piano stool. Bunches of climbing ropes, tumbling mats, the hated leather horse with the vaulting board propped against it, dust swirling in the broad shafts of sunlight that penetrated the windows on the north wall.

Alison's stomach fluttered. Her mouth was dry.

She had lied to Jim. She wasn't calm at all.

She had appeared before the whole school several times before. She had read the Bible lesson, had even made a little speech once on behalf of the pupils when Miss Syme was gravely ill. Somehow today felt different, though. While she'd waited in the classroom for Jim to summon her she'd become quite tense and sad. This was surely the last time she'd appear before her schoolfellows, Head Girl in everything but name. In twelve weeks she'd be right back at the beginning, an insignificant fish in the sea of Glasgow University. Not a prospect she enjoyed.

She nodded to Smailes, who looked glum, and to Dave Wallace who looked as if he was about to be sick.

The boys' obvious nervousness settled Alison down. *She* wouldn't stammer. *She* wouldn't stutter. *She* wouldn't fumble in her pocket for her notes. She would speak out clearly, tell everyone that she had been accepted for the course in medicine at the University of Glasgow, thank Mr Pallant and all her teachers and step down. And then she'd be gone and – like Walter – forgotten in no time at all.

She could smell strong peppermint on Jim's breath as he leaned across her and pushed the door ajar.

Dave groaned, 'Oh, Jeeze,' then murmured, 'Sorry, Mr Abbott.'

'*Ssshhh*,' Jim whispered. 'Listen, Alison, listen for your cue.'

Mr Pallant was on his feet.

He looked, Alison thought, more ethereal than ever in the cascade of sunshine. He was not at all grave, though, and suddenly she realised just what the little ceremony meant to the headmaster, how proud he was of his pupils and his school. And then she heard Mr Pallant mention her name and felt Jim's hand on her arm, gripping tightly.

'And so, ladies and gentlemen, boys and girls,' Mr Pallant was saying, 'it is *my* honour and *my* privilege to present to you now the winner of the Tuxford Prize, Alison Burnside.'

She heard applause, cheers and whistles, saw Dave Wallace grinning, the grudging smile on Smailes's pale face. She felt Jim's hand slide to her shoulder and give it a squeeze, even as he pushed her towards the door.

'Jim, I didn't—?'

'You did,' he said. 'It's all yours, Alison. Go get it.'

'What did you think when you saw us?' Trudi asked.

'I nearly died.'

'Well, I don't know how you did it, darlin'.' Alex had an arm about her shoulders. 'I mean, them not tellin' you. I've never been so proud in all my life, seein' you standin' up there an' all those important men shakin' your hand.' He sniffed, released her and reached for the handkerchief that Ruby had at the ready. 'You sayin' all those nice things about Mr Abbott. He must've been fair pleased.'

'He was, believe me,' Jim Abbott said.

They were strolling in a group down Wingfield Drive, passing among schoolbags and skipping ropes and a general slouch of pupils which parted if not reverently at least with a mild display of respect for the heroine of the day.

'Why did none of you warn me?' Alison said.

'Sworn to secrecy,' said Henry.

'The school isn't supposed to inform the winning student until after the Tuxford Trust makes its announcement to the newspapers,' Jim explained. 'Mr Pallant decided not to abide strictly by the rules. In fact, he arranged everything perfectly.'

'Includin' that board,' said Alex.

After Alison had received the prize cheque and had expanded her prepared speech to include the sponsors of the Tuxford, she had been treated to the sight of the school's first memorial board, a huge block of varnished wood with Smailes's and her names emblazoned upon it in gilt letters: *Head of Girls' School – Alison Burnside, Winner of the Tuxford Prize, 1930*. She was more proud of that than anything, a fixture which would still be here when she was an old lady. She had, however, retreated into a strange state of melancholic euphoria and was relieved when all the congratulatory fuss was over and she was free to join her family and set off for a celebratory tea which Trudi had laid out at home.

In a week's time she would be able to throw away her grey skirt, green cardigan, and ridiculous pudding-basin hat, a prisoner of that uniform no more. She wondered what would happen to her then, what would happen to them all when Dad was married and the house belonged to Henry and she had finally stepped away into student life.

How she longed to take Jim's hand.

Instead she walked sedately down Wingfield Drive by Henry's side with Jim a half step behind, and listened to her praises being sung. Tomorrow her name and her achievement would be reported in the press, a nine-day wonder, and then it would all move on and she would be herself again.

'Isn't she a marvel, Ruby, eh?' Alison heard her father say.

Glancing round Alison saw how Brenda's mother bit her lip before she replied and realised that all her little triumphs would surely have a price if she remained here much longer, at home in Flannery Park.

It was Ruby who unintentionally applied the old Scots term 'a penny wedding' to her nuptials. The first time she used the phrase, in the middle of a conversation about steak pies and sausage rolls, Alex had taken umbrage. He was riled by the belief that his beloved had implied a mercenary aspect to their coming union. Not so, Henry had quickly explained. All that Ruby meant was that neighbours and friends seemed bent on donating so much food and drink towards the celebration and that there would be enough left to keep the happy couple fed for weeks afterwards. Mollified, Alex swiftly came round to the view that a bridal shower made up of comestibles was no bad thing and would serve the budget better than nineteen new frying pans and a dozen or so baking bowls. What, after all, did you give to a man and a woman who were already well established domestically and who appeared to have everything?

Besides, the celebration party, which had started out as a family affair, seemed to have swelled unmanageably. Henry was talking about hiring trestle tables to put on the lawn and Trudi added to her stock of teacups and drinking glasses practically every time she went shopping. The awkwardness of celebrating the marriage of a widow to a widower appeared to have been swept away by neighbourly enthusiasm for Flannery Park's first 'at home' wedding reception.

'It used to be just like this in Perthshire when I was a boy,' Jim Abbott said. 'When a farmer got married the entire community would gather in the stackyard or the barn and get absolutely sloshed.'

'Henry,' Alex said, straight-faced, 'better see if you can hire a barn.'

'Be cheaper to pray for a nice dry day,' said Alison.

'June?' said Bertie. 'Not a hope. Last Saturday in June's always wet.'

'Who says?'

'I read it in the *Mercury*.'

'In that case it must be true,' said Alex. 'Tell me, Jim, what else did these farmer buddies do, when you were a lad?'

'There would be a fiddler, of course, and dancing.'

'Aye, and they'd kill a sheep, roast it and eat it with their bare hands,' Bertie put in, scathingly.

'Sounds good to me,' said Davy. 'Henry—'

'I know. Order a sheep.'

'Aye, Bertie can pluck it,' Alex said.

'Hah-hah!' said Bertie.

'Listen, Dad,' said Davy, 'just how many folk are comin' to this do?'

Alex with an apologetic shrug said, 'Hundreds, I reckon.'

'Where are we gonna put them all?'

'Outside.'

'God!' said Bertie. 'What a public exhibition – just for a lousy weddin'.'

'A penny wedding, remember,' Alison said.

'Come one—' said Davy.

'Come all,' said Alison.

Scratching his ear thoughtfully, Alex said, 'Henry, what does a fat sheep cost these days?'

And Bertie cried out, 'Aaawww!'

There was more awkwardness across in Foxhill Crescent than among the Burnsides. Although Brenda had finally emerged from her long dark mood she remained disenchanted by her mother's forthcoming marriage. She refused to be cajoled into being fitted for a pretty pink frock and be trailed to the altar as a bridesmaid, along with Ally Burnside.

'But I don't *have* anyone else, Brenda.'

'You should have thought of that before,' Brenda said. 'Anyway, it isn't right, being married in a church an' showin' yourself off like you were a pair of flamin' sweethearts.'

'We are a pair of sweethearts. Age has nothin' to do with it.'

'What does the minister have to, you know, say about it?'

'Provided Alex and I take an instruction class beforehand

the minister is perfectly agreeable to us bein' married in the Congregational.'

'An instruction class? The facts of life?'

'Brenda!'

'Well, it's all wrong. An' if you think I'm wearin' that daft pink frock while shufflin' down the aisle with a bunch of bloody violets in my hand then you can think again.'

'Oh, Brenda, don't spoil it.'

'Anyway, who's gonna give you away?'

Ruby hesitated.

She and Alex had given the problem much thought. She had no close male relative to whom she could turn for assistance and it would not have been proper for Henry to be a surrogate father of the bride.

'Mr Abbott,' Ruby said.

'*What?*'

'He volunteered.'

'Bloody hell!' said Brenda, savagely. 'We all know why *he* volunteered.'

'He's a nice chap. I shan't mind bein' given away by him.'

'He volunteered 'cause he's after Alison.'

'What's wrong with that?' said Ruby.

'You don't seem, you know, surprised?'

'Why should I be? I'm not blind.'

'He's fancied her since she was fifteen.'

'Can't blame him. She's an attractive young lady.'

'Meanin' I'm not?'

'Brenda, this is beside the point.'

'Get Trudi to do it. Matron of whatsit. You don't need me.'

'Aren't you going to turn up at all?'

'Nope.'

'Jack will be disappointed,' Ruby said smoothly.

'Jack?'

'Yes, he was askin' me just last night what you'd be wearin'.'

'Was he?'

'He assumes you'll be there. He'll be awfully put out if you're not.'

'Will he?'

'Of course he will. He's too bashful to say so but it'll spoil his whole day if you're not there.'

'You're pullin' my leg.'

'He's had his dance band suit specially cleaned an' pressed an' Trudi bought him a new shirt. He's goin' to look a real treat, believe me.'

Brenda hunched her shoulders and neatly nipped her cigarette between finger and thumb. 'Will he be playin' his trumpet?'

'Afterwards, at the party. He's the band.'

Brenda inhaled and, holding smoke in her lungs, scowled at the swathe of garish silk chiffon that Ruby draped delicately across her arm.

'Pink, for God's sake!' Brenda said, coughing.

And Ruby sighed with relief that another little hurdle had been crossed and that her darling daughter, moaning all the way, would be present at the wedding after all.

As a weather prophet Bertie was a wash-out. Saturday, twenty-eighth of June dawned fair and warm. In fact by early afternoon the temperature had risen to the low eighties and there were flushed faces and frayed tempers galore within the precincts of 162.

In the kitchen Trudi was surrounded by pots, pans and baking trays. The oven had been going full blast since early morning and great clouds of steam billowed from the back door. The hired trestles arrived on the back of a van along with two kegs of beer. Henry and Jack put them away in the brick shed and covered the kegs with wet towels to keep them cool. Bertie and Alex should have been similarly treated for they were at each other's throats from the moment Bertie arrived home from the Co-op at half past twelve.

The squabbling was at its worst on the stairs. Everyone, it seemed, wanted into the bathroom at once and the Burnsides' enraged shouts could be heard not only by the Rooneys but by half the neighbourhood too.

Trudi, usually so calm, lost her temper about half past two o'clock. Head turbanned in a towel and housecoat flapping about her bare knees, she screamed, '*I am sick of you, sick of you all*,' flew from the bathroom into the bedroom and slammed the door so hard that the whole house shook as if a bomb had gone off nearby.

'What's wrong with her then?' Jack asked as he picked lint from Bertie's dark blue lapels and adjusted the knot in his brother's tie.

'Women!' Bertie answered with a shake of the head. 'They're all the same. Time of the month, I expect.'

'The what?'

'Never mind.'

Alison had had the foresight to request the use of Mrs Rooney's facilities. At a quarter past two she slipped next door with her frock, stockings, shoes and hat in a bundle in her arms like a refugee.

Mrs Rooney, with Juliette slung on her hip, was icing sponge cakes in the kitchen and in the living-room Mr Rooney was blowing up coloured balloons with the assistance, so called, of the rest of the tribe.

He looked at Alison and winked. 'Who's winning?'

Alison shook her head ruefully. 'I am, I think.'

Twenty minutes later, bathed, powdered and dressed in pink silk chiffon Alison descended into the comparative calm of the Rooneys' front room to allow Mrs Rooney to apply the finishing touches to her toilet and to tell her how beautiful she looked.

A few minutes later, stepping carefully, Alison returned to the back door of her house to be greeted by her father's cry, '*Where's the car? Ruby's car should be here by now. Is it not time we were off? Henry, is it not time we hit the trail? Jeeze, these bloody collar studs'll be the death of me,*' and Henry, in his best officer-of-the-line voice, saying, '*Stand still. Stand still, will you,*' then shouting, '*Damn it, Dad, can you not stand still for two bloody minutes?*'

Trudi was popping about the kitchen like a ping-pong ball, hair straggling from under her hat, gloves tucked into her bodice while Davy, leaning on the sink, slyly eyed the huge pyramid of ham sandwiches that reposed under a muslin shroud.

'*Touch von of those,*' Trudi hissed, '*and I vill kill you.*'

'Trudi, I'm starvin'.'

'*Kill you. You got it, right?*'

Davy nodded penitently. 'I got it, right.'

Out in the garden, under the raspberry canes, Pete lay asleep, forepaws folded across a hambone that Jack had unearthed to keep the dog happy. The Wilsons' wireless set was broadcasting a programme of symphonic variations from a concert hall in Kensington which seemed, somehow, a million miles away, as remote from Flannery Park as the planet Jupiter. On the clothes poles Mr Rooney's balloons expanded in the heat and bobbed like giant grapes on stems of hairy brown twine.

Mr Rooney and Mr Johnstone, from next door but one, were to put up the tables and attend to the kegs and Mrs Rooney and Mrs McAlmond, Ruby's downstairs neighbour, would put the finishing touches to the wedding feast, both indoors and out.

Everything, it seemed, was in order. Alison, standing alone on the edge of the grass, wondered why she felt so forlorn. Logic told her that her family was not so very much different from ten thousand others spread across the new suburban estates, strugglers and strivers, winners and losers, each beating against the flow of circumstance if not with fortitude at least with energy and humour.

She missed her mother. She even missed her grandmother. There would be no Gilfillans at the penny wedding. To Alison's disappointment they had refused point blank to attend. She thought too of Jim Abbott loitering by the gate of Ruby's house, waiting not for his own bride but to give away in marriage a woman he hardly knew.

'Ally?' a voice said. 'Alison?'

She turned to discover that her father had come up behind her.

He seemed perfectly in control of himself, unhurried, unabashed in the brand-new blue suit that Trudi had bought from the Co-operative's Clydebank emporium. Everything about him was shiny new, from his polished black shoes to the lick of Brylcreem that flattened his unruly grey hair. He looked paler than he had a year ago but his features were unchanged, the pitted little scars that hot rivets and hard metal flakes had inflicted over the years just as ugly and as handsome as they had always been.

'Daddy?'

'Got to go now, sweetheart.'

'Is Ruby's car here?'

'Waitin' at the gate. We'll be leavin' in a couple of minutes.' He was awkward with her now. 'You look lovely, darlin', so you do.' He stepped closer and lowered his voice. 'You'll still be my wee girl, won't you?'

'Aye, Daddy.'

'Aye? Who says "aye?" like that?'

'Me. I do.'

'We have to go now.'

'I know.'

For a fleeting moment she was tempted to punish him for forsaking her, for letting go all that had gone before. She held her ground, unmoving, unmoved by his last split-second appeal. Then she saw that none of it had gone, that it had simply expanded like the balloons on the poles, realised that it would always be thus between them, father and daughter, that neither would ever be far from the other no matter the weight of miles between.

Feeling just a little silly in the sweetie-pink frock and hard little cardboard-lined hat, taller than he was too, she put her arms about him and gave him a hug and a kiss on the cheek.

'Better?' she said.

'Fine now,' Alex Burnside said and, linking his arm with hers, led her through the close to join her brothers for the short walk to the church.

'My God, Jack,' Brenda said, 'that's some lip you've got on you.'

'I've been playin' for the best part of four hours. What d' you expect – velvet?'

'I didn't say I didn't like it.' Brenda kissed him again and rubbed the remnants of her floral corsage against his shirt front. 'Fact, I think it's very, you know, manly.'

'Like bein' kissed by a vacuum cleaner?'

'I never said that.'

'No, somebody else did.'

'Somebody else? Who?'

'A girl I once knew.'

'Aw, so you do have a murky past?'

'Well, hardly murky,' Jack said.

'Who was she? Anybody I'd know?'

'Nope. Just a girl.'

'Was she your girlfriend?'

'Nah.'

'Haven't you ever had a girlfriend?' Brenda said.

'Never seem to have the time to find one.'

They were standing at the hedge by the gate in Foxhill Crescent. It was almost midnight now but the sky was lit by mid-summer afterglow and the silhouettes of the houses stood out against it as if cut from black paper. Across the park the lights in 162 were all ablaze and in the still night air you could hear Burnside voices calling goodnight to neighbours and friends and Bertie, who had taken a drop too much to drink, yodelling the chorus from 'The Sheik of Araby' over and over again.

'Some party, wasn't it?' Jack said.

'Aye, they'll not forget it round here in a hurry.'

There had been no hitches at all. The service in the Congregational had gone off smoothly, the family dinner's toasts and speeches too. Then Mr and Mrs Alexander Burnside had stepped out into the garden to thank the neighbours for their generosity and, soon after, the tranquil evening had been enlivened by the sound of Jack's four-man dance band warming up.

Within half an hour everyone who was anyone had arrived, some bearing gifts for the happy couple, others simply drifting in to listen to the music, to dance a reel on the trampled lawn or join the Conga line that snaked through the closes and along the paths, to scoff the sandwiches, dumpling and cakes which appeared in endless supply from the kitchen doors. And at half past eight bride and groom had made their departure.

There was much in the way of flying rice and ribbons, tin-cans and confetti but no strenuous flinging about of the groom or tormenting of the bride, the rough sort of send-off that a younger couple would have had to endure. The honeymoon – three nights in the Sunray Guest House in Largs – had been paid for by the proprietors of the Argyll Hotel in recognition of Ruby's marriage and retirement. On Monday night it would be back to work for Alex, though, and memories of the penny wedding would gradually fade as new rhythms and rituals took over.

Brenda said, 'Are you not comin' in, Jack?'

'What for?'

'Cocoa.'

'Oh! Do you not want to be on your own? You could sleep in our house, if you like.'

'In your bed?'

'Sharin' with Alison.'

'Huh! Come on. I'm not tired. I'll make us both cocoa.'

'I should really be gettin' back.'

Jack glanced sidelong towards the lighted house across the way while Brenda rubbed against him again, kissing his cheek with soft little brushing motions. He swallowed the lump in his throat. He had been watching her all evening long, watching her while he played, and the sight of her had somehow made him play more sweetly.

She wasn't wee Brenda McColl from round the corner now. Actually she was probably his sister. But he couldn't think of her in that way. He knew what she thought of him. He wasn't *that* daft. What Brenda offered was the sort of love he had longed for under Rothesay's palm trees; yet he was wary of the strain of pity he still felt for her and sensed danger in his need to please and protect.

'For what?' Brenda said. 'What's over there for you?'

'The washin' up?'

'You've done your bit,' she said, giving his arm a tug. 'Nobody's gonna miss you, not now your daddy's gone. Anyway, we're supposed to be, you know, just one big happy family. So come on.'

He allowed her to coax him down the path and mount the doorstep then he said, 'Brenda, do you have a key?'

She turned the handle, pushed open the door.

'My door's never locked,' she said and, with a knowing little laugh, drew Jack after her into the warm, dark house and closed the door behind him before he could escape again.

It was so late and the streets of Flannery Park were so quiet that discretion seemed pointless and Jim did not resist when Alison reached for his hand. He was tired but it was a relaxed sort of tiredness. Tomorrow he would lie long, breakfast late. He would attend church in the evening not the morning. He did not need to go to church at all, really, but something Ruby had said, only minutes before he'd escorted her out to the hired motorcar that afternoon, had struck home.

'I've waited thirteen years for this day,' Ruby McColl had told him, 'and, by God, it's been worth it.'

'Waited for Alex Burnside, do you mean?' Jim had asked in surprise.

'Nope. Just waited, waited patiently for something good to happen.'

'How could you be sure it ever would?'

'Never doubted it,' the woman had told him.

Ruby had been surprisingly calm. They had been ready a good half hour before the motorcar was due and even Brenda, slouched in a wicker chair in the front bedroom, had been unexpectedly passive. He had offered to act as father of the bride on a whim and had been surprised when his offer had been accepted. Only then had he realised how empty Ruby McColl's life had been and had found himself observing her with increasing respect.

'I'll tell you a secret, though,' Ruby had said, 'I used to pray nearly every night. Pray I'd meet a man who'd change things for me – just a wee bit of change, not too much. A man who'd take me at face value. Do you know what I mean, Mr Abbott?'

'Only too well,' Jim had said.

'It's different for men, I suppose.'

'Some men perhaps, not all.'

'Sometimes I thought I was kidding myself on. But I just kept waiting, trying to be patient about it.' When she'd touched the back of his hand he'd experienced an uncomfortable empathy. 'Harder for you, though, Jim.'

'I'm not sure what you mean.' Jim had said.

'She's very young.'

'If you mean Alison—'

'She's going places.'

'Oh, I know that.'

'Be patient, Mr Abbott, that's my advice.'

When the party had ended and the guests dispersed Alison and he had lingered in the garden while Henry and the boys had collected empty glasses, dismantled tables and rolled away the empty beer kegs. Seated on a rug on the grass, backs resting against the shed, they had contrived to ignore the activity around them. They had talked quietly together, talked and talked until Alison had finally run out of words just as the long northern twilight and the first false streaks of dawn met and mingled overhead.

'Walk me part of the way home,' he'd said.

'I'll walk you all the way, if you like?'

'No, to the Kingsway will do.'

They walked slowly, her hand in his.

The streets were uncannily still, as if the entire population of Flannery Park, lulled by the heat, lay lapped in Sabbath sleep.

Alison could feel the warmth of the night air in her lungs, the material of the bridesmaid's dress brushing against her limbs. Another memory, another moment that would be held for ever in her memory. So many of them now crowding upon her, so many experiences gathered into her history.

When he spoke his voice startled her.

'Alison,' he said, 'would you ever consider marrying me?'

'Yes,' she said without hesitation. 'I would.'

'Are we being grammatically correct here?'

'Very, Jim, very grammatically correct.'

'You don't need me now, you know.'

'Oh, but I do. I need you more than ever.'

'It's that damned money,' he said. 'That put the kibosh on everything.'

Alison was tempted to pretend that she had given no thought to the money and the freedom that two hundred and fifty pounds could buy, for financial independence did indeed complicate matters which were already complicated enough. The ease with which her life had turned itself around, the manner in which she had willed a man to fall in love with her, and the way she had fallen in love, alarmed her. She was too shrewd to take good luck for granted, though. Daughter of cocky Clydesiders, hard men and practical women, she was linked to a heritage which she would never entirely shake off, with Jim or without him.

'Yes,' she said. 'It did rather.'

'I presume you've guessed what I had in mind,' Jim said, 'until the money came on the scene, that is?'

'To see me through university?'

'To put you under an obligation, yes,' Jim said.

'I wish we didn't have to talk like this. It seems so calculating.'

'Alison, I have to be sure.'

'If I'm worth waiting for?'

'No. If *I'm* worth waiting for.'

'What if I tell you I don't want to wait?'

'Then I'd have to advise you to think again.'

'What a predicament, Jim,' she said. 'You know I love you, but I don't know what to do about it. It seems so unfair to ask your advice.'

'I'll wait,' he said.

'For six years?'

'Four or five. Six if I have to.'

'What do we do in the meantime?'

'Grin and bear it.'

'Six years is an eternity,' Alison said. 'I'm not sure I can stand it.'

'You'll have plenty to keep you occupied, believe me,' Jim told her, a trace of schoolmaster in his tone. 'You'll have to work hard to graduate with a good degree. You've no idea how hard.'

'It might be easier just to marry you and forget the rest.'

'No,' he said sharply.

'But I love you *now*,' Alison said. 'I want you *now*.'

'No, you don't.'

'How do *you* know what I want, what's good for me?'

'God,' Jim said, 'if I don't know, who does?'

'All right,' Alison said. 'If you were to ask me to marry you here and now I'd have no hesitation in accepting your proposal. You'd have to ask my Dad, or my brother Henry, of course, but they wouldn't turn you down. We'd be engaged for six months or a year then we'd marry and live in your house and you'd carry on teaching and I'd stay at home and have babies.'

'And spend the rest of your life regretting your lost opportunities and perhaps hating me for it?'

'No, never, never that.'

'I can't take the risk,' Jim said.

'You don't *want* me to be just an ordinary sort of wife, do you?'

'You aren't ordinary, Alison.'

'I wish I was. Oh, God, how I wish I was.'

'There's no obligation, be clear on that point.'

'I *want* there to be an obligation, don't you see?'

It had not been his intention to drive her to tears.

She was close to them now. He put his arm about her and for the first time kissed her lips and held her close. Her body was shockingly strong and youthful. He could feel the breath in her lungs, the rise and fall of her ribs, the lithe muscles of her back when she leaned against him, one long coltish leg held out for balance. He was flooded with desire for her and for that very reason gently pushed her away.

'I don't want to lose you, Jim. I don't want you to let me go.'

'I'll be here,' he said. 'I'm not going anywhere. But I can't hold you, Alison, and even if I could I would not.'

'You're not really in love with me.'

'Oh, yes. Yes, I am.'

'Then why don't you stop treating me as a child?'

'You mean why don't I tell you what to do?'

'Yes, just *tell* me to marry you and I will.'

'What if I tell you to go on with your career?'

'I don't want to. I don't want to. Not now.'

Even as she spoke, though, Alison realised that she was not telling the truth. She had been deceived by Jim's cleverness and betrayed by her own emotions. In that instant she saw precisely what Jim Abbott meant. If he had given her an ultimatum, if he had forced her to choose marriage there and then she *would* have resented him for it. She was angry only because he had allowed her liberty, because he had treated her like a woman with a mind of her own.

She was caught in the trap of wanting too much, too soon. To choose to act upon her own initiative – and to be responsible for the consequences – was *not* the same as reacting to what others required of her. Even a faint glimmer of what that might mean for her future was intimidating.

She stepped back with a sudden sharp little intake of breath.

All Jim said was, 'No?'

She shook her head. 'You're right, of course.'

Her tears suddenly evaporated. She looked at Jim Abbott not with longing but with love, a friendly affection, very clear and unsentimental.

'Medicine?' he asked.

'Medicine,' she agreed.

'You won't regret it.'

'No. Will you?'

'I might,' Jim said. 'Unfortunately, I might.'

There was dawn light in the sky before Trudi and Henry retired at last to their bedroom. Trudi had brought up a teapot and cups and the couple sat on the edge of the bed and shared refreshment in the cool air from the half-open window.

'Are they all come home?' Trudi asked. 'Since it is our house now we are responsible, no?'

'Can't you hear them?'

'I hear Bert, how he is snoring.'

503

'God, yes, what a skinful he had tonight.'

'Why is it that he cries so much?'

'Just that type, I suppose,' said Henry.

'Davy?'

'Dead to the world.'

'Jack?'

Henry sipped tea thoughtfully. 'He can take care of himself.'

'And, of course, we know how safe Alison is,' said Trudi with a smile.

'Why doesn't Abbott just go home?' Henry said.

'He is too much in love to be sleepy.'

Henry shook his head. 'I don't know what will come of this, Trude.'

'Do you not approve of him?'

'No, I *do* approve of him. Abbott's a nice guy. That's the trouble. I feel sorry for him.'

'As once you felt sorry for me?' Trudi said.

She wore a cream-coloured nightgown, had let her hair down and looked demure, not seductive, in the lamplight.

'No, I never felt sorry for you, Trudi. What I felt for you was something quite different.'

'What do you feel for me now?'

Henry put the teacup on to the saucer with a little *plink* and lit a cigarette. He wafted away the waxy smoke from the match and leaned back, one elbow upon the pillow like a Roman emperor.

'You shouldn't have to ask,' he said.

'But I do ask,' Trudi said. 'Wedding days—'

'Enough about wedding days,' Henry said.

She chuckled and, putting the tray to one side, leaned her weight against him. He could feel the warmth from her and smell again that clean, exciting perfume from her body. He could still remember how she had been in the railway carriage. Rich, elegant and aristocratic. Wickedness personified. How different now, like a pale blonde angel in the simple cotton gown.

'Are you not sure of me, Henry?'

'No. No, I'm not, not quite.'

'Do you not know what that is, my boy?'

'No.'

'That's love,' said Mrs Trudi Burnside.

And Henry, in his wisdom, knew then that she was right.